EWE COMPLETE ME

COMMON THREADS BOOK #6

SUSANNAH NIX

WWW.SMARTYPANTSROMANCE.COM

COPYRIGHT

CHAPTER ONE

CHLOE

I was a reliable person. Solid, trustworthy, dependable. *Good old Chloe Carpenter*, people said, *always there when you need her.*

Not the most exciting sort of reputation to have, perhaps, but I took pride in being considerate of others. Growing up with busy, distracted parents who frequently let me down had given me strong feelings about the importance of dependability. When I made a commitment to someone, I showed up. I didn't want to be anything like my parents. And I most certainly didn't intend to *date* someone like my parents.

Seeking inner stillness to calm my frustration, I breathed out slowly through my nose while I checked my phone again. My date was fifteen full minutes late now without a message of explanation. How much longer should I give him?

Things happened. Unavoidable things. Accidents. Traffic. Delayed trains. Maybe he'd had car trouble or stopped to help someone else who had. Maybe he'd gotten sick and dropped his phone in the toilet so he couldn't message me to let me know. Maybe he'd hit his head and was wandering the streets of Chicago with amnesia and no idea he'd left me sitting here at this overly trendy rooftop bar.

Or maybe I was making up fanciful excuses for him when he was just another inconsiderate jerk who didn't respect other people's time.

Honestly, I didn't know why I kept bothering with online dating. I could be at home in my favorite sloth pajamas right now crocheting in front of the TV instead of sitting on this uncomfortable faux-industrial stool sipping a watered-down margarita.

Why did I keep setting myself up for disappointment? I'd even curled my hair and taken extra time with my makeup this morning. Not that you could tell after eight hours of hauling inventory around at work. I'd also worn my cutest bra today, which happened to be my least comfortable. The underwire had practically fused with my ribs. I'd probably need to have it surgically removed.

And for what? To be stood up by a stranger named Bran.

So much for my perfect match.

To be honest, I'd had my doubts about his perfection from the moment the notification from FindUrPartner hit my inbox. For starters, his name was Bran. Not only did it bring to mind high-fiber laxatives and regular bowel movements, it sounded like the kind of one-syllable name favored by too many of the douchebags I'd known in high school. What was it about guys with names like Brock and Bryce and Beck that they seemed to grow up into entitled jerks?

On top of that, Bran was a law student, and every law student I'd ever met was a competitive, self-absorbed overachiever. Which was the exact opposite of what I wanted in a boyfriend. Not to mention, my father was a lawyer, so…yeah. I had some not-good feelings about men who wanted to be lawyers.

I should have swiped left based on the law student thing alone, but I'd been lured in by Bran's profile photo. He'd had a nice smile and kind-looking eyes, so I'd given him a shot. That would teach me to judge a book by its cover. *Actual* kind eyes never would have stood me up. That probably wasn't even him in the picture. Those were likely some stock photo model's kind eyes that I'd been suckered into meeting for a drink.

Deciding I'd waited long enough, I clambered off my stool and turned to make my escape…only to find myself face-to-face with the very pair of eyes I'd been ruminating over, along with the dark hair, chiseled cheekbones, and square chin I recognized from Bran's profile photo.

Wowza. Definitely not a stock photo.

His eyes were even more arresting in person, a lovely mix of brown, emerald green, and gold. When they locked onto mine, I felt an odd, disorienting sensation—like the floor had unexpectedly tilted—and my heart kicked into my throat.

An excited and completely irrational voice in the back of my head whispered, *It's him. He's the one.*

You could blame the romance novels I'd pilfered from my grandmother's bedroom at the much-too-young age of eleven for my belief in *Princess Bride*–style true love. Come to think of it, you could probably blame my childhood obsession with *The Princess Bride* for it too, as long as we were assigning blame. Stupid Westley, giving me unrealistic expectations.

That Westley-loving little girl who still lived inside me believed in soul mates and fairy-tale happily ever afters despite overwhelming evidence to the contrary. Somewhere out there in the big, wide world, I wanted to think my One True Love was searching for me and I'd recognize him the instant we finally met. Call it intuition or love at first sight or whatever, I'd always imagined it would feel a lot like this peculiar sensation I experienced as I stared into Bran's eyes for the first time.

Huh.

There was no sign of the nice smile in his photo, but he did have the most alluring mouth I'd ever seen on a man. His upper lip had a lovely, pronounced curve to it that gave the impression of a permanent sexy pout.

"Chloe?"

"That's my name!" I chirped too loudly, feeling weirdly light-headed. Maybe that margarita hadn't been as watered down as I'd thought. "You must be Bran."

Beneath his lush, wavy hair, a pair of dark eyebrows that fell somewhere between Robert Pattinson and Dan Levy on the thickness scale drew together, creating two deep creases between them. "Were you leaving? I'm not that late, am I?"

"Twenty minutes." Despite my annoyance, I continued to stare at him in a sort of daze. Maybe Franz Mesmer had been onto something with that animal magnetism theory after all. Or perhaps my date was secretly a centuries-old Transylvanian noble with hypnotic powers who slept in a box filled with dirt from his homeland in the Carpathian Mountains.

"Sorry," Bran offered in a brusque tone with no hint of contrition. He broke eye contact to remove his suit jacket, releasing me from my besotted trance. "I got caught up at work and lost track of time."

Funny, I had also gotten caught up at work, and yet I'd still managed to show up to our date at the appointed time rather than leave him waiting on me for twenty minutes. Go figure.

As Bran helped himself to a seat at my table and directed his attention to the drink menu, I was sorely tempted to cut my losses and leave him to it. What were the odds this rude, unsmiling law student in a suit and tie was my perfect match? Surely they must be astronomical.

That weird feeling I'd experienced a moment ago had merely been my hormones overreacting to the presence of a physically attractive man—biology, not destiny. A pretty pair of eyes did not a soul mate make.

Did I really want to sit here for the next hour trying to make conversation with this guy? I'd much rather be at home, curled up on my grandmother's old denim sofa with some yarn and a crochet needle, listening to her catcall Tom Selleck while she watched the latest episode of *Blue Bloods*.

Maybe I should just give up on internet dating and lean fully into the Victorian spinster lifestyle, which would free up more time to work on my fiber art portfolio so I could apply to MFA programs like I kept saying I was going to do.

What did I need with a man anyway? I didn't want kids, so what did they have to offer other than sex? And there were plenty of high-tech substitutes available for that. Honestly, the innovations in the sex toy industry these days were nothing short of amazing. Even at the higher price points you'd more than make back your investment with the long-term time and aggravation saved by not being constantly disappointed by men.

While I was in the midst of thinking about sex toys, Bran casually unbuttoned the cuffs of his white dress shirt and rolled the sleeves up to his elbows.

Well, damn. Male forearms were a fatal weakness of mine. And Bran's were outstanding examples of the form. Strong and ropey but not too muscular, tapering to thick wrists, and covered with a layer of fine dark hair I wanted to run my fingers through. A veritable forearm feast for the eyes.

It couldn't hurt to stay for one more drink. Might as well give the guy a proper chance, right?

As I hopped back onto my stool, a server appeared out of nowhere to take Bran's drink order. She didn't acknowledge my existence until Bran had given his order and asked me if I wanted anything. Only then did she seem to notice me, appearing surprised to find me sitting across from him.

Admittedly, we did make an improbable pair with him in his suit and me in my hand-knit patchwork cardigan and olive-green overalls, with my undercut and multiple ear piercings—not to even mention all the tattoos covered by my clothes. It was hard to imagine a more mismatched couple than the two of us.

"I'll have another margarita," I said, feeling dispirited.

"Separate checks or together?" the server asked.

"Separate," Bran answered automatically.

Although I wholeheartedly approved of his answer, I couldn't help feeling it might have been nice if he'd at least offered to pay. Not that I expected him to—I was capable of buying my own drinks and preferred to do so. Still, the quickness of his reply felt like a brush-off, as if he'd already decided I wasn't worth wooing. It seemed his hopes for tonight weren't any higher than mine.

"Well," he said, giving me a businesslike smile once the server had departed. "Here we are."

"Here we are," I agreed, shifting on my uncomfortable stool. One of my butt cheeks had gone partially numb while I'd been waiting on him and was still in the pins-and-needles phase of waking back up.

"Your dating profile didn't tell me much about you."

That had been an intentional choice. You never knew when a harmless-seeming dude on the internet might turn into a stalker. The last thing I needed was some freak turning up at my house or place of work because I'd stopped responding to his messages. So my profile only included ambiguous facts about my personality and worldview rather than specific biographical details.

One of the things that had appealed to me about FindUrPartner was the confidential personality test you filled out when you signed up, which was used to rank your matches on a compatibility scale from one to one hundred. I'd liked the idea of getting to know someone brand-new, but with a higher probability you'd hit it off.

In theory, anyway. In practice, either people were lying their asses off in their personality tests or the FindUrPartner algorithm sucked donkey balls. My matches so far had been more like cautionary tales than boyfriend material. But Bran was my first compatibility match in the ninetieth percentile—my "perfect" match, according to the app. That, as much as his nice smile and kind eyes, had piqued my curiosity enough to swipe right and propose a meeting.

"Your profile didn't tell me much about you either," I pointed out.

"Really?" His dark eyebrows slashed downward. "I thought it was quite comprehensive."

Maybe if this had been a job interview instead of a date. I knew from Bran's profile he was twenty-four—the same as me—and a law student at UChicago. I knew he majored in political science at Princeton, used to volunteer for the ACLU, and was interning at a law firm this summer. But it hadn't said anything about his tastes, interests, or hobbies. I'd bet a hundred bucks he'd copied and pasted it from his LinkedIn profile.

"It read like a résumé," I said. "I'm more interested in who you are than what you've done."

"At least it offered something more concrete than the fact you like grilled cheese sandwiches and smiling."

That curve to his upper lip that I'd thought looked like a sexy pout? It could also look an awful like a lot like a sneer.

"My bio says I like to *make* people smile and I believe in the healing powers of a grilled cheese sandwich, which says a lot more about my personality than my undergraduate major."

His eyeroll was subtle, but not subtle enough. "What was your undergraduate major?"

My chin tipped up. "Who says I even went to college?"

He looked surprised, as if it hadn't occurred to him the world was full of people walking around without college degrees. Or maybe he was just shocked that he'd been matched with one. *Quelle horreur.* "Did you?"

"What if I didn't? Would that be a deal breaker for you?"

His hesitation made me think he was trying to decide whether to lie or tell the truth. "No," he finally said. "It's just a single data point."

I suspected that in addition to being inconsiderate and a snob, Bran was a liar. But since I wasn't, I answered his question truthfully. "I have an art degree."

"From what school?"

"I never share personally identifying information on a first date. I'm sure you can understand why a woman might need to be cautious with strange men she's met on a dating app."

He blinked, looking contrite for the first time. "Of course. It's smart to be careful."

Since he'd called me smart, I decided to throw him a bone. "I went to college out of state. Not Ivy League like you though."

Bran picked up his phone and typed something before setting it down again. "Are you from Chicago originally?"

"Born and bred. What about you?"

"I grew up in Lakeview."

Our server reappeared with our drinks. When she'd finished running our cards and departed again, Bran reached for his pint glass. He'd ordered an IPA, and our high-top table was small enough that I could smell the sharp tang of the hops in his beer.

As he swallowed, my gaze dropped to the stubble-shadowed column of his throat, and I winced inwardly, imagining the bitter flavor on my own tongue. The last guy I'd gone on a date with had been obsessed with IPAs and certain they would grow on me if I just gave them a chance. They hadn't, and neither had he.

I must have had some kind of look on my face because Bran's eyebrows twitched upward when he set his beer down. "Is something wrong?"

"Nope, nothing at all." I forced my smile back into place. "My mind was wandering someplace else, sorry. How's your IPA?"

"Adequate. How's your margarita?"

I reached for it and took a sip. "Delicious."

As I licked the salt off my lips, Bran's eyes focused on my mouth with an intensity that sent an unexpected sizzle down my spine. I felt his stare on the surface of my skin as it slowly traveled down my arms to where my hands curled around my drink, then made its way back up again, lingering on my chest before returning to my face. Goose bumps shivered down my arms inside my sweater, even as my face grew hot under his scrutiny.

"You seem to have spilled something on your...overalls," he said.

I looked down with a jolt of embarrassment. He hadn't been admiring me like I thought. He'd been cataloging my flaws.

Disconcerted, I pulled my cardigan over the coffee stain I'd forgotten about. "I had a run-in with someone else's coffee on the L this morning."

"You look different than your profile photo."

"How so?" I asked, certain I wouldn't like the answer.

"In your photo you looked more put together."

So real-life me was an unattractive slob? Was he implying I'd used a misleadingly flattering profile photo to trick him into going on a date with my pathetic, gross self?

I breathed out a long, slow breath and reached for more inner stillness. "The picture was taken at a friend's wedding six months ago, so I was more dressed up. I came here straight from work today and didn't have time to change."

"I don't remember your hair being..." He gestured at the side of my head. "Like that."

My undercut wasn't particularly obvious when I wore my long hair down like this, but he must have noticed the buzzed section behind my ear. I turned my head and lifted my hair to show off the shaved patch that wrapped around the base of my skull, giving him a view of the lotus tattoo on the back of my neck while I was at it. "This, you mean?" I asked brightly, pretending not to have noticed the disdain in his tone. "I just did this a month ago, but I haven't decided if I'm going to keep it or not. What do you think?"

I found it easier to pretend mean people weren't being mean than to call them out on it. Most of them were doing it to get a reaction out of you, and I'd just as soon deny them the satisfaction. If I acted oblivious enough, they often gave up and cut it out. Occasionally, if I projected enough niceness at them, I could even shame them into behaving better.

"It's your hair," Bran said gruffly. "What matters is whether you like it."

Letting it fall back into place, I faced him again and smiled even wider. "I kind of want to shave it into a mohawk, but I'm afraid it might be too cold in the winter."

"You could always wear a hat." His gaze dipped to scrutinize my clothes again, and the curve of his upper lip tipped farther into sneer territory. "That's an interesting sweater."

It didn't sound like a compliment, but I pretended to think it was. "Thanks! I made it myself."

"What kind of work do you do, if I'm allowed to ask?"

Here we go, I thought, bracing myself for more judgment. "I work in retail."

Bran picked up his phone again and started typing. "Do you enjoy that?" he asked in a dust-dry tone, as though he found it inconceivable that I might.

"Yes, as a matter of fact I do." It was getting harder to keep up my cheerful act and pretend he wasn't sitting there looking down on me. "I love talking to new people every day and helping them find the things they're looking for."

"Where do you see yourself in five years?" he asked without looking up. "Doing the same thing or something different?"

"I don't know," I said, feeling an uncomfortable twist in my stomach. Thinking about the future stressed me out. Being an artist wasn't exactly a secure career path. "I don't really care as long as I'm happy."

"Are you religious?" he asked, still typing.

I didn't understand why he was asking all these questions when he was so disinterested in my answers. "I like to think of myself as a spiritual agnostic."

The corner of his mouth quirked slightly, but otherwise his attention remained on his phone. "Did you vote in the last presidential election?"

"Yes." I narrowed my eyes. "Did you?"

"I vote in every election," he said as his thumbs tapped on his phone screen. "Who did you vote for?"

"Am I keeping you from something?"

Bran shook his head as he continued to type. "I'm just making some notes."

"Notes about what?" I asked, as confused by his answer as I was by his bizarre rapid-fire questions. This was starting to feel more like a marketing survey than a date. "You're not making notes about *me*, are you?"

His head jerked up with a guilty expression that said he was doing exactly that. Before he could respond, I reached across the table and snatched his phone out of his hand.

My stomach plummeted as I scanned the document open on the screen. Not only had he been reading his questions directly from it, he'd noted down my answers as well as his opinions of them. Next to *Profession* he'd written *Retail - no ambition?* and next to *Religion* he'd made a note that said *Possibly new age or kooky.* Worst of all, beneath the heading *General Impressions* he'd written only a single word: *Unsophisticated.*

I flinched like I'd been slapped, not by his hand but by the harshness of his condemnation. "What *is* this?"

He grabbed his phone back. "You're not meant to see that."

"No shit," I said. "What the hell, man?"

"It's to help me organize my thoughts. I made a list of questions that focus on five key areas of compatibility. Whenever I go out with someone new, I input their answers into a spreadsheet so I can rate them by a metric designed to indicate whether it's worth my time to go on a second date."

"Wow," I said, gaping in disbelief. "*Wow.* You keep a *spreadsheet* to rank the women you go out with?"

"What's wrong with that?"

"Are you kidding me?" I whisper-yelled, not wanting to make a scene in a public place. "We're supposed to be on a date and you're over there making snap judgments and typing snide comments into your phone. It's seriously shitty."

So much for not calling people out on their bad behavior. Even I had my limits.

Bran's mouth tightened. "You shouldn't have looked at my phone."

Oh *hell* no. Screw inner stillness and screw this jerk. My hands shook as I got to my feet, but I drew my outrage around me like a blanket, letting it insulate me from his hurtful opinions.

What did he know anyway? This guy didn't know anything about me. He was just taking out his own insecurities and miserable personality on the nearest warm body.

"Are you leaving?" He had the nerve to look surprised. As if I'd stick around after seeing what he thought about me.

It doesn't matter what he thinks. You didn't like him anyway. His good opinion isn't worth having.

I wasn't hurt. He didn't have the power to hurt me unless I let him.

Setting my jaw, I cleared my stinging throat. "I wouldn't want to waste more of your precious time since I'm so unsophisticated. I obviously don't live up to your high standards."

At least he had the grace to wince. His mouth opened, but he snapped it shut again without a word. Apparently I didn't even rate an apology. What an asshat.

"It's been thoroughly unpleasant meeting you, Bran. Have a nice life." I turned my back and walked out of the bar, comforted by the knowledge that I'd never have to see him again.

CHAPTER TWO

CHLOE

Yarn was better than therapy. Okay, maybe that wasn't *technically* true. But it sure was a heck of a lot more pleasant. For starters, yarn never made you cry, which wasn't something you could say about therapy. Then there was the squishiness factor. Therapists never let you squish them, but yarn begged to be squished. Was there anything more happy-making than scrunching your fingers into a fluffy, cloudlike hank of soft merino or alpaca?

Everyone did it when they came into Mad About Ewe, the yarn store where I worked. All day long I watched customers wander around, taking in all the bright, beautiful colors as they fondled different fibers to assess their touchability. When they found a yarn that struck their fancy, they'd rub it against their cheek, and their eyes would fall closed in an expression of perfect bliss.

Could a therapist do that? No.

Squishing yarn always improved my mood. Hence why I was currently knuckle-deep in a chunky cashmere/merino blend. What better way to shed the lingering bad taste of my awful date last night than the dopamine release of squishing luxury fibers? Men might be jerks, but yarn would always love me.

I'd been trying to put Bran out of my mind, but it wasn't so easy to shake off someone else's poor opinion of you. Not for me, anyway. My father said I was oversensitive, and my grandmother called me tenderhearted. According to my high school therapist, I was what was known as a highly sensitive person, due in part to a lack of parental warmth growing up. Basically, it meant I felt things more than most people, which left me extra susceptible to both my own emotions and those of others around me.

Knowing that was supposed to make it easier to manage, but sometimes I wondered. Just because I knew I shouldn't internalize the negative feelings of others didn't mean I could magically stop doing it. It didn't make Bran's words hurt any less. I still felt what I felt.

"You get any fresher with that yarn, you're gonna need to buy it a drink first."

I looked up to find Linda, one of our regulars who came into the store every morning to knit and drink the complimentary coffee, watching me from her favorite armchair by the front window.

I grinned, unashamed of my yarn-cuddling. "You're one to talk. I saw you canoodling with the new Madelinetosh Pashmina we got in last week."

Linda snorted. "Canoodling? I thought that word went out of fashion with pillbox hats and white kid gloves."

I spotted my coworker, Angie Ellis, lugging a garment bag and giant cardboard box down the sidewalk outside the store window, and I unhanded my emotional support yarn to hold the door open for her. In addition to being an artist and crafter active in the Chicago maker community who sold her handmade fashion accessories on Etsy, Angie created all the window displays for Mad About Ewe.

"Is this everything?" I asked as I took the box from her. It was more bulky than heavy and seemed to be full of white tulle.

She nodded as she tucked her silver-streaked black bob behind her ear. "Dawn's not coming in until noon, which gives us two hours to get everything set up."

Angie and Dawn Botstein, the store's owner, had been besties since high school. Dawn was getting married in a month, and Angie was surprising her with a new window display in honor of her upcoming nuptials.

"Did you finish the tuxedo jacket?" Angie asked me.

"It's in the back." She'd recruited me to help her with the new display. I was in charge of dressing the groom in our wedding tableau while Angie handled the bride.

"I'm going to miss the rainbows," Linda said as we started taking down the old window display to make room for the new one. For Pride last month Angie had made rainbow-striped knitted animals holding rainbow-colored umbrellas beneath a huge garter-stitch rainbow suspended from the ceiling.

"Yeah, but you're gonna love this. Get ready to laugh your ass off." Angie unzipped the garment bag and pulled out a frothy white wedding dress.

"Is that *your* wedding dress?" I asked as I marveled at the vintage puffed sleeves and sweetheart neckline. Never in a million years would I have pictured Angie in such a traditional gown. Dawn had shown me a photo once of the two of them back in high school when Angie had been deep in her goth phase, sporting dramatic dark eye makeup with her jet-black hair teased around her head like a lion's mane. Even in her late forties, Angie's fashion sense remained offbeat. Her outfit today, for example, was a black-and-white polka-dotted dress over colorful floral tights paired with a quilted patchwork jacket she'd made from upcycled clothes, and an eclectic statement necklace and spangly earrings she'd also made herself from repurposed estate jewelry.

Angie laughed at my stunned reaction. "Ridiculous, isn't it? Thanks to you Zoomers bringing back nineties fashion, I guess this thing's considered retro cool now."

"But it's so…" I struggled to find the right word to describe the princessy white confection.

"Hideously conservative?" she suggested. "Boring? Ugly?"

"It's beautiful," I said, shaking my head. "Just more conventional than I expected."

Angie shrugged as she fluffed the crinoline underskirts. "My parents wanted me to have a traditional wedding, and since they were footing the bill, my mother got to dress me up like a meringue. You know what though? I secretly loved it. It made me feel like Princess Di."

"What are you going to do with it? Please tell me you're not planning to *Pretty in Pink* this beautiful dress."

"Give me a little credit for having better sense than that. I love that movie, but Molly Ringwald should have gone to jail for what she did to that beautiful vintage prom dress Annie Potts gave her."

"Amen," Linda chimed in.

"No harm will come to the dress," Angie promised as she draped it over the couch. "You'll see. It's going to knock your socks off."

I admired and envied Angie's confidence. She never seemed to doubt herself or give a damn what other people thought. If they liked her style, great. If not, she didn't let it get to her. Not the way I did. I could only hope by the time I was Angie's age I'd have developed half as much self-confidence.

"Come on." Angie shook my shoulder. "Help me carry this stuff into the back. We need to get a move on if we want it done before Dawn gets in."

The two of us spent the next two hours setting up the new window display. We lugged two antique dress forms to the front window, and I dressed one of them in the mock tuxedo sweater I'd knit. A pair of Angie's husband's black dress pants and a crocheted flower boutonniere completed the groom's outfit.

Meanwhile, Angie had tugged her wedding dress over the other mannequin and was busy pinning together hanks of pastel yarn that she draped in bouffant layers over the skirt. In between helping customers, I hung white tulle from the ceiling to make a wedding arch and set a small antique table in front of the bride and groom to hold their wedding cake and the bride's bouquet, both of which I constructed out of skeins of yarn, ribbon, and knitting needles tied together with ribbon. By the time Dawn got in shortly before noon, the new display was pretty much done.

"Angie, oh my God!" Dawn exclaimed when she walked in the door and saw it. "It's your wedding dress! What have you done?"

Angie grinned up at her from the floor where she was putting the final touches on the yarn skirt. "We thought the window this month should celebrate your wedding."

"I can't believe you did all this." Dawn dropped her purse on the couch as she came over for a closer look. "Look at this cake. And the yarn bouquet. They're amazing!"

"That's all Chloe's wizardry," Angie said as she got to her feet and brushed off her butt. "She did most of the work while I was fussing with this damn skirt. It was a lot easier in my head than it turned out to be."

"Well, I love it," Dawn said, pulling her BFF into a hug. Her eyes shone as she turned to hug me next. "Honestly, you two. You're the best."

Dawn gave great mom hugs. Or what I imagined mom hugs should feel like, anyway. My mother had always been a stiff, reluctant hugger, just like my father. My grandmother wasn't too big on physical affection either, so my childhood had sorely lacked the kind of awesome hugs my boss gave out. Being hugged by Dawn was even better than squishing yarn. I could have stood there for an hour soaking up the feeling, but since that would have been super weird I made myself let go before it got awkward.

Dawn's finely attuned mom senses picked up on my clinginess, and she reached up to push my hair out of my face. "Everything all right with you?"

A lump rose in my throat at the casual maternal gesture, and I turned to straighten the satin ribbon holding the top tier of the wedding cake together. "Yep. Everything's dandy."

"How did your date go last night?"

I wrinkled my nose in distaste. "A new personal low. The guy was a total jerk."

"What did he do?" Angie asked in the hard, dangerous tone of someone already plotting the best way to dispose of a body.

"First, he was late. Then he told me I didn't look as good as my profile photo."

"He did not!" Angie's eyes flashed with homicidal intent, and I could practically hear the chorus of "Goodbye Earl" running through her head.

"He said I looked different because I wasn't as dressed up, but it was obvious what he meant. And you should have seen his face when I told him I worked in retail. He was a total snob who spent the whole date cataloguing all my flaws."

Dawn gave me a sympathetic look. "Oh, honey, I'm sure he wasn't."

"No, he literally was. He kept typing on his phone, which was rude enough by itself. But then I got a look at the screen and saw he'd been making these sneering notes about me."

"What kind of notes?" Dawn asked, frowning. "What did he say about you?"

"He called me unsophisticated and kooky. And apparently I lack ambition because I work retail."

"What a jagweed," Angie said with a scowl. "I hope he gets a fungus on his scrotum that doesn't respond to treatment."

"Get this—he told me he keeps notes on all his dates and inputs them into a spreadsheet so he can assign us all a rating. Can you believe that?"

"Wow, that is scuzzy," Dawn said. "He sounds like a little Mark Zuckerberg wannabe."

"Well, what do you expect?" Angie said. "That's what you get for listening to a computer algorithm when it comes to matters of the heart."

Dawn rolled her eyes at her friend. "Easy for you to say. The last time you went on a first date *Seinfeld* was still on the air and smartphones didn't even exist. You have no idea what it's like out there these days."

"Angie's right though," I said with a sigh. "I should have swiped left as soon as I saw he was a law student."

"Hey, my son's in law school." Dawn elbowed me lightly. "Not all law students are jagweeds."

"Barack Obama went to law school," Angie pointed out as she scooped up unused yarn hanks, tossing them into the box with the extra tulle. "You wouldn't turn your nose up at a young Barack Obama, would you?"

"He was a hottie," I agreed. "But realistically, I don't think Barack and I would have made a good match either. You don't get to be president unless you're super ambitious, and that's not the kind of man I'm looking for."

"What are you looking for?" Dawn asked.

"Someone who'll love me enough to make me a priority. I don't want to come in second to anyone's career." I'd gotten enough of that from my parents growing up. They'd both been so caught up in their own lives, they'd treated their own children like an afterthought. "I want to be the most important thing in someone else's life. That's not too much to ask, is it?"

"Hell no," Angie said, winging a hank of yarn into the box of tulle. "Hold out for a man who thinks you hung the stars in the sky. Don't you dare settle for anything less."

"If only I'd been as wise as you when I was your age." Dawn let out a wry chuckle. "Maybe I wouldn't have wasted twenty years being taken for granted by my first husband."

"Hey, but you've got Mike now, and he worships the ground you walk on." Angie slung her arm around her friend's shoulders. "Sometimes the universe wants us to take the scenic route and make an extended detour past the world's largest peanut before we find our soul mate."

Dawn stifled a snort as she retrieved her purse from the couch. "Jerry does kind of look like a peanut, doesn't he?"

"We live and learn." Angie hoisted the box of leftover supplies off the floor. "If anyone had told me twenty-five years ago that Mike Pilota would turn out to be a major upgrade over Dr. Gerald Botstein, I would have thought they were out of their gourd."

I smiled as I watched them disappear into the back of the shop. The two of them were a big part of why I loved working here so much. Dawn was like the mother I wished I'd had—generous, caring, full of good advice, and always willing to listen and offer a hug. While Angie was the wacky, protective aunt who'd help you key the word "dildo" onto the car of someone who'd done you wrong. I adored them both to the moon and back.

Stooping, I gathered the stray yarn bands left on the floor and carried them over to the counter. When the bell above the shop door jangled, I turned to greet the newly arrived customer and my smile froze on my face.

It was *him*.

The rude, snobby jagweed from last night. Bran the Judgmental.

How the hell had he found me? More importantly: What did he want with me?

He stopped short inside the door, doing a startled double take that at least laid to rest any fears this might be a stalker situation. The stunned expression on his face might as well have been accompanied by a record-scratch sound effect.

"What are you doing here?" he demanded. As if I'd committed an offense against him when *he* was the one who'd showed up at *my* workplace unexpectedly.

"I work here," I shot back. "What are you doing here?"

"I'm here to pick up my mother," he said, looking confused.

I blinked, trying to make his words make sense. "Who's your mother?"

"Brandon!" Dawn emerged from the back and broke into a huge smile as she flung her arms wide to hug him.

Brandon?

Wait a second.

Hold the phone.

Bran my terrible date was Dawn's son Brandon?

Oh, hell.

CHAPTER THREE

BRAN

As I hugged my mom, I frowned over her head at Chloe.

Who apparently *worked* here. The Chloe I'd matched with on FindUrPartner was the same person as the Chloe who worked for Mom. The Chloe I'd been hearing about for the last year, whom I'd always assumed was the same age as my mother.

As Chloe glared back at me with eyes cold enough to give the warm summer day a bitter chill, my neck flushed with a mix of shame and indignation. I felt bad about hurting her feelings last night—even though she'd had no right to grab my phone and invade my privacy. My unfiltered first impressions hadn't been meant for anyone's eyes but mine. I'd only been taking notes to help me focus on the conversation and aid my recall later. Apparently in her eyes that made me some kind of creep, but I didn't see why the same strategies I used to manage my ADHD in school and at work couldn't be employed in social situations as well.

It wasn't as if she'd been any more generous in her assessment of me. She might not have written her opinions down, but she'd made it clear how unimpressed she was from the moment I arrived. If the frozen look on her face when she'd first laid eyes on me hadn't been enough of a clue, her defensive, insincere manner had communicated her feelings well enough to dismiss any doubt that I'd been judged and found wanting.

My mom stepped back, holding me at arm's length as she peered into my face. "Are you feeling all right, sweetheart? You're not getting one of your headaches, are you?"

"No, I'm feeling fine," I assured her, dredging up a smile.

"Good." She hooked her arm through mine and dragged me over to Chloe.

The instant my mom turned around, Chloe's entire demeanor changed. Gone was all the hostility, replaced by a smile so beautiful and warm it felt like stepping into a beam of unfiltered sunshine. You'd never suspect those bright, toffee-colored eyes had been shooting murderous daggers at me a half second ago.

The sight of her smile did something to my chest. Chloe's pointed chin, upturned mouth, and deep-set eyes were too striking to be considered anything as ordinary as pretty. She was attractive in a way that was interesting to look at, like a piece of art. But when she smiled like that, her beauty took my breath away.

Why didn't she smile at me like that last night?

"Chloe, I'd like you to meet my older son, Brandon," Mom said. "Brandon, this is Chloe Carpenter."

I braced myself for Chloe to tell her we already knew each other and what a terrible date I'd been last night.

"Nice to meet you," she said instead, extending her hand as if we'd never met before. The wattage of her smile didn't change as she focused it on me, but it lost most of its warmth, going from a full-spectrum LED to a cool fluorescent. "Your mom talks about you all the time."

I stared, too surprised to react as my mind tripped in confusion. Did she expect me to play along with her pretense and pretend last night hadn't happened? Why wouldn't she want my mom to know we'd met?

Struggling to re-center my disoriented thoughts, I reached out to shake Chloe's hand before the moment dragged out into awkwardness. When my fingers wrapped around hers, a tingling jolt raced up my arm and into my chest. All the nerve endings in my body perked up and stood at attention, causing a fresh flush of heat to climb my neck.

I cleared my throat. "Mom speaks highly of you as well."

As Chloe slipped her hand out of mine, I noticed the tattoos on her arms, which had been covered by her sweater last night. A constellation dotted the inside of one forearm, a spray of pink flowers decorated her upper arm, and a delicate vine twined around the opposite arm, starting at her wrist and disappearing under the sleeve of her T-shirt. An inappropriate impulse to trace my fingertips over the intricate designs forced me to ball my hands into fists as I wondered how many other tattoos she had hidden under her clothes.

I had to remind myself that she despised me. Maybe if I'd never downloaded that cursed dating app and we'd met for the first time just now, we might have had a chance. Maybe I would have made a better first impression. Maybe if we'd been introduced this way first, she would have been more inclined to give me the benefit of the doubt.

Probably not. More likely I would have found a different way to piss her off. Despite what FindUrPartner's clearly flawed algorithm claimed, I found it difficult to believe the two of us could be compatible. Attraction aside, Chloe wasn't any more my type than I was hers. Free-spirited art majors with tattoos and shaved hair lived in a different world than the one ruled by somber-colored suits and conservative haircuts that I'd chosen for myself.

"It's crazy we've never met before this," Chloe said. "What brings you to the store today of all days?"

"We're going out to lunch," Mom answered for me.

"Oh? What's the occasion?" Chloe's eyes narrowed as if she thought I might have an ulterior motive for going out to lunch with my own mother.

"No occasion," I replied, disconcerted by her suspicion.

"Brandon just started an internship at a law office downtown," Mom said proudly. "Now that he's working nearby, I'm hoping I'll get to see more of him."

"That would sure be nice." Chloe's demeanor was outwardly friendly, but her eyes held no warmth at all.

"Are you ready to go?" I asked my mom, eager to escape this uncomfortable encounter. "I've only got an hour for lunch."

"Let me just grab my purse and jacket real quick." Mom squeezed my arm and disappeared into the back of the shop.

"Wow. So you're Dawn's Brandon." Chloe dropped all pretense of a smile as soon as the two of us were alone. "I should have guessed."

"Why?"

She shrugged. "It just seems odd that I've worked here a year and this is the first time I've seen you set foot in the store."

"It's a yarn store. I don't have a huge need for yarn in my life."

"Yeah, why would you want to visit the business your mom cares so much about when there's nothing in it for you? You're much too busy to do that, just like you were too busy and important to show up for our date on time."

"Now who's being snide and making snap judgments?" I shot back as her words shaped themselves into a hot, prickly ball that stuck in my chest.

"Doesn't feel so good, does it?"

"You don't know anything about me."

"If you say so," she replied with another shrug.

"Ready!" Mom trilled, reappearing from the back of the store.

Once again, Chloe's expression warmed as she turned to face my mom. "Enjoy your lunch."

"I'm sure we will," Mom said, fiddling with the collar of her jacket. "I'll be back in an hour."

I reached out to straighten it for her as I followed her to the door.

"Nice to meet you," Chloe called out. Purely for my mother's sake, I assumed.

"You too," I tossed over my shoulder for the same reason.

"Apparently no one has bridal showers anymore," Mom said as she stabbed her fork into her Cobb salad. "It's all couples showers these days. That's what Angie says, anyway. I certainly wouldn't know."

We were having lunch at a deli that was only a five-minute walk from her store. I did my best to focus on Mom's wedding talk while I picked at the Reuben I didn't feel like eating, but my thoughts kept rubber-banding back to Chloe.

Being disliked was nothing new to me, but despite what she seemed to think, I didn't go around trying to hurt people's feelings. This internet dating thing was brand-new to me, and clearly there was still room for improvement. Any kind of dating at all was more or less a foreign concept to me. I'd only ever had one girlfriend. We'd been together for seven years, through half of high school, then long-distance through all of college. Neither of us had been old enough to drive when we started dating, much less go to a bar, so there hadn't been much actual dating involved. While all my friends had been hooking up and playing the field in college, I'd stayed faithful to the woman I'd assumed I'd one day marry.

How was I supposed to know how to date? I'd missed my window of opportunity for learning. It had taken me months after the breakup to talk myself into signing up for a dating app. Last night had only been the third attempt of my dating experiment. The first two hadn't gone so great either, but at least no one had stormed off in a huff.

If Chloe wanted to think I was a terrible person based on one bad date, so be it. She was entitled to her feelings in that regard. But I resented her insinuation that I didn't care about my mom. She didn't even know me. Who did she think she was to make that kind of accusation? I called my mother every Sunday and went home for dinner at least once a month. Did that sound like someone who didn't care?

Well…

I called my mom *almost* every Sunday. I did occasionally forget. But only because I'd barely been managing to keep my head above water since I'd started law school. My mom understood that. She never put demands on my time or complained if I didn't see as much of her as she'd like. When I forgot to call, she knew it was because of my ADHD and not because I didn't love her. Besides, she'd been busy with her new boyfriend—now fiancé—anyway. It wasn't as if she'd been lonely.

A gentle touch on my hand snapped me back to the present, and I realized I hadn't been listening to a thing she'd said. One look at her face told me she knew it too. It had happened so many times before, she'd long ago learned to recognize the signs.

"I'm sorry," I said as a flush of guilt heated my neck. "I didn't mean—"

"I know you didn't. It's all right. I was rambling on anyway."

"You really weren't. It's just me being me." Her easy understanding only made me feel worse. She deserved better than a son who didn't pay attention to her.

That was what Chloe had been getting at, wasn't it? She thought I'd been ignoring my mom because I hadn't come by the store more often to see her. Maybe she had a point. Maybe I wasn't making enough of an effort.

Mom had given up her career to stay home with me and my younger brother, so she'd been a constant, devoted presence in my life. One that I'd admittedly taken for granted sometimes growing up, as children often did. But since my parents' divorce a few years ago, she seemed to have built this whole new life for herself that didn't involve me.

Until they split up after I left for college, I assumed my parents had a happy marriage. But I guess Mom had only been pretending to be happy, biding her time until my brother and I grew up so she could finally have a life of her own. First she'd opened the yarn store, then last year she'd started dating this guy named Mike who she'd known in high school. Now he'd moved in with her, and this person I barely knew was living in my childhood home and had made himself so comfortable he seemed to belong there more than I did.

I wasn't sure I even knew who my mom was anymore. But maybe I'd never known who she was apart from being my mom. I'd assumed she didn't need much from me with everything else she had going on, but maybe I should have made more of an effort to be part of the changes in her life.

"I'm sorry if it seems like I don't pay enough attention to you," I said, feeling another churn of guilt.

"Oh, sweetie. I don't think that." Mom's expressive green eyes softened as she reached across the table again to give my hand a reassuring squeeze. "I know you're doing your best."

Was I though? And what if my best wasn't good enough? I could probably try harder. And I would, I vowed.

"We should make lunch a weekly thing," I said. "At least for the rest of the summer while I'm working nearby."

"I think that'd be lovely, but only if you have time. I know you'll be busy with your internship, and I don't want you taking on additional stress for me."

"Having lunch with you isn't stressful."

She smiled as she tucked her copper hair behind her ear. "We can have lunch as much as you want. You know I'm always happy to see you. I just don't want to be one of those parents who makes you feel guilty for having a life of your own."

"You don't have to worry about that. School and work is pretty much all the life I can handle right now."

My unsuccessful ventures into the world of internet dating were more of a test exercise than a serious effort to find a girlfriend. I didn't have time to devote to a new relationship, and wouldn't for the next several years if my law career proceeded as I hoped. The only reason I even bothered was that I didn't want to end up in my thirties with no dating experience. If I could squeeze in the occasional date now, when it wasn't a high priority, it'd be a low-risk way of getting some experience under my belt.

"You're so much like your father," Mom said, shaking her head. "But with him it was his medical career consuming his life instead of the law." Her smile wavered as her eyes got a faraway look for a second before she refocused on me. "How is your internship going so far? Are you enjoying it?"

Only if your definition of enjoyment involved constant stress, anxiety, and feelings of inadequacy.

"It's not too bad," I said, trying to put a positive spin on it so she wouldn't worry. I always struggled with changes to my established routines, as my mom knew from all the years she'd spent consulting doctors, ferrying me to and from my therapy appointments, and talking me down whenever I got overwhelmed. It required constant vigilance to manage my ADHD and would for the rest of my life. Whenever I let up even a little bit, like a moment ago when my mind had wandered while my mother was talking, my attention deficit reared its ugly head and made a mess of things.

"I'm still adjusting, but I'm sure it'll be fine," I told my mom. It would be fine. Eventually. Once I found my stride.

Mom's head tilted to the side as she studied my face, and I fought the urge to squirm. "Have you been taking care of yourself?"

"I'm taking my meds, if that's what you're asking."

"What about sleeping?"

"As best I can. Same as always." My ADHD meds made it hard to sleep. Some nights my brain refused to turn off and let me relax.

"And eating?" Mom cast a pointed look at the half-eaten sandwich on my plate.

"You know the meds suppress my appetite." Stifling a flicker of annoyance, I picked up my sandwich and forced myself to eat another bite. There was no hiding anything from my mom's perceptive gaze.

"I'm sorry," she said. "I don't mean to be a nag. You're a grown man now who's more than capable of managing your own life. I just forget sometimes that you're not my little boy anymore."

I rubbed my chest, hating that I'd let my petty irritation make her feel bad. "I know, Mom. It's okay."

Did it even count as nagging when I needed the reminders? Mom had gotten into the habit of micromanaging me because I'd needed her to do it, even if it sometimes annoyed me. Part of the reason I'd gone out of state for college was to get away from her constant fussing. I'd wanted to prove that I could take care of myself without relying on someone else to check up on me.

"I'm sorry for being cranky," I said. "I guess I have been pretty stressed about the new job." I forced myself to take another bite of sandwich even though I didn't feel hungry.

Mom watched me, considering. "Have you had any migraines lately?"

"Last Friday," I admitted with a wince.

The migraines were a fun new thing that had started in college. People with ADHD were more likely to suffer from migraines, but the reason why remained an unknown variable. By keeping a migraine journal, I'd identified some of my triggers. Stress, dehydration, skipping meals, and lack of sleep were a few of the big ones. All things I'd experienced more of since the start of my internship.

Mom's soft gaze moved over me, but she didn't say anything. She didn't have to.

"I take your point," I muttered. "I'll try to be better."

"You don't need to put any more pressure on yourself. It's not about being good or bad. Maybe just try to set aside more time for self-care. You know, Angie made this Spotify playlist that she uses for meditation. I've been listening to it in the mornings when I do yoga. I could send you the link if you want."

"That'd be great," I said. "Thanks." I was willing to try anything that might help. Meditation hadn't worked all that well for me in the past, but maybe if I found the right music or tried a different visual stimulus... Maybe I'd given up too easily before. There were so many different meditation techniques... I could do some research, make a list of all the ones that seemed the most promising and test them out, recording my results in a spreadsheet.

"You're so goal-oriented, like your father," Mom said, and I yanked myself out of my thought spiral to focus on her again. Her mouth had turned down at the corners the way it always did at the mention of Dad. Even thinking about him seemed to make her unhappy. "I worry about you pushing yourself too hard. The world's not going to end if you're not the best at everything. It's okay to give yourself a break sometimes, Brandon."

I nodded, staring past her head at the window behind her. Everyone on the sidewalk outside was hurrying to get somewhere. Do something. *Be* someone. None of them were taking a break. If I let up on myself, they'd all outpace me.

Rationally, I understood the wisdom of Mom's advice. But what she was really suggesting was that I let myself fail, which wasn't something I knew how to do on purpose. On accident? Sure, I failed all the time. That was why I had to constantly push myself so hard to be the best.

When I didn't say anything, Mom reached out and laid her hand over mine. "I'm so proud of you and everything you've accomplished. You know that, right?"

"Yeah, Mom. Of course I know that."

She was a big believer in positive reinforcement. Even when I'd been failing classes and falling apart, she always found something to praise. Unlike my dad, a world-renowned pediatric pulmonologist who expected excellence from everyone around him, and liberally dispensed his weighty scowl to let you know when you'd fallen short. Dad's stinginess with his approval had made me that much more desperate to earn it. While I appreciated Mom's faith in me, it didn't hold as much weight because I'd never had to fight as hard for it as for one of Dad's rare pats on the back.

"Just remember that accomplishments aren't the only thing in life that's important," Mom went on. "When you get to be my age you'll realize that a good life is about the people you surround yourself with and the time you spend with them—not a bunch of lines on your résumé. I don't want you to look back on your youth with regret because you didn't take time to enjoy yourself along the way."

"I've been dating," I blurted in an attempt to relieve her worries. Then instantly regretted it.

Mom perked up. "Really?"

I felt the weight of all her hopes and expectations in the eagerness she injected into that one word. They sank into the pit of my stomach like a rock as I thought about how disappointed she'd be if she knew how badly it was going.

"Nothing to get excited about," I said, trying to manage her expectations. "I signed up for an app just to try it out a little. I've only been on a few trial dates."

"You haven't liked any of the people you've met so far?"

"Not really." More importantly, they hadn't liked me. My chest tightened as I recalled the hurt in Chloe's face when she'd read the notes on my phone.

"But you're trying, that's what matters," my mom said with her irrepressible optimism. "It's nice to see you putting yourself out there again. I know you took it hard when you and Marisa broke up."

My lips pressed together as I brushed away an errant breadcrumb from the table. The girlfriend who'd dumped me wasn't my favorite topic of conversation.

"Enough talking about me," I said, taking charge of the conversation in what was meant to be a cheery tone of voice but came out sounding like the sort of demented birthday party clown who struck terror in the hearts of children. "Tell me what's going on with you. How've you been?"

Mom gave me a sympathetic smile, one that said *I know what you're doing, but I'll take pity on you and indulge your avoidant tendencies this time because I love you.* The woman had a real gift for conveying entire paragraphs with the crinkles around her eyes. "I've been wonderful. Up to my ears with wedding preparations, but it's a fun kind of busy so I can't complain. Mike and I swore we were going to keep it small and simple, but things always have a way of getting more complicated than you planned."

"Is there anything I can do to help?" I offered. And not just to prove Chloe wrong. Although that certainly factored into it, along with a heaping dose of guilt over my mixed feelings about Mom's upcoming nuptials. I knew it was childish, but I looked forward to watching my mom marry a man who wasn't my father with about as much enthusiasm as I anticipated my first colonoscopy. But that was my issue to get over, and I wasn't going to let it cast a pall over my mom's happiness.

"Oh no, Mike and I have it all under control." She dismissed my offer with a wave of her hand. "Between Angie and Chloe, we've got all the help we need."

Great, so Chloe had been helping my mom with her wedding preparations while I'd petulantly avoided getting involved. No wonder she thought I was a self-involved asshole who didn't care about my mom. "You can always ask me to help, you know. I'm available if you ever need anything."

"I know, honey." She gave another careless flick of her hand that meant she had no intention of doing any such thing.

"I'm serious, Mom. I'll get my feelings hurt if you don't let me help."

Her tinkling laugh was only slightly self-conscious. Mostly she seemed pleased, which made me feel a little better. "Okay, I promise to let you know if anything comes up. There's the shower in two weeks, obviously, but Angie's handling all of that and refuses to let me do any of the work. Do you think you'll be able to make it?"

Right, the wedding shower. That was what Mom had been talking about when I'd tuned out earlier. Something about it being for couples? Which apparently meant I was expected to attend. There was probably an invitation buried in the stack of unread mail piling up at home. Presumably Mike would be there too. Yay, another opportunity for my future stepfather and me to awkwardly attempt to bond. Even better, I assumed Chloe would be there as well. *Wonderful.*

I must have looked traumatized because Mom quickly added, "You don't have to come if you're too busy. Everyone will understand if you can't make it."

The fuck they would. What she meant was *she'd* understand, even though I could tell she really wanted me there. No way in hell was I disappointing my mom, whether or not she was willing to let me off the hook. "I'm coming to the shower, Mom. Of course I am."

She looked so pleased I felt like a real asshole for dreading it so much.

CHAPTER FOUR

CHLOE

I did not expect to see so many penises and boobs at Dawn and Mike's wedding shower. No matter which direction I looked, there they were. Penises and boobs everywhere.

Not real ones, mind you. I was talking about the decorations. Penis garland festooned the ceiling, bouquets of breast- and penis-shaped balloons hovered in every corner, and penis confetti had been scattered over the buffet table. Angie must have cleaned out the whole naughty section of the party supply store.

Another thing I hadn't been prepared for? Cocktails strong enough to knock a heavyweight boxer on his ass. The shower hadn't even started yet, and I was already tipsy thanks to the lemon drop Janie Sullivan had foisted on me when I arrived to help set up.

I hadn't planned on drinking, but you didn't say no to Janie. She was six feet tall, intimidatingly smart, and married to Mr. Sullivan, who not only owned the retail space that Mad About Ewe occupied but also happened to be Mike's boss.

Unfortunately, I'd guzzled my lemon drop too quickly, and now I had to concentrate extra hard not to accidentally dice my fingertips with the tomatoes for the taco bar. Oh right—I forgot to mention the shower featured both a taco bar and a hot dog bar in keeping with the genitalia theme.

As Dawn's matron of honor, Angie had organized the shower, but Fiona Archer had volunteered to host it at her apartment in the building above Mad

About Ewe. Fiona was a regular customer at the store, but she also worked with Mike at Mr. Sullivan's company, Cipher Security.

"What do you think?" Fiona's husband Greg asked from the ladder where he was hanging another swag of penis garland across their dining room ceiling. "Is that enough dicks, or do we want more?"

Fiona glanced up from the penis-shaped cake she was icing. "I'd make a dick joke right now, but I don't want to come off as cocky."

"Nice," her husband said, grinning at her.

Tilting her head, Fiona studied the dining room he'd been decorating. "What if you hung some penises from the chandelier above the buffet?"

"Coming right up," Greg replied and climbed down from the ladder.

The doorbell rang as I was washing my hands after finishing the last of the food prep. "I'll get it," I said and dropped off the bowls of tomatoes, lettuce, and shredded cheese at the buffet table on my way to the front door.

I opened it to find Sandra Fielding, another regular customer at the store who also lived in the building, accompanied by a younger man carrying two covered trays.

"We come bearing phallic food!" she declared in cheerful greeting.

"Oh good." I stepped back to admit them. "I was afraid we might not have enough."

"Chloe, this is my husband, Alex." Sandra gestured at the man behind her as she breezed into the apartment. "Alex, this is Chloe, a ruthless enabler of my luxury yarn addiction who works in the shop downstairs."

"Nice to meet you," I said to Alex.

He nodded his head in solemn greeting as he moved past me. "Hey."

"We brought chocolate-covered bananas," Sandra declared as I trailed her and Alex into the kitchen.

"And figs," Alex added, setting the trays on the island. "Don't forget the figs."

Sandra peered over Fiona's shoulder with an approving nod. "Nice penis cake."

"Why figs?" Janie asked, joining them at the island. "How do they fit into the theme?"

"Because the inside of a halved fig looks just like a vag." Sandra peeled back the foil covering one of the trays and held out a fig for Janie's inspection.

I leaned in for a look along with everyone else. Sure enough, the sliced fig did have a certain Georgia O'Keeffe look to it.

"Did you know every ripe fig has a dead wasp inside it?" Angie announced, causing everyone to turn and stare at her.

"Um…*what?*" Sandra wore a horrified expression. "That's not true, is it? Please tell me I haven't been eating dead wasps."

Angie shrugged. "There was a post about it on Facebook. Apparently fig trees are pollinated by female wasps that tunnel inside the immature fruit to lay their eggs. But they lose their wings burrowing into the fig and get trapped there. When the eggs hatch, the baby wasps all fly away, and the pollinated fig grows around the body of the dead mama wasp that's left behind."

"That's true," Janie said. "Some figs species are dioecious—meaning each tree has either male or female reproductive organs—and rely on a particular species of wasp for pollination."

"Okay, well, I'm never eating a fig again." Fiona sent an apologetic look at Sandra. "No offense to your figs."

"Fig wasps are much smaller than common wasps," Janie said, as if that made it fine to eat them. "And the fig produces an enzyme that breaks down the insect carcass. It essentially digests the wasp during the ripening process, so figs could be considered carnivorous."

Fiona wrinkled her nose. "That's not any less disgusting."

Janie reached over and helped herself to a fig. "If the thought upsets you, you might be comforted to know the vast majority of fresh figs currently sold in the United States are grown from parthenocarpic cultivars, meaning they don't require pollination."

"Oh thank God," Sandra said, laying a hand over her chest. "I was afraid I might have to give up figs."

"Doesn't bother me either way. I still love figs." Alex smirked as he popped a fig in his mouth. "Sandra introduced me to them, and now they're one of my favorite things to eat."

"Yeah, I'll bet they are," Greg said with a snort. "But do you think you could unhand the figs for a minute and hold the ladder so I can hang more penises over here?"

Sandra started unwrapping the chocolate-covered bananas. "If anyone knows any disgusting banana facts, I'll thank you to keep them to yourself."

Fiona glanced at the bananas and clapped a hand across her mouth to smother a laugh. "Sandra, you didn't."

"Oh yes I did." Sandra held up one of her bananas to show it off. "I'm really pleased with how they turned out."

She'd cut a strawberry in half around its equator and fastened the pointy tip to one end of the chocolate-covered banana, and the bulbous top of the strawberry to the other, using a skewer to hold the whole thing together. Put together like that, it looked uncannily like a circumcised penis and ballsack.

The doorbell rang again, and I went to go answer it. This time it was Linda from the store. "I made itty-bitty titty cookies," she said, shoving a covered plate at me. "I was told there would be cocktails."

I directed her toward Janie and her pitcher of lemon drops, then went to set Linda's sugar cookies decorated with disturbingly realistic icing nipples on the dessert table. I'd just finished arranging them when the guests of honor showed up.

Dawn burst out laughing when she got a look at the decor, while her fiancé Mike, a big, beardy, lumberjack-looking guy, turned adorably beet red. "Sakes alive, where are your kids?" she asked Fiona and Greg. "Tell me they're not about to come popping out of their bedrooms any second."

"Never fear. All the kids are safely upstairs at Elizabeth's with Nico's mom," Fiona said.

"Although they did help blow up some of the balloons before we exiled them," Greg added proudly.

The guests started arriving in full force not long after that, and the Archers' apartment filled up with people sipping lemon drops and enjoying the raunchy-themed foods. Some of the shower guests were regular customers I knew, but there were quite a few I didn't know, many of whom worked with Mike. Mr. Sullivan himself showed up, looking as grouchy and terrifying as usual, followed shortly thereafter by the aforementioned Elizabeth and Nico, who I knew from their frequent visits to the store.

Elizabeth was a doctor who used to work for Dawn's ex-husband, so she and Dawn had known each other for a long time. She was married to Nico Moretti, a famous comedian who also happened to be an avid crocheter and regular purchaser of yarn.

As I mingled with the party guests, I kept one eye on the front door in case Bran showed up. He and his mother had been meeting for lunch regularly, but he hadn't been back to the store since that first time. I couldn't help wondering if he was intentionally avoiding me, though it was hard to imagine my existence mattered enough to factor into Bran's decisions. More likely he didn't think about me at all.

I wished I could say the same. Ever since I'd found out my awful internet date was Dawn's son, he'd been taking up way too much real estate in my head. My stomach dipped with apprehension at the thought of seeing him again. Even if he didn't show at the shower today, he'd be at the wedding next month. Dawn and Mike were having a destination wedding at a winery estate in northern Michigan. What were the odds I'd be able to avoid Bran during the three whole days of meals and activities planned for all the guests? Slim to none, I expected.

I forced my attention away from the door and back to the two women I'd been talking to. I knew Marie from her frequent visits to the shop, while Tess was a high school friend of Dawn's who'd taken one of our knitting classes with her daughter Erin last year.

"What do you get when you cross a penis and a potato?" Marie asked, grinning over the rim of her lemon drop. Inspired by the party decor, she and Tess had been trading dick jokes and trying to top each other.

"I don't know," Tess said. "What?"

"A dick-tater," Marie replied, earning groans from me and Tess. She pointed a finger at me. "Fine then, let's hear you do better, Chloe."

"What did the left nut say to the right nut?" I offered, throwing my hat into the dick joke ring. "Don't talk to the guy in the middle. He's a real dick."

"Not bad," Marie conceded, raising her glass in salute.

"What do a penis and a Rubik's Cube have in common?" Tess countered. "The more you play with it, the harder it gets."

"Okay, that's a good one," Marie said, snickering. "Extra on-brand points for slipping in a Gen X reference."

"Slipping in." Tess snorted and clinked her martini glass against Marie's. "Nice."

They were both extra giggly thanks to Janie's lemon drops. Having learned my lesson after the first one, I'd been nursing my second drink for the last hour and only had a mild case of the warm fuzzies at the moment.

The sound of Dawn's animated voice drew my attention, and my stomach dropped when I saw her talking to Bran. Annoyingly, he looked even more handsome than I remembered. Instead of a suit, tonight he wore a light-blue oxford paired with a beautiful Fair Isle sweater-vest. Both were impeccably fitted, pulling tight across his shoulders and torso. Combined with a pair of thigh-hugging jeans, the outfit looked way hotter on him than any sweater-vest had the right to, no matter how beautifully knitted. I hadn't realized he'd been hiding such a nice body under his starched dress shirts.

Gah! What was I doing? I shouldn't be standing here admiring his body. Especially not while he was talking to his mother.

Dismayed, I excused myself and made a beeline for the dining room before Bran caught me staring. In need of a distraction, I busied myself tidying up the buffet, then collected all the dirty dishes and carried them into the kitchen.

Was I doing it to hide from Bran? Yes. Yes, I was. I knew if I went back out there, I wouldn't be able to stop myself from staring at him. What if he noticed and got the wrong idea? Or worse, what if he tried to talk to me? Better to stay as far away as possible.

When Dawn eventually found me in the kitchen, I'd nearly finished hand-washing all the dishes. "I was wondering where you'd disappeared to. You're not here to work, you know. You're off the clock tonight."

"I know," I said, rinsing off a plate. "I just thought I'd help out by getting a head start on the cleanup."

"The cleanup can wait." Dawn shut off the water and handed me a dish towel. "You're supposed to be enjoying the party with the other guests. Come on, young lady." Taking me by the arm, she marched me into the dining room and over to someone picking through the cooler next to the drinks table. "Zach."

He straightened and turned to face us, arching his eyebrows slightly. "Yes, Mom?"

I started, realizing this must be Bran's younger brother. The two of them looked nothing alike. I assumed Bran took after his father, while Zach was one hundred percent his mother's son. Same copper hair and freckled skin, same twinkling green eyes, same sunny smile.

"Say hello to Chloe Carpenter," Dawn ordered, tugging me forward.

Zach shifted his attention to me, and his sunny smile grew even warmer as he looked me up and down. "Hi there, Chloe Carpenter."

Whoa. He was cute. Feeling my cheeks flush, I opened my mouth to respond, but Dawn spoke before I could.

"Would you do me a favor? Get Chloe a drink and then keep an eye on her so she doesn't try to do any more work?"

"Nothing would make me happier."

"Thank you, sweetheart." Dawn rose on her toes to kiss his cheek before leaving the two of us alone.

"What would you like to drink?" Zach asked me. "There seems to be a variety of beers, assorted flavors of sparkling water, and a pitcher of unidentified yellow liquid."

"That would be the lemon drops," I said. "And I'll have one of those." Probably not a good idea, but hey, Dawn had told me to enjoy the party. Who was I to defy her wishes?

"Coming right up." Zach turned to the drinks table and hesitated over the selection of glassware.

"You can use one of the martini glasses," I told him. "And there's sugar for the rim. Here, I can do it."

"Ah ah." He held up a finger to stop me. "You might be willing to flout my mother's orders, but I am not. I'll be getting your drink, for good or ill. Sorry in advance for my poor bartending skills."

I laughed and raised my hands in surrender. "Fine. Just press the rim of one of those martini glasses into the sponge, then lightly dip it in the saucer of sugar."

He followed my instructions and handed me a brimming glass of lemon drop. "Your drink, madam."

"Thank you." I watched his thigh muscles flex beneath his faded jeans as he bent over to get himself a beer. He was stockier than Bran and not quite as tall, but equally as attractive in his own very different way.

Zach's attention zeroed in on me again as he sipped his beer. "So…you're the famous Chloe."

"Famous?"

"Mom talks about you so much that I feel like I already know you."

My smile grew as his words sank in. "She does?"

"I confess to being a little jealous. I'm starting to think she likes you more than me."

My cheeks flushed. "Oh, no, that's not— She doesn't really—"

"Don't worry," he said, eyes twinkling playfully. "I promise not to hold it against you. Too much."

"Your mom talks about you too, you know."

"To take my name in vain, I'm guessing."

I laughed. "Not at all. She adores you."

"That's because I'm naturally adorable," he said with another eye twinkle. "But I've also been known to make her tear her hair out a time or two, which I'm willing to bet you've never done."

"Since she's my boss, it's in my financial interest not to."

Zach's attention shifted to something behind me that caused him to narrow his eyes. "Now, that's curious."

"What is?" Since Bran was likely back there somewhere, I refused to turn and look for myself.

"My brother seems to be giving one of us the evil eye. Usually I'd assume it was me, but I can't think of anything I've done to piss him off this week."

"That would be my evil eye," I said, scowling into my lemon drop. Now I *definitely* wasn't turning around to look. "You're in the clear this time."

Zach's eyebrows jumped upward. "You're already acquainted with Brandon's charms, are you?"

"You could say that."

Zach leaned in closer, his soft breath warming the side of my neck as he dropped into a conspiratorial whisper. "Don't keep me in suspense. I thought we were friends."

"We only met five minutes ago," I pointed out, reminding myself that Zach was still an undergrad, the same age as my younger brother, and entirely too charming to boot. Guys who were this good at flirting rarely meant anything they said.

His lips pursed in mock disapproval. They weren't as full or shapely as Bran's but were nice enough in their way. "The deep, meaningful bond we've forged transcends such mundanities as time. Now spill, bestie."

Was Bran still watching us? My neck hurt with the strain of not turning around to look. "If I tell you, you have to promise not to breathe a word to your mother."

"Ohh! The plot thickens." Zach's eyes sparked with delight. "Color me even more intrigued."

"I'm serious," I said, giving him my sternest look. "I don't want your mom to know about it."

"It'll be our little secret. You can trust me." With utmost gravity, he raised his hand in an oath-swearing gesture. "On my honor. I'll take it to my grave."

"Bran and I may have sort of gone out on a date."

The corner of Zach's mouth pulled into a smirk. "May have sort of? Sounds like a real banger."

"It definitely was not that."

He gave a knowing nod. "So what did my brother do to offend you?"

"What makes you so sure he did anything wrong?"

"Because I've known him all my life. Brandon's what you might call an acquired taste."

I let out a wry laugh. That was certainly one way of putting it. "Let's just say we mutually failed to hit it off."

Zach's lips twitched as his gaze flicked past me again. "Judging by the looks he keeps giving you, I'm guessing there's a lot more to the story than that."

My insides churned with mixed emotions. Being the object of anyone's antipathy made my stomach sink with anxiety, and yet there was also this odd little flutter of excitement at the thought that Bran was as preoccupied by me as I was by him.

"So?" Zach pressed, studying me. "Come on. What happened?"

"It's possible I stormed out in the middle of our date," I admitted, feigning an excessive interest in the surface of my drink.

"Now I'm *really* going to need more details."

I didn't want to tell him more. Even now, just thinking about the things Bran had written about me—*flaky, unsophisticated, no ambition*—made my chest feel hollow and achy. They weren't even all that bad, objectively. There were far worse things he could have said, words that would have been far more hurtful and insulting. But the words he'd used had hurt enough.

Unfortunately, Zach refused to let it go. He continued to pester me in that friendly, cajoling manner of his until I gave in finally. As I described how Bran had fired odd questions at me while typing on his phone, Zach's smile shifted to a sympathetic frown. I skipped over the part where I saw what he'd written about me, but when I recounted Bran's admission that he kept a spreadsheet for scoring all his dates, Zach seemed to find it more amusing than outrageous.

He shook his head, chuckling to himself. "I wish I could say that didn't sound like him, but…that sounds exactly like something he would do."

"Really?"

Zach shrugged. "Brandon's always been a bit of a judgmental prick. He's like a walking Rotten Tomatoes commenter." He cocked his head, leaning in as if to share a confidence. "As someone who's been on the receiving end of his fault-finding my entire life, allow me to tell you a little secret that helps it go down easier."

"Okay." I leaned toward him, eager to receive any insider information that might help make sense of Bran's odd ways.

"The thing to know about my brother is he's a fanatical perfectionist, which means there's no one in the world he's harder on than himself. He picks apart his own flaws and mistakes so much that it's second nature for him to identify everyone else's shortcomings as a side gig. I think he honestly believes he's being helpful instead of a dick."

I frowned, disappointed by Zach's so-called secret. It didn't make me feel any better or explain why Bran was the way he was. "I'm still skeeved about the dating spreadsheet. That's giving some serious HOTorNOT incel energy."

Zach laughed. "Brandon's love affair with spreadsheets is actually one of his more endearing personality quirks. He uses them for everything from planning his meals to keeping track of all the books he's read. The only way he knows how to function is by slotting everything into neatly labeled boxes in a hopeless attempt to enforce order on a chaotic world. It's adorable, really."

Yeah, no. Keeping a reading spreadsheet might be a little bit adorable. But recording contemptuous opinions of me in a document he used to rank me against the other women he dated? Not so much.

Zach broke into a grin as his gaze flicked past me. "Oh goodie. Brandon seems to be coming over here. This should be interesting."

CHAPTER FIVE

BRAN

It figured that Chloe and my brother would get along. If she were just a few years younger, she'd be exactly his type—quirky and eye-catching. Much like a crow, Zach had never been able to resist beautiful, shiny things.

The age difference didn't seem to be stopping him from slathering on the charm, I couldn't help noticing. I tried not to pay attention, but my eyes kept drifting that direction of their own volition. Chloe wasn't easy for me to ignore.

I'd tried to put her out of my head over the last several weeks, but she'd infected my brain. A highlight reel of our two unsettling encounters had been playing on a recurring loop, haunting my idle moments. I didn't understand it. I barely knew her. She should have been easy to forget, yet thoughts of her had haunted me as I lay in bed battling insomnia every night. Her biting words needled at me while the image of her soft brown eyes shimmering with hurt spiked shamefully through my gut.

I'd known she would be at the shower tonight, but the sight of her had blind-sided me nonetheless. Despite my vow to stop by Mom's store more often, I'd avoided going back there. I told myself it was to spare Chloe's feelings, but it was just as much to spare mine. Yet I'd instinctively looked for her tonight as soon as I'd walked into the party.

When I'd first glimpsed her honey-gold hair, for a moment everything seemed to stop. My heart. My breathing. My brain function. The bright purple outfit she wore made her easy to spot in the crowd. My eyes were drawn to her like a compass needle no matter how hard I tried to resist the pull. She'd disappeared into the kitchen for a while, but instead of enjoying the reprieve from her distracting presence, I'd continued to scan the room, watching for her reappearance.

When I finally spotted her again she was deep in conversation with Zach, and the two of them looked as cozy as old friends. They stood off to themselves in a corner of the dining room, affording me an unobstructed view of Chloe from behind. Initially I'd thought she was wearing a floor-length dress, but now I could see her purple one-piece was actually long, billowy pants. The outfit's thin straps zigzagged across her back, leaving acres of bare skin exposed and cursing me with the knowledge she wasn't wearing a bra. It also afforded me a better look at the tattoos on her upper arms, as well as a tantalizing partial view of a previously unseen one on her shoulder blade—a puffy dandelion with its seeds turning to birds as they blew away stretched across her upper back, disappearing under the fall of her hair.

I didn't like how close Zach was standing to her or the way his gaze kept dipping to her chest. He shouldn't be looking at her like that, like she was a candy bar he wanted to unwrap.

His eyes briefly met mine, and his white teeth flashed in a self-satisfied smile I would have loved to smack right off his irritating face. My jaw clenched when he rested his hand on her shoulder and leaned in close to speak into her ear. I wanted to walk over there and tell him not to touch her, but Chloe didn't seem to mind my brother's attention.

I tried to refocus on the story Mike's sister and her husband were telling about their kid's Little League team, but it was hard to pay attention when Zach kept smirking at me over Chloe's shoulder. Every time I glanced their way his eyes would shift to meet mine, and his mouth would quirk with knowing smugness.

Were they talking about me? Probably. No doubt she'd told him about our disastrous date, and they were having a chuckle at my expense.

Zach leaned in to invade Chloe's personal space again, and I saw her shift toward him in response. A red haze filmed my vision when he threw his head back with a cackling laugh that rose above the din of voices. Before I could think better of it, I excused myself and headed toward them.

When he noticed my approach, Zach murmured something to Chloe, and I saw her stiffen as she turned to face me.

"Hey, big brother! Nice of you to join us." Zach grinned as he clapped a too-firm hand on my shoulder. "I'd introduce you two, but apparently you know each other already."

So they had been talking about me. Ignoring my brother, I addressed myself to Chloe. "It's good to see you again."

"Is it?" Zach asked before she could respond. "To hear Chloe tell it, you two got on like pancakes and ketchup."

"Did you ask Mom's permission to have that beer?" I returned testily.

Zach's jaw ticked. He loved to goad me but didn't enjoy being goaded back nearly as much. "Did you seriously come over here to play narc? I'm three months shy of twenty-one, and Mom doesn't give a shit."

"Which one of us is pancakes and which one is ketchup?" Chloe broke in.

"What?" Zach blinked at her, momentarily distracted from picking a fight with me.

A smile curved Chloe's lips as she gazed up at him through her lashes. "You said Brandon and I got on like pancakes and ketchup, so am I supposed to be the pancakes or the ketchup?"

"You're pancakes," I said, wishing I knew how to get her to smile at me like that.

Her eyes met mine, and I felt a peculiar jab below my ribs. "Why?"

"Because you're sweet," Zach answered for me.

Chloe's gaze stayed on me. "Is that why?"

I shook my head. "A tablespoon of ketchup contains the same amount of sugar as a full-size pancake."

"Then why?"

"Because ketchup has vinegar in it."

"Excellent point," Zach agreed. "Between the two of you, Brandon's definitely the sour one."

"I don't know," Chloe said, pinking slightly. "I've got some vinegar in me when I get riled up."

My mouth twitched as I remembered how she'd told me off. "Very true."

"Okay, but everyone likes pancakes," Zach said. "You can't say the same about Brandon."

I pressed my lips together, unable to deny the accuracy of his statement.

"I'm not sure any food is universally liked." Chloe looked at me again. "Do you like pancakes?"

"Too much gluten gives me brain fog."

"Well, there you go," she said, smiling tightly.

A too-long silence ballooned in the awkward atmosphere between us until Zach clapped me on the shoulder again. "Wow. Some party, huh?"

"Yes," I agreed. "It definitely is a party of some kind."

"Are you having a good time?" Chloe asked me, working hard to maintain the appearance of civility.

"Not really."

"Right." Her lips pinched together.

"Brandon doesn't like parties," Zach explained. "Or people. Or fun. He'd rather be home studying, right?"

I shrugged, unable to deny it.

"Okay, but how much are you loving the decor?" he asked me. "Be honest."

I glanced up at the sex-themed decorations I'd been trying to ignore. Like any sane person, I preferred not to think about sex and my mother in the same context. That went double for not wanting to think about my mother and her fiancé having sex. "About as much as you are, I'd imagine."

Zach's mouth twisted wryly. "I've actually had anxiety dreams where I'm trapped in a room with Mom and her new lover surrounded by giant inflatable penises, so you could say it's a real dream come true for me."

Chloe gave him a bemused look. "Don't tell me you're embarrassed by sex?"

"Heaven forfend," Zach said with a snort. "Why wouldn't I want to celebrate the fact that my mom's getting boned by some dude?"

Chloe was fully frowning now, and I found myself relieved that someone else had put their foot in it for once.

Zach wisely changed the subject. "So Chloe, please tell me you'll be gracing us with your presence at the wedding next month?"

She nodded as she sipped her drink. "Dawn's closing the shop for the weekend, so I'll be able to make the trip. I assume you'll both be there?"

"Absolutely. With bells on." Zach's gaze cut meaningfully to me. "Right, Brandon?"

"Of course. I wouldn't miss Mom's big day." I directed my attention to Chloe. "Could I speak to you in private for a moment?"

"Well I guess that's my cue to fuck off." Zach turned to Chloe with an expansive smile. "It was lovely meeting you. I hope our paths cross again very soon." He shot me a pointed look before leaving us alone.

"What did you want to talk about?" Chloe asked with a wary expression.

"I'd like to apologize."

"For what?"

"For the way I behaved on our date. I didn't treat you with the respect you deserve, and I regret that."

"Okay. Well...thank you?" Her brow furrowed. "Just so I know, which part of your behavior are you referring to exactly?"

I'd imagined this conversation in my head numerous times, but now that we were having it, it was difficult to remember what I'd planned to say. This was why I needed to write things down. "All of it? Anything I might have done that made you unhappy."

"Does that include those things you wrote about me?"

"Yes," I said with a grimace. "I regret you saw that."

"Uh-huh."

I sensed from her tone I'd said the wrong thing. "I mean—"

"I understand what you mean."

I tried again because I didn't think she did. I seemed to be doing this badly. "I regret that I wrote those things down at all. I realize now that taking notes while on a date could be construed as rude."

"*Could* be construed as rude?"

"*Was* rude," I corrected. "It *was* rude."

"Well, great," she said with false brightness. "Better late than never, I suppose."

"If it makes you feel better, I've decided to revise my approach to dating based on your feedback."

Her fake smile tightened. "How nice for you and all your future dates. Glad I could be the catalyst for your evolution as a human being."

"You still sound angry." The conversation we'd had in my head had gone a lot better than this.

"I'm not angry. I'm over it."

"You're lying."

She inhaled sharply, and I sensed she was fighting to hold her emotions in check. "I accept your apology. How about we leave it at that and move on?"

"If that's what you want."

"It is. Your mother means a lot to me, and you mean a lot to her, so I think it's best if we both forget the whole date thing ever happened and pretend to get along for her sake."

Which meant she hadn't forgiven me and still thought I was an asshole. I wasn't entirely surprised, but I wished there was a way to wipe the slate clean and start over. I wished I had Zach's knack for making people like me. I wished I could be someone a woman like Chloe would want to know.

"Can we do that?" she asked, giving me a pleading look.

"Sure," I said reluctantly. I didn't want to pretend to get along. I wanted her to not hate me.

"Great. Thank you."

We stared at each other in uncomfortable silence, the distance between us insurmountable.

"Well," she said, edging away. Eager to escape my company. "I guess I'll probably see you around." Her false smile made it clear how little she looked forward to it.

I might as well accept it. The two of us would never be friends.

I didn't know why that bothered me so much. But it did.

CHAPTER SIX

CHLOE

It was pouring rain when my Uber pulled up in front of Dawn's brick two-story house in Lakeview. The wedding was in less than two weeks, and I'd offered to help make the paper flowers that would decorate the DIY centerpieces and gift bags for the guests making the trip to Michigan.

Of course I hadn't thought to bring an umbrella because it hadn't been raining when I'd left my house ten minutes ago. It was one of those summer thunderstorms that seemed to come out of nowhere and douse random parts of the city in a concentrated, short-lived deluge. Just the dash from the car, through the iron gate, down the front walk, and up the steps to the relative shelter of Dawn's front stoop left me soaking wet and shivering like a half-drowned cat.

"Oh goodness, you're drenched to the skin," Dawn said when she opened the door and pulled into the house. "It's really coming down in buckets, isn't it?"

"Little bit," I agreed as I pushed my dripping hair out of my face. I looked down at my feet and winced at the puddle forming on the shiny wood floor of her foyer. "Sorry for making a mess."

"Don't worry about that. Here, give me your sweater." Dawn helped me peel my wet cardigan off my arms and hung it on a coat hook to dry. After I'd toed off my soggy Chuck Taylors, she herded me into the downstairs bathroom and pushed a towel into my hands. "You're probably freezing, poor thing. I'll go get you a sweatshirt while you dry yourself off."

I loved coming to Dawn's house. It was the kind of house I used to dream of living in, not because of the upscale decor, but because the signs of Dawn's caring nature were everywhere—the scent of coffee and baked goods in the air, the cozy knitted throws and pillows that invited you to make yourself at home on her plush couches, the framed photos documenting her children's journeys through infancy and adolescence, and the childish handmade gifts and drawings she still displayed with pride. This was a house that belonged to a loving family, a warm, welcoming place that was nothing at all like the stark downtown penthouse I'd grown up in that my father had treated like a hotel and my mother like a prison.

I stared at my disheveled reflection in the mirror as I blotted the water from my hair. Thank God for waterproof eyeliner and mascara. My canvas joggers had done a halfway decent job of repelling water, and my sweater had largely saved my tank top from getting too wet. It was just my hair that had taken most of the hit. Once I'd towel-dried it as best I could, I twisted it up into a knot on top of my head.

"Here you go. Put this on," Dawn said, reappearing with a heather-gray zippered hoodie.

I shrugged into it as I followed her out of the bathroom. It was huge on me and wonderfully warm. At first I thought it had just come out of the dryer, but the subtle manly scent I detected on the fabric made me think it more likely her fiancé Mike had donated the sweatshirt off his back. I opened my mouth to thank him as I trailed Dawn into the spacious kitchen, but stopped short and snapped it shut again when I saw Bran sitting at the breakfast bar.

What was *he* doing here? Surely he wasn't helping with the decorations too. Except that appeared to be exactly what he was doing as he sat next to Angie with a pair of scissors in his hand and a stack of lilac crepe paper in front of him.

Bran looked up, and his green eyes connected with mine. I swallowed, painfully aware of how bedraggled I looked. *Unsophisticated*, just like he'd said. I could only imagine how much he was looking down on me right now.

"How about some tea to warm you up?" Dawn offered as she crossed the kitchen. "Or would you prefer coffee?"

"Tea would be great," I said, tearing my gaze from Bran. "If it's not too much trouble."

"Here, I'll do it." Mike smoothed his hand down Dawn's back as he took the kettle from her. "What kind of tea do you want?"

While he rattled off the tea options, I looked down at the hoodie I'd just put on and saw the word PRINCETON written across my chest.

This wasn't Mike's hoodie. It was Bran's. That was *his* body heat that had warmed it, and his manly scent I'd detected.

"Chloe? Any of that strike your fancy?"

I looked up at Mike and made myself smile. "Chai, please. Thank you."

"Come on then, sit down," Angie ordered with an imperious wave of her hand. "These flowers aren't going to make themselves."

Dawn had claimed the stool next to her, so the only empty seat left at the bar was the one by Bran. He was so intent on the paper he was cutting, he didn't so much as glance my way as I seated myself beside him.

"Thank you for loaning me your sweatshirt," I said, watching him cut a petal out of the crepe paper. "I assume it's yours, anyway."

He nodded without looking at me.

Angie leaned around him to slide me a pair of scissors and a stack of colored crepe paper. "You didn't take the bus, did you, hon?"

"No, I took an Uber," I said as I picked up a piece of crepe paper. "Thank God, because I didn't expect it to rain, and it would have been a seriously miserable walk here from the bus stop."

"You could have simply checked the weather," Bran commented. "The forecast called for an eighty percent chance of rain tonight."

I bristled but pretended to laugh it off. "That would have been the smart thing to do, wouldn't it?"

"You don't have a car?" he asked, deigning to direct a glance at me finally.

"No." I took a page from his playbook and focused on folding my crepe paper. "I'm doing my part for the environment." I'd chosen to rebrand my driving anxiety as an ethical stance so I could pretend to be a good person instead of a nervous wimp.

"Speaking of which…" Angie exchanged a look with Dawn before turning to me. "I know I said Charles and I could give you a ride to the wedding, but it turns out he can take the whole week off work, and we were thinking it might be nice to drive up on Tuesday with Dawn and Mike instead of Friday like we originally planned."

"That's great," I said, swallowing my disappointment. "You can make a whole vacation week out of it. You should definitely do that."

The store would be closed Friday through Sunday, but Dawn needed me to work Tuesday through Thursday to hold down the fort for her. If Angie and her husband drove up on Tuesday instead of Friday, I'd need to find another way to get myself to northern Michigan.

"But I wouldn't want to leave you in the lurch," Angie said.

"Don't worry about that," I told her. "It's no problem. It's totally fine."

It was a problem, and it was not fine. The cost of the two-night stay at the wedding hotel was already eating up a big chunk of my savings. I'd been counting on getting a ride with Angie to save me the added expense of airfare. But that was my problem, not Angie's.

Mike gave me a sympathetic look as he set my tea in front of me. "Here you go."

"Thank you." I cradled the warm mug in both hands and inhaled the spicy, comforting scent.

"Are you sure?" Angie said, watching me. "I don't *have* to go up early. Charles and I are perfectly happy to stay and drive you up on Friday if you need us to."

"No, no. Don't do that," I said. "You guys should go up whenever you want to. I can get myself there."

"How?" Dawn asked, peering down the counter at me.

"I can always fly." Although the last I'd looked, flights had been close to four hundred dollars. And that was a month ago. The price might be even higher now. "Or I can borrow my grandmother's car and drive myself there."

Bran cut a frown at me. "I thought you didn't drive."

"I *can* drive," I said, glaring at him over my tea mug. "I just don't like to."

"That's an awful long way to drive alone." Mike was frowning now too as he scratched his beard. "Especially for someone who doesn't like to drive."

"I'll be fine," I said with false optimism. I'd figure something out. Somehow or other.

"I'm driving up Friday morning," Bran said. "You can ride with me if you want."

I nearly choked on my tea.

"Yes!" Dawn cried. "That's a perfect solution. You and Brandon can keep each other company on the drive."

"Oh no," I blurted. "I couldn't. That's—"

Shit. I couldn't think of a reason to object. Other than the fact that I'd rather sell my own blood for airfare money than spend hours alone in a car with Bran. But that wasn't something I could say to his mother.

"You don't have to do that," I told him helplessly. "I wouldn't want to put you to any trouble."

"It's no trouble, is it, Brandon?" Dawn went on before he could answer.

"And I won't have to worry so much if I know the two of you are riding up together. I have to say, I didn't love the idea of Brandon driving all that way by himself."

"I don't mind giving Chloe a ride," he said with a shrug.

Seriously? He didn't mean that, did he? There was no way he could possibly want to spend that much time alone with me.

"As long as she's okay with it." His eyebrows twitched upward as if he was daring me to refuse his offer.

"Yeah, of course," I lied. "I'm happy to ride with Brandon."

"It's settled, then," Dawn announced. "Perfect."

Two hours, six floral centerpieces, and forty gift bags later, I carried my empty tea mug to the sink and announced I was going outside to wait for my Uber.

"I'll walk you out," Bran said, pushing his chair back.

After his unexpected offer to drive me to the wedding, he'd spent the rest of the evening more or less ignoring my existence. In fact, he'd barely spoken at all unless someone addressed him, so his sudden chivalry took me by surprise.

Bran waited while I hugged Dawn, Mike, and Angie goodbye, then trailed me silently to the front door. As we passed a framed collage of his and Zach's elementary school pictures, I stopped to take a closer look. Instead of stopping with me, Bran continued to the front door, leaving me behind.

Now that I'd met both brothers, it was easy to tell which was which in the photos. Young Zach showed off a familiar gap-toothed grin in all his school pictures, while tiny, dark-haired Bran glared at the camera as if its very existence was an affront. He was wearing the exact same expression when I found him waiting impatiently by the front door with his sneakers on already.

"Thanks for the loan," I said, handing him back his hoodie.

"You're welcome," he replied gruffly as he hung it on the coatrack.

After I'd pulled on my still-damp shoes and grabbed my sort-of-dry sweater, Bran held the door open and followed me outside onto the stoop. It'd stopped raining, but the air outside was chilly enough to make me shiver.

As he shut the door behind us, I struggled to pull on my clammy cardigan. "I don't understand you at all. What's your game?"

"What do you mean?" He took hold of my sweater to help me into it.

I sucked in a startled breath when his fingers grazed my arms, leaving a searing trail on my skin. I could sense his body right behind me, a solid, beckoning wall of warmth just inches away. The nearness of him was so potent it made my knees feel weak. I swayed a little and almost leaned back against him but managed to control myself. Thank God.

After Bran had pulled my sweater over my shoulders, he straightened it with a couple of fussy tugs before stepping back. "Why would you think I have a game?"

I spun to face him, searching his face for answers. Instead I got distracted by his stubble, which was thicker and darker today than the other times I'd seen him, giving his already handsome face an unfairly sexy roughness.

Ugh. Focus.

"Why did you offer to drive me to Michigan?"

Two tiny lines formed between his eyebrows as they pulled together. "Because you need a ride."

"So you offered out of the goodness of your heart?" I said dubiously.

He blinked, and for a fraction of a second he almost looked wounded before his expression shuttered. "Is that so hard to believe?"

Yes.

Since I already seemed to have insulted him, I kept the thought to myself. Maybe I wasn't being fair. Maybe Bran was more generous than I'd given him credit for.

"I just find it hard to believe you'd want to be stuck in a car with me for that long."

"Because you dislike me so much, you mean?" He said it with calm indifference, as if my opinion of him didn't affect him in the least.

My back teeth clicked together as something hot and itchy tightened around my chest. His assertion might be true, but I didn't like hearing him say it out loud.

He seemed to be watching my reaction closely, and I found being the focus of his scrutiny even more unnerving than his blunt assertion.

Folding my arms across my chest, I forced myself to meet his penetrating gaze. "Because *you* don't like *me*."

His jaw ticked, confirming I'd hit the truth nail on the head. "If you didn't want to ride with me, all you had to do was say so."

"You know I couldn't do that."

"Why not?"

"Because I don't want to disappoint your mother."

"Neither do I."

"Is that why you offered me a ride? To make your mom happy?" That, at least, was a motivation I could understand.

He shrugged. "I honestly didn't give it that much thought. You need a way to get to the wedding, and I've got plenty of room in my car. It'd be selfish not to offer you a ride." His dark eyebrows lifted. "Or did you assume I was that selfish?"

I pressed my lips together, taking the Fifth on that one.

"You did, didn't you?" He let out a dry laugh as he shook his head. "Of course."

Guilt pinged against my rib cage, and my hand instinctively reached out for him. "I'm sorry. I'm being a jerk. I appreciate you offering me a ride. Really."

His stare fastened to the spot where my fingertips were touching his forearm. "Does that mean you're taking me up on it or not?"

I drew my hand back. "I guess I am."

"Give me your phone number." He dug his phone out of his jeans, and I recited it for him. "I'll text you about our departure time closer to the date. I prefer an early start if that's all right."

"Whatever you want." I was at his mercy. God help me.

His gaze flicked to the empty street. "How far away is your Uber?"

I checked my phone. "Only four minutes out. You don't have to wait with me."

"I'm going to do it anyway."

"Suit yourself."

We stood side by side watching the street in total silence for four minutes until the flash of headlights heralded the approach of my Uber driver's Prius. *Thank the baby jeebus.*

"Well…good night." I tossed a glance over my shoulder as I shot down the steps.

Bran nodded stiffly. "Good night."

CHAPTER SEVEN

BRAN

In an unshocking turn of events, I was running late despite my best efforts to the contrary. I'd packed for the three-day trip to Michigan last night, laid out everything I'd need to get dressed this morning, and set my alarm to wake me in plenty of time to get ready and eat breakfast before I needed to leave to pick up Chloe.

But then I'd lain in bed unable to fall asleep as my mind raced in anticipation of the long drive and stressful weekend of socializing that loomed ahead. I kept thinking of things I'd forgotten to pack and had to get up to add them to my suitcase. It took hours longer than usual for me to finally drop off to sleep.

When my alarm went off this morning, it felt like I'd only been asleep for a few minutes instead of a few hours. I'd dragged myself out of bed, feeling even more foggy than usual and in desperate need of a caffeine fix. That was when I discovered I'd forgotten to preset the coffee maker last night like I usually did.

On my first attempt at making coffee, I forgot to add grounds and instead made a pot of vaguely coffee-tainted hot water, which I didn't notice until twenty minutes later because I got distracted checking my email "really quick for just a second." Cursing myself, I started the coffee a second time and went to take a shower.

Thanks to my time blindness, another twenty minutes somehow passed before I finished what should have been a five-minute shower because I'd stood under the hot spray zoning out and lost track of how long I'd been in there. After that, I had to rush to get dressed and pack up my last-minute toiletries. I no longer had time to eat, so I poured my coffee to go and set a protein bar next to my travel mug to take in the car. Then somehow, in the last-second bustle to get out of the apartment with my luggage, I managed to leave both my coffee and my breakfast sitting on the counter.

Welcome to life with ADHD brain. Never a dull moment because nothing ever went as planned.

I pulled up in front of Chloe's place twenty minutes late, undercaffeinated, and veering into hangry. The address she'd given me was in Avondale, in what turned out to be a small single-family house rather than an apartment like I'd expect for someone our age. It occurred to me she might live with her parents, so I was only a little surprised when a gray-haired woman in a fluffy pink robe and slippers opened the door to my knock.

"Good morning," I said, affixing a polite smile on my face. "I'm here to pick up Chloe."

The woman regarded me with narrowed, flinty eyes surrounded by a lifetime's worth of wrinkles. "You're Dawn's son Brandon, huh? The one who's driving my granddaughter to Michigan."

"Yes, ma'am." I tried not to fidget under her steely inspection. "Nice to meet you."

"You got a good driving record?"

"For crying out loud, Grammy!" I heard Chloe yell from somewhere in the depths of the house. "Will you just let him in?"

The woman grunted and stepped back to admit me.

"My driving record is spotless," I said as I moved past her into a cozy but cluttered living room. The sound of the *Today* show blared from a large television in the corner, and the house smelled pleasantly of coffee and toast, reminding me of my empty stomach.

"You'd better go back there and put a fire to that girl's feet if you plan to get on the road anytime today." The woman waved her hand toward a hallway leading into the back of the house. "Second door on the right."

I thanked her and proceeded as indicated, passing the open doorway of a bathroom emitting humid, coconut-scented air. The next doorway revealed Chloe rummaging through a closet in what looked like it might once have been a bedroom before someone turned it into an indoor landfill.

"You're not packed," I said, taking in the absolute chaos of Chloe's room. I wasn't sure what I'd expected, but it wasn't this dizzying level of disorganization.

A half-full suitcase lay open on the parquet floor, surrounded by messy piles of shoes, toiletries, and clothes. Still more piles of clothes and toiletries lay scattered across the unmade twin bed, along with a towering basket of laundry that teetered on the verge of an avalanche. A folding card table shoved into one corner of the small room hosted a disorderly collection of art and craft supplies, while clear plastic bins and paper bags bulging with yarn took up nearly half the limited floor space.

"Yeah, well, you're late," Chloe fired back. Her hair was still damp from the shower, hanging in loose, curling strands that clung to her shoulders and the sides of her neck. The cropped black tank top she wore bared a good four inches of skin above the waist of her loose cotton pants. As I stared, she yanked a shirt from its hanger and tossed it in the general vicinity of the suitcase. *Again.*

My eye twitched as the presumably clean shirt landed in a heap on the floor. "All the more reason you should be packed by now. Was your place tossed by the mob or did an extremely localized tornado touch down?"

She shot me a dirty look as she snatched another shirt out of the closet and leaned over the suitcase, shoving things into it with a haphazardness that made my molars grind together. "I was up late finishing your mother's wedding present and accidentally slept through my alarm, okay? I'll be ready in a minute."

Her estimate seemed highly improbable—nay, impossible—given the state of things. I glanced at my watch and grimaced. So much for my hopes of getting through the city before morning rush hour hit its peak. Still, we had plenty of time to spare. Even with traffic delays, we should make it to the winery by midafternoon, and the rehearsal dinner wasn't until seven tonight.

As my gaze wandered around Chloe's room, my attention caught on a brightly colored tapestry draped over the back of a chair. It looked like an expressionist painting, but made out of swirling chains of yarn that formed a likeness of two people I immediately recognized as my mom and Mike. They were posed in profile gazing at each other, and despite the abstract nature of the portrait, the love in their expressions was rendered so vividly I felt an unexpected tightness in my chest. The need to get a closer look drove me to pick my way across the minefield of Chloe's bedroom floor. "Did you make this?"

She didn't answer right away. "Yes, that's the wedding present I finished last night. I know it doesn't look that great right now, but it'll look better after it's stretched over canvas and framed."

"Are you kidding?" I said wondering how she could be so hard on something so impressive. "It's extraordinary." The sounds of her harried packing stopped, and I glanced over my shoulder to find her standing stock-still with an odd look on her face. "What's wrong?"

"Nothing." She shook her head and resumed packing. "That's the first time you've ever paid me a compliment."

"As opposed to the many compliments you've paid me."

"Fair point," she conceded. "And thank you."

I returned to my contemplation of her yarn portrait, bending down for a closer study of the technique. My fingers ached to touch the intricate, textured whorls of yarn that made up the design, but I resisted for fear of doing it damage. "Is this knitting? I've never seen anything like it before."

"It's a form of crochet. Although it uses a nontraditional technique."

Straightening again, I turned to face her. "How did you learn to do that?"

She shrugged as if it was nothing special and tossed two mismatched shoes into her suitcase. "I've always been crafty. My grandmother taught me to sew, knit, and crochet when I was a kid. When I was doing my textile arts degree, I worked with lots of different fibers and techniques—weaving, embroidery, quilting." She grew more animated as she spoke, her passion for the work making her whole face glow from within. "For the last few years my focus has mostly been knitting, but I've started experimenting more with free-form crochet lately because it lets me do curves and abstract shapes. With knitting you're mostly limited to geometric shapes."

My gaze fell on a blanket peeking out from underneath the clutter on the bed. "Like this bedspread, you mean? That's knitting, isn't it? I assume you made that as well."

It was a patchwork of irregular rectangles in a chaotic mix of patterns and colors stitched together like a quilt. Its beauty lay in its randomness, which was completely different from the wedding gift she'd made for my mom, and yet it was somehow obvious they'd both been made by the same artist.

"That's right," she said.

"And the sweater you were wearing when we first met." I recalled it had been done in a style much like the bedspread.

"Yes." She turned her back to crouch in front of her suitcase. The position accentuated the delicate curve of her waist and enticing swell of her hips exposed beneath her crop top.

"You do beautiful work." I definitely was not staring at her ass, nor was I imagining what it would feel like to slide my hands over her satiny, bare skin. And my dick was absolutely not hardening against the fly of my jeans. All of that would be completely inappropriate.

Chloe stilled for a second, then went back to shoving things in her bag with more force than necessary. "You didn't think so the first time you saw it."

I jerked my gaze away from her ass. "That's not true."

She let out a dry laugh. "You called it interesting."

"It is interesting."

"It didn't seem like you meant the good kind of interesting." The fall of her hair concealed her face from me, but it couldn't hide the waver in her voice.

A pang of regret speared through me. "Chloe."

She stilled again, her posture tensed for an attack. "What?"

"I meant exactly what I said. Your work is beautiful *and* interesting. The good kind."

When her eyes lifted to mine, I felt that unsettling punch in my diaphragm again. A jumble of emotions—tenderness, self-reproach, and the urge to protect her—tumbled around inside me. And then she smiled. It was more hesitant than the smile she'd beamed at my brother, but it was warm and genuine enough to rob my lungs of all their oxygen.

"Thank you for saying that." She ducked her head shyly, taking her smile away from me again.

Easy come, easy go.

Something squeezed tight deep in the center of my body, a pang of longing so sharp I had to reach up and rub my sternum.

Chloe zipped her suitcase shut and pushed herself to her feet. "All right, I'm ready to go."

"Great," I said, still rubbing the hollow ache in my chest. "Let's get on the road."

CHAPTER EIGHT

CHLOE

It figured that Bran would drive a Honda Accord, the most sensible car in existence. I also wasn't surprised to find it was in near-mint condition despite not being particularly new. Of course his car would be as orderly and impeccable as he was. He even had one of those automobile trash cans hanging over the back of the passenger seat—with a built-in tissue holder, no less—because he couldn't possibly just throw his trash on the floor of his car like lesser humans did. Heaven forbid.

I slipped off my shoes and pulled my knees to my chest while Bran programmed our destination into his phone and clipped it into a holder on the dash. After he'd finished, he put his hand on the gearshift and aimed a sidelong look at me.

His eyebrows seemed to have two primary settings: frowning disapproval and frowning consternation. Right now they were serving a heavy dose of the former. Earlier, when he'd stopped being appalled by my messy room long enough to compliment my art, his eyebrows had been all about the consternation, as if he was as bewildered as I was that he'd found something nice to say about me.

I dropped my socked feet to the floor with an eyeroll, and Bran shifted the car into drive. Today was going to be super fun, I could already tell.

"I mapped out the trip last night," he said with businesslike brusqueness as he followed the GPS directions to the expressway. "There's a printout in your door."

"A printout? And here I thought my grandmother was the only person in the world who still printed out maps." Leaning forward, I peered down into the passenger door compartment. "Hey, Mr. Neat Freak. Did you know someone left a water bottle over here in your pristine car? And a granola bar too. Tsk tsk."

"They're for you," Bran said, cutting an irritated look at me. "For the trip."

My jaw dropped. "You got me trip snacks?"

He nodded without taking his eyes off the road. "The granola bar was made in a nut-free facility."

I stared, even more astonished. "How did you know about my nut allergy?"

"My mom mentioned it."

Pretty soon I was going to have to accept that Bran was a pretty good guy. I didn't want to do it, because it was easier to live with the fact that a jerk disliked you than it was knowing a genuinely nice person didn't care for you. But holding on to my grudge was starting to feel unfair at this point. If I could stop being so touchy around him, maybe we could get to be friends. Maybe that was even what he wanted, in his own peculiar way.

"Thank you," I said, clutching the granola bar like a cherished birthday present. "That was really thoughtful of you."

"It's a five-and-a-half-hour trip, which can be divided into two equal legs of two hours and forty-five minutes," Bran continued as if he hadn't heard me. So maybe not so much interested in being friends after all. "But I thought it would make more sense to do three and a half hours on the first leg to get us past Grand Rapids before we stop for a brief bio break in Rockford or Cedar Springs. If you can wait that long?" He flicked a glance my way, showing off one of his eyebrows' variable sub-settings: questioning. It was only marginally less frowny than the two primary settings.

"I guess we'll see, won't we?" I shrugged as I used my teeth to tear open my granola bar. I hadn't had time for breakfast, and my stomach was growling its displeasure. I spat out the sliver of wrapper and shoved half the granola bar into my mouth. "You can't force the call of nature to conform to a timetable."

Bran's lips pressed together as he braked for a red light. Even thinned their pronounced curve resembled a sexy pout. Honestly, it was beyond unfair those lips had been wasted on a man who didn't even wear lipstick, while I'd been cursed with thin, flat lips that looked like they'd been drawn by a fifth grader.

While I was still staring at his lips, he said, "I made a spreadsheet of the lunch options between Rockford and Cedar Springs that seemed to offer the best combination of convenience, palatability, and clean bathrooms."

"Of course you did." I reached down to scratch my leg, then stopped myself and shoved my hand under my thigh instead.

"I texted you a link to it, if you want to have a look."

"Cool." Did he ever loosen up and let himself have fun? Like, at all? He'd probably never done anything spontaneous in his life. Imagine what his blood pressure was going to be like in ten years. The guy needed to unclench and let off some steam or he was going to give himself a stomach ulcer. And boy, would I give a lot to see him lose some of that buttoned-up composure. "Hey, Brandon?"

"Only my family calls me Brandon. I prefer Bran."

"Gotcha," I said, filing the information away. "Do you mind if I put on some music?"

His eyebrows went back into disapproval mode. "I'd rather you didn't. I find the noise an irritating distraction when I'm driving."

Did that mean he expected us to pass the entire trip in silence? Were we even allowed to talk to each other or was that too much of an irritating distraction too?

I leaned over for a look at the GPS on Bran's phone. Estimated time remaining until we reached our destination: five hours and forty-three minutes.

Fantastic.

I sank down in my seat with a sigh and stared out the window.

After several minutes of silence had passed, Bran cleared his throat. "So… you live with your grandmother?"

Oh, so talking *was* allowed while His Highness was driving. How generous.

"I moved in with her after college," I said, sitting up in my seat a little. "I went to U Mich, by the way. There's no reason to protect my identity anymore. If you try to stalk me, I'll just tell your mom on you."

Bran didn't react to my attempt at a joke. I wasn't sure he'd even recognized it as a joke. After an awkward pause, he cleared his throat again and said, "Is it just you and your grandmother living there?"

"Yep." I was trying not to worry about her being on her own all weekend. She'd be fine. I knew she would. Even if she did take advantage of my absence to eat all the saturated fats and salty foods she could get her hands on. A few french fries wouldn't be the end of the world. "She had a stroke. That's why I came back to Chicago."

"I'm sorry," Bran murmured, his thick, dark eyebrows drawing together.

"It was a minor one, but the doctor said she needed to make some lifestyle changes to reduce the risk of having a not-so-minor one." I reached down to check the Band-Aid on my ankle, making sure it was still in place under my sock. "I was planning to stay in Ann Arbor after graduation and get an apartment with some friends, but I came back to Chicago instead so Grammy would have someone to keep an eye on her. She was always there for me when I was growing up, so I wanted to be here for her."

Bran nodded absently. After another long pause he said, "Do you have any other family?"

"I have a brother Zach's age. Noah's at Indiana." I smiled. "Zach reminds me a lot of him, actually."

Another uncomfortable pause followed. "What about your parents?" Bran asked eventually.

I didn't want to talk about my parents. Talking about my parents depressed me. But I appreciated Bran's clearly Sisyphean attempts to make conversation with me too much to discourage him. "They're divorced. My mom lives in New York, and Dad's busy with his own life. It was me or no one."

Bran sliced a frown at me. "You weren't busy with your own life too?"

I snorted and rubbed my shin, trying not to scratch it. "I work in retail, remember? It's not like I'm doing anything important."

"I think my mom would disagree with that."

Perhaps, but he wouldn't, would he? Bran had already made his feelings about that clear. My lack of ambition had cost me points in his little dating rubric. Why would he want to waste his precious time with someone who wasn't on the fast track to a corner office and a big fat salary like he was?

"What about your art?" he asked when I didn't say anything. "Isn't that important?"

"I'm not a real artist yet."

It earned me another frown. "I'm not a real lawyer yet. That doesn't mean what I'm doing now isn't important."

"You're in law school and interning at a big downtown firm. I'm working at a craft store and playing with yarn in my spare time."

His fingers drummed the steering wheel. "What do you need to do to consider yourself a real artist?"

"Build up my portfolio a lot more. Get my MFA. Have a gallery show eventually."

"What's stopping you?"

I stiffened at the implied rebuke I heard in his question. Why wasn't I working harder? What had I been doing with myself? Was I actually trying or just drifting aimlessly? They were the same questions that haunted me constantly.

"Time and money," I said, staring out the side window. "I've been waitressing part-time in addition to working at the store to save up for grad school, but that doesn't leave a lot of free time for building up my portfolio."

"Shit," Bran muttered as he slowed the car.

The Kennedy Expressway had turned into a sea of red brake lights ahead of us. Traffic headed toward downtown was bumper-to-bumper as far as I could see.

"So much for beating morning rush hour," I said as our lane came to a standstill.

A muscle ticked in Bran's jaw. "Looks like we've managed to hit it right at the peak."

Which would be my fault. "Sorry."

"Can you look at my phone to see how much farther this slowdown lasts?"

I reached over to zoom out the GPS map on his phone. When my arm brushed against his, he jerked it away like I might give him cooties.

"It's solid red all the way to 55," I reported glumly.

In the silence of the car I could hear Bran's jaw pop. "Right."

I re-centered the map and sank back into my seat. "Sorry."

"You said that already."

"We could get off the freeway and try taking surface streets?" I suggested.

"That'll be even slower," he gritted out.

"Are you sure some music wouldn't help you relax?" I said when he reached up to rub the tension out of his neck.

"Positive."

"What about a podcast?" I tried, desperate for something to lighten the mood in the car.

"No."

I gave up and kept my mouth shut. Irritation rolled off him in buffeting waves that made me want to ball up like an armadillo. Since I hadn't been blessed with an armored shell or the ability to roll myself into a sphere, I had to settle for crossing my arms and staring out the window.

We sat in miserable silence as we crept along the congested freeway, moving forward a few feet at a time before stopping again. Forward. Stop. Forward.

Stop. Repeat ad nauseam. I squirmed in my seat, feeling guiltier and more wretched as I sensed Bran's frustration grow with every passing minute.

"Dammit," he growled when he had to slam on the brakes after a pickup truck darted into our lane.

"This is all my fault," I said miserably.

"You didn't cause rush hour."

"No, I just caused us to be stuck sitting in it."

He didn't respond, but the way his knuckles whitened as he squeezed the steering wheel said plenty.

"I'm sorry."

"You've already apologized," he snapped.

"I know I have, but I'm still sorry," I snapped right back at him. "It's my fault we got stuck in all this traffic, and now you're in a bad mood, so I'm going to keep saying sorry as long as I keep feeling bad about it, which is probably until we get out of this stupid traffic jam. And I'm sorry about that too, because clearly it annoys you as much as everything else I do!"

In the ringing silence that followed my outburst, I wondered if it was too late to buy a plane ticket. The freeway was at enough of a standstill, I could probably jump out of the car easily enough. I might even be able to Frogger my way to the shoulder without getting flattened.

"It's not your fault I'm in a bad mood," Bran said.

"Sure," I scoffed.

He let out an aggrieved sigh and squeezed the steering wheel even harder. "If you'll remember, I was running late too. I'm in a bad mood because I accidentally left my coffee and breakfast on the counter this morning, so I'm hungry and undercaffeinated."

"I can't believe it."

"What?" he said, cutting a glance at me.

"Did you actually just admit to being less than perfect?"

His expression darkened into a full-on scowl. "I'm about as far as you can get from perfect. Believe me."

The bitter emphasis he placed on the last two words reminded me what Zach had said about him, that Bran was even harder on himself than he was on others. I sensed I'd accidentally struck a nerve.

"If you were hungry, why did you let me go and eat that granola bar?"

"It was your granola bar. I got it for you."

"Okay, but you could have mentioned you were hungry," I said as I dragged my purse into my lap and rummaged through it. "I would have shared it with you. Or better yet, we could have taken a few minutes to eat before we left my house since we were running late anyway." I found an old granola bar at the bottom of my bag that was only slightly smooshy and hopefully not too stale. I tore the wrapper open and held it out to Bran. "Here. Eat this, Hangry Hulk."

Bran accepted it with a sheepish look. "Thank you."

"Unfortunately, my purse isn't a TARDIS or a Bag of Holding, so I can't magically pull a cup of coffee out of it. But we could get off at the next exit if you need to stop and caffeinate yourself."

He shook his head as he swallowed a bite of granola bar. "I'll be fine."

"Suit yourself," I said, looking out the window again.

After a long moment of silence, Bran cleared his throat. "I'm not annoyed by everything you do."

I snorted softly. "Okay."

"I'm sorry I make you feel that way. It wasn't my intention. It's just this thing I do unconsciously—it's like resting asshole face but for my whole person-ality. Particularly when I'm hangry." He slid a cautious look at me to gauge my reaction.

Warmth spread through my chest at the remorseful, chagrined expression he wore, and my lips curved with a flicker of a smile. "So what you're saying is it's only *most* things I do that annoy you, not all of them?"

His mouth twitched with what could have been consternation or amusement. At this point I was willing to admit I couldn't tell the difference. I decided to give him the benefit of the doubt and assume amusement.

"Only a very few things you do annoy me," he said, gazing straight ahead again as our lane inched forward. "And they're minor annoyances at worst."

I rolled my lips together to hide my growing smile. "Careful, Bran, or I might start to think you enjoy my company."

He made a face like he'd stubbed his toe.

Ah well.

Maybe we weren't destined to become best friends, given our diametrically opposing personalities. But perhaps we could at least achieve some kind of mutual understanding so our interactions didn't have to be so contentious all the time. It'd be nice if we could negotiate a cessation of hostilities for the duration of the car trip. Or even for the entire three-day wedding weekend.

A girl could dream.

CHAPTER NINE

BRAN

The traffic finally cleared up once we made it past downtown. A half hour later, when we crossed the state line into Indiana, I breathed a sigh of relief. One state down, two more to go. We were making good progress now. If we could keep it up, we might even make back some of the time we'd lost to rush hour traffic.

"IHOP!" Chloe said, speaking up suddenly. "Can we stop for breakfast?"

She'd been so quiet since we'd left Chicago, I thought she'd fallen asleep. But maybe she'd simply lost all interest in talking to me after my earlier bout of surliness.

Not that I could blame her. I'd let my frustration and low blood sugar get the better of me and inadvertently hurt her feelings again. My foul mood earlier hadn't been directed at her, but she seemed convinced I didn't like her, and interpreted everything I did as an intentional slight.

She couldn't be more wrong, but I didn't know how to persuade her of that. I doubted she'd believe me if I told her how much I enjoyed her company. Or that I'd offered her a ride to the wedding because I wanted the chance to spend more time with her. I'd hoped if we got to know each other, she might grow to like me more. But the opposite seemed to be true.

I rolled my shoulders, keeping my eyes on the road. "The plan I mapped out doesn't call for us to stop until lunch."

"And I'm sure it's a super efficient plan you put tons of thought into," she said. "But the fact is we're both starving right now and lunch is hours away."

"You had a granola bar," I pointed out.

"It was really small and I'm still hungry. You know you're hungry too. There's no way one little granola bar is enough to tide you over for the next three hours. So can we please stop? Please?"

On the one hand, the thought of deviating from the plan so soon into the trip when we were already behind schedule made my temple throb, and IHOP would entail a far longer stop than I'd meant for us to make. But on the other hand, I wanted to see Chloe smile, and maybe this would make her like me more.

"Please, Bran. Please, please, please. I'm *so* hungry."

I sighed and put on my turn signal. "Fine."

"Yay!" Chloe cheered, bouncing in her seat as she clapped her hands. "I love IHOP. You're the best."

I sure hoped she meant it.

At nine-thirty on a weekday morning, the IHOP in Hammond, Indiana, was mostly empty, populated only by a few senior citizens and exhausted-looking truck drivers. Like every other IHOP in existence, every conceivable surface was sticky, as if they regularly sprayed down the interior of the restaurant with aerosolized syrup. Maybe they did. Maybe they cleaned the place with syrup instead of disinfectant. It was the only thing that could explain the sheer magnitude of stickiness.

Our middle-aged server had the look of someone who'd rather be anywhere else in the world this morning, and I shared the sentiment. She mumbled a disconsolate greeting as she slapped two paper placemats in front of us before ambling off to get our coffee.

"I know what I want," Chloe announced as I flipped through the absurdly large menu. Which was sticky, of course. So sticky. "Chocolate chip pancakes. The kind with the smiley face."

"I don't think they do the smiley face for adults." My earlier hunger had dissipated, leaving me vaguely queasy. Nothing in the laminated color photographs looked the least bit appetizing.

"Why wouldn't they? Adults need smiles as much as kids. Probably more, to be honest."

Our server came back with two coffee mugs and filled them from a plastic thermal carafe that I estimated to be older than I was. She set it on the table, letting out an audible sigh as she plucked a pen from behind her ear. "You two know what you want?"

"I'd like the chocolate chip pancakes, please." Chloe beamed a smile sunny enough to melt an iceberg. "And could I possibly get them with a smiley face? I know it's supposed to be for kids, but it reminds me of my grandmother because she always used to bring me here when I was little."

The server nodded as she scribbled on her pad. "Sure thing, hon. You want a full stack or a half stack?"

"I'll probably regret it, but I'll have a full stack, please. Thank you so much" —Chloe canted her head to read the server's name tag—"Vera. You're my hero today."

So much for me being the best. I'd been dethroned by smiley face pancakes. Vera flicked a weary look at me, and I requested a veggie omelet with a side of dry toast.

"I love your tattoo," Chloe said as Vera collected our giant menus.

"Thanks." The barest hint of a smile creased her face as she nodded at Chloe's arms. "I like yours too."

Chloe's smile glowed warmer still. "Do you mind—could I take a closer look at it? I'm always on the lookout for inspiration."

"Sure, I guess." Vera extended her forearm to show off the ink on the inside, which appeared to be some kind of tree with its roots twined around a human heart.

Chloe leaned in to study it. "Oh wow. That's great workmanship. The shading is really nice."

"It looked better when it was new. It's been more than a few years now."

"The words in the branches—are those your kids' names?"

Vera nodded. "Those are my babies, Destiny, Angel, and Rosa. They're all grown now, of course, off living their own lives, but they're always with me."

Chloe continued to question Vera, who grew increasingly lively the longer the two of them chatted and compared tattoos. I watched them as I sipped my truly terrible coffee, fascinated by Chloe's seemingly effortless ability to make friends with anyone. Even Vera's desolate mood couldn't withstand Chloe's smiles.

"You're good at that," I said after Vera finally left to put in our food order.

"What?" Chloe looked up as she dumped cream in her coffee.

"Getting people to like you. Making friends."

"Not *that* good at it," she said, aiming a pointed look at me.

I frowned. "I don't dislike you, if that's what you're implying."

"Okay." She offered me a conciliatory but disbelieving smile.

What would it take to change her first impression of me? Or at least get her to stop thinking I disliked her? Not for the first time, I wished I had Zach's knack for charming people into liking me. Or Chloe's for that matter.

"Can you teach me how you do it?" I asked.

"Teach you what?"

"How to be more likable. Like you."

She barked a laugh. "Please. You don't want to be like me."

The way she said it troubled me. It sounded like she didn't think *anyone* would want to be like her. Didn't she realize how incredible she was? I doubted anyone could spend five minutes in her company and not fall under her spell. Even I had, and I was a notorious curmudgeon.

I frowned. "Why not? I'm sure you'd agree my peopling skills could use some improvement."

Her tawny eyes searched my face. "You're serious."

"I almost always am."

"I'm not sure what I do can be taught," she said, tracing the condensation ring around her water glass. "I'm an empath, so I have an intuitive gift for reading energy."

"Reading energy?" I repeated, envisioning multicolored auras, tarot cards, crystals, and other metaphysical flights of fancy.

She nodded and sipped her coffee, barely even grimacing at the dreadful taste. "According to my high school therapist, I have a higher-than-average level of empathy, which makes me hypersensitive to the emotional states of people around me."

I knew better than to ask why she'd seen a therapist in high school, but it was hard not to. My own adventures in therapy made me curious to explore this potential common ground between us. Instead, I leaned forward and rested my forearms on the sticky table as Chloe dumped even more creamer into her coffee. The tarry brew swallowed it up with no discernable change in color.

"It's both a blessing and curse," she said, tapping her spoon on the rim of the mug. "Being able to feel what other people are feeling makes it easier to connect with them." She shrugged lightly as she sipped her coffee again. "Like Vera—I sensed she was feeling low when she came over to our table."

"Even I could tell that much. It was obvious from her body language."

"Yes, but to you it was just an observation. It didn't have any impact on you because you're strangers, so her state of mind is none of your business—which is as it should be. You might have felt sympathy, but you didn't feel compelled to act on it."

"That's true," I agreed.

"The thing about being an empath is I'm not just a neutral observer of other people's emotional states. It's like their emotions are contagious, so I feel whatever they're feeling."

My brow furrowed as I tried to understand. "You mean you literally feel it? Like some sort of psychosomatic transference?"

"Sort of," she said. "Have you ever seen someone get hurt and winced in response or maybe even felt a sympathetic physical sensation in your own body?"

I thought about it and nodded, remembering when one of my college roommates had cut his hand while slicing a bagel. Looking at the wound had made my stomach clench up, but I'd thought I was just being squeamish. "Yeah, I guess I have."

"That's your empathy at work. Humans are social creatures, so we all unconsciously take on each other's emotions to some extent. Except psychopaths, sociopaths, and narcissists—they're all on the low end of the empathy spectrum. I'm on the high end, so I have an unhealthy tendency to internalize the feelings and pain of others and experience it as my own. I can't help it most of the time. That's why it can be a curse. If I'm around someone in a negative mood, it'll infect me."

"That's what happened in the car earlier." The realization came with an acute stab of regret. "When I was hangry and irritated by the traffic, it made you upset, didn't it?"

Chloe's eyelashes lowered as she cradled her coffee mug. "Like I said, feelings are contagious."

"I'm sorry. I didn't mean to—"

"It's not your fault. My emotional state is mine to manage."

"Still." I felt lousy nonetheless.

"It's no big deal." She gave me the smile she so often gave me, the one that felt false and failed to reach her eyes. Would I ever earn more of her genuine smiles? The incandescently warm ones she seemed to offer so easily to everyone but me.

"So there's no hope for me." From my own extensive adventures in therapy, I already knew I fell slightly below median on the empathy bell curve, which was one of the reasons I struggled so much with socializing. "That's what you're saying."

"I wouldn't go that far. There's always hope." Her expression grew thoughtful as she studied me. "Where's this coming from anyway? What makes you think you need to change anything? You seem to be doing excellent exactly as you are."

I grimaced at her overestimation of me and considered how to respond to her question. There were two different answers I could give, both of them true but neither of them appealing. I could offer the embarrassing admission that my attraction to her had made me wish to be more likable. Or I could offer the embarrassing admission that I was struggling at my internship.

I settled on the latter, afraid it might make her uncomfortable if I confessed my feelings for her. Correction: *more* uncomfortable around me than she already was. Assuming she even believed me, which seemed unlikely.

"You know how I've been doing an internship at McCurdy Becker?"

"I don't know what that is, but sure."

"It's one of the top corporate law firms in the country."

"What exactly is corporate law? Is that, like, protecting corporations from the consequences of their actions?"

"It's the body of law that governs the formation, ownership, and operation of corporations."

"So I was right," she said nodding.

I ignored her and continued. "A friend of my mom's recommended me for this internship, and—"

"Which friend?" she asked, interrupting me again.

"Donal Larkin. He's a partner at McCurdy Becker."

"Oh, right. His girlfriend Tess and their daughter Erin took knitting lessons together at the store. Erin's baby is so unbelievably cute. When she brings him in to the shop she lets me hold him, and he does this adorable thing—"

"Anyway," I cut in, trying to get the conversation back on track before I lost my nerve and gave up altogether. "Donal's been mentoring me, and he suggested that my interpersonal skills might be hurting my chances of getting a postgraduate job offer with the firm. Apparently I've alienated the other summer associates because I correct them too much."

"Imagine that," Chloe murmured.

"What am I supposed to do when I hear them make an inaccurate assertion or notice a mistake in one of their memos? Would they prefer I let them turn in sloppy work or repeat erroneous information that makes them look foolish?"

"Probably, yeah."

"Really?" I asked in disbelief.

Chloe shrugged. "Are you their supervisor or responsible for training them? Is it part of your job to correct their mistakes?"

"No."

"Did they ask for your help?"

"No."

"Then they probably don't want it."

"I don't understand that." I'd spent most of my life trying to improve myself and seeking advice from anyone willing to offer it to me. I didn't resent people for pointing out the errors in my work. I accepted the correction gratefully and tried to learn from it. "Why wouldn't they want to fix their mistakes? Shouldn't they be welcoming constructive criticism?"

"Criticism isn't constructive when it's uninvited," Chloe said.

I frowned, shaking my head in disagreement. "The context in which the critique is delivered doesn't negate its objective usefulness. If the criticism is helpful, it shouldn't matter who delivers it or how."

"Ah, but it does. See, most people aren't robots, and they have these pesky things called feelings that get in the way of rational behavior."

"I'm aware of that," I said, not appreciating the implication I was an unfeeling robot. "I'm bruising their pride, is what you're saying. I need to find a nicer way to tell them when they've done something wrong."

"Or maybe—here's a thought—don't do it at all. Or at least not until you've established a rapport with them. Once you've earned their trust and respect, they'll ask for your help. Until then, you're just some stranger pointing out their inadequacies, and that's going to feel like you're tearing them down so you can feel superior."

I sensed she wasn't just speaking hypothetically. Rather, she was describing how I'd made her feel. "That wasn't what I was trying to do," I said. "To them or to you."

"Maybe. But people don't have any reason to believe that until you've let them get to know you better."

A dark laugh burst out of me. "You say that as if getting to know me better will make me more likable."

"Oh come on. You're not *that* bad."

"High praise. Maybe that's what they'll put on my tombstone—*Not that bad.*"

The corner of her mouth quirked. "I'm sure you have your charms."

"But if I do, you haven't seen any sign of them, right?"

"I didn't say that." She tsked and shook her head at me. "There you go, making assumptions again."

"Careful. I might start to think you enjoy my company."

Amusement danced across her lips, threatening a smile. "What does it matter if the other summer interns don't like you anyway? I thought all this lawyer stuff was supposed to be cutthroat. Aren't you competing with each other for the same few jobs?"

"To some extent." I sat back as I picked up my coffee. "The summer associate program at a big firm is basically a ten-week job interview. They want to see what kind of work we can do, but there's a huge social component on top of that." I made a face as the bitter brew hit my tongue. "It's nonstop lunches, dinners, cocktail parties, and quote-unquote *fun* activities. Last weekend it was a booze cruise on Lake Michigan, Tuesday we watched a White Sox game from the firm's luxury suite at Guaranteed Rate Field, and tomorrow they're going to an escape room, which I'm missing for the wedding."

"Yikes." Chloe made a face. "Thank God your mom's getting married so you only have to spend the day trapped in a car with me instead."

"Indeed." I hid my smile behind another sip of coffee. "All that wining and dining is meant to give us a sense of the firm's personality, but it's also to give them a sense of ours. They want to see if we're a good fit for the culture by observing how we carry ourselves, how we get along with the firm's partners and full-time associates, and how we get along with each other."

"Ahh," Chloe said with a nod of understanding. "It's like a reality TV show. It's not just about spanking your competitors at the challenges. You have to mug for the camera and put on a good show while you're doing it, or the judges will find a reason to eliminate you in favor of a contestant with a better TV personality."

The aptness of the analogy impressed me. "That's exactly what it's like. Those who prove they can perform well under pressure and play the game with poise get offered a postgraduation position with the firm. The ones who don't will have to scramble to find another job."

Chloe peered across the table at me as she rested her chin in her hand. Under the glare of the restaurant lights, the scattering of freckles across her nose and cheeks looked like she'd been dusted with cinnamon powder. "You really were trying to help, weren't you? You were trying to keep them from making mistakes that could hurt their job prospects."

I grunted in confirmation. "And all it got me was ostracized."

"Well, yeah. No surprise there. Your problem's obvious."

"People don't like me?" I said dryly. "Yes, I'm aware."

"Like has nothing to do with it. They're intimidated by you. Instead of seeing you as a potential ally, they're perceiving you as a threat because you're so…" She waved her hand vaguely.

"What?" I asked, trying to guess her meaning. "Intense?" It was something I'd been called before, usually with the word *too* in front of it. Too intense. Too uptight. Too rigid. Just generally too much.

"I was going to say terrifyingly competent. You've probably got all the other interns wetting themselves."

"You're vastly overestimating how impressive I am. Every single person chosen for this program is terrifyingly competent, or else they wouldn't be there. I promise you none of them are intimidated by me."

"Obviously they are, or their egos wouldn't be bruised." Chloe's head tilted to one side as she regarded me. "You really have no idea how you come across, do you?"

"How do I come across?"

"Like someone who's the best at everything he does."

I snorted. "Hardly."

"I'm serious. I can totally picture it. I'll bet you rolled in there like a machine, all stern and businesslike with your organized spreadsheets, well-researched plans, and methodical systems, spouting arcane knowledge like it's second nature and homing in on each and every one of their mistakes. I guarantee you they're intimidated, no matter how good they think they are."

What Chloe had described was so far removed from my own self-image that I found it difficult to comprehend. Inside my own head, my life looked more like Chloe's bedroom: a jumbled mess that constantly threatened to bury me in an avalanche of chaos despite my efforts to impose order. I assumed my shortcomings and struggles were as glaringly obvious to everyone else as they were to me. "That's really how you see me?"

"At first, absolutely."

"And now?" I had to ask, although I was a little afraid to find out the answer.

She regarded me for a painfully long time while I sweated under her scrutiny. "Final results are still pending, but I'm beginning to suspect there's a human being hiding behind those well-oiled gears after all. A pretty decent one, even."

It wasn't exactly a sweeping declaration of affection, or even a compliment, really, but it was a start.

CHAPTER TEN

CHLOE

"You haven't eaten much," I said when Bran pushed his plate away and leaned back against the booth. "Did you not like your omelet?"

His lip curled in a clear expression of disgust, but all he said was, "I'm not that hungry."

"You were about to turn into Low Blood Sugar Hulk an hour ago," I pointed out as I scooped up a forkful of whipped cream. "One measly granola bar can't have filled you up that much." His eyes tracked the movement of my fork as I brought it to my lips, and I saw his jaw clench as I licked the whipped cream off. Jeez, the guy was a finicky eater.

"My ADHD meds suppress my appetite. It makes it hard to eat, even when I know I should."

I paused mid-lick. "You have ADHD?"

"Yes." His brows drew together as his gaze lifted from my mouth to my eyes. "Why do you look so surprised?"

"I just wouldn't have guessed it." It didn't fit my image of him at all. Or at least not who I'd initially thought he was. I kept having to revise my original impression the more I learned about him.

"Why? Because I'm not the stereotypical impulsive chatterbox who can't sit still?"

"Well...yeah, sort of." I shrugged as I picked up a chocolate chip with my fork. "That's what the people I knew in school with ADHD were like."

"There's more than one type of ADHD. The hyperactive-impulsive type is easier to recognize, so it's often diagnosed earlier." He straightened his placemat as he spoke, adjusting it until it was perfectly parallel to the edge of the table. "I have inattentive type ADHD, so I struggle with distractibility, disorganization, follow-through, attention to detail, short-term memory issues, and poor listening skills. Instead of the kid getting in trouble for talking out of turn and jumping off the desks, I was the kid quietly staring off into space during class and forgetting to do my work."

"Wait," I said, lowering my fork. "No, but you're so—"

"What?" He tensed like he expected a blow.

"Organized."

Bran's shoulders drooped as his mouth took on a bitter twist. "Why do you think that is? It's a coping strategy it took me years to train myself into."

"I thought you just liked to be in control," I teased.

Rather than smile as I'd hoped, he stared down at his hands and rubbed his thumb across his palm. "I do, but only because it never feels like I am," he said in a flat, detached-sounding voice. "You know why I'm always running late? Time blindness. I literally don't perceive time passing. When I let myself get distracted, I'll look up and realize an hour has passed when it only feels like a minute to me. I have to organize every aspect of my life with spreadsheets, schedules, alarms, and calendar reminders to stay on top of everything, and it's still not enough. Some of it always gets away from me anyway."

"Zach said you were a fanatical perfectionist."

Bran's scowl at the mention of his brother made me wonder if the tension I'd sensed between them was just the usual sibling rivalry or something more than that. "I've had to be to get where I am," he said. "When you're as prone to making careless mistakes as I am, you have to be extra diligent to avoid them."

The self-reproach I heard in his voice made my heart hurt for him. I understood now what Zach had meant when he said Bran was far harder on himself than anyone else. "Or you could accept that mistakes happen sometimes and give yourself a break for being human," I suggested gently.

"If I'd given myself a break, I wouldn't have finished high school, much less gotten into college or law school."

I nodded as I brought my coffee to my lips. "Well, I suppose it explains the dating spreadsheet."

He cringed. "I was only trying to be efficient. It didn't occur to me how offensive it might be to the women I was attempting to date."

"Efficiency being the most important part of falling in love, as everyone knows."

The corners of his mouth curved as he shook his head in wry amusement. "I deserve that."

Bran didn't smile much or often, but it was a beautiful thing to see the way it softened the hard edges of his expression. It made me want to bring out more of that side of him now that I knew it existed. To find ways to make him smile more often.

When his smile faded, I felt like I'd been deprived of something. Like someone had shown me a present and snatched it away.

"Sometimes I get so inside my own head I lose perspective," he said, rubbing his brow. "I guess I don't realize how different the view from in here is from the view out there."

It was a jolt to realize a lot of the displeasure I'd felt coming off Bran from the moment we first met had probably been self-focused and not, as I'd assumed, about me at all. Zach had tried to tell me, but I'd been too caught up in my hurt feelings—too inside *my* own head—to really get it.

I set my coffee cup down and leaned forward. "And meanwhile, other people don't realize how different things are in that head of yours than they appear from the outside. That's the real issue you're having with the people at your internship. They think you're one thing when you're something else altogether." Exactly like I had.

"I don't know what to do about that," he said, sounding dispirited.

"Guess it's lucky for you I do, then."

Bran lifted his eyes, gazing at me through his incredibly dark and unreasonably long eyelashes. It was inexcusable—offensive, really—how long and thick they were. They were so distracting that I lost my train of thought.

"Well?" he said. "Are you going to tell me, or do I have to buy a vowel?"

I pulled myself together. "It's like I said before. You have to let them see who you really are."

The face he pulled in reaction made me laugh. You'd think I'd stuck a spoonful of the foulest-tasting medicine on the planet under his nose and told him to open wide.

"It won't be that bad," I said.

"Easy to say when you have the personality of a Disney princess."

"I can't decide if that's a compliment or an insult."

"It's a compliment." He sounded irritated, but maybe it was self-consciousness. I was having a hard time recalibrating my perception of him. "Everyone likes Disney princesses. That's the whole point of them."

Do you? I wanted to ask and had to bite my lip to keep from blurting it out. Bran didn't really strike me as the princess-loving type. Or the Disney-watching type for that matter. He'd probably meant everyone *else* liked princesses but not him. Although my insides very much wanted to believe otherwise.

"I do have an absentee father and a wicked stepmother," I said. "But I'd like to know where my wisecracking animal sidekicks are. It's a rip-off that I have to braid my own hair."

Bran's smile made a return, faint but divine. For a second, all I could do was stare while my heart thumped against my ribs.

Focus, I chided myself. "Look, just let them see it doesn't all come easy to you," I suggested, returning to the subject at hand. "Once they realize you're a mere mortal like the rest of them, they won't be so threatened by you. They might even give you the benefit of the doubt."

"Or they'll swarm like a school of piranha who've caught the scent of blood in the water."

"Well, that is also a possibility," I conceded. "We're talking about future lawyers, after all. Although I have to assume most of you at least start out as human beings."

His brow furrowed. "You really don't like lawyers, do you?"

"Bad firsthand experience," I muttered. "It's nothing against you personally." I could feel Bran watching me as I poked at my pancakes with my fork. Before he could work himself up to ask a question I didn't want to answer, I shoved my plate toward him. "Do you want some of my pancakes? I can't finish them."

He looked torn. I remembered what he'd said at the shower about gluten giving him brain fog and felt bad for tempting him. Just as I was about to take back the offer, he pulled the plate toward him.

"Yeah, okay," he said. "Fuck it."

By the time we paid the check—halfsies, since Bran refused to let me cover him as a thank-you for the ride—and got back on the road, it was nearly ten o'clock.

He only grumbled a little about the overthrow of his carefully laid bio break plans. The chocolate chip pancakes he'd finished off for me seemed to have improved his mood. He didn't even blink when I took my shoes off and propped my socked feet on the dash.

The sun shone bright in the cloudless skies overhead as we drove past the steel plants and oil refineries lining the industrial lakefront. I pushed my seat all the way back and wiggled my toes in the warming rays, feeling peaceful. Next to me, Bran's posture was loose and easy as he navigated the relatively light traffic.

"You can play music if you want," he said after we'd driven through Gary.

"Will it bother you?" I asked, studying his profile. Silhouetted against the window, it was a masterpiece of classical proportions, all graceful curves and strong angles. I wished I'd brought my sketch pad so I could draw it. Instead I'd just have to settle for staring at it all day long. What a hardship. "Be honest."

"A little," he admitted. "But if it would make you happy—"

"What were the other questions on your first-date survey?" I asked, cutting off his sweet but unnecessary attempt to martyr himself for my sake.

"What?" His mouth pulled into a distracted frown as he changed lanes.

I was learning to identify the subtle differences between his frowns. There was a whole continuum of them, as it turned out. What I'd taken for disapproval could just as easily be a frown of concentration, contemplation, preoccupation, or something else I'd yet to identify. "Your dating spreadsheet. I'm curious what else you would have asked if I hadn't stormed out on you. What kind of criteria would I have had to meet in order to qualify for second-date status?"

"Nothing too onerous," he said. "Just a simple credit check, blood draw, and Myers-Briggs personality test."

"Perfectly reasonable and not at all deranged," I said with a smile. I loved his dry, blink-and-you-miss-it sense of humor. It took me by surprise every time. "I'm an ENFP, by the way."

"Shocking."

"Let me guess—you're an ISTJ." I laughed when I saw his lips purse. "Nailed it. But I prefer the Enneagram over Myers-Briggs. I'm a Two, if you're wondering. I'll bet you a million bucks in Kohl's Cash you're a Five."

"I don't know what that means."

"When's your birthday?" I asked, whipping out my phone.

He cut a suspicious sidelong glance at me. "Why?"

"I want to compare our star signs, obviously."

A sneer curled his upper lip, and yet it still looked as lickable as ever. "I should have known you were an astrology girl."

"That sounds awfully judgmental coming from the spreadsheet guy."

He shook his head. "I don't see how anyone can believe their birthdate determines who they are. As if every human being in all of history born during the same calendar month could possibly share a common temperament and destiny."

"You're a Taurus, aren't you? That's such a Taurus thing to say." My gaze drifted downward from Bran's face to his lean, strong arms. Hello, why was I only just now noticing the tightness of his shirt? I wouldn't ordinarily consider a polo shirt sexy, but the way the fabric strained across his biceps and shoulders awakened certain feelings. The oatmeal color was also nice, the way it brought out the green in his eyes and made his skin look golden and sun-kissed.

"Horoscopes are a scam," he said. "Some lifestyle blogger who doesn't believe in vaccines makes up a random list of generic personality traits and vague prognostications that could apply to literally anyone, and people act like it actually means something."

While he was busy ranting, I might have been staring at his lap, admiring the fit of his jeans, the way they hugged his thick thighs, and the muscles I could see shifting underneath the denim. Not to mention the visible bulge that hinted at the riches that lay between those thighs. *Heaven have mercy.* My mind should not be going there.

"Now I'm really dying to look up your ascendant and planet signs," I said as I twisted the dial to lower the temperature in the car. Because of reasons. "I don't suppose you know the exact time you were born?"

"If I did, I wouldn't tell you. I don't need to hear which giant space rock circling the sun is supposedly ruining my life, thanks all the same, astrology girl."

"That's fine." I lifted my phone again. "I can just text your mom."

"Do it and I'll pull off at the next rest stop and leave you in Indiana."

I gasped. "You wouldn't."

"Try me."

I doubted he meant it, but he had a mighty good poker face. "And after I gave you a granola bar. For shame."

"I gave you one first," he said as a hint of a smile tugged at his lovely lips. Sadly, it faded as soon as he started talking again. "The problem with astrology is it starts out as a bunch of harmless fun with memes and shit, but the next thing you know it's turned into an obsession, and you're consulting charts before making any decision and blaming all the problems in your life on some planet in retrograde instead of accepting culpability for your own actions."

My eyebrows rose. "That's, uh…oddly specific."

Bran squirmed in his seat, somehow managing to scowl and look sheepish at the same time. "My ex-girlfriend got really into astrology a few months before she broke up with me."

"Ahh," I said gently. "Now it all makes sense."

"I may still be a bit oversensitive about it." He peeled one of his hands off the steering wheel and rubbed it on his thigh. "We were together for seven years."

My jaw dropped. *"Seven years?"* Seven years was the entirety of our adult lives and then some. I didn't even own shoes that went that far back. "So you were seventeen when you met?"

"Fifteen, actually."

"Wow. That's…wow." Mind. Blown.

"We started dating in high school and stayed together while I was at Princeton and she was at Northwestern."

"Jeez, that's a lot of long distance." Four years. Damn. How'd they manage it? I'd known a few couples who went to different colleges and tried to stick it out, but not a single one of them had lasted more than a year.

Bran nodded absently, his attention locked on the highway straight ahead. "She ended things a few months after I moved back to Chicago for law school." A muscle ticked in his jaw. "I guess she liked dating me better when we were in separate states."

"I'm sorry. That really sucks."

"We didn't break up because of astrology, but she did tell me she'd compared our star charts and concluded we were hopelessly incompatible."

"Ouch."

"It was just an indication of how much we'd grown apart by then. I probably should have seen it coming, but I—" He cut himself off, wincing as he rubbed the back of his neck. "That's really why I started the dating spreadsheet, to help me analyze potential partners more objectively by identifying incompatibilities before either of us became emotionally invested."

I could almost sort of understand it. It wasn't how I would have reacted to a breakup, but to each their own. Not that I'd ever experienced anything comparable to the kind of breakup he'd gone through. My relationship history was pretty damn meager. I'd had sexual partners aplenty, but people who actually wanted to stick around long-term? Not so much.

"Okay, so I'd obviously get a demerit for being an astrology girl," I said, trying to lighten the mood by getting us back to the original subject. "What else is in your test that would have gotten me weeded out?"

Bran frowned slightly as he traded hands on the steering wheel. "It's not a test. It's a survey to highlight areas of common and diverging interests."

"Such as?"

"Basic getting-to-know-you stuff. Like your favorite book, for example."

"Unfair question. I couldn't possibly choose just one."

"Favorite movie, then."

"Ditto."

"I also ask about food preferences and aversions."

"You mean like how I hate mayonnaise?"

He looked surprised. "You hate mayonnaise?"

"Yes, as any right-thinking person should. Don't tell me you like it?"

"It's my favorite condiment."

I screwed up my face in disgust. "It's just as well we didn't make it past the first date. I could never love someone who likes mayonnaise."

"Seems a little harsh."

"You're the one with the dating rubric. How do you feel about pineapple on pizza?"

His sexy sneer made a return appearance. "Fruit doesn't belong on pizza."

"Okay, but have you actually tried Hawaiian pizza?" I licked my lips as I stared at his. *Lord have mercy.* "It's delicious."

Bran made a face like the one I'd made a moment ago. "It's really not."

I snickered as I pulled my knees to my chest. "People put pineapple on baked ham all the time. It's tradition."

"That's just as bad," he said. "Fruit should never be hot. Ever."

"Why not? What's wrong with—wait…" I snapped my head around to goggle at him. "What about pie?"

"Custard pies are fine, but I despise fruit pie."

"You hate apple pie?" I said in disbelief. "That's un-American. The FBI probably has you on a watch list."

"All hot fruit is disgusting," he declared with a stubborn thrust of his chin. "A fresh apple is crisp, delicious, and perfectly sweetened in its natural state. Why would you want to douse it in unnecessary sugar and heat it until it turns into unappetizing mush? It's sadistic."

Huh. Clearly this was a subject he had very strong feelings about.

"Okay, but how do you feel about candy corn?" I asked him.

His brow furrowed as he mulled the question. "I don't think I have feelings about candy corn."

"See, in my experience the world can be divided into two kinds of people: those who like candy corn and those who hate it with every fiber of their being."

"I guess I like it okay."

"Proof you have no taste," I said, staunchly anti candy corn myself. "I'll bet you also like marshmallow Peeps and those peanut butter toffees in the orange waxed paper."

"Says the person who tried to defend the most universally reviled kind of pizza."

"Which brownies are better, edge pieces or centers?" I fired back.

"Edge pieces," he answered automatically. "Obviously."

My head fell back against the seat as I laughed. "Wow, we really don't agree on anything, do we? We're like England and France."

"See, you mocked my spreadsheet, but you have to admit figuring out all these red flags on the first date saves everyone from wasting time and energy on a relationship that's doomed from the outset."

Shaking my head, I stared out the window at the passing landscape. Other than the trees and grass lining the interstate, there wasn't much to look at in this part of southern Michigan. "There's a fatal flaw in your spreadsheet strategy, Dr. NerdLove."

"Which is?"

My gaze slid to Bran, then flitted away again before I answered. "I don't want to date someone exactly like me who shares all the same interests and opinions. I can't think of anything more boring."

"You *just said* you couldn't love anyone who likes mayonnaise," he countered with an exasperated huff.

A smile pulled at my lips. "Mayonnaise is my line in the sand. Just about everything else is negotiable."

"Don't you think relationships are easier when you enjoy the same things and have similar goals and priorities?"

It felt like a dig at my lack of goals and priorities relative to him, but I tried hard to not take it personally. Because I was capable of growing as a person. *Suck it, insecurity.* "There's a flaw in the premise of your question. Easier doesn't necessarily equal better."

"You want your relationships to be hard?"

"No, of course not, but I wouldn't want it to be completely frictionless either.

There's something to be said for opposites attracting. Your soul mate isn't going to be an exact copy of you."

He snorted. "Of course you believe in soul mates."

"Watch it with the eyeroll, buddy."

"I suppose you believe in love at first sight too." He darted a glance my way and his brow arched, the tiniest glimmer of a teasing smirk dimpling the corner of his mouth.

"There's science to support both ideas, you know."

"Simple math says soul mates are statistically impossible. Even if you make the highly improbable leap that your lifetimes will coincide in the same sliver of human history, the odds of bumping into one specific person on a planet of seven billion people are astronomical."

"Only if you discount the role played by destiny," I said. "If you're willing to accept we're all enrolled in some sort of metaphysical matchmaking service, then you also have to figure there's something more than random chance moving us around the chessboard."

His lips pursed. "I *don't* accept any of that."

"Neither do I, for the record." I stretched my legs out on the floor and scooched down in my seat. "I'm not saying we've all only got one perfect soul mate out there with our name tattooed into their DNA, and if yours happens to be a hermetic monk living in the Swiss Alps then you're out of luck. I just think there are certain people who happen to be a natural match for us. Whether that's because of pheromones, brain wave patterns, entangled particles affecting us at the quantum level, or some other kind of subconscious recognition we don't understand yet doesn't mean it's not real."

"I guess," Bran said dubiously.

"The way I figure it, people have different wavelengths just like colors do. No matter where you land on the color wheel, there's a corresponding spot opposite yours that's your complementary color. That's all a soul mate is—someone who's the right wavelength so when the two of you are brought together you make white light that contains the entire visible spectrum of color."

"That's kind of a nice metaphor, actually."

I turned my head toward Bran and smiled. "I'm going to take that lukewarm endorsement as a compliment coming from you."

His lips twitched with a flicker of an answering smile. "You should."

"So if we apply my metaphor to your compatibility metric," I went on happily, "your soul mate—or complement, if that makes you less eyerolly—isn't a color close to yours. They'll be diametrically opposite. They're supposed to be your missing half, the oddly shaped piece that molds itself around your weird quirks and fills in your gaps. They should have strengths and weaknesses you don't have, so the two of you together make a whole that's better than either of you are on your own. That means they won't think exactly like you. They'll challenge your assumptions and shake up your world, which might not always be comfortable or easy."

Bran's frown was mighty, not with displeasure, but because the thinking gears in his head were turning extra hard. "It sounds like you're saying you need to be in a relationship in order to be whole."

Was that what I was saying? I reached up to scratch the back of my neck as I thought about it. "No," I said after some consideration. "It's not like I think I'm insufficient or defective on my own. I don't necessarily *need* a relationship to complete me. But I do think love can make you better, whether it's love between family, friends, or romantic partners. So even though I'm fine as I am, I'd still like to fall in love and find a partner one day, and I think that partner should be someone who brings things to the table that I don't already have."

Bran nodded. "That's fair, I suppose."

"Look at it this way. If two people who both think brownie edge pieces are the best get married, they'll always want the same pieces. For the rest of their lives, whenever they bake brownies someone will have to settle for eating the least favorite pieces. But if I'm a sane person who knows the gooey center brownies are where it's at, and I end up with a weirdo who likes nasty dried-up edges, we'll always be able to divide up the brownies so we both get exactly what we want. Having opposing tastes makes us a good team and means we're happier together."

His perfect lips spread in the most glorious of smiles. "I can't argue with that reasoning."

Oh man, that smile…the things it did to me.

I was in so much trouble.

CHAPTER ELEVEN

BRAN

I felt the first foreboding twinge of pain not long after we left I-94 for 196. As I tilted my head from side to side and rolled my shoulders, I told myself it was just tension. I'd stiffened up, that was all. I hadn't been moving around enough.

Chloe had fallen asleep about a half hour ago when the mountain of sugar she'd consumed finally caught up with her. Left to my own thoughts in the silent car, I'd been dwelling on parts of our previous conversation. Her theories about complementary personalities made enough sense I was forced to concede that dating someone too similar to me might not be ideal after all. If we shared the same weaknesses and limitations, wouldn't we be reinforcing our disadvantages and potentially even exacerbating our flaws? Perhaps instead I should be looking for someone whose personality balanced mine, with strengths that compensated for my deficiencies. The possibility had me deep in thought, reexamining all of my compatibility criteria.

Despite its name, ADHD didn't cause a deficit of attention so much as an inability to regulate it. I was easily distracted from mundane, unpleasant tasks, but when something claimed my interest I could throw myself into it with absolute, single-minded concentration. When it could be harnessed for good, my ability to hyperfocus was practically a superpower. I became so focused I'd forget to move, drink, eat, or do anything else, sometimes for hours at a time.

That was what had happened as I contemplated which qualities I should be seeking in a partner to offer the optimal counterpart to my own. With part of my brain occupied by the mundane task of driving, the rest had been engaged in some heavy thinking, and I hadn't moved a muscle in the last thirty minutes. Not until the dull ache in the base of my skull grew persistent enough to puncture my focus.

As I reached up to rub the back of my neck, I darted a look at Chloe. She was turned toward me, curled up sideways in her seat with her phone clutched in her hand. A soft snore parted her lips, and she snuggled into a tighter ball.

Reluctantly, I dragged my gaze back to the road. In my attempts to imagine an ideal romantic partner, my thoughts had repeatedly circled back to her. All the differences I'd previously considered proof of our incompatibility now felt like signs of how good we might be for each other. Was there real potential there? Or did I just want to believe there was to justify my attraction to her?

The flash of brake lights in the distance interrupted my deliberations again. Something had caused the cars on the highway up ahead to slow down. I lifted my foot off the gas and gently tapped the brake.

Well, shit. Traffic wasn't just slowed, I realized as we neared the trailing end of the bottleneck. It was at a near standstill.

The car's deceleration caused Chloe to rouse. "What's the matter?" she asked in a sleepy mumble.

"I don't know. Traffic's stopped."

She rubbed her eyes and sat up, stretching her arms out in front of her. "Ow."

I cast a glance at her. "You okay?"

"Crick in my neck," she said, wincing as she moved her head around. "I must have slept on it funny."

We were at a dead stop for the moment. I took one hand off the steering wheel and reached over, pushing her hair aside to rub the back of her neck. "Does that help?"

"Yes," she moaned, leaning into my touch. "Oh my God. Please keep doing that."

I smiled, keeping my eyes on the road as my fingers probed her muscles and massaged the tight spots away. After the rocky start we'd gotten off to, I couldn't help marveling at how much more comfortable things had become between us. Spending time together wasn't awkward anymore. It was peaceful.

"Thanks," she said when traffic started edging forward again. "It feels much better."

Taking my hand back, I glanced at the GPS and saw it had added an extra twenty minutes to our estimated arrival time since the last time I'd checked. "Will you use your phone to see if you can figure out what's going on?"

While she was doing that, I squinted into the distance. It was hard to make out much ahead with the sun reflected in blinding glints off every windshield, but I could see a portable roadside message sign flashing a warning that was too far away to read.

"Looks like it might be construction," I said. "Maybe a lane closure."

Pain pulsed behind my eyes, and I reached up to rub my forehead, using my hand to block out some of the glare in my field of vision.

"You're right," Chloe said as she studied her phone. "There's construction up ahead. According to the map, it's like this all the way to Saugatuck."

"Great," I muttered with a sigh of frustration.

At least traffic seemed to be moving, albeit intermittently and at a snail's pace. As we inched along in a cloud of automobile exhaust, the pulse of pain in my head progressed to a steady throb. The next time our forward momentum dwindled to a full stop, I squeezed my eyes shut and pressed my fingers against my eyelids.

Please don't be a migraine. Please don't be a migraine. Please don't be a fucking migraine.

My pleas were pointless. I already knew this was the beginning of a migraine. Triggered by the glare, possibly. Or lack of sleep. Or not eating enough. Or too little caffeine too late in the day. Take your pick of any or all of the above. All that gluten and sugar in Chloe's chocolate chip pancakes probably hadn't helped either. I'd known better than to eat them, but I'd done it anyway. This was what I got for giving in to temptation and letting myself enjoy something for a few goddamn minutes.

Fuck. Why couldn't I do anything right? I knew what my migraine triggers were and what I needed to do to avoid them, and I'd still managed to do all the wrong things. It shouldn't be this hard to stay on top of basic stuff like food and sleep, but I kept failing at it over and over.

Every reflected flash of sunlight seared into my vision like red-hot pokers. I squirmed in my seat, growing more restless and uncomfortable by the minute. It felt like we'd already been in the car for an eternity, and we hadn't even made it halfway to our destination. There were hours of driving still to do, but at this rate I'd be balled up in the fetal position long before we made it to the hotel.

"What's the matter?" Chloe asked.

"Nothing," I answered, trying to sound relaxed.

"Did you know your right eyebrow twitches when you lie?"

"It does not."

"Bran," she said in a softer voice than she'd ever used with me before. "Tell me what's wrong."

"I don't want to." I was thinking about how she'd said she could feel other people's pain. I didn't want my migraine affecting her the way my bad mood had affected her this morning.

"Why not?"

"Because I don't want to make my problem your problem."

"Too late. I can already tell something's bothering you. Just tell me what it is, and maybe we can fix it together."

"I'm getting a migraine is all. There's nothing you can do."

She picked up her purse and started digging through it. "I think I have some Advil in here."

"That won't be enough to help."

"Okay, what does help, then?"

"My migraine medicine and a nap, but I obviously can't do that right now." I'd just have to power through it. There wasn't any other choice.

"Put these on," Chloe said, passing me a pair of sunglasses. "They'll help with the glare at least."

They were huge pink cat-eye frames with rose gold reflective lenses. I put them on and glanced in the rearview mirror. Yep, I looked ridiculous. But they dimmed the sunlight enough to make the pain behind my eyes recede a little. "Thank you."

"Do you have your migraine medicine with you?"

"It's in the trunk, but it makes me drowsy. I won't be able to drive."

"I can drive."

I shook my head. "You hate driving."

"I don't enjoy it, but I can do it when I need to. And I'd say this qualifies as a need-to situation."

"I'll be okay." My head didn't hurt *that* bad. I could deal with it long enough to get us there. If I kept repeating that to myself, it might be true.

"Your twitchy right eyebrow says otherwise."

"Fuck off," I grumbled without heat, holding my hand to the side of my face to hide my turncoat eyebrow.

Chloe laughed and picked up her phone again. After studying it for a minute she said, "If we take the next exit, it looks like we can use local roads to detour around the construction."

"All right," I said, putting my turn signal on. I was getting nauseous from the exhaust fumes and constant stopping and starting. Getting off the highway sounded like a terrific idea.

It took some maneuvering in the bumper-to-bumper traffic to get into the right lane. By the time we finally made it to the freedom of the exit ramp, my migraine had upgraded from a steady throb to screaming bloody murder inside my skull.

"Take a right," Chloe said, directing me from the map on her phone. "Can we pull in at that gas station for a minute? I'm about to pee my pants."

I complied with her request, relieved for any excuse to take a break from driving and close my eyes for a few minutes.

While Chloe went inside, I stayed in the car and tipped my head back against the seat. Hello, blessed darkness. So much better. Not pain-free, but more manageable. Too bad I couldn't drive with my eyes closed. I tried doing some meditation breathing techniques, hoping they'd help reduce the pain. When Chloe opened my door a few minutes later, I was so deep in my own world I nearly jumped out of my skin.

"I got you a Coke," she said, placing a cold plastic bottle in my hand. "They used to help my mom when she had migraines."

"Thank you," I mumbled around the lump of gratitude that clogged my throat. Chloe watched with worried eyes as I gulped down half the bottle and wiped my mouth with the back of my hand. "I'm feeling better," I told her, trying my damnedest to smile. "I can keep going."

"Nice try," she said. "A for effort, but that was even less convincing than Ben Affleck's Batman."

"Low blow," I muttered as I pressed the heel of my hand against my eye.

"Okay, so here's what we're going to do," Chloe announced in a pleasant, take-charge voice that reminded me of an elementary school teacher. "You're taking your migraine medicine, and I'm going to drive us the rest of the way there while you sleep this off."

Like hell. I'd volunteered to drive Chloe to the wedding, and I'd be damned if I was making her do the driving while I took a fucking nap.

"No way," I gritted out through clenched teeth.

She folded her arms across her chest and gave me a look that might have been intimidating if she wasn't so fucking cute. "I mean it, Bran. I can handle this, okay? It's only city driving that makes me anxious. And honestly, I'll be way less stressed doing the driving myself than riding in a car with you behind the wheel in this condition."

I shook my head and immediately regretted it when pain lanced through my skull. Okay, maybe she had a point.

Grunting in surrender, I hauled myself out of the car so she could slide behind the wheel. After I dug my migraine meds out of the trunk, I sank into the passenger seat and washed them down with another slug of pop.

Chloe wriggled out of her patchwork sweater and tossed it into my lap. "You can cover your head with this to block out the light."

The sweater was warm from her body heat, and I clutched it to my chest as I handed her back her sunglasses. They looked a hell of a lot cuter on her than they had on me.

"Lie back and try to sleep," she said as she fastened her seat belt. "I've got this."

Stubbornly, I tried to stay awake. If I was forcing Chloe to drive despite her anxiety, the least I could do was remain alert enough to offer moral support. Although it quickly became clear she didn't need my moral support. She was handling it just fine. Still, I gritted it out until the sunlight became so unbearable I finally gave up and pulled her sweater over my face.

Chloe's scent enveloped me as the world went blissfully dim. She didn't wear perfume, so it was just the sweet, clean smell of her skin. It formed a pleasant, protective bubble around me, blocking out the unpleasant stimuli of the world beyond. I closed my eyes, feeling myself relax as I breathed the comforting Chloe scent deep into my lungs.

As the migraine meds kicked in, the dulling drowsiness brought some relief from the pain. The movement of the car as Chloe drove us over farm roads and through a series of small towns kept me from falling into a deep sleep, but I slipped into a half-conscious doze for a while. My drugged mind conjured a comforting dream about being in bed with Chloe and having her arms wrapped around me and my face nestled against her soft, warm skin.

I jolted back to reality when I felt the car pull off the road and stop. Dragging Chloe's sweater off my face, I sat up and blinked at our surroundings. "Why did we stop? What's going on?"

Chloe twisted in her seat to face me. "Change of plans."

"Oh good. Something I always enjoy."

"Don't sass me," she said, smiling, and a wistful warmth suffused my chest as I remembered how good it had felt to have her body wrapped around mine in my dream. "I had an idea, but you don't have to do it if you think it's stupid or you hate it."

I scrubbed my hands over my face, trying to wake myself up. "Okay?"

"I was wondering if I should find a rest stop or somewhere else we could park, so you could sleep for a while in peace. And then it came to me. What's someplace calming and restful where you're allowed to lie down and fall asleep for an hour?"

My brow furrowed. "A dentist's office?"

Her lips quirked in amusement as she shook her head. "You and I have very different ideas of calming and restful."

"An hourly hotel frequented by sex workers?"

This time she rolled her eyes. "You'd call that calming and restful, would you?"

"Not really, no."

"Then what about option C?" She gestured at the building we were parked in front of, something called the Art & Soul Wellness Day Spa. "When I saw the sign for this place, it felt like fate had led us here for a reason."

"You want me to get a facial?"

"No, you goof. A massage!" She reached over and flicked me on the arm. It was the sort of playful, casual touch you'd give a friend you felt comfortable with, and it made me smile. "I've heard it can help relieve migraine pain. At the very least, an hour lying facedown on a massage table in a quiet room might make the rest of the drive more bearable for you. And before you say anything, even with the delays we still have piles of time. Look." She turned my phone to show me the GPS. "We can afford to stop for an hour and still make it to the hotel in plenty of time for the rehearsal dinner tonight."

"We don't have an appointment," I said, surprised to find I was actually considering it. To be honest, it sounded damned appealing. A hell of a lot more appealing than getting back on the road did at the moment.

Chloe shrugged. "If they can't fit us in, they can't. But why don't we at least go inside and ask? I have a feeling about this place, like we're supposed to stop here. If fate brought us here, I'll bet they have an open appointment."

"All right," I said, unfastening my seat belt. "What the hell." I didn't subscribe to Chloe's fate theory, but maybe some of her spontaneity was rubbing off on me. My whole plan for this road trip was totally fucked at this point anyway, so what did it matter?

Despite being located next to a blueberry farm ten minutes from Lake Michigan, the inside of the Art & Soul Wellness Day Spa had the vibe of a hippie New Mexican art gallery. Chloe explained my situation to the middle-aged woman draped with beaded necklaces who greeted us from behind the reception desk. She clucked sympathetically and perched a pair of lime-green reading glasses on the tip of her nose to peer at the reservation book. "We're usually booked solid on Fridays, but you're in luck—we just had a couples massage cancel their one o'clock appointment."

Chloe grinned as she flicked me on the arm again. "I told you fate brought us here."

"We'll take it," I told the receptionist before I had time to talk myself out of it.

"But it'll just be for him," Chloe said. "Not both of us."

"It's a couples appointment," the woman said with an apologetic smile. "In order to book you in the double room, we'll have to charge you the couples rate for two massages whether you use them both or not."

"If I'm doing this, you're doing it with me," I told Chloe. When she opened her mouth to protest, I said, "This is clearly what fate wants you to do. You wouldn't flout fate's plans now, would you?"

"Fine," she said, huffing a reluctant sigh.

We were offered tea and directed to a waiting area decorated with cacti, a large stone water feature, and a collection of Southwestern landscape paintings that appeared to be for sale. While Chloe wandered around looking at the art, I sank into a cushy leather recliner and closed my eyes. The soothing burble of running water and ambient New Age music playing in the background must have lulled me to sleep, because I started awake to the sound of Chloe's voice saying my name and the feel of her warm hand on my arm.

I rubbed my eyes, and her face came into focus. Her expression suffused with warmth as she smiled down at me, looking so beautiful my heart kicked up into my throat.

"They're ready for us."

A woman who introduced herself as Annika led us to a private room deco-rated like a honeymoon suite. Only then did it begin to sink in exactly what I'd signed us up for.

A couples massage was supposed to be romantic. Intimate. Sensual.

Oh God.

The lights had been dimmed, and a small table covered with candles bathed the room in a flickering yellow glow. Two massage tables that had been made up with pillows and blankets sat side by side like a matched pair of twin beds from an old black-and-white TV show made in the days of the Hays Code.

At the far end of the room was a whirlpool tub surrounded by yet more candles and what I was pretty sure were rose petals.

Oh no.

"Make yourself comfortable," Annika said. "You'll find robes, slippers, and undergarments in the wardrobe. Once you've had some time to change and relax, I'll be back with Katrina, who'll be doing your treatment with me today."

Oh fuck.

"Did she say undergarments?" I asked after Annika had left us alone in our lovers' paradise.

"Yep. Yep, she did." Chloe wandered over to the open wardrobe where a pair of white terrycloth robes hung on the insides of the doors. "Oh, look. Disposable underwear."

This was the problem with spontaneity. You tried to be a good sport and go with the flow, and the next thing you knew you were being asked to change into disposable underwear in front of a girl you liked.

I cleared my throat. "I'm almost afraid to ask, but—why can't we keep our own underwear on?"

"I think it might be because of the massage oil. So it doesn't stain our clothes."

"Right," I said. "Of course. Very sensible."

"Isn't it?" Chloe looked like she might also be having some regrets.

"Have you ever had a massage before?" My throat had gone so dry my voice came out sounding weird.

"Uh, nope. Never. I'm guessing the blue underwear is yours and mine's the pink. How very gender normative."

"So…we're supposed to strip down all the way?" I cast my eyes around the room, hoping to find some sort of changing area or privacy screen, but it was one big open space. The only piece of furniture you could reasonably hide behind was the wardrobe, but you'd have to contend with the pair of giant potted palms flanking it. Not exactly practical or dignified.

"I believe that's the idea," Chloe said.

"You think it's too late to sneak out the back door?" I asked, only half kidding.

CHAPTER TWELVE

CHLOE

Bran's self-consciousness was totally adorable and made me feel a heck of a lot better about my own discomfort with the situation. Getting a couples massage with him had definitely *not* been part of my plan. It was supposed to be him in here all by himself while I chilled out in the waiting room.

I usually avoided spas. I couldn't risk letting a stranger touch my legs, so pedicures and waxing were both out of the question.

I didn't like having my legs and feet on display at all if I could help it. It was easier to keep them covered under long pants and socks, so I didn't have to deal with stares and questions about why they looked the way they did. But I'd agreed to do this.

It's only embarrassing if you act embarrassed.

With my grandmother's sage advice ringing in my head, I put on a show of false bravado and shot Bran a grin. "Don't be a wimp," I said and peeled my top over my head.

His gaze dropped to my cotton bralette. The one I'd put on this morning for comfort rather than sex appeal, never imagining I'd be showing it off. He swallowed thickly before his eyes snapped back to my face.

Nice to know he wasn't immune to the magical power of boobs, at least. With any luck, he'd be so preoccupied by the rest of my body he wouldn't even look at my legs.

Clenching his jaw, Bran yanked one of the robes off its hanger. "I'll just, uh —I'll go over there and give you some space."

He walked a few steps away and turned his back before tugging his shirt off. My jaw unhinged as I stared at his muscley back. Holy hell, his body was gorgeous. He had that perfectly proportioned Dorito shape: strong, broad shoulders and upper back tapering to narrow hips.

His jeans were halfway down his butt cheeks before I remembered I should probably avert my eyes. Regretfully, I turned my back on the sight of his naked ass and concentrated on changing out of my own clothes.

After I'd stripped down and exchanged my underwear for the spa's—*so* not sexy—I pulled the robe on and carefully eased my socks off, making sure not to displace the Band-Aid on my blistered ankle. I slipped my feet into the spa's slippers, tied my robe closed, and turned around to find Bran similarly attired and waiting with his back politely turned.

"It's safe to look now," I said. "I'm decent."

He turned around slowly, and his eyes lifted to meet mine. We stared at each other for a silent, awkward moment, both of us painfully conscious that we weren't wearing anything but matching robes and paper underwear.

"I feel like I should apologize for pressuring you into doing this," he said with a wince. "I didn't exactly think it through."

I cracked a smile to break the tension. "You mean it didn't occur to you we'd have to get naked together in a romantic candlelit room?"

Bran cleared his throat, blushing all the way to his hairline. "I, uh...understand now why you didn't want to do the couples massage."

"It's fine," I said with a shrug.

"Did you know you've also got a tell when you're lying?"

"I do?" I lifted my hand to my face as if I'd be able to feel it. "What is it?"

"You can't expect me to give up my advantage so easily."

"Unfair," I said with a pout. "I told you yours."

Bran's gaze moved over my face before fixing on my mouth. "Your smile gets a glassy quality to it. It's hard to describe exactly what's different, but it's clear as day now that I've noticed it."

I swallowed, trying to maintain my chill exterior. "If I didn't know better, I might think you'd been making a study of my face."

"Maybe I have," he said, and I felt my eyes widen. He looked away and cleared his throat again. "But I promise not to ogle anything that might happen to be exposed for the next hour."

"Only for the next hour? What about after that? Ogling's back on the table?"

His gaze met mine again, and the corner of his mouth twitched. "I make no guarantees as to future ogling."

Heat flooded my chest, leaving me in sudden, urgent need of some water. I crossed to the pitcher and glasses sitting out on the sideboard. "I'm not very ogle-worthy in this glamorous disposable underwear anyway."

"I hate to break it to you, but you'd be ogle-worthy even if you were wearing a plastic trash bag."

I was glad I had my back turned, so Bran couldn't see my cheeks flame at the compliment. I took my time pouring two glasses of cucumber water to give my thudding heart a chance to quiet down.

"What are we supposed to do now?" he asked when I handed him a glass of water. My stomach tightened as his fingers touched mine. "Just sit here and wait for them to come back?"

Feeling dangerously light-headed, I hopped up onto one of the massage tables. My legs were in full view as they dangled over the edge, but I refused to be self-conscious about it. Bran was bound to notice eventually, so there was no point trying to hide them. "I think we're supposed to enjoy some of this refreshing cucumber water, listen to the calming music, and get into a relaxed state before the massage starts."

He sat on the table across from me, mirroring my position. "If they wanted me to relax, they shouldn't have made me wear paper underwear."

I looked down at the water in my hand to hide my smile. "You do have to wonder how couples are supposed to feel romantic wearing these things."

"What? You don't find the luxurious feel of paper against your genitals an aphrodisiac?"

A laugh sprang out of me, and the corners of his mouth curved in response. He looked so pleased with himself, it gave my heart a little flutter. But then I saw his attention catch on the bandage on my ankle. Briefly, I considered yanking my robe open and flashing a boob in a desperate, last-ditch attempt to distract him, but I knew it was already too late.

"Did you hurt yourself?"

I tried not to stiffen as I watched him take in the patchwork of bright red scars and lesions covering my lower legs. "No. It's just a—it's like a rash. Don't worry though, it's not contagious."

"It looks painful."

"It's not that bad. I'm used to it."

His brow furrowed, but he didn't say anything else. He was too polite for that.

"Go ahead and ask," I said when I couldn't stand the weighty silence anymore. "You know you want to."

"Only if you want to tell me."

Now that he'd seen, the worst part was over. It was easier to talk about it after the initial "ew, yuck" moment I dreaded so much had passed. My opinion of Bran had changed so much over the last few hours that I wasn't even afraid he'd say something insensitive. He'd turned out to be a lot kinder and more considerate than he'd seemed at first.

"I have a rare genetic condition that makes the skin on my lower legs unusually fragile. It's called dystrophic epidermolysis bullosa. Any sort of minor abrasion turns into a big, ugly blister, like this one on my ankle."

He leaned forward when I turned my foot to give him a better view of the blister showing around the edges of the Band-Aid. "It looks like a burn blister."

"Kind of, yeah. My legs are just really extra, like those overdramatic soccer players who throw themselves to the ground at the slightest foul, yelling and crying like they're mortally injured. If I accidentally bump my ankle or get a tiny little scratch, my skin gets all melodramatic and acts like I've got a second-degree burn."

"That must be a pain to live with."

I shrugged. "It's been like this my whole life, so I've never known any other way to live. I got used to it a long time ago. And it could be a lot worse. I'm lucky I've only got it on the fronts of my legs and ankles. Some people get it on the bottoms of their feet or all over their body—even inside their mouth and throat. The really bad cases of it can be debilitating and cause disfigurement or even death."

Bran looked stricken. "Jesus, Chloe."

That was pretty much how I felt when I let myself think about what my life could have been like with a slightly different roll of the dice. "Like I said, I'm lucky I only have a mild type of it. Mostly it's just an inconvenience. I can't shave my legs, which isn't that much of a sacrifice. I usually try to wear long pants and socks to protect my skin, but otherwise it doesn't interfere with my life that much. Not the way your ADHD or migraines do. It's just that my disorder's out in plain sight instead of invisible like yours."

A pair of creases formed between his brows. "That's why you didn't want to get a massage, isn't it?"

I looked down at the glass I was clutching and nodded. "I didn't want you to see my ugly legs."

"Nothing about you could ever be ugly."

My heart flipped like it was inside a dice popper on a Trouble board, but I told myself he was just being nice. "Not even my janky toenails?" I joked as a deflection. "They're pretty ugly."

"What's janky about them?" he asked, frowning at my feet.

I stuck my foot out, pointing my toes to show them off. "See how weird and tiny they are? It's another fun symptom of my condition."

He studied them with an adorable seriousness. "I don't think your weirdly tiny toenails are ugly," he pronounced when he'd completed his examination. "I think they're cute."

A jolt of pleasure warmed my chest and pulled my lips into a smile. Bran smiled back at me, and *oh boy*, when he full-on smiled it was like a shaft of sunlight breaking through a storm cloud. The green in his eyes seemed to glimmer as his face transformed into something so boyish and eager my heart jumped straight into my throat.

A knock on the door startled the smile off his face, and I mourned the loss of it as Annika returned with a second massage therapist in tow. "Ready to get started?" she asked cheerfully. "Let's get those robes off and get comfortable."

Oh, goodie. Time to get naked.

No problem. I could handle this, right?

I could sort of handle this.

I might not be able to handle this.

CHAPTER THIRTEEN

BRAN

One upside of having a migraine was it pretty much killed any possibility of inconvenient erections.

Usually.

Not so much when Chloe was topless next to me with her bare breasts compressed beneath her as she lay facedown on the massage table. Only a single thin sheet covered her lower body, leaving her bare back exposed all the way to…

Don't think about it.

I'd turned my back when she'd slipped off her robe to lie down on the table. But while I'd been climbing onto the table next to hers, I'd accidentally gotten a generous eyeful of sideboob.

The vision lingered behind my eyelids, burned into my retinas like a flash-bulb afterimage. I hadn't even properly recovered from the sight of Chloe stripping her shirt off in front of me yet. That blush-pink cotton bra she'd been wearing was so thin her nipples had shown right through it. Jesus, I'd wanted to tug it aside and put my mouth on her perky little—

Nope. Nope. Nope.

Shame thrummed under my skin as my dick gave a threatening twitch. Things were going to get awkward fast if I couldn't redirect my thoughts away from Chloe's naked body. I balled my hands into fists and tried to distract myself by reciting Article I of the Illinois State Constitution in my head.

All men are by nature free and independent and have certain inherent and inalienable rights among which are life, liberty, and the pursuit of happiness. To secure these rights and the protection of property, governments are—

"You're wound up like a jack-in-the-box," Katrina, my massage therapist, said as she worked on my shoulders. "Stress contributes to migraines, you know."

Yes, I was aware of that. Oddly, having a total stranger rub my back while I tried not to get hard because a woman I liked was naked a few feet away wasn't exactly a stress-free activity.

How did other men do this? The entire concept of a couples massage was seriously problematic and fraught with hazards.

Great, Chloe was making *noises* now. Whatever Annika was doing to her was causing Chloe to let out little moans and groans that sounded an awful lot like sex noises. I really did not need to know what Chloe sounded like when she was about to have an orgasm. Now that it was in my head, I'd never be able to stop thinking about it.

What had started out as a minor, mildly irrational attraction was quickly turning into something much more. Something I didn't fully understand. Watching her let her guard down and slowly warm up to me felt terrifyingly good. Finally earning some of her incandescent smiles had made me feel more hopeful, more alive than I'd felt in a very long time.

I wasn't new to being friends with women. I'd had enough practice at it in college. A man in a committed long-distance relationship made for a safe, nonthreatening friend who could walk you home from the library at night or help you move furniture without trying to get in your pants. What I felt around Chloe was completely different than that. I wanted to be the guy who made her feel safe, but I also wanted to get into her pants. Problem was, going from friends to more than friends wasn't something I knew how to do anymore. And I wasn't convinced it was something I should try for anyway.

Just because she'd grown to tolerate me—maybe even like me a little—didn't mean she felt the same attraction I did. I doubted I was Chloe's vision of ideal boyfriend material.

"Oh my gaaaawd." The purr of her low, breathy voice sent all the blood in my body rushing straight toward my cock. "Right there. Don't stop."

Kill. Me. Now.

As if in answer to my silent prayer, Katrina found a spot in my trapezius that shocked me with a stab of pleasure-pain so intense I nearly jumped off the table.

"There it is," she said, sounding pleased with herself. "That's where you've been carrying your tension."

She dug her thumb into the spot again, and now I was the one groaning uncontrollably. The pain brought tears to my eyes, but it also felt insanely good, like lancing an infected wound to relieve the pressure.

"It's amazing, isn't it?" Chloe said. "It hurts but in a crazy good way, right?"

I turned my head to find her grinning at me. All I could manage in response was a jerky nod that got cut off by another incoherent groan as Katrina sank the pointy tip of her elbow into my muscle. I wanted to be embarrassed by the sounds coming out of my mouth, but the sensation was so intense it was hard to think about anything else.

I might have actually blacked out a little after that. At the very least I went into a sort of trance as Katrina worked her way across my upper back, rooting out all the knots and ruthlessly digging deep into the tissue.

"Okay, that's the worst of it over with," she said eventually, and I breathed out a sigh of relief. "Trust me, you're going to feel like a whole new man after this."

I'd have to take her word for that. Right now I felt like I'd been hit by a truck. Or possibly trampled by an entire football team offensive line. Hard to believe a woman as average-sized as Katrina could inflict so much damage with just her hands and an occasional elbow.

She had me roll over next, which turned out not to be so easy. My limbs were weak and shaking, leaving me with all the coordination of a deboned fish. "Now I'm going to work on your face and scalp," she said once I'd made it onto my back. "This will feel a lot more pleasant and should take care of that migraine."

Boy, she was not wrong. The firm, soothing strokes of her fingertips melted away tension I hadn't even known was there as she worked her way from the base of my skull to my hairline, leaving my head pleasantly tingly. As she moved on to my temples and forehead, my mind emptied of coherent thoughts and I drifted in a blissfully blank daze.

I must have fallen asleep at some point. I dreamed that Chloe was whispering in my ear. The warm touch of her breath made my heart hammer in my chest, and I reached out for her, wanting to hold her in my arms, but my hands found nothing but empty air.

"Bran."

My eyes snapped open to find Chloe's warm toffee eyes gazing into mine. I blinked, half expecting her to disappear like mist along with the other hazy remnants of my dream. But no, she was really there, smiling down at me. Her hand was on my arm, her slim, soft fingers exerting gentle pressure I could feel with every nerve ending in my body.

She seemed to realize where her hand was a second after I did and jerked it back, to my tremendous disappointment. "Sorry, I didn't mean to startle you," she said. "Our time's up. We need to go."

I sat up on the edge of the table and rubbed my eyes. Chloe was already dressed, and we were alone in the room. "How long was I asleep?"

"About fifteen minutes. How do you feel?"

"Amazing, actually." My head felt thick and stuffed with cotton like it always did after taking my migraine medicine, but there was no pain at all.

Chloe smiled. "I'm really glad."

I smiled back. "You fixed me."

"That was probably the migraine medicine," she said. "With an assist from Katrina. I didn't do anything."

"You made both of those things possible."

"I guess I do occasionally have a pretty good idea." She softened her sarcasm with a wink that made my stomach flutter unsteadily. "I'm going to go and let you get dressed. I'll meet you in the waiting area."

As the door closed behind her, I thought about her putting her own clothes back on while I'd been lying here asleep just a few feet away. Dreaming about her, no less.

Shaking the thought out of my head, I went to collect my clothes. We still had a long way left to go and hours of driving ahead of us. Now wasn't the time for fantasies and daydreams.

CHAPTER FOURTEEN

CHLOE

"I can take over driving again," Bran said as we walked toward his car.

I shook my head at the hand he held out for the key and brushed past him, making for the driver's side. "Not a chance."

He followed me, putting his hand on the door before I could open it. "My migraine's completely gone now. You don't have to keep driving."

I swiveled to face him, but he was standing closer than I'd expected. *Really* close. The fronts of our thighs touched as I found myself staring directly at Bran's mouth. I backed up until my butt hit the car at the same time as he edged away a little. Not a lot. Just a little. He was still close enough I could smell the faint odor of massage oil coming off his skin and hear the sharp breath he drew into his lungs.

Ignoring all the many things his proximity was making me feel, I lifted my chin to stare him in the eye. "The medicine makes you drowsy, remember? I'm not putting my life in your hands. Besides, I don't want to risk your migraine coming back when you've got your mom's rehearsal dinner tonight. Therefore, I'm driving and you're riding in the passenger seat so you can close your eyes if you need to."

His jaw clenched as he pressed his lips together. So reluctant to give up control. The way his brow furrowed, I expected an argument. But all he said was, "Are you sure you're okay with driving on the highway?"

"I guess we'll find out."

The furrows in his brow deepened into bottomless crevices. "Chloe—"

"I'm kidding!" I said, rolling my eyes. "I'll be fine."

Bran's gaze roved over my face, the gold flecks in his eyes picking up the sunlight. "Promise me something."

Oh, jeez. I was already having a hard enough time keeping my breathing steady under his examination. Throw in that soft, rumbling voice he'd just used, and I was ready to promise just about anything he asked. "Okay."

"If at any point you don't feel fine about driving anymore, promise me you'll say something. I don't want to worry you're hiding it from me."

"You mean the way you tried to hide your migraine from me?"

"Exactly."

Well, at least he was honest.

"I promise," I vowed, suppressing the smile trying to tug at my mouth. "If we need to trade back, I'll let you know."

He exhaled a deep breath I felt on my forehead. "Thank you."

"You're welcome," I said. "Now move so I can drive us to your mom's wedding."

I could do this. I *was* doing this. I was driving without stressing the fuck out.

Look at me, totally rocking this driving thing and being chill as hell about it. *Boo yah!* Driving wasn't so bad when you weren't in the city with pedestrians, dogs, and bicycles coming at you out of nowhere and impatient drivers honking because you'd hesitated at an unprotected left turn into oncoming traffic and possible death.

I'd figured driving at higher speeds on the highway might stress me out more than the farm roads had, but I'd wanted to see if I could handle it, both for Bran's sake and for mine. I wanted to prove I could be capable and actually useful for something. And hey, it turned out not to be that bad at all.

To be quite honest, I'd worried Bran might stress me out a little too. When I'd taken over driving earlier, on the back roads, he'd been in too much pain to judge my driving and make me nervous. Plus, I'd been so concerned about him it had kept me focused and distracted me from my driving anxiety.

Now that I was driving on the highway, he was feeling better and a lot more alert. He had plenty of attention to spare for fretting about me being behind the wheel. I'd sort of expected him to armchair quarterback or sit there all tense and glowery, waiting for me to screw up so he could point it out. That was what my father had done whenever he'd ridden with me, and I'd assumed Bran would be similar.

But that wasn't Bran at all. He wasn't anything like my father, even if they did share a chosen career. I should have known that by now.

Bran didn't seem to be fretting in the least. I could feel him watching, but not in a nervous way that made me nervous.

I glanced over at him just to make sure. "I'm still fine, in case you were worried."

"I wasn't worried. You're doing great."

Wow. Bran thought I was doing great. So there. Anxiety could suck it. And while I was kicking things to the curb, my dad could suck it too.

"Maybe I only have city-driving anxiety," I said. "Is that a thing?"

"I don't see why not."

I bit my lip. "I passed my driving test in high school with no problem whatsoever. I even aced parallel parking. My first year as a licensed driver, everything was totally fine. Until I had my first accident." My hands tightened on the steering wheel as I remembered the sound of the impact and the shock of adrenaline that followed. "It was just a minor fender bender. No big deal. No one was hurt, and my car was barely even damaged. My dad gave me one of his usual lectures about being careless and not taking anything seriously enough, and that was that." Shrugging, I peeled one of my hands off the wheel and rubbed it on my thigh. "I got right back in the driver's seat with no problem. And I tried really hard to be extra cautious so I could prove my dad wrong about me."

We were passing a slow-moving van, and I glanced at my rearview mirror as a shiny red sports car zoomed up behind us, impatiently riding my bumper. Ignoring him, I waited until I'd safely passed the van before moving over to the right. The sports car accelerated obnoxiously and blew past us.

"Jerk," I muttered. "I hope you get a ticket." I cleared my throat, conscious of Bran's gaze on me. "Anyway. A month after my first accident, I had another one. Only that time it wasn't my fault. Some guy ran a red light and broadsided me."

"Jesus," Bran murmured.

"It was fine," I said quickly, shooting him a smile. "I was fine. He wasn't going that fast, so it wasn't bad. The passenger door got a little mangled, but other than some minor bruises and burns from the airbag going off, I wasn't hurt at all. My dad was out of town, so I didn't even have to listen to a lecture that time."

"Was your mom around back then?"

I shook my head. "My parents split up when I was ten, and she moved to New York right after that." I didn't mention that she couldn't wait to get away. Or that she'd relinquished all her custodial rights in exchange for more money in the divorce. My dad had paid her to give up my brother and me, and she'd been only too happy to sell her right to be our mother.

"So you had to deal with the accident all by yourself?"

"No, Grammy came and picked me up, since they had to tow my car. She took me to IHOP for chocolate chip pancakes that night," I added, shooting another smile at Bran.

He met it with a frown. It drew his dark eyebrows together, creating those two little lines between them. My smile waned as I directed my attention back to the road. I knew he wasn't frowning at me. He was frowning *for* me. Out of sympathy. Or maybe even a sense of protectiveness. Which was sweet. It made my stomach feel a little fluttery. But I also didn't like knowing he was upset.

"Is that when your driving anxiety started?" His voice was much softer than usual.

I nodded, tightening my grip on the wheel. "I hated driving after that. I'd be so tense and stressed out the whole time, my neck and shoulders would seize up with muscle cramps. I started avoiding it as much as I could. Then I went off to college, and it was an easy thing to avoid it completely by leaving my car behind. I told my dad to give it to my brother, and I haven't had a car since."

"Have you driven at all?"

I nodded. "A few times, taking my grandmother to doctor's appointments. I can do it when I need to. It's not like I get panic attacks or anything bad. I just really hated it."

"You used the past tense," Bran pointed out.

"I know," I said, feeling my smile return. "I don't know why, but I haven't been nervous at all today. Maybe it's only city driving that scares me. Or maybe it's you. Maybe having you in the car is keeping me calm."

He grunted. "That seems unlikely."

"You actually have a very reassuring energy when you're not all cranky."

"I do, do I?" He sounded amused.

"It's true. You project a lot of confidence."

"Entirely an illusion."

I shot him a look. "No, it's not. You're kind, sensible, and competent. The sort of person who's good to have around in a tight spot."

"I'm not sure I've ever been told that before."

"So how are *you* doing?" I asked him as I signaled a lane change and checked my sideview mirror. "Any signs of your migraine coming back?"

"All clear so far."

"Good." I moved into the left lane and re-engaged the cruise control to pass a tractor trailer. "You can close your eyes if you want. I've got this."

"I know you do," he said. "I will if I feel like I need to."

I smiled and settled back in my seat, getting more comfortable. "This is nice. Who'd have thought we'd make a pretty okay team when we put our minds to it?"

Bran responded with a grunt. "Do you want me to put on some music?"

"Won't that bother you?"

"Only when I'm driving. I like listening to music. It's just that I find it too distracting sometimes when I'm edgy or trying to concentrate on something."

"Brains are so weird, aren't they? I usually focus better when I listen to music. In college I made different study playlists for every class. Or sometimes I'd just leave the TV on. Background noise always seems to help somehow."

"I think that's pretty common," Bran said, taking his phone out of its holder on the dash. "A lot of people with ADHD use different kinds of background noise to help with focus. Just not me. Everyone's different. What do you feel like listening to?"

"It won't make your migraine come back?" I darted a glance at him, but he had his head bent over his phone.

"If it feels like it's going to, I'll say something, won't I? So come on. If you were making a road trip playlist, what would be on it?"

"Hmmm." I chewed on my lip as I thought about it. What was I in the mood for? Something upbeat and energizing? Or something more mellow and soothing? Maybe something in between. "Will you judge me for requesting Taylor Swift?"

"Why would I judge you for that? Do you want a particular album or a 'best of' mix?"

"How about *Lover*?" I said as I rolled my shoulders. "Lots of guys make fun of girls for liking Taylor Swift. It makes me basic, I guess. Just another one of those girls who likes Uggs, mimosa brunches, and pumpkin spice lattes." Some of my art major friends had teased me for liking Taylor too. Most of them had been into edgier, more esoteric stuff.

"So what?" Bran said. "There's nothing wrong with any of those things. People should be able to enjoy whatever they want. Any guy who'd make fun of you for something you like is an insecure, misogynist dick who isn't worth your time."

I couldn't help grinning at his angry rant. "Excuse me, but aren't you the same person who was mocking me for being an astrology girl just a few hours ago in this very car?"

"I didn't mock you," he said defensively as the first song on the album started playing over the car's speakers. "I simply explained why I didn't like it, and then I admitted I was oversensitive about it because of Marisa." He exhaled. "But you're right. I was judging you for liking something fun and perfectly harmless, and I shouldn't have done that."

I cast a sidelong glance at him. He was staring out the window with his jaw tight and his arms folded across his chest. I turned Taylor down a few notches and reached over to knuckle the side of Bran's leg. "Hey, I was just teasing. I'm not upset about it."

"You should be." Out of the corner of my eye, I saw him turn his head toward me. "You shouldn't tolerate any man who makes fun of you."

"Then I guess it's a good thing you didn't. I'd hate to have to kick you out of your own car. Talk about awkward. How would I explain that to your mother?"

His answering grunt sounded almost amused.

"So…" I said after a lengthy moment of silence. "Marisa was your girlfriend, huh?"

"Yes."

"Did she like Taylor Swift and pumpkin spice lattes too?"

"No. She was more of a Mitski and matcha smoothies person."

Knowing her name and that little bit about her personality made Bran's ex feel more real, and her presence seemed to loom a lot larger. I could almost imagine her sitting in the car with us.

Sliding another glance at him, I saw he'd gone back to staring out the window. "It must have been hard letting go of someone who was an important part of your life for that long."

It took him a good long while to answer. "She was my best friend. Even with as much time as we spent apart, I used to feel like she was the only person who really knew me."

My throat tightened at the loneliness I heard in his voice. "I'm sorry."

He didn't say anything else, and I figured he was probably done talking. I decided to give him some space with his feelings, and we sat in silence through two incongruously upbeat songs that made me wish I'd picked one of Taylor's moodier albums.

Out of nowhere, Bran spoke up as if we were still in the middle of a conversation. "She wanted to have kids."

I swiveled my head in surprise at his sudden truth bomb.

"I think that's the real reason Marisa broke up with me." His voice sounded flat and detached, as if he was talking about someone else's ex. "She wanted a certain kind of life, and I wasn't the guy who was going to give it to her." He paused. "Or maybe she just realized she didn't like me that much anymore. I don't know."

"You don't want kids?" I wished I could see his face, but he still had it turned away from me.

"Being a success at the career I want is going to take up most of my time and energy. I can't afford to prioritize a family as much as they'd need. Besides, I have a hard enough time managing my own shit. I don't think I could deal with managing children on top of that. I don't *want* to deal with it, anyway. Maybe that makes me selfish."

"That's the opposite of selfish. Selfish is having kids you don't want or have time for and making them feel like an inconvenience." I winced after I blurted it out, realizing how bitter I sounded.

In my peripheral vision, I saw Bran's head swivel toward me. I fidgeted under the inescapable weight of his attention.

"Is that what your parents did?" His voice sounded strained. Like he was fighting to hold back anger.

Part of me wanted to look at him, to see the expression on his face. But another part of me was afraid to see it and make it real. To distract myself, I reached up to unnecessarily adjust the rearview mirror.

"My mom wasn't much into the mom thing," I said, focusing on the road again. "She gave up all her custody rights in exchange for a bigger divorce settlement, and moved to New York. I've only seen her twice in the last five years. But even when she was around, she always seemed distracted and impatient, like she wanted to be somewhere else. Noah and I spent a lot of time with nannies or our grandmother. My dad works long hours, so sometimes we'd go days without seeing either of our parents because they came and went while we were asleep."

"I'm so sorry you grew up that way," Bran said.

"It's okay." I tried to sound light. "We were always looked after. It's not like we were mistreated or anything."

"Don't do that."

I flinched at the sharpness of his tone. "What?"

"Don't say it's okay. You *were* mistreated. What you're describing is emotional neglect."

"Funny, that's exactly what my therapist said." I shot a sidelong smile at Bran, but he didn't appear to appreciate the humor.

His hands were balled into fists and his expression was dark with a combination of outrage and sorrow. My stomach tried to churn and flutter at the same time seeing him so upset on my behalf. It made me feel like I was bouncing over whitewater rapids on an inner tube.

Impulsively, I reached across the center console and squeezed his hand. "Hey."

His fingers uncurled and wrapped around mine. His touch spread warm tingles over my skin and through my body. It took all my willpower to sever the contact after a few seconds and put my hand back on the wheel.

"All I mean is we could have had it a whole lot worse," I said as I checked the mirror to see how pink my cheeks looked. Pretty darn pink. "But you're right, it wasn't okay. It's why my little brother seems to be trying to drink his way through college, and why I'm oversensitive and insecure. So anyone who tries to call you selfish for not wanting to have kids can go fuck themselves, and that includes Mitski-loving Marisa and her matcha smoothies."

Bran made an odd, strangled sound. When I cut a concerned look at him, I realized he was smothering a laugh.

Something loosened in my chest as I felt myself smile. "Sorry, did I go too far?"

"No, that was perfect," he said, his voice vibrating with laughter. "You're perfect."

"Perfect, huh?" My smile tugged wider as I stretched out the fingers on my right hand, which still prickled with phantom tingles from Bran's touch. "Hey, so here's a question. Where should we stop for lunch?"

CHAPTER FIFTEEN

BRAN

I resisted the urge to check the time. I refused to think about it or stress over how long we planned to stop for lunch on top of all our other unplanned stops today.

Chloe had wanted to eat at Culver's, so that was where we were, in Cedar Springs, twenty miles north of Grand Rapids. I didn't give a damn where we ate or how much farther behind schedule it put us as long as it made her happy. Right now, making Chloe happy was my only goal in life.

And it did seem to make her happy. She chattered cheerfully while we stood in line to order and waited for our food. I loved seeing her so animated, her eyes sparkling and her lips tilting with smile after smile. It was like someone had turned on a faucet of sunlight. Compared to how reserved and mistrustful she'd been at the beginning of the trip, only letting her brightness out in meager dribs and drabs, it was the difference between winter and summer.

She was loveliness personified. The silvery lilt of her voice made my heart feel lighter. Every time she let out a bright chime of laughter, my breath caught. If I let myself look at her too closely, her beauty stole the air from my lungs.

My time blindness rendered me oblivious to the advancing of the clock while we lingered over our food, talking as easily as old friends. She stole fries off my tray after she'd finished off her cheese curds. When she went back for frozen custard, I didn't worry about the lateness of the afternoon or how many miles we still had to go. I could have stayed there all day watching Chloe drag her tongue over that cone of creamy chocolate custard. If she'd asked me to, I would have.

I'd put myself in Chloe's hands earlier, and it had turned out better than I'd expected. So why not keep doing it? It actually felt pretty good to give up control and let someone else take the reins for a while. There was something freeing about it. I decided to embrace the peaceful feeling that had stolen over me and go with it. Chloe knew what time the rehearsal dinner started and how important it was to my mother. I trusted her not to let us miss it. If she wanted us to take our time and loiter over lunch, I'd let her decide when we needed to get back on the road. If she wanted to drive the last leg of the trip, more power to her. She'd tell me if she wanted to trade. I was just a passenger on the train Chloe was driving. The sidekick to her protagonist, bobbing happily in her wake.

When we finally got back in the car, I slipped my shoes off and reclined my seat. I used my phone to pull up the music Chloe requested, but I didn't look at the GPS, ignoring the impulse to check our ETA. I was on vacation from worrying. We'd get there when we got there. In the meantime, I planned to sit back and enjoy the journey.

Halfway through our second Taylor Swift album of the day, Chloe slipped her sunglasses off and passed them to me. "Will you put these in my bag?"

As I tucked them into the purse at my feet, I cocked my head to peer through the windshield at the bank of heavy clouds that had cropped up, dimming the sun. "We might run into some rain up ahead."

"Looks like it," she said, appearing unconcerned.

I tried to follow her lead. She was in control. If she felt comfortable driving in the rain, that was her call to make.

"You want me to take a turn driving?" I offered anyway, unable to help myself.

"Nope," she said, tapping the steering wheel in time with the music. "I'm fine."

The sky continued to darken as we drove northward. The patch of gray clouds in the distance became a low-hanging ceiling of leaden sky surrounding us.

"You sure you want to drive in the rain?" I asked as the first fat drops started to hit the windshield.

"I can do this," Chloe said, her jaw set in determination.

I reached for my phone to check the weather radar. Forget that being-passive bullshit. What Chloe needed right now was a good copilot. But either the cell coverage was crap in this part of Michigan or the storm had affected the signal.

The radar image was taking an interminable time to load. Impatiently, I refreshed the map again, cursing the failure of modern technology.

As the rain picked up, Chloe eased off the accelerator, keeping a sensible distance between us and the car ahead. The harder it rained, the more we slowed. Most of the other traffic on the highway slowed down with us. Except for one asshole in a pickup who sped by on the left, his oversized tires kicking up a sheet of water.

Chloe flinched as the spray hit our windshield with a loud smack, obstructing visibility until the wipers cleared the view. Her hands tightened on the steering wheel as she leaned forward, redoubling her concentration.

"You're doing great," I told her. "You're doing everything exactly right."

She gave a distracted nod.

"Still feeling okay over there?"

"I might be just an eensy bit stressed," she confessed with a tight smile.

"Any time you want to pull over and trade places, we can do that. It's your call."

"It's not that bad," she said after a pause. "I can handle it. Facing your fear is supposed to be good, right?" The little nervous laugh she let out pulled a tight band around my ribs.

"You don't have to prove anything." Not to me, that was for sure. She'd already impressed the hell out of me.

"I want to though." Her chin lifted stubbornly. "I want to do this."

I could understand why she felt she needed to do it for herself. Conquering a mental challenge was something I related to all too well. "Okay. Like I said, it's up to you. You're doing a great job."

Her teeth worried at her lower lip. "How are we for time?"

"Don't worry about it. We've still got plenty of time. No worries, okay?" We were probably okay. I didn't actually know or care. It didn't matter. Getting Chloe through this rain mattered. Everything else could get fucked.

I refreshed the radar map again. It sure would be nice to know how big this storm was.

"How's the music?" I asked as I waited on the map. "Say the word if you want me to turn the volume up or down."

"It's okay." The skin around her eye crinkled. "You're being really nice to me."

"Is it helping or freaking you out?"

"It's helping. You should feel free to keep doing it as much as you want. Like, all the time," she added, rolling her lips together.

I checked my phone and saw the radar image had finally drawn in. "Hey, Chloe," I said quietly as I took in the dark-red rain cell directly ahead of us on the map. "The radar doesn't look good."

"How not good?"

"I think we should pull over and wait it out."

She must have heard something in my voice because she didn't argue. "Okay. I'll get off at the next exit."

The next exit wasn't soon enough. Less than a minute later we drove into a solid wall of water. Rain pounded the car with a deafening roar and turned the windows opaque. Chloe's back went rigid as she twisted the windshield wiper control. Even on the highest setting, it only allowed intermittent glimpses through the glass. It was like looking at the world through a zoetrope projector. In the gaps when the windshield wasn't obscured, the visibility through the sheeting rain was only a few yards.

"I can't see the road." A tremor of panic ran through her voice as she raised it to be heard over the rain. "I have no idea where my lane is or if I'm even in it." Her arms shook as she inhaled an unsteady breath. "I want to slow down but if I lose sight of the car ahead of us, I'll be totally blind."

"You could try to pull over." It wasn't a great option, but neither was driving with no visibility. There were no good options.

"Where?" Chloe's voice cracked as she shouted over the rain. "I can't even see where the shoulder is, much less if it's clear. I could hit the barrier or drive us into a ditch."

"You could do it carefully. We know the shoulder's got to be there. It doesn't matter if you hit the barrier as long as you're going slow enough." I didn't give two shits about getting scratches on my car.

"And then what?" she asked. "Won't we be sitting ducks, waiting for someone to come along and rear-end us?"

"Maybe."

She drew herself up even straighter. "I think I have to keep going."

"I think you're right. I'm sorry." I cursed myself for not insisting on driving. If I had, she wouldn't be in this situation. I doubted I'd be doing a better job than she was, but at least it'd be me suffering instead of her.

Her head bobbed jerkily. "I'll just keep following those two red lights up there and hope like hell that guy knows where he's going."

"That's a good plan. It's the only thing you can do."

She clenched her jaw as her head bobbed again.

I peered at the road ahead of us, but there was nothing to see but that single pair of red lights gleaming weakly through the impenetrable grayness. Giving up, I turned my attention back to Chloe, watching her watch the invisible road. Her body was taut as a steel cable, her limbs vibrating with tension as she held the wheel in a two-handed death grip. Otherwise, she was still as a statue. Too still.

"Chloe." Gently, I touched the top of her leg to get her attention. "Chloe, you need to breathe. You're holding your breath."

Her lips parted, and she pulled in a shaky lungful of air. "Oops," she muttered as she exhaled.

I withdrew my hand. "You okay?"

"Sure," she said, shaking her head to indicate the opposite. "Forgetting how to breathe is always a good sign."

Despite the terrifying circumstances, I had to smile at her spirit. "You've got this."

"I really don't."

"What can I do?" My instinct was to bundle her up in my arms, but that would almost definitely get us killed, so it probably wasn't the best idea. "Tell me what would help."

She drew her lower lip between her teeth. "It's going to sound weird."

"I'm totally fine with weird."

"Will you put your hand on my leg again? It made me feel calmer when you did it before."

I laid my hand on top of her leg again. "Like that?"

"Yes." She gave a jerky nod.

"You're okay," I said, squeezing my fingers gently to exert a little more pressure. "You can do this. Just remember to breathe."

"Right. Breathing. Passing out right now would definitely be bad."

"Yes it would." I swallowed as the heat of her skin soaked into my palm through her pants. "Blinking is important too. Make sure you blink."

"Keep talking to me," she said. "Tell me something funny."

"Funny. Okay." I quickly flipped through my mental scrapbook of embarrassing moments until I landed on one I thought would make her laugh. "At one of the mixers I went to in my first year of law school, I was introduced to a federal district judge. And instead of addressing her as 'Your Honor' like anyone of sound mind would, I accidentally called her 'Your Majesty.'"

"You did not."

"Hang on," I said, giving Chloe's leg a light squeeze. "I'm not through yet. So this judge, she looks at me, clearly having heard exactly what just came out of my mouth, and she very politely says, 'Excuse me?' Giving me a chance to pretend it never happened and correct my humiliating mistake. And so you know what I did?"

"What?" Chloe asked.

"I repeated it."

Her mouth gaped in disbelief. "You called her 'Your Majesty' twice?"

"To my absolute despair, that is precisely what I did."

"I assume you haven't been able to enjoy a night's sleep since then."

"Obviously."

Chloe broke into a smile that wrapped itself around my chest. At the very same moment, the downpour let up, almost as abruptly as it had kicked off. The percussion of the rain beating on the car dropped by twenty or so decibels, and a once-more discernable Taylor Swift song drifted softly through the quiet left in its wake.

"Oh thank God," Chloe said, releasing a long breath as the surface of the highway once more became visible. "We have lanes again! I missed you so much, lanes. Never ever leave me again."

"Well done," I said, giving her leg a congratulatory squeeze. "Not many people would have kept their shit together so well under those conditions."

She shook her head, peeling her fingers off the wheel one hand at a time and wiggling them to get the blood flowing. "I can't believe I actually made it through that."

"I never doubted you for a second." Now that the rain had slowed to a placid drizzle, I reluctantly took my hand off her leg, figuring she didn't need the physical reassurance anymore.

As I drew it back to my lap, she reached out to catch it. "Thank you," she said, her voice quiet and full of feeling.

My throat tightened as her hand squeezed mine. "Your fingers are cold," I said gruffly and tried to rub some warmth into them.

"I couldn't have gotten through that without you. You know that, right?"

"You underestimate yourself," I murmured, liking the feel of her touch more than I should. It was dangerous to like something too much when it wasn't yours.

Now that I knew how it felt to hold Chloe's hand in mine, I'd opened myself up to disappointment if it never happened again. It was like having one of the best meals of your life in a city you weren't ever likely to return to, and knowing you'd probably never taste it again.

Chloe cut a glance at me. Her lips tilted as she focused on the road again, and she slid her fingers over mine, stroking my knuckles. My heartbeat tripped at the slow, purposeful caress as a spark of hope flared within me. Did that mean she—

My phone went off, ringing loudly over the car's speakers. We both startled at the jarring noise, and Chloe jerked her hand back.

"It's my mom," I said apologetically as I took the call off Bluetooth before lifting it to my ear. "Hi, Mom. We're fine. Everything's fine."

As I'd guessed, she'd gotten worried that we were so far behind my estimated arrival time. She was used to me running late, but not usually quite this late. I explained we'd made a couple of unplanned stops and run into some weather but were getting close to the hotel now. Less than thirty minutes away, according to the GPS estimate. I told Mom we'd see her at the rehearsal dinner and ended the conversation with a promise to text her as soon as we got in safely.

"Sorry," I said to Chloe, starting the music up again.

"Was your mom worried?"

"She's fine." I was far more concerned about Chloe after that harrowing stretch of driving she'd had to do. I scrutinized her profile for signs of shock or exhaustion. "How are you? Do you want to let me finish the drive?"

She shook her head, stubborn as ever. "I'm good."

"Hey." I reached over to touch her leg again. "You've already proven you're a superhero. The way you drove through that storm was incredibly impressive and brave." When her hand dropped from the wheel to curl gratefully around mine, I had to swallow before continuing. "But bodies don't just shake off an adrenaline spike like that. It's okay to let someone else take over now."

"We're so close," she said. "I want to finish it myself. I just need to know I can beat my fear and get us all the way there without giving up."

I didn't try to talk her out of it since it was so important to her. But I did continue to keep a close eye on her. She left her hand on mine for the rest of the drive, and I happily let her hold it there.

Twenty minutes later, she turned into the vineyard where the wedding was being held, and parked in front of the small, quaint inn on the property. The clouds had thinned during the final few miles of the journey, uncovering patches of pink-tinted sky. As we both climbed out of the car, the sun peeked out through one of the holes in the clouds and bathed the rain-speckled buildings and vineyards around us in a shimmering golden glow.

While I walked around the car to open the trunk, Chloe threw her head back, flung her arms into the air, and let out a victory whoop.

"Heck, yeah! I totally crushed it!" She spun around in a circle, doing a little celebratory dance, then bounded over and unexpectedly threw her arms around my neck.

Taken by surprise, I stiffened for a split second before my arms instinctively wrapped around her middle. Her body pressed against mine as she leaned into the embrace, resting her cheek against my chest. Overwhelmed by her closeness, I tried to catalogue every sensation—the softness of her hair against my neck, the heat of her skin soaking through my clothes, and the gentle rise and fall of her chest when she breathed out a long sigh that warmed me through and through.

It was just an innocent hug, I told myself. A show of friendship. But as Chloe's hands smoothed over my back, my insides wanted to believe differently. My insides took off on a journey of imagination, conjuring up fantasies that went way beyond the bounds of friendship.

I banished those fantasies from my thoughts as Chloe pulled away and smiled her incandescent smile up at me. We were friends. That was what her smile meant. It was what she'd been telling me with that hug and also with the decisive step back she'd taken when she ended it. Friends but not more than that.

"Let's get this wedding weekend started," she said cheerily, plucking her bag out of the trunk before I could retrieve it for her.

My heart thumped unwisely against my chest as I watched her sashay off toward the inn, and I reminded myself that winning Chloe's friendship wasn't something to lament. It was a triumph. An honor. My brain knew that. It was just the rest of my body that needed to get the message.

CHAPTER SIXTEEN

CHLOE

A giddy lightness filled my chest as I got ready for Dawn's rehearsal dinner. You'd think after nearly ten straight hours of forced proximity with Bran, I'd be relieved to finally have a break from him. But you'd be abso-freaking-lutely wrong.

I couldn't stop smiling as I played back moments from the day we'd spent together. I'd already been looking forward to this weekend, but now my stomach fizzed with a whole new kind of excitement at the promise of seeing more of Bran.

The way we'd parted had left me unsettled. We'd both been in a hurry to get to our rooms to change for dinner, so we'd gone our separate ways without fanfare. Watching Bran stiffly turn and walk away after delivering a perfunctory goodbye had felt like an anticlimactic ending to the adventures that had brought us so much closer together.

He'd seemed to grow more subdued after we got out of the car. I wanted to believe he'd simply been tired and distracted, but I worried there might be something else behind it.

Had it been the hug? Maybe Bran wasn't a hugger. I probably should have asked before launching myself at him. I'd definitely felt him stiffen at first, but he'd seemed to relax into it after that. Had I made him uncomfortable? Should I apologize?

Or maybe I was overthinking everything as per usual.

Despite my eagerness to get to the rehearsal dinner, I took my time doing my hair and makeup. I'd be lying if I said I wasn't thinking of Bran while I did it, wanting to look good for him. Although I wasn't sure what I was actually hoping for or what these feelings I was having meant. There were only three things I knew for sure.

Number one: I enjoyed spending time with Bran.

Number two: I wanted to spend more time with him.

Number three: Bran was objectively attractive.

Given those three facts, it made sense that I felt an attraction to him. But was it merely an abstract appreciation or did it mean I wanted to be more than friends? My feelings were still too new to say for certain, and Bran's were even harder to decode. I felt pretty confident he liked me enough to be friends—or at least friend*ly*, if not actual friends who regularly sought out each other's company—but anything beyond that was a big fat question mark. There'd been several moments when I could have sworn I sensed a vibe, but I didn't trust my instincts where Bran was concerned. Maybe what I wanted to believe was attraction had simply been kindness.

My head continued to swim with distracted, dizzying thoughts of Bran as I wandered through the winery grounds in search of the restaurant where Dawn and Mike's rehearsal dinner was being held. There were three restaurants on the property, and by the time I finally found my way to the right one, I appeared to be the last to arrive. The private party room at the back was filled with the chattering voices of two dozen or so guests seated at a long table that appeared to have only one vacant seat—the one between Zach and Bran.

The sight of Bran in a suit shouldn't have had such an effect on me. I'd never found men in suits all that attractive to begin with, and it wasn't as if I'd never seen Bran wearing one before. I hadn't been that impressed the last time, so why should now be any different?

It would have to go on the list of feelings in need of examination because *hoo boy*. Color me impressed. My body had an instant visceral reaction to Bran and his charcoal-gray suit. My skin grew warm, my pulse jumped, and there was some definite tingling happening in places that were best not spoken of in polite company. But that was nothing—a mere blip, a minor flicker, only an errant whisper of feeling—compared to the vertiginous drop my stomach took when Bran looked up from his seat at the far end of the long table and his eyes collided with mine.

His expression was frustratingly impenetrable. I couldn't tell if he was

126

pleased to see me. I thought I'd gotten better at reading him, but I was at an absolute loss. His face might as well have been written in Welsh. It was all consonants and no vowels. Maybe my brain had shorted out, because the longer our eye contact lasted, the more the room seemed to waver around me as I floundered for equilibrium like a drunken sailor taking his first steps on dry land.

"Chloe!"

Dawn's beckoning cry tore my attention from Bran, and I went to greet the bride-to-be sitting beside her fiancé at the center of the table. After I exchanged hugs with Dawn and Mike, they peppered me with concerned questions about my terrifying driving adventure. Apparently Bran had already filled them in on the highlights of our day. I tried not to look at him, but the back of my neck itched with an unrelenting awareness that he was only a few yards away and potentially watching me talk to his mother.

My overblown reaction to being back in Bran's presence clarified at least one aspect of my feelings in three-dimensional relief. I'd developed a full-blown case of mancrush on Mr. Brandon Botstein. The thought of spending the next few hours seated next to him inspired a mix of heady excitement and pulse-pounding jitters. So yeah, I'd say I was definitely attracted to him, all right.

After we'd spent a few minutes catching up, Dawn waved me toward the remaining empty seat with instructions to relax and enjoy dinner. When I turned around, Bran was deep in conversation with Tess and Donal, who were seated to his left. Knowing Donal was Bran's professional mentor, I made my way past them silently, not wishing to interrupt.

Bran glanced up to offer me a fleeting smile before returning his attention to the conversation. At just that brief, halfhearted greeting my heart did a flying loop the loop in my chest.

Oh man, I was gone, gone, gone.

As I slipped into my chair at the corner of the table, Zach greeted me with a broad, bright smile. "There she is! The legendary hero has arrived at last, having survived her arduous ten-year journey across the treacherous wine-dark sea." He leaned over to pluck a bottle from the center of the table. "I'm guessing you could use a drink."

"God yes," I said. "Please."

After he'd filled my glass with a generous helping of red wine, he lifted his own in a toast. "To making it here alive—and in one piece, even."

I clinked my glass against his and took a long, much-needed drink before sinking against my chair with a sigh. "I take it you already heard about our day."

"Brandon treated us to the story when he got here. I expected a six-hour drive with my brother would be traumatic, but not literally life-threatening."

My gaze involuntarily flicked toward Bran, whose body was angled away from us, his attention fully occupied by something Donal was saying.

Zach watched me as I gulped down another drink of wine. "Having any PTSD? Should I be worried about you?"

I produced a smile as I shook my head. "Nope. I'm fine. Just relieved it's over."

"I believe that's a common refrain among women who've spent time in Brandon's company."

I opened my mouth to speak in Bran's defense, but he beat me to it.

"I'd tell you to go fuck yourself, Zachary, but according to the women you've dated that would be cruel and unusual punishment." Bran's knee brushed up against mine under the table as he swiveled in his seat to face us.

"Savage burn, bro." Zach looked strangely delighted. "I had a hunch you might be listening."

Bran's eyes narrowed. "Careful, baby brother. People might think you're obsessed with me the way my name always seems to be in your mouth."

"But of course you know better," Zach replied with an arch smile.

"Are you two always like this?" I asked them, already exhausted by their sibling taunting.

"Only when we're together," Zach said cheerfully.

Bran's attention shifted to me, and his gaze softened as it swept over my face before dipping lower to take in my floral halter top romper. "You look beautiful."

"Thank you," I said as the skin on my chest prickled with heat.

"Oh, so you *did* notice she was here," Zach said, watching us. "It was hard to tell."

Bran shot a glare at him. "You have the rest of your life to be an insufferable little shit. Why not take one night off?"

Zach's smile showed off his teeth. "Has anyone ever complimented you on your infectious personality?"

"No," Bran replied flatly.

"You should change your dating profile to 'Spreading misery wherever I go.'"

"And you should change yours to 'Not reaching my potential since 1999.'"

"Tonight's going to be a real hoot," I mumbled into my wineglass, fighting an urge to sink down in my chair and slide under the table. "I can already tell."

"Isn't it just?" Zach said with a mischievous gleam in his eyes. "Nothing warms the heart cockles like some good-natured fraternal bonding. It's a teaspoon of castor oil for the soul."

"What exactly is a cockle?" I mused aloud. "And do hearts actually have them?"

"I think you have to have a heart first," Bran said with a pointed look at Zach.

"Hey, here's a fun fact," I piped up with a tense smile. "Have I ever mentioned how conflict averse I am? Any whiff of strife sends my stress levels into overdrive."

Bran's lips thinned as he offered me an apologetic look.

"So what you're saying is we should stop acting like a pair of asshole toddlers?" Zach said, leaning back in his chair.

"I can behave like an adult if you can," Bran said to his brother.

Zach's shoulders lifted in a shrug. "I never have before, but I suppose there's a first time for everything." At Bran's glower, he put his hands up. "I kid! Mea culpa. I promise I'll be good for the sake of poor Chloe's frazzled nerves."

"Sorry," Bran said, pressing his knee against mine under the table. "You've had enough stress in your day already."

"Let's talk about something more pleasant," Zach proposed as he topped off my almost-empty wineglass. "So Chloe…what do you like to do when you're not slinging yarn at our mother's store?"

"She's a textile artist," Bran said. "She's incredibly talented too." Although his words were addressed to Zach, his gaze was locked on me. There was no pretending he didn't notice the way my cheeks flamed at his praise.

"Wow, you really must be good for Bran to bestow one of his rare compliments," Zach said.

I braced for Bran to swipe back, but his focus remained on me. "You should see the wedding present she made for Mom."

As Zach proceeded to pepper me with questions—about my art, my background, my aspirations—Bran leaned back in his chair and quietly sipped his wine. But his knee remained pressed against mine in a way that couldn't have been an accident, and his attention never seemed to waver from my face.

When Zach broached the subject of my family, I deflected by turning the conversation back to him and his family, hoping that would encourage Bran to contribute more. Alas no. Although I sensed Bran's watchfulness intensify when Zach brought up my parents, he remained frustratingly silent on this and all other subjects. Even after the first course of the meal arrived, Bran merely listened while Zach engaged me in conversation.

I was disappointed and annoyed. While I found Zach to be a pleasant and lively dinner companion when he wasn't actively antagonizing his brother, I would have much preferred to talk to Bran. I would have preferred to be doing pretty much anything with Bran, truth be told.

Sitting between the two of them only drove home how strong my feelings for Bran were. Zach was also objectively attractive. Some people might even call him more attractive than his dark-haired older brother, although I, for one, considered those people misguided. Zach did nothing for me. My heart didn't race at the feel of his eyes on me, my stomach didn't kick when he smiled, and my thighs didn't tingle when his arm accidentally brushed mine. I felt no attraction to him whatsoever, despite his bounty of charms.

Meanwhile, every nerve ending in my body was tuned in to the square inch of my leg being touched by Bran's knee. It felt like there was an electrical current pouring through that small point of contact and lighting up my spine like a Christmas tree.

I just really wished Bran would talk to me. About anything at all.

"How's your food?" I asked him after the main course arrived.

"It tastes like chicken," he said, dabbing at his mouth with his napkin.

"It is chicken," I pointed out.

His lips twitched with the barest hint of a smile. "That explains it, then."

I tried to think of another question to draw him into conversation, but I got distracted staring at his mouth. His lips were like two delicious pillows I wanted to sink into face-first. What would it feel like to kiss them? It was a mystery I ached to unravel.

While my thoughts went on a mini-vacation fantasizing about Bran's lips, Zach started talking about a book he was reading for one of his philosophy classes. Zach was just too damn friendly and easy to talk to. It was hard not to get swept up in conversation with him. And yet somehow Bran managed to avoid it with seemingly no trouble, lapsing into another lengthy silence.

He didn't speak again until Zach topped off my wineglass as the dessert plates were being cleared. "How many glasses is that?" Bran asked as his eyebrows downshifted into heavy disapproval mode. "Maybe you should slow down."

"Let her live," Zach said with a roll of his eyes. "She's entitled to cut loose a little if she wants to."

"Yeah," I said, shooting Bran a defiant look. "I'm entitled to cut loose."

"I wouldn't want you to make yourself sick," he said as his frown deepened.

"That would imply you cared," I answered back a lot more sharply than I meant to. *Big yikes.* Maybe he was right and I should ease off on the wine.

My insides knotted as Bran's spine stiffened, his expression shuttering like a storm window. *Fuck.*

"Sorry," I mumbled, feeling like a piece of shit.

He avoided looking at me as he shook his head. "Your alcohol consumption is your business. I'm the one who should apologize."

The same wine-fueled recklessness that had made me snippy also made me bold. I reached into Bran's lap underneath the table and squeezed his hand. "I didn't mean it. I know you care."

"Do you?" he asked as his fingers twined with mine, unleashing a storm of butterflies in my stomach.

I smiled at him and nodded. "I like that you care."

An answering smile curved his lips as his thumb caressed a slow path across my palm, and my thighs clenched involuntarily.

Zach cleared his throat. "I'm thinking we all could stand to stretch our legs. I hear this place has some pretty nice scenic paths leading down to the beach. What do you say we get some fresh air and check them out?"

I didn't care about scenic paths or stretching my legs, and I *really* didn't care to go anywhere with Zach right now. All I cared about was the way Bran was looking at me—like he was as smitten as I was—and the fact that he was holding my hand.

Dismayingly, Zach didn't seem interested in what we thought. Without waiting for an answer, he shoved his chair back and took Bran and me each by an elbow. We were both so dazed we didn't resist as he herded us to our feet, forcing me to release Bran's hand. "We're going for a walk," he called out to his mother as he steered us outside.

There was a perfectly nice deck just behind the restaurant, but Zach urged us past it and onto a gravel path illuminated by landscape lighting.

"Isn't this lovely?" he said as he marched us along the rather unexceptional path. "You've got trees and plants and the moon overhead. It's an ideal setting for a romantic stroll."

"What's happening?" I asked. "What are we doing out here?"

"We're taking a walk and admiring the view," Zach said. "Duh."

"What view?" Bran asked dryly. "It's dark."

"This view," Zach said as the path opened up into a small, sheltered garden surrounded by flowering trees and shrubs.

I had to admit it was a bit nice. Though really my interest in nighttime horticulture was minimal at best.

"Chloe looks cold," Zach said, shoving Bran and I together so we were standing shoulder to shoulder. "Maybe do something about that," he called back at us as he wandered off to look at a spindly tree covered with lacy flowers. "Wow, look at this tree! It's so…arboreal."

I looked at Bran, whose lips were pursed in an expression of intense annoyance. "Do you know why he dragged us out here?"

"Unfortunately, I do," he said, shaking his head as Zach stooped to examine an unremarkable shrub with a bizarre amount of interest.

"Care to share with the class?"

"I really don't."

"I like this shrub," Zach commented. "This is an excellent shrub."

"Are you cold?" Bran asked me, ignoring his brother.

I crossed my arms in an attempt to hide my goose bumps. "No, I'm okay."

Bran made a growly, exasperated noise and shrugged out of his suit jacket.

"Thank you," I murmured as he draped it around my shoulders. His close proximity and the scent of his cologne made my head swim. Or maybe that was all the wine I'd consumed, because I was definitely feeling a little tipsy.

He adjusted the jacket until he'd deemed it acceptably straight. Once he was satisfied, he smoothed his hands down my wool-cloaked upper arms. "Better?"

I nodded. My mouth went dry as his gaze took a slow journey down my body before sliding back up to my face.

"Gee, I wonder where this path goes," Zach called out, sounding farther away now. "I'm just going to go do some exploring on my own. No need to follow me. I'm sure you two can find your own way back to your rooms from this secluded, romantic setting. You're welcome, by the way!"

The retreating crunch of his footsteps petered out into silence as he left us. Alone. Together. In a secluded, romantic setting.

CHAPTER SEVENTEEN

CHLOE

Ohhhh!

I mentally smacked myself in the forehead. I almost *literally* smacked myself in the forehead but checked the instinct just in time.

Sheesh, was I dense. And apparently more than just a little tipsy because I should have figured it out sooner. Zach hadn't been cockblocking. He'd been trying to play wingman in his own diabolical way.

Now that we were alone, Bran was very determinedly *not* looking at me.

"I get it now," I said, unable to stop myself from giggling. "He ships us."

Bran's grimace somehow managed to convey irritation, embarrassment, and amusement all at once. "I sincerely apologize for my wretched little brother. He delights in giving me new reasons to regret his birth."

"You guys had me totally fooled earlier. I thought you genuinely couldn't stand each other."

"I assure you we can't. Your first instinct was the correct one."

I shook my head, rejecting his bullheaded refusal to admit to the affection beneath their surface rivalry. "If he didn't care about you, why would he be so determined to set you up? Huh? Answer me that," I said, poking Bran in the chest.

Whoa. That was one firm chest. I poked it again, just to be sure I hadn't imagined the impressiveness of his chest muscles. *Nope.* Not my imagination. Definitely rock-hard pecs. *Nice.*

Bran's lips twitched as he stared down at my finger, which was still pressed against his chest. *Oopsie.* I snatched my hand back and shoved it in my armpit so it wouldn't misbehave again. Sheesh, I really was drunker than I thought.

"He did it to humiliate me," Bran said in answer to the question I'd posed. "Obviously."

I didn't buy it. Zach's matchmaking had to mean that deep down he wanted Bran to be happy. Even if he had a bizarre way of showing it.

Unless…

Unless Bran's embarrassment wasn't just about his brother's heavy-handed methods.

Unless the reason he was so embarrassed was that Zach had attempted to fix him up with someone Bran had no interest in pursuing.

Oh no.

If Bran had wanted to pursue me, he would have made an effort to do it himself, right? He wouldn't have needed Zach's intervention. But Bran hadn't made an effort.

If Zach knew that, then he *had* been punking Bran. And using me and my embarrassingly obvious crush to do it.

"Oh my God," I said, covering my face as my stomach turned to lead. "I'm such an idiot."

"No," Bran said, sounding panicky. "No, I didn't mean—"

"It's okay." Mortified, I waved my hand to cut him off. "I get it now. Ha ha. Zach really got you good. I just, um—I need to—" *Leave. Not be here anymore. Get away from Bran and this stupid romantic garden before I make even more of a fool of myself.*

I spun around and started walking, not knowing where I was going and not caring as long as it took me away from this place.

"Wait. Chloe—" Gravel crunched behind me, echoing my steps as Bran followed in my wake. "Where are you going?"

"Back to my room," I tossed over my shoulder. Then stopped a few steps later. I had no idea how to get there from here. I didn't even remember which of the paths leading away from the garden we'd come from. "Which way is the hotel?"

"I'll walk you back."

"I don't need you—" My voice broke. *Dammit.* Why did I drink so much? It made it too hard to control my emotions. I blinked back tears of frustration and scrubbed my hands over my face. I wasn't crying. I *wasn't.* "It's fine. It's not your fault. I didn't actually expect you to—I mean, if you'd been interested in me like that you would have done something about it yourself. Duh. I just really want to—"

Bran pulled me against his warm, solid chest and wrapped his arms around me. I didn't want to, but God help me, I melted into his embrace because it felt too good to do anything else. Stupid comforting man muscles.

"Chloe." The sound of my name rumbling through his chest in that sexy, growly voice was too much. It churned up a surge of feelings that threatened to break the dam and drown me.

I gulped, trying to shove them back down again. "I'd just really like for today to be over," I whispered, hiding my face.

"I know," he said. "I know, I'm sorry."

God, now he was stroking my hair. The tenderness of it tore a sob out of me. I didn't want him to pity me. It was humiliating. The urge to flee trembled through me, but Bran only held me tighter. I had no choice but to cling to him and burrow farther into his chest to muffle the crying I couldn't seem to stop.

"Please don't be sad," he murmured, rubbing soothing circles on my back. "I didn't mean to make you cry."

There was something so intensely intimate about the way he was holding me. It made me feel safe. And wanted. Which was confusing. Because he didn't want me. And that made me feel vulnerable. Which didn't feel safe. Basically I didn't know what to make of anything. My feelings were all kinds of messy.

"I think I might be drunk," I mumbled. Jesus, I was getting tears and snot on his nice silk tie and pristine dress shirt. I pulled back and tried to wipe off his shirt. "God, how embarrassing."

"You have no reason at all to be embarrassed." Warm hands cradled my head and gentle fingers slid into my hair. "You're perfect."

I winced. "Hardly."

Bran's thumbs stroked away the tears on my cheeks. "But you are. You should never doubt that."

How could he say that? He didn't mean it. He couldn't. Unless I was wrong…

I blinked up at him. Moonlight illuminated the beautiful features of his face. It was pinched with concern, but there might have been something else there as well. I couldn't tell anymore. It was all too confusing.

It didn't get any less confusing when he bent his head and kissed my forehead. My lungs expelled a long, deep sigh as the soft caress of his lips turned me into a quivering puddle.

"I'm sorry I'm not very good at this," he murmured against my skin.

"Are you kidding?" A semi-delirious laugh bubbled out of me as I clutched at his waist. "That was a top-notch hug. One of the best I've ever had. You're a master hug-giver. You could take gold in the hug Olympics."

He drew back, amusement crinkling the corners of his eyes. "Is that right?"

"Damn straight." I wished I was more sober. In my muddled state I couldn't be sure what I saw in his eyes was real. Or that it actually meant what I wanted it to mean. Maybe it was just an illusion, like the moonlight making his green eyes look dark and silvery.

"I should take you back to your room." At my nod of enthusiastic agreement, he wrapped an arm around my shoulders and tucked me against him as he steered me out of the garden.

"You're a good friend to put up with my tipsy messiness."

He grunted.

I poked him in the side. "We are friends, aren't we?"

"Of course we are," he said, grabbing my poking finger. "If you're sure that's what you want." Instead of releasing my hand, he held it trapped against his stomach.

"Is that what you want?" I asked, fighting the urge to fondle the ab muscles I could feel under my fingers.

"Yes."

Had he hesitated or had I imagined it?

"Are you sure?" I asked, squinting up at him.

"Of course I'm sure." His fingertips stroked the back of my hand.

"Okay, good." I let out a relieved breath and leaned into him. "I want us to be friends."

At a branch in the path, we paused for Bran to read a sign pointing the way toward the inn and continued onward until a familiar building came into view. We hadn't been as far from the hotel as I'd thought.

Bran took us through a courtyard and through the back entrance, releasing me to swipe his keycard and hold the door open. He followed as I hurried through the lobby and up the carpeted stairs, then down the hallway to my room.

"This is me," I said, slipping off his jacket and holding it out as I turned to face him. "Thanks for the loan. And the escort."

He folded the jacket and laid it over his forearm. "Do you have your keycard?"

I plucked it out of my pocket to show him. As he nodded again, his eyes locked onto mine, and my breath caught in my throat. His lids lowered as something shifted in the green depths, and suddenly the air between us felt different. Electric. Sparking with potential.

Risky.

I didn't want to get my hopes up and have them dashed again. I'd been getting some seriously conflicting signals from Bran all night. No, scratch that. Ever since I'd first laid eyes on him, it'd been nonstop mixed messages. My gut had already proven useless at deciphering them. I couldn't trust anything it was trying to tell me.

Bran and I were friends. That was what we'd said. It was an established fact. Anything beyond was mere speculation and liable to lead me into trouble.

Friends could give each other hugs though, and I could really use one of those right now.

I stepped forward and wrapped myself around Bran's torso, resting my cheek against his chest. The deep breath he let out as his arms encircled me sounded a lot like relief.

The knots in my stomach loosened as we stood there clinging to each other. I'd been a bundle of jangling nerves all night, but they'd all gone quiet as soon as I'd stepped into Bran's arms. Hug therapy was even better than yarn therapy. Way better.

"This is nice," I said, wondering how long I could reasonably keep this hug going. Forever was probably unrealistic.

"Yes." His rough voice was almost a whisper. He didn't seem in any more of a hurry to end the hug than I was.

"It's been a weird day, hasn't it?"

This time he didn't answer except to let his head rest heavily against mine. Which was pretty much an answer. It felt good to be this close to him and feel the strength of his arms holding on to me. As if he needed me too. It wasn't just me being needy. We were each other's life preservers.

The pad of his thumb rubbed back and forth over my shoulder blade, giving me goose bumps. Shivering, I slid my hands up his back, following the thick columns of muscle.

He rubbed his nose against my hair, inhaling a lungful of the scent. "You smell good."

"So do you."

Since he didn't seem to mind, I let my hands wander higher up his back, sweeping over the curves and plateaus of muscle. His thumb continued its short arc across my skin as the fingertips of his other hand inched downward. They followed my spine down to my waist before reversing direction and traveling back up until they reached bare skin, skimming along the edge of the fabric and dipping ever so slightly inside it.

All this soothing, perfectly innocent touching lulled me into a peaceful sort of trance, so I wasn't really thinking about it or about much of anything at all. I was just enjoying the nice feeling while my mind drifted aimlessly. We were friends being friendly. That was all.

Until I started to feel him harden against me. And then I became extremely conscious of the heat between my thighs, the way my breasts were pressed against his chest, and the friction on my tight nipples every time I breathed.

Okay, maybe not just friends being friendly.

We weren't exactly rubbing on each other, but we weren't *not* rubbing either. Bran didn't seem to be trying to hide his reaction to me. That had to mean something, didn't it? In addition to the fact that he'd had a reaction in the first place. So maybe he was a little attracted to me.

"Do you really think I'm perfect?" I couldn't help myself. I had to know if he meant it enough to say it when I wasn't blubbering all over him.

"Yes." He spoke with no hesitation. Just put it out there, clear and strong. Not unlike the erection nudging my lower stomach.

I tilted my head up to look at him. His eyes were dark and heavy, the pupils blotting out all the colors in his irises. I swallowed as his gaze traveled slowly over my face. When it found my mouth, my lips parted, trembling in anticipation, and I heard Bran's breath quicken as he tracked my reaction.

God I wanted to feel those gorgeous lips. To taste them. My fingers curled into his back, maybe possibly tugging on him a little, and he made a sound deep in his throat when our hips pressed together.

"Chloe…"

One of us was trembling. I couldn't tell which one. Maybe it was both of us.

"What?" Too impatient to wait for him to answer, I surged up to press my lips against his.

I didn't make it there.

Bran jerked backward. His hands grasped my shoulders, pushing me back down and firmly away. "That's not a good idea."

"Shit," I croaked, burying my face in my hands. I couldn't stand to have him look at me. Ever. Again. The only cure for this level of humiliation was moving to another country and changing my name.

"Chloe—"

"Don't say a word."

"But—"

"I mean it."

Silence. Finally.

Without letting myself look at him, I spun around and fumbled my room key out of my pocket. Of course I couldn't get it to work. Every time the little red light came on and it made that awful error sound, I got more frantic. I could feel Bran behind me, itching to step in and do it for me, but I didn't want him that close. I needed to *get out of here*. Finally the lock took pity on me and I was rewarded with a green light and a satisfying click.

"Are you okay?" Bran asked as I yanked on the door handle.

"Yeah, I'm great," I snapped, pressing my forehead against the door. I squeezed my eyes shut and tried to pull myself together.

"I'm really sorry, I—"

"Can you do me a favor?" I said, cutting him off again.

"What?"

"Let's forget this ever happened, okay? In fact, it would be great if we could forget all of tonight happened. Let's just write it off as one big, embarrassing drunken mistake that will never be spoken of again. Can we do that?"

He hesitated. "But—"

"*Please*," I croaked, desperate to avoid drawing out my humiliation by rehashing it while he attempted to make me feel better about his rejection.

He swallowed thickly in the agonizing silence. "I'm sorry, but no. We're not doing that. We're definitely going to talk about this tomorrow when you're sober."

"Fine. Great. I guess I'll see you tomorrow, then." I pushed into the room and shoved the door shut behind me.

"Chloe," he said just before it closed with a satisfying *thunk*.

I walked over to the bed and crawled into it face-first, vowing never to drink around someone I had a crush on ever again.

CHAPTER EIGHTEEN

BRAN

How many different ways could one person bungle a romantic opportunity with the same girl? At this point I'd lost count of all the times I'd fucked up with Chloe. Surely I had to be approaching some kind of world record by now.

After the way we'd left things last night, it was hard to imagine her ever trusting me again.

Fuck.

I didn't regret stopping her attempt to kiss me though. I'd wanted that kiss so bad every bone in my body still ached for it, but she'd been drunk. I couldn't regret not taking advantage of her. Not even a little bit.

What I regretted was that my rejection had wounded and embarrassed her. Guilt had opened up a hole in my chest that was still making it hard to breathe this morning. I also regretted not cutting that second hug short a hell of a lot sooner. I shouldn't have let it go so far beyond the boundaries of a platonic hug. Maybe I shouldn't have even let her hug me in the first place, but she'd seemed to need it, and I'd claimed to be her friend. Refusing to hug her would have made a liar out of me and hurt her feelings even more.

Though I loathed myself for hurting her, some part of me couldn't help wondering if it wasn't for the best that last night might have killed any chance between us. Realistically, I didn't have much to offer Chloe. The same issues that had driven Marisa away—my lack of free time for her, my perpetual distraction and exhaustion, my dislike of going out to parties and bars at night—would plague any relationship I attempted. I wouldn't be able to make Chloe any happier than I'd made Marisa. She deserved better than that.

Even so, I needed to talk to her. To apologize and try to explain. I couldn't stand the way we'd left things. I'd texted her last night and again this morning, but she hadn't responded. I took it as an indication she didn't want to talk. Showing up at her room unannounced seemed unlikely to win me into her good graces, so instead I'd staked out the breakfast buffet, hoping she'd show up.

It was the first thing on the wedding itinerary today. I arrived early to be sure I didn't miss Chloe. For once lateness hadn't been a problem since I'd been lying in bed wide-awake since four o'clock this morning. I claimed a seat with a good view of the buffet and settled in to wait.

My soon-to-be stepfather was one of the first to make an appearance, flanked by his best man and another friend, all three of them dressed as if they'd just come from the gym. I watched as he piled his plate with as much protein as it would hold and then attempted to balance a Danish atop the precarious mountain of eggs.

Mike was a brawny, lumbering sort of guy. If you put him in a red plaid shirt and handed him a roll of paper towels, he could model for the label. Unsurprisingly, he'd been a football player in high school. My mom had been infatuated with him back then, but he'd rejected her because she wasn't one of the popular crowd.

They'd both laughed when they told me the story last year after they'd reconnected and started dating, but I hadn't found it particularly endearing. The fact that my mom was marrying a twice-divorced former jock who used to think he was too good for her didn't thrill me. She claimed Mike had changed a lot since high school, and as far as I'd been able to tell he doted on my mom these days. But I couldn't shake the feeling he wasn't good enough for her.

Nevertheless, Mike was who my mom wanted, so I'd kept my opinion to myself. Even I couldn't deny that he seemed to treat her well and make her happy. So when Mike spotted me sitting alone and made a beeline to join me, I made my best attempt to appear friendly as I greeted him.

"Your mom's sleeping in," he said as he lowered himself into a seat across from me at the large round table. "We were at the bar until pretty late last night."

"And yet you still managed to make it to the gym," I observed. "That's dedication."

"Old habits die hard, I guess." His companions had gotten distracted by the options at the mimosa bar, and he darted a glance at them before his attention returned to me. "You know, I think this might be the first time you and I have ever been alone together."

"I think you're right." We'd always had my mom around as a buffer, and I found myself desperately missing her presence now.

He nodded as he unwrapped his napkin. "This must all be pretty weird for you. Watching your mom get married to someone who isn't your dad. If I were in your shoes, I'm not sure I'd be handling it half as well as you."

"It's fine," I said, feeling cornered and panicky. The absolute last thing I wanted to do right now was talk about my feelings with Mike. "As long as Mom's happy, I'm happy for her."

"Uh-huh," Mike said in a tone that let me know he wasn't the least bit fooled. "I'm just saying, I don't expect you to be unreservedly overjoyed about what's happening today. It's okay for you to feel loyal to your dad. I wouldn't blame you if you resented me for taking his place in your mom's life."

I opened my mouth to deny it, but he cut me off before I could.

"I just want you to know that," he said, spearing me with a look. "And I also want you to know how much I appreciate that you've tried to give me the benefit of the doubt anyway and put up with me for your mom's sake. It means a lot to her, and it means a lot to me too. Okay?"

I nodded, rendered speechless by Mike's unexpected bluntness and sensitivity.

He picked up his fork and focused on pushing his eggs around his plate. "You don't have to say anything. Heart-to-hearts give me indigestion, but I just thought I should put that out there before I marry your mom today."

"I really am happy for you both," I said. "Or at least I'm trying really hard to be."

"You're doing a good job," he said, flashing a cockeyed grin. "Don't worry about it."

"I'm already having mimosa regret." Mike's best man Deon set his plate down in front of the seat next to Mike. I'd met him last night before the rehearsal dinner, along with his husband Andrew. "I think the peach was a mistake."

"Told ya you shoulda got the grapefruit," the other man with him said in a South Boston accent, claiming the seat on Deon's other side.

"Only if I wanted to punish myself," Deon retorted. "Grapefruit is the Devil's juice."

"That's Stan," Mike told me, cocking his thumb at the third man. "He's a friend of mine from work."

"Brandon here is Dawn's oldest son," Deon explained to Stan.

"Nice to meet ya," Stan said with a nod.

"I think he prefers Bran," Mike said around a mouthful of bacon. He glanced at me for confirmation. "Don't you?"

"That's true," I said, surprised he'd noticed. "Brandon's what my parents call me, so it makes me feel like I'm in trouble."

"You're up disappointingly early," Deon commented, giving me an appraising look. "Judging from those bags under your eyes, I'd say you either had a rough night or a *very* good night."

"Definitely not the latter," I muttered, reaching for my coffee.

"Does that mean things didn't work out with that girl?" Stan asked.

I went still. "What girl?"

"Maybe we should drop it," Mike suggested.

"The pretty one seated next to you at the rehearsal dinner," Deon said, totally not dropping it. "The one you've got a crush on."

"Chloe," Mike supplied, avoiding looking at me.

I stared at him. "Why would you think I have a crush on Chloe?"

Mike's eyes lifted to mine. "I've seen the way you look at her. But also…" He paused, wincing. "Zach showed up at the bar last night. He might have been bragging about setting you and Chloe up."

"Of course he was." I rubbed my forehead as I contemplated the most painful death I could arrange for my meddling brother. Shooting him into the vacuum of space seemed impractical, but pushing him in front of a bus would be letting him off way too easy. Perhaps there was some way to arrange for him to be torn limb from limb…

"Did you crash and burn?" Stan asked, giving me a sympathetic look. "It's okay. We've all been there, kid."

"Whatever Zach's intention might have been, he did more harm than good." I cut a disconcerted look at Mike. "Does Mom know? Was she around when Zach was—"

Mike shook his head. "No. And I didn't mention it to her either."

"It was just us guys," Deon confirmed.

"Just the three of you?" I asked hopefully.

"Pretty sure Alex and Matt were there," Stan said in between bites of Danish.

"And obviously Andrew," Deon said.

"And Donal," Mike added.

Donal, my professional mentor. *Terrific.*

"You still haven't told us what happened," Deon pointed out. "Was it that bad?"

Mike elbowed him. "Leave the kid alone. He doesn't have to talk about it if he doesn't want to."

Deon rolled his eyes. "Okay, but my imagination is just going to fill in all the blanks if I don't know the real story. And I have a very vivid imagination, which means I'll be thinking it's something way more shocking than it probably was. Just so you know."

"Nothing shocking happened," I said. "Zach put us both in an uncomfortable position by trying to force something that wasn't meant to be, with the entirely predictable result of making things extremely awkward between us."

"Does that mean you didn't even try to shoot your shot?" Stan asked, looking disappointed.

"Or did you swing and strike out?" Deon wanted to know.

"What do you mean 'not meant to be'?" Mike asked, frowning.

I rubbed my temples. "There was no shot to shoot. She'd had a rough day and a lot to drink with dinner. Even if I'd wanted to, nothing was going to happen last night."

Stan gave me a nod. "Good on you, kid."

Deon raised his hand. "I'd like to revisit the part where you said 'even if I wanted to.' Does that mean you're not interested in the lovely Chloe after all?"

"I don't have room in my life for a girlfriend," I said, staring down at the uneaten remnants of my breakfast.

"Bzzzt," Deon said. "Nonresponsive. That's not an answer to my question."

I could feel Mike watching me, and it made me wonder what he thought he'd seen. Had I really been that obvious? I cleared my throat. "Chloe's a great person, but we're better off as friends."

Mike set his fork down and rested his forearms on either side of his plate. "Okay, I'm just gonna say one thing, and then we're going to change the subject and give poor Bran a break." He spoke in a firm, no-arguments tone I'd never heard him use before, and shot a warning look at Deon and Stan before turning his full attention to me. "You like Chloe. Chloe likes you. Those are facts." When I opened my mouth to argue, he raised a hand to silence me. "Those are facts, whether you choose to admit it or not. Now, you're still young, so you probably don't realize how rare it is for two people to really dig each other and feel a connection." Mike glanced at his friends. "Am I wrong?"

"He is not wrong," Deon said, shaking his head.

"Nope," Stan agreed as he bit into a piece of toast.

Mike turned back to me. "When you trip over something rare and special lying in the road, it's a mistake to leave it there and keep on walking by. Even if you weren't looking for it, you shouldn't pass up a treasure. Because it might actually turn out to be exactly what you need. And what if it never comes along again, and then you've missed your chance?"

"Unless it's a cork-lid trapdoor spider," Stan said. "Then you're in for a nasty surprise."

Mike shook his head while keeping his focus on me. "If you and Chloe like each other enough, you'll find a way to figure out all the other stuff. If you don't, you won't. But you'll never know whether you could have made it work if you never even try." He leaned back, picking up his coffee. "And that's the last we're going to say on the subject because your mom's coming, and she's got Chloe with her."

It took a second for his last sentence to sink in. When it did, I stiffened and swiveled my head around in time to see Chloe and my mom walking past the windows on their way to the door.

"Oh damn," Deon said, looking cheerful. "Drama."

Mike elbowed him again before raising his hand to wave at my mom as she walked into the restaurant.

Mom waved back at us, which was when Chloe saw me sitting there. She froze in place, looking like she wanted to turn and run. But Mom didn't give her the chance, hooking her arm through Chloe's to herd her to the buffet.

"Breathe, kid," Stan helpfully reminded me.

Right. Breathing. Oxygen was useful for cognitive function and a lot of other things I couldn't think of right now because I'd forgotten to breathe.

CHAPTER NINETEEN

CHLOE

The back of my neck itched with the awareness of Bran's eyes watching me as we stood at the waffle bar. I knew I should have skipped breakfast. I'd planned to slip in, grab a few croissants from the buffet, and flee back to my room, but I'd bumped into Dawn on the way and now I was trapped.

"Did you enjoy yourself at the rehearsal dinner?" she asked me.

"Yep," I said, bending to examine the syrup so she wouldn't see me lying. "It was lovely. More importantly, did *you* enjoy yourself? This weekend is all about you. And Mike. But mostly you."

Dawn laughed as she spooned sliced bananas onto her plate. "The whole week has been absolutely wonderful. It's just gotten better and better as more guests have arrived. What's not to love about having all my favorite people in one place?" She beamed a smile at the table where Bran sat with Mike before turning it on me. "You and the boys seemed to be chatting it up last night. I can't remember the last time I saw Brandon and Zach getting along so well."

"Mmmm," I hummed noncommittally.

She held her plate out to receive the waffle the chef had just pulled off the iron. "I'm so glad you're all becoming friends. I was worried you younger kids would be bored out of your minds hanging out with us old fogies this weekend."

"Stop it. You're nowhere near old fogy status," I said as I held out my own plate for the other waffle.

"Here, have some of these bananas," Dawn said, spooning them on top of my waffle. "You look like you might have overindulged in the wine last night."

I pressed my hand to my brow to shield my bloodshot eyes. "God, do I look that bad?"

"No, sweetheart, you're perfect." Dawn smiled as she tucked a lock of hair from my extremely messy bun behind my ear.

My affection-starved heart squeezed at the gesture, which showed more tenderness than I'd ever gotten from my parents. At the same time, the word *perfect* shivered down my spine, reviving the memory of Bran saying it last night and leaving me to fight off a stew of mixed-up emotions I wasn't prepared to handle this morning.

"You look as lovely as ever," Dawn went on, blessedly turning away as I felt my throat burn. "Just a bit dehydrated is all. I suspect we're all feeling a little rough around the edges this morning. Can you believe Mike and I closed down the bar last night? I'm not used to being such a party animal."

She continued to chatter cheerfully about all the fun things they'd done this week leading up to the wedding as she herded me to the juice bar for some much-needed electrolytes. And then it was time to face the moment I'd dreaded. My feet felt heavy as I trailed Dawn to the table to join the others.

I mumbled a response to their greetings without meeting Bran's eyes. Mike stood to kiss Dawn, pulling out the chair next to him for her. Meanwhile, his best man Deon jumped to his feet and insisted on giving up his seat to me while he went to get another mimosa. This put me directly across the round table from Bran. Reluctantly, I slid into the offered seat between Mike and another man who introduced himself as Stan.

I avoided looking across the table by talking to Stan about his job at Mr. Sullivan's security company, and our mutual acquaintances among his colleagues and their friends and spouses. A few of them had come up for the wedding, like Sandra and Marie and their husbands, though most had been unable to make the weekend trip because of children or other obligations.

While we talked, I felt Bran's apprehensive eyes watching me, but I refused to acknowledge or return his stare. I wasn't any more interested this morning in talking about what happened than I had been last night. Maybe we wouldn't have to if I could avoid being alone with him. I had no need to hear his uncomfortable apology. If we didn't dwell on it, the sting would fade, and eventually we'd be able to forget it ever happened. Maybe we could even get back to being sort-of friends again.

Deon returned with a tray of mimosas for the table. When I tried to decline, he set one in front of me anyway, saying a little hair of the dog would do me good. Apparently my hungover state was obvious to everyone.

When I'd consumed as much food and coffee as my churning stomach could take, I pushed my chair back and announced I was heading back to my room. To my dismay, Bran stood up with me and asked if we could talk. Everyone at the table fell quiet, riveted by our interaction. Caught on the spot, I had no choice but to agree and let Bran accompany me out of the dining room.

I walked tensely ahead of him, stopping in the lobby once we were out of sight of the dining room windows. "What?"

"Not here," he said with a glance at the other people walking through the lobby around us, many of whom were here for the wedding. Pressing his hand against my back, he steered me toward the door we'd come in last night. "Come on."

An unpleasant sense of déjà vu haunted me as Bran guided me through the courtyard. But instead of taking the gravel path to the scenic walk, we ducked down a narrow stone walk and through a vine-covered arch that led to a small sheltered area surrounded by rose-covered trellises.

"What?" I demanded, no longer attempting to hide my annoyance. "What do you want?"

"We need to talk," Bran said.

"No," I said through gritted teeth. "We don't. Like I told you last night, I'd prefer to forget it."

"Chloe, you can't even look at me. At least let me apologize."

I hugged myself as I shook my head. "You didn't do anything wrong. It was all me. I had too much to drink and my mouth made bad choices. I'm sorry for trying to kiss you when you're clearly not interested in me like that. But you don't have to worry. It won't happen again."

"You're wrong," Bran said.

"No, really." If we were going to have any chance of salvaging our friendship, I needed him to believe me so we could move past this. "I learned my lesson. I won't be throwing myself at you anymore. You're safe, I promise."

"That's disappointing."

I stared at him in bewilderment. "What is?"

"You're wrong about me not being interested in you like that."

I continued to stare, not trusting myself to correctly interpret what he was saying. "I'm going to need you to explain exactly what you mean by that."

A smile curled at the corner of his lips as he shook his head. "For someone who claims to be able to read people's energy, you sure misread mine a hell of a lot."

"Do you have any idea how closed off you are?" My voice rose in frustration. "You keep all your feelings locked down behind these impenetrable walls. I feel like I've actually been doing pretty well, considering."

"Then I'll have to get better at telling you what I'm feeling from now on. Starting right now."

My heart hammered in my chest as Bran unwrapped my arms to take both of my hands in his.

"Chloe." The soft, uncertain way he spoke my name sent my stomach tumbling into free fall. "All I could think about all through dinner last night and for most of the day before that was how much I wanted to kiss you. It almost killed me to walk away from your room."

"Then why did you?"

"Because you were drunk."

"I wasn't *that* drunk."

"Well I didn't happen to have a Breathalyzer on me, so I figured better safe than sorry." He paused, taking an unsteady breath. "I didn't want our first kiss to be something you regretted in the sober light of morning."

"I'm not drunk now," I said, still not quite able to trust he meant what it sounded like he meant. "Do you still want to kiss me?"

He licked his lips as his gaze dropped to my mouth. That, along with the hungry desperation on his face, gave me a pretty good idea what his answer was before he managed to say it. "More than ever."

I fought to hold myself still as every cell in my body strained toward him. "You'd better do it, then, before something else happens to mess it up."

A loud breath gusted out of him, and he released my hands to take hold of my face.

When his lips pressed against mine, I discovered they were even softer and lusher than they'd looked. My insides dissolved into goo as Bran's mouth moved over mine in a worshipful caress.

I moaned and melted against him, weak with relief. He banded a strong forearm around the small of my back, holding me up and flattening our bodies together. Meanwhile, his other hand slid into my hair, angling my head the way he wanted it as his lips plied mine open with a husky growl.

My God, that growl. Heat sizzled through me as he licked deep into my mouth like a man finally getting exactly what he wanted.

And what he wanted was me.

I'd never in my life tasted anything as sweet as his eager need. His mouth devoured me like he couldn't get enough, his tongue sliding over mine with an urgency that left me breathless and limp. I clutched at his shirt, grateful for the arm around me, which was the only thing keeping me from sliding to the ground.

Bran drew back just enough to allow us both to pull gasping breaths into our lungs. His forehead rested against mine as we stood locked together, our chests heaving in tandem.

"Wow," I whispered, at a loss to come up with a coherent thought. *"Wow."*

"Was that okay?" He actually sounded serious. Like he expected me to deliver a detailed, well-reasoned critique of his method and approach.

"Did you not just hear me say 'wow'?" I said, lightly pinching his chest. "I said it twice! That means it was a lot better than just okay."

When he laughed, I decided to fulfil my fantasy of plunging my fingers into his thick hair to play with the silky strands. *So soft!* Oh, man. How was I supposed to stop myself from touching his hair all the time now that I knew how wonderful it felt?

"How was it for you?" I asked, a little afraid he'd actually offer constructive criticism.

Nuzzling his nose against mine, he dragged his thumb slowly over my cheek. "Even better than I imagined."

I let out a breath and closed my eyes. After all the uncertainty between us, it felt good to quietly soak in this new closeness. Bran's firm body pressed against mine in so many places it made me flush to catalogue them all. And his scent, so manly and clean with a subtle hint of spice, gave me a dizzying buzz.

"Chloe," he whispered as the pad of his thumb rubbed back and forth across my cheek, sending goose bumps skittering down my arms.

"Mmm?" I replied, skimming my fingertips over his stubble. So rough and prickly. *Yummy.*

His lips brushed gently over mine. "Can you sense what I'm feeling right now?"

"I think so." I pushed up on my toes, seeking more of his lips.

He gave me the kiss I wanted, stroking his tongue into my mouth as he yanked me against him. "How about now?" he murmured, lifting me up to grind our hips together.

"Definitely," I croaked around a stifled moan. "Yep. That's pretty clear, I think."

Our mouths melded again, and I took his breath into my lungs. This time our kiss was slow and savoring. His hips rocked against mine, the torturous friction driving us both into a fevered state until we were moaning with every taunting thrust.

God, we fit together so perfectly. I could only imagine how well we'd fit without so many clothes on and in a much less public place. I wanted to do more than imagine it. I wanted to *know*.

"This way?" a woman's voice said on the other side of our little shelter of vegetation.

Bran broke off the kiss and sucked in a ragged breath. I stared at his mouth in a daze, waiting for my brain's ignition to catch.

"Are you sure?" the voice said, and this time I was able to identify its owner. It was Angie, Dawn's best friend and matron of honor at the wedding that was happening later today.

Shit.

"This is the way Tess said she saw them go," said a second voice. And that one belonged to Bran's mother.

Double shit.

CHAPTER TWENTY

CHLOE

Bran and I jumped apart, staring at each other in wild-eyed alarm.

"I'll just text her," Angie said.

I fumbled my phone out of my pocket and double-checked that the ringer was silenced. It vibrated in my hand, and I thrust it into my armpit to muffle the sound.

Bran's eyes glittered as he rolled his lips together to suppress a smile.

"Let's just take a quick peek around here," Dawn said, sounding closer.

I stared at Bran's mussed hair and damp, kiss-swollen lips, knowing I must be in an equally incriminating state. Then my gaze dropped lower, and I realized his current state was much more incriminating than mine.

At the sound of approaching footsteps, I surged forward and made a quick swipe at smoothing his hair before spinning around and putting myself between Bran and anyone coming down the path.

Just in time.

Dawn and Angie came into view, ducking under a low-hanging swag of vines. They stopped short when they saw us standing there.

"Oh, here you both are," Dawn said, breaking into a smile.

Angie stepped out from behind her, smirking as she rested her hands on her hips. "Here they are, all right. Whatcha been up to back here, huh?"

I felt myself redden all the way down to my shoes. It had to be obvious exactly what we'd been doing. This was not how I wanted Bran's mother—*my boss*—to find out about us. I didn't even know if there was an "us" yet. We'd barely finished our first kiss. There hadn't even been time for it to sink in.

Bran cleared his throat behind me. "Were you looking for us, Mom?"

"For Chloe, actually." Dawn was smiling from ear to ear as her gaze darted back and forth between us. She practically vibrated with unasked questions—questions Bran and I hadn't even had time to ask each other. But instead of interrogating us, she visibly clamped down on her curiosity and said, "Angie has some news."

"Oh?" I said, trying to sound nonchalant. This was fine. Everything was fine. Nothing out of the ordinary happening here.

Dawn looked expectantly at Angie, who was so busy enjoying our obvious discomfort she didn't appear to have heard. Dawn elbowed her. "Angie?"

"Oh right," Angie said, shaking herself out of it. "I got an email this morning from a friend of mine who owns a gallery in River North. He's putting together a mixed-media exhibition that opens next month, and one of his artists just had to drop out. He's scrambling to find a replacement and wanted to know if I knew anyone who'd be able to step in on short notice." Angie lifted her eyebrows at me expectantly.

Everyone was looking at me, but I couldn't move. I didn't even seem to be breathing.

An art show. My work hanging in a real gallery. On display to the public. Part of an exhibition. Covered by the local art press. This could give me the kind of visibility and legitimacy I'd been afraid to even let myself dream about.

"Isn't it exciting?" Dawn burst out. "Your first show! Only just the first of many, I'm sure."

"Roland will obviously want to see your work before he offers you the slot," Angie said. "But it'll be a no-brainer. He's going to go nuts for you as soon as he gets a look at your stuff."

I shook my head as reality came crashing down, all but extinguishing my initial surge of excitement. "I don't have that much to show him."

For over a year I'd been saying I needed to expand my portfolio, but I hadn't actually gotten around to it. I kept finding reasons to put it off. Making excuses not to prioritize my art. And now a once-in-a-lifetime opportunity had dropped into my lap, and I wasn't prepared.

"Don't worry about that," Angie said. "He only needs a sampling to give him a taste of what you can do. If you just show him the wedding present you made for Dawn, he'll be tripping over himself to get you into the show."

Panic snaked through my insides. "I'm not ready. I don't have enough finished work for a show."

"It's a group show, so you won't need that much," Angie said. "Anyway, you've got a month to get ready."

Bran's hands settled on my shoulders and he shifted closer, bringing his solid warmth against my back. "You can do this. I know you can."

I wanted to have as much confidence in myself as he inexplicably had in me. But I knew better than he did how much it would take to get ready for a show. I knew what the expectations would be, and I knew my own limitations.

Angie glanced at her phone and nudged Dawn. "We've got a manicure appointment to get to. Come on," she said, beckoning to me. "Come with us and get your nails done, and we can talk about it some more."

"That's a great idea," Dawn said. "Come get wedding nails with us."

"Oh. Well, um…" I would have preferred to stay with Bran, but it was Dawn's wedding day. If she wanted me to get a manicure with her, I couldn't very well say no.

"Go on," Bran said, giving me a gentle push. "Go have fun."

As Dawn and Angie led me away, I cast a longing look over my shoulder. "I guess I'll see you later, then?"

His heart-stopping smile made me feel a thousand times better. "Definitely."

I wasn't a big manicure girl. Art could be murder on the nails, as could working retail. Why waste time and money getting my nails painted for it to chip off by the end of the day? But I had to admit my freshly painted nails made me feel like one of those sophisticated, confident women who had all their shit together.

If I'd been picking a color to suit my own tastes, I probably would have chosen something darker or more eye-catching. Instead, I'd gone with the same lilac as Dawn and Angie to coordinate with the wedding colors. But it was still awfully pretty.

"So how about it?" Angie asked from her pedicure chair. She and Dawn were getting the full works—pedicures with a hot stone massage and paraffin treatment—while I'd stuck to my simple manicure on account of my legs. "Can I call Roland and set up a meeting?"

She'd been doing her level best to hype me up about this gallery show, but I remained conflicted. Most of the finished pieces I had were from college and not especially representative of my current interests or skills, but Angie seemed to think a month was plenty of time to whip up a couple of small new projects. Between that and my existing portfolio, she was convinced I could pull something worthwhile together.

I wasn't so sure about that.

In the same way I didn't want to show my immature older works, I didn't want to show something I'd thrown together in a rush at the last minute. What was the point of showing my art at all if I wasn't putting my best foot forward?

The idea of showing the work I was proudest of for people to judge was scary enough, but showing sloppy, second-rate work would only increase the chances of it being dismissed and derided. As well as being my own personal nightmare, a poorly received show could kill my chances of ever getting another one. Wasn't it better to wait for the next opportunity to come along than rush into this one before I was ready and invite public mockery?

On the other hand, there might not be another opportunity. What if this was my only shot, and I turned it down? Wouldn't I regret that for the rest of my life?

I chewed on my lip as I studied my shiny nails. They might give me a little more confidence, but not nearly enough for this. "Can I think about it?"

"For how long?" Angie asked. "If we don't jump on this quick, Roland might find someone else to take the slot while you're making up your mind."

I felt my phone vibrate and slipped it out of my pocket. It was a text from Bran.

You OK?

Just knowing he was thinking about me helped calm my nerves.

"What about this?" Dawn said. "What if Angie gets back to Roland and tells him she's out of town at a wedding but has the perfect person in mind and can she get back to him on Monday? That gives you two days to think it over, and hopefully Roland won't give your spot away in the meantime."

"That sounds great," I said as I typed a reply to Bran.

Everything's good.

"Okay," Angie said. "I'll text Roland as soon as I can take my fingernails out of these dryers."

Dawn leaned around her aesthetician to make eye contact with me. "I know you think you're not ready, but the thing about taking risks is that you're never going to feel ready. At some point you have to trust in yourself enough to take the big, scary leaps."

"She's right," Angie said. "And I *know* you're ready. You just need to test yourself to find out how strong you really are."

"Maybe," I mumbled. Or maybe I'd crash and burn and be so scarred by the experience I'd lose what little confidence I had. Frankly, that outcome seemed the most likely.

"We'll get off your back now," Dawn said. "No more pressure."

My phone vibrated with another text from Bran.

I still like you. (Just in case you were having any doubts.)

"What's got you smiling like that?" Angie asked. "Or should I say who?"

"Nothing," I said, trying to hide my face as I typed a reply to Bran.

I still like you too.

"Look at that girl over there mooning over her phone as if we can't guess who she's texting with." Angie looked at Dawn. "Aren't you ever going to ask what's going on with her and Brandon?"

"I certainly am not," Dawn said. "It's none of my business."

"Fine. I'll ask. What's going on between you and Brandon, huh?"

I kept my lips firmly pressed together, refusing to respond. Fortunately, a new text from Bran gave me an excuse to look back down at my phone.

I want to kiss you again.

"She doesn't have to answer that," Dawn said. "You don't have to answer that, Chloe."

Another text followed quickly after the last.

So much.

"No way," Angie protested. "Chloe always fills us in on all her romantic exploits so we can live vicariously through her. It's not fair to start keeping us in the dark now."

My heart spun in my chest, making my hands shake as I typed a reply.

Where are you? I can ditch your mom and make that happen…

"It was different when it wasn't my son. I'm sure you can imagine why Chloe might not want to fill Brandon's mother in on any exploits she may or may not have had with him."

"Well fine, then." Angie huffed. "I'll just wait until you're not around and drag the story out of her myself."

"Don't you dare." Dawn shot a warning look at Angie. "I'm sure they'll tell us whatever they want us to know whenever they're ready for us to know it." She turned her head to arch an eyebrow at me. "Right, Chloe?"

"Uh-huh," I mumbled, getting up from the drying station. "You know, I think my nails are dry enough now, so I'm just gonna—"

Dawn jabbed a finger at me to cut me off. "Sit your little heinie back down. The three of us are getting facials next. And after that we're doing the champagne lunch in the garden. I'm the bride. You can't say no to me today."

My phone vibrated with Bran's reply.

I wish. I have to do a bunch of pre-wedding stuff with Mike today.

Oh well. At least we'd see each other tonight at the wedding.

I ended up spending most of the day with Dawn and Angie. After lunch in the spa garden, Mike's sister Kelly showed up with the mother of the groom to join in on the pre-wedding pampering, and we all had our hair and makeup done. It was actually pretty great. For one afternoon, at least, I could pretend to be part of the kind of family I'd always wanted to have.

By the time we'd all been coiffed and made-up, it was time to get dressed for the wedding. I thanked Dawn for including me in her special day and hugged her tightly as I wished her the best, getting teary over the fact that the next time I saw her she'd be walking down the aisle. The champagne had been flowing freely all day at the spa, and I blamed the two glasses I'd indulged in for making me so emotional.

Angie whisked Dawn off to the bridal suite to get ready, and I went back to my own room to change. Tonight I was wearing a new outfit I'd bought for the occasion, a silky turquoise jumpsuit with swishy wide legs and a convertible top, which I styled into a deep-V neckline that twisted down my back and tied around my waist with a side bow. I usually tried to wear ankle boots for dressy occasions, but since it was an outdoor summer wedding I opted to brave flats instead, hoping the billowy pants legs would mostly hide the fresh Band-Aids I'd applied to protect my vulnerable ankles.

Looking at myself in the mirror, I felt prettier than usual. My hair had been styled into a high bun with a loose side-crown braid, showing off my undercut and ear piercings. The shimmery rose-gold shades the makeup artist had applied to my eyes, lips, and cheeks were softer and prettier than the dark, smoky eyes I usually favored. The whole effect was more fairy princess than I was used to, but still had a hint of edge to it that felt like me.

The ceremony was taking place on a lawn overlooking the lake below, just past the rustic barn-style building where the reception would be held. I got there early hoping to see Bran, who was serving as an usher. As I followed the stone path around the side of the barn, I got my first breathtaking glimpse of the spectacular view that would provide the backdrop for the ceremony.

I lost my breath again when I spotted Bran in a gray wedding suit and lilac tie, looking impossibly handsome as he escorted a wedding guest down the aisle. Seeing him felt like that eye-popping moment at the top of a roller coaster when the world seems to drop away as you teeter on the precipice of a thrilling downward swoop.

The regular texts he'd been sending all day reassured me we were headed for *something*. But what, exactly, still remained to be seen. The possibilities filled me with giddy anticipation. Our interrupted hot-as-hell make-out session had also left me restless and horny as heck. If the occasion had been anything less significant than his mother's wedding, I definitely would have tried to drag him off behind the barn to deliver that kiss he'd wished for earlier.

As it was, the best I could hope for was some brief conversation and an opportunity to cling to his arm while he escorted me to my seat. Tragically, I was denied even that much when his brother swooped in while Bran was having his ear talked off by another guest. *Curses!*

Zach greeted me warmly and presented his arm with a flourish. I accepted it reluctantly and with a lukewarm smile.

As he walked me past the rows of folding chairs, he leaned in to speak in a low voice. "I've been told I need to offer you an apology for butting in last night." He paused, turning to search my face. "Are you mad at me?"

"That depends on why you did it. Were you trying to embarrass Bran?"

Zach's lips pursed. "I can't pretend I didn't know it would embarrass him, and I may have enjoyed the thought a little, but that's not the reason I did it."

"Then why?"

He glanced over his shoulder to check that Bran was still occupied elsewhere. "You're the first girl he's actually seemed interested in since his ex knocked him sideways. I figured he might need a little help to do something about it."

"In that case, I'm not mad—as long as you never do it again."

His eyes crinkled with a smile that looked just like his mother's. "I really am sorry if my scheming caused you any discomfort. I hoped you might appreciate the results."

"Go help Cousin Vivian find a seat," Bran said, appearing behind Zach. The bottom dropped right out of my stomach as his gaze zeroed in on mine.

"Hi," I whispered, feeling my lips curve in a smile.

"Ugh, look at you two." Zach made a face as he transferred my hand to Bran's arm. "You're giving me a cavity."

Neither of us paid him the slightest attention as he absented himself.

"Hi." Bran swallowed thickly as his gaze dipped to the exposed skin between my breasts. "You look incredible."

"So do you," I said, letting my own eyes take an appreciative wander down his body. "Nice suit."

"I'm glad you like it, but these pants are going to become disconcertingly revelatory if you don't stop looking at me like that."

"Sorry, no can do. You're too hot for my eyes to handle."

Shaking his head, he ushered me down the aisle. "I saved you a good seat."

I leaned in to speak in his ear, letting my nose graze his neck while I took the opportunity to inhale a lungful of his amazing scent. "I hope it's in your lap."

"Behave," he ground out through a tightly clenched jaw.

We reached the end of the second row, and he gestured for me to sit. This was it already. The end of our too-brief interaction. "I'll see you after the ceremony?" I asked.

He nodded. "I have to do a bunch of wedding stuff, but I'll come find you at the reception after I'm done."

"Okay." I bit my lip as I squeezed his arm, reluctant to let go.

"You're killing me," he murmured, brushing a kiss to my cheek before returning to his usher duties.

I moved down to take one of the seats in the middle of the empty row. Before long I was joined by Sandra and Alex on one side and Stan from breakfast on the other.

I'd thought it slightly odd that Bran had seated me on the groom's side, but as soon as the male members of the wedding party took their places for the ceremony, it became clear why. Bran smiled at me as he stood just a few feet in front of me waiting for the bride to come out. Not only would I have a great view of the wedding from here, I'd have a great view of him as well.

Next to me, Sandra slipped in earbuds and started a video call with her friend Elizabeth, who hadn't been able to make it to the wedding. When the processional started, Sandra aimed the phone so Elizabeth could watch from home.

Dawn looked beautiful walking down the aisle in an ankle-length lace sheath gown with delicate flutter sleeves. Just the look on Mike's face as he watched her walk toward him had my vision blurring with tears before a word of the ceremony had even been spoken.

"Here," Stan whispered, passing me a tissue. He shrugged when I murmured my thanks. "I never come to a wedding without them. Someone around me always seems to need them."

"Give me one of those," Sandra hissed, and Stan handed another one down for her.

My gaze repeatedly drifted to Bran during the ceremony, pulled there by the gravitational force he seemed to exert on me. It made me smile to remember it had been that way from the first moment I saw him. Even before I'd known him, I hadn't been able to tear my eyes away from him.

He stood watching his mother's wedding with a solemn expression on his face. I wondered what he was thinking. We hadn't talked much about it, but I thought I'd detected some ambivalence hiding behind his efforts to appear supportive.

The tears started up again as Dawn and Mike recited the vows they'd written. Stan passed out more tissues, then eventually handed the whole pack over with a mumbled, "Just keep it."

Trying not to mess up my makeup, I dabbed at the corners of my eyes when the officiant declared Mike and Dawn husband and wife. Boisterous applause broke out at their first kiss as a married couple. As I rose to cheer them on, my eyes strayed to Bran, and I was surprised to find him looking at me. The raw, searching expression on his face made me ache to charge up the aisle and give him a hug. I restrained myself, however, staying where I was as the wedding party followed the bride and groom back up the aisle. Bran sent me a half smile as he passed, and I lifted my hand in a wave.

The "barn" hosting the reception turned out to have a charming rustic elegance, but the polished wood floors made it clear no animals had been anywhere near it for a long while—or possibly ever. Chandeliers and strings of cafe lights hung from the rafters, and fairy lights wrapped the rough-hewn pillars. Half the space was taken up by long wooden tables set for the sit-down dinner, decorated with the paper flower centerpieces Bran and I had helped make at Dawn's house weeks ago. The other half of the space was open, providing a place for mingling and presumably dancing later.

After acquiring a glass of wine, I circulated through the milling crowd of guests, growing increasingly impatient as the minutes ticked by with no sign of the wedding party. Pretty soon I'd developed a crick in my neck from craning it so often to search for Bran.

Eventually, we were encouraged to find seats at the tables, and I ended up sitting next to Marie and Matt, across from Tess and Donal. When the bride and groom finally made their appearance, they took their seats, along with the rest of the wedding party, at a perpendicular table way up at the head of the room. I could barely see Bran from where I sat, but if I leaned way back, I could just catch a glimpse of his dark hair.

I'd always loved weddings, but as I sat through seemingly endless speeches and toasts, followed by an interminable multicourse meal, I repeatedly cursed the ponderous pace of wedding traditions. It was far from the slowest reception in history, but it began to feel that way the longer it conspired to keep Bran and me apart.

Rationally, I knew my restless need to be near Bran again was an unreasonable reaction to the relatively short time we'd been separated. I wasn't usually this clingy, and I blamed it on the fact that we'd been interrupted just when things were starting to get good.

Really, *really* good.

I hadn't had time to get used to this new reality between us before we'd been prematurely separated. All these new feelings Bran had stirred in me this morning remained stirred up. Unsettled. Agitated. Unresolved. It was like having the internet go out right as you were getting to the exciting part of a movie you'd never seen before.

We had business to finish, dammit. More talking and more kissing and hopefully all the stuff that came after the kissing. Boy, was I hella eager to get to the part that came after kissing.

I wasn't normally this much of a hostage to my sex drive. Most of the time I could easily weather months-long dry spells without even missing sex with another human being all that much. But right now I was itching for it something awful. I couldn't stop trying to imagine what sex would be like with Bran. The nonstop fantasies made it difficult to concentrate or sit still. I was way too conscious of the rubbing of my nipples against my top as anticipatory shivers danced down the back of my neck. Not to even mention the swelter happening between my thighs.

How long could a person exist in a state like this before they spontaneously combusted?

Asking for a friend. Who is me. Hi. I'm the friend. It's me.

As the servers descended to sweep away the entrée plates, I craned my neck toward the head table. Some members of the wedding party were already on their feet and milling around. I leaned back, trying to spot Bran, but he didn't seem to be in his seat anymore. I didn't see him standing around either.

"Hey," said a deep voice close enough to tickle my ear.

I startled as my brain's emergency alert system issued a proximity warning, and I swung my head around to find myself staring into Bran's eyes.

"Sorry." He laid a mollifying hand on my arm as he crouched beside my chair. "I didn't mean to sneak up on you."

"I was just looking for you," I said, smiling like an utter goober. *Rein it in, freakazoid! Don't make it weird!* I attempted to turn down the wattage, but it was hopeless. I was a beaming fool.

"I thought dinner would never end." Bran's fingertips stroked slowly down my arm in a way that might have been soothing if it hadn't been so freaking arousing.

"Me too." It came out as a rasp thanks to my suddenly dry mouth.

His gaze dipped to my lips, and I instinctively leaned closer, thirsting for a kiss.

I startled again when the sound system let out a fuzzy, earsplitting thump. He stood and turned as the DJ beckoned everyone to come watch the bride and groom's first dance, sparking a clamor of chairs pushing back from the tables.

"Come on." Bran took my hand and pulled me to my feet.

Threading my fingers through his, I let him pull me along with the migration toward the dance floor, absurdly happy just to be standing near him and holding his hand. When we reached the end of the table, he veered off from the crowd, releasing my hand (boo!) to slide his arm around my waist (yay!). His hand held on to my hip, his thumb rubbing back and forth over the bare skin of my lower back as he led me toward the head table and through a doorway behind it. A little way down the hall beyond, he opened a door, guided me into some kind of sitting room, and closed the door behind us.

"What is this place?" I asked, peering around curiously.

Instead of answering, Bran pressed me up against the door and gave me the kiss I'd been dying for all day.

CHAPTER TWENTY-ONE

BRAN

After an entire day of wedding-related activities and forced socializing that had left me raw and exhausted, kissing Chloe was like sinking into a hot, rejuvenating bath. The taste of her, the feel of her body against mine, the little moan she breathed into my mouth—it all worked some kind of magic that simultaneously soothed and invigorated my frayed nerves.

I cupped her jaw with one hand, angling it to taste her deeper while my other hand slid over her waist so my fingertips could explore the soft, alluring skin exposed there. Ever since I'd first caught sight of her in this outfit, it was all I could think about. All that bare skin on display—down her back, up her sides, between her breasts—had been torturing me for hours.

I was nearly out of my mind with urgency as I pushed her up against the door. I didn't remember ever needing to be close to a woman this much. Was I pressing too much of my weight against her? Worried I'd been too rough, I eased back a little, though I couldn't bring myself to stop kissing her. Not yet.

Chloe's hand snaked around to grip my ass, tugging me against her again as her fingernails raked over the back of my neck. So maybe I hadn't been too rough after all. Experimentally, I leaned into her even more, pinning her with my body weight. Her needy whimpers let me know how much she liked it, and I dragged my thumb down her throat so I could feel the vibrations of them as I ground my hips against hers.

If we kept up like this much longer, she'd end up underneath me on the couch. Was that what she wanted? I didn't have a fucking clue what was expected in a situation like this. But the way her hips rocked to meet mine made me think she wouldn't mind.

Were we really going there this fast?

No, we damn well weren't. Not here. Not like this. I didn't want our first time to be a stolen quickie someplace where anyone could walk in on us.

The thought chilled me enough to break the kiss. We'd already suffered one embarrassing interruption today. That was more than enough.

We both strained for breath as I rested my forehead against hers. "You have no idea how much I needed that."

"I think I have some idea." Chloe's eyes met mine with a hazy smile. "I needed it too."

I traced her kiss-swollen lower lip with the pad of my thumb, trying to talk myself out of kissing her again.

"You're missing the first dance."

I nodded, only distantly aware of the music that had started up. "I really don't care."

She took my face in her hands, stroking her fingers over my jaw as she studied me with soft, concerned eyes. "How are you holding up with all the wedding stuff today?"

"Fine," I murmured, giving in to temptation and pressing my mouth to the side of her neck.

"Bran." She squirmed with a shiver as I sucked at the tender skin. "Now why don't you try telling me how you're really doing?"

I dropped my head to her shoulder with a sigh, letting it rest there heavily. "Exhausted."

Her fingers sank into my hair, pulling a groan out of me as they lightly scratched my scalp. "Is it hard watching your mom get remarried?"

"Not so much hard as weird. I'm not sure how I'm supposed to feel about it."

"How *do* you feel about it?"

My hands settled on Chloe's hips as I considered the question, trying to parse the emotions I'd been carrying inside me all day. "Better than I did a few days ago." It was the closest I'd ever come to admitting my misgivings out loud. "Today was the first chance I've had to spend any real time with Mike. I think I might have underestimated him. I'm coming around to the idea that even though he's not who I pictured my mom with, he's who makes her happy."

Chloe turned her head to kiss my temple, and I banded my arms around her, pulling her into a hug. It had never occurred to me before how well human bodies fit together. Aside from the obvious reproductive body parts, that is. Hips made perfect handholds, waists were ideal for wrapping arms around, and heads nestled into that curve between the neck and shoulder like it had been designed as a landing area.

It was as if our bodies were made for hugging. Maybe that was why it felt so good—like plugging into a charging station. As I held on to Chloe, I could feel restorative energy flowing from her body into mine, breathing new life into tired limbs, lifting flagging spirits, and lightening the weight of burdens.

"How did your day go?" I asked, pulling back to look at her.

"Good."

"Really?" I searched her face for the truth.

She nodded. "I had a great time with your mom today. It was really nice."

"Did she ask you about us?" My mom wasn't typically the kind to pry too much into my romantic life, but I worried she might feel freer to pester Chloe, given their prior friendship.

"No, but Angie did. Or tried to. Your mom told her to cut it out."

"I hope it didn't make you too uncomfortable."

Chloe's lips curved. "It could have been a lot worse, given where things were headed when she found us."

A shudder traveled through me at the thought, and she laughed as she stretched up to kiss me. Her laughter resonated against my lips and straight into my chest, pulling a smile out of me. I grasped the back of her neck as my mouth slanted over hers hungrily.

When she sagged against me with a moan, I knew we needed to get out of this room soon or we'd never leave.

With a muttered curse, I dragged my lips away from hers, squeezing her nape. "We should probably get back out there before we're missed."

She nodded, and we took a moment to make ourselves presentable again before I led her back into the reception hall where the cake cutting was happening. We blended in with the crowd to watch my mom and Mike smear cake on each other's faces.

Chloe knew more people at the wedding than I did, and she mingled with ease, finding something to talk about with everyone she encountered. Despite having long since depleted my social battery, it wasn't difficult to stand at her side and watch her hold court. I marveled at how well she seemed to fit in while I felt like an awkward interloper. Though I felt somewhat less so with her at my side, introducing me to everyone and skillfully drawing me out of my shell.

After we'd been circulating like that for almost an hour, I noticed her attention wandering wistfully to the dance floor and realized I'd been negligent.

"Would you like to dance?" I asked, and her eyes lit up as she answered with an enthusiastic nod.

I took her hand and led her to an empty spot among the people slow dancing to "Time After Time." Deon and his husband were clenched together on one side of us, and Donal was dancing with his girlfriend on the other. He gave me a wink as I slid my arms around Chloe's waist.

"I haven't done this since high school," she said as we found a rhythm swaying along with the music.

"Me neither." I mostly remembered feeling gawky and clumsy back then. But dancing with Chloe didn't make me feel like that at all. Whatever magic she had in her made it seem easy and comfortable, like everything else we did together.

"That would have been with Marisa, I'm assuming."

"That would be a correct assumption. What about you?" My fingertips stroked the exposed skin at the small of her back. "Who did you slow dance with in high school?"

"Austin Moran." Her nose wrinkled. "He ditched me halfway through our senior prom to get stoned in the parking lot with his drama club buddies and ended up making out with the guy who'd played Puck in *A Midsummer Night's Dream*."

"Ouch."

"Yeah, not exactly a night to remember. But we'd only gone to prom together as friends, so it wasn't like I was brokenhearted or anything."

"Did you date much in high school?"

"Not exactly. There was never anyone serious. The guys I really liked never liked me back." She let out a small, tight laugh. "Story of my life."

I frowned. "What do you mean?"

Her eyes lowered. "The people I wish would care about me usually don't." Another brittle laugh escaped her. "Sorry. I didn't mean to get so cringey on you. Forget I said that."

My arms tightened around her, holding her close. "Is that why you had such a hard time believing I liked you? Or was I just that bad at showing it?"

"Maybe," she said, nestling into my neck.

"Maybe which?"

"Maybe some of both." This time her laugh sounded more natural.

"Are you saying you've never had a serious boyfriend?" I asked, finding it hard to believe no one had ever tried to hold on to her.

"Pretty much, yeah." Chloe lifted her head to peer at my face. "Why do you sound so surprised?"

"Because I am. Someone as amazing as you should be able to have your pick of any man you want."

"Do you think you could go back in time and tell that to every guy I've ever had an unrequited crush on?"

"So one of them could end up here dancing with you instead of me? Absolutely not. If they can't appreciate you on their own, they don't deserve you."

The song ended, but we stayed put when another slow one followed. It was the song from the end of *Pretty in Pink*, one of my mom's favorite movies, and I saw Mike tug her to the dance floor and wind his arms around her.

"They look happy," Chloe said, following my gaze.

"Yes, they do." I didn't feel any discomfort anymore as I watched them. I could simply feel glad for Mom that she'd found someone to love her.

The reception went on for another hour before the DJ encouraged all the single women to gather for the throwing of the bouquet. There turned out not to be that many single women there, and my mom managed to wing her bouquet directly into Chloe's hands.

Shortly after that, the newlyweds took their leave, and we showered them with birdseed as they headed off to the honeymoon suite. When Chloe and I went to see if Deon and Angie needed help with the final wedding duties, they gave us identical knowing smirks and said we were free to go.

As I led Chloe out of the reception hall, it sank in that the rest of the night was finally ours. To do whatever we wanted. My initial surge of relief wilted under a ripple of uncertainty. Once again, I was reminded how out of my depth I was. I had next to no experience dating as an adult. Was dating even what we were doing? Or were we just "hanging out," which I'd gathered was more casual than dating? Would Chloe want to have sex tonight? If we did, would that imply this was only a hookup? *Was* it only a hookup or was she looking for something more? How the fuck did people negotiate all these murky decisions?

Chloe's shoulder bumped against mine. "I lost you, didn't I?"

"What?" I stopped, turning to look at her.

"Your brain is totally spinning out into space right now, isn't it?"

I nodded as I scrubbed a hand over my jaw. "Sorry. It does that sometimes. More so when I'm tired."

"Right." Her head dipped as she shifted the bridal bouquet from one hand to the other.

Seeing her deflate, I realized it had probably sounded like I wanted to end the night here. *Shit.* Not what I wanted. Not at all.

I reached for her free hand, threading my fingers through hers. "I was actually just wondering if I should invite you back to my room or hope you'd invite me back to yours."

Her smile was slow and magnificent. "Bran, would you like to come back to my room?"

"More than anything."

CHAPTER TWENTY-TWO

CHLOE

As soon as I opened the door to my room, I had major regrets.

Why on earth had I invited Bran to chaos central? I could have suggested he take me to his room instead, which was undoubtedly far tidier. Meanwhile, mine looked like my suitcase had exploded, hurling clothing shrapnel in every direction. There was so much stuff scattered across the bed, housekeeping hadn't been able to make it up.

If I'd bothered to think ahead even a little, I could have predicted I might end up bringing Bran back here and made some effort to clean up first. Woe unto me, I did not think ahead.

I stopped on the threshold and spun around. "On second thought, maybe we should go to your room instead."

Bran's hands caught me by the waist, blocking my attempt to dodge around him. "I already know you're messy. I've seen your room at home, remember?"

Letting out a groan, I dropped my head against his chest. "I'm sorry I'm not as much of a fussbudget as you."

He walked me backward into the room, kicking the door closed behind him. "I don't care that you're messy. I think it's cute."

I looked up and swallowed when his intense green eyes collided with mine. *Have mercy.* The man was just stupidly handsome, and he was here, in my room, looking at me like I was dessert. I was *so* ready. Unbelievably ready.

This. Was. Happening.

In one fluid motion, I swept my arms across the bed and sent everything on it tumbling to the floor. "There," I said, turning back to Bran. "We're good now."

He wasn't looking at me like I was dessert anymore. In fact, he looked kind of frozen.

Oh, shit. Maybe this wasn't happening. Had I jumped the gun big-time?

"Uhhh," I said, floundering, "were we not— Did you not want to—"

Bran cupped my face and kissed me. It wasn't at all like the hungry kiss he'd given me before. This one was so careful and tender it almost felt reverent. I'd never been kissed like that before. It wasn't the sort of kiss you got from a casual fling or friends-with-benefits situation, and none of my brief, unsatisfying attempts at more serious relationships had included any kisses like that. I didn't know what to make of it. Was Bran trying to let me down easy or—

"I didn't expect this," he murmured, still cradling my face.

I blinked up at him. As per usual, when those green eyes stared into mine, my brain ceased functioning. "Expect what?"

"You." He pressed a kiss to the corner of my jaw. "I didn't think we'd end up here." His husky voice whispered over my skin as his lips skimmed down my throat. "I didn't expect you to want me." He paused, those two adorable lines appearing between his brows as he lifted his head. "That's assuming you do."

"I do. I really do."

Relief washed over his face, but not enough to chase away all the hesitation in it. "I want to take you to bed more than anything."

An unspoken *but* hovered at the end of that sentence. I searched his face, trying to understand what was holding him back. If it wasn't desire, then what? And then it clicked.

"You haven't slept with anyone since your ex, have you?"

"She was the last," he confirmed, watching my reaction. "And also the first."

Now it made sense. He was probably nervous. Or possibly not ready yet. Maybe for him, sex was only for meaningful, committed relationships.

"We don't have to do anything," I said. "We can do as much or as little as you want, okay?"

Bran's head jerked from side to side as his hands flexed on my waist. "I want to do *everything* with you." His heavy gaze burned right through me. "And *to* you."

My lips parted as all the air left my lungs in a whoosh. I was fully down with that plan. One hundred percent. So said the excited flutter in my tummy and the insistent throb between my legs. Sliding my hand around the back of his neck, I pulled his mouth to mine. "Okay. That works also."

His chest hitched as my lips skimmed over his, but when he sought to deepen the kiss, I spun us around and pushed him backward until his calves hit the bed. He blinked at me in surprise as I guided him down onto the edge of the mattress.

I nudged his thighs apart to stand between them, and his gaze zeroed in on my breasts, only a few inches from his face. My nipples turned to points, aching to feel more than just his gaze on them. When I reached for the bow at my hip, he tracked my movement, swallowing as I unwound the fabric wrapped around my waist.

"Here," I said, placing the two loose ends in his hands and turning my back to him. "Can you help me with these?"

He let out a soft exhale I felt between my shoulder blades. "This outfit's been tormenting me all night," he murmured as he unwound the twists at the small of my back. Tingles sparked on my skin everywhere his fingers grazed. "It's like unwrapping a present."

I felt the tension holding the fabric against my breasts release when he finished the last twist, letting the two separated lengths of fabric hang down my back. A husky breath escaped him as he gently stroked the skin between them like he was savoring the feel of me, reveling in the fact that I was his to touch.

Bran's fingers slowly glided up to my shoulders, and my heart thumped as he pushed the fabric off them one at a time, baring me to the waist. I started to turn around, but his hands gripped my hips, keeping me where I was as an impatient sound rumbled in his chest.

Once I stilled, his fingertips skated up my back again and over to my shoulder blade, where a single finger dragged a slow, methodical path across my skin. He was tracing my tattoo, the pad of his finger following the path of the ink. When he'd finished, his fingers skimmed back down my spine and traveled along the curve of my waist.

My breath grew uneven as they dipped inside the back of my jumpsuit, tugging at it gently. I swayed a little as I realized he was testing its give and searching for hidden fasteners. Once he'd established there was nothing but a bit of elastic holding it up, he began to ease it down my hips.

"Chloe," he said hoarsely when he uncovered my thong. "Fuck."

Desperation hurried his movements as he dragged my jumpsuit down my thighs, letting it fall to the floor around my feet. I kicked it and my shoes away, stifling a shiver of self-consciousness when the hotel room air chilled my exposed skin.

Bran grasped my hips again, breathing heavily. "You're gorgeous," he whispered as he smoothed his palms down over my butt cheeks, stroking and squeezing the pliant flesh. "So beautiful."

A shudder racked me when he pressed a prickly, open-mouthed kiss to the center of my back. His palms smoothed up my rib cage, and he groaned as his big hands cupped my small breasts. He squeezed, just this side of rough, and my body jolted at the drag of a callus across one of my hard nipples.

"You like that?" he asked, his voice strained and gravelly.

"Yes," I whispered, arching into his touch.

His thumbs circled the stiff peaks, slow then faster, caressing one moment and pinching the next, alternating gentle touches with rough until I was panting and shaking.

"Do you like it when I touch you?" he asked like it was a serious question. As if there could be any doubt.

My gasping intake of breath was the only answer I could manage to make.

He pulled me down into his lap, settling me on his thighs as he held me against his chest. I was naked except for my thong, and Bran was still fully dressed, still wearing his shoes and jacket even, the wool rubbing my bare skin and his erection pressed against my ass.

"Have you thought about it?" he asked in a growly whisper as he ran his hands over my body. "Have you thought about me touching you?"

I nodded jerkily and squirmed in his lap.

A groan reverberated through his chest when my ass rubbed against his hard cock. "I've dreamed about it." Bran's mouth latched onto my neck as his hands smoothed over my hips, then down my thighs, pushing them apart and quickening my breath. "I've dreamed about holding you just like this."

"Bran." It came out as a needy whimper.

He spread his legs beneath mine, opening me wider while his fingers teased a trail up my inner thighs. "Tell me you want this too."

"Y-yesss." I threw my head back as my hips pitched forward, straining toward his touch, utterly raw and defenseless but unable to think about anything except how badly I needed him.

"Shhh," he murmured against my neck as he traced his index finger over my damp thong and tugged it aside. "I've got you."

Relief rippled through me as his thumb circled my clit. "Oh God," I gasped. "Bran."

His breath heated my neck as his fingers explored me mercilessly. Teasing, testing, and stroking. Lavishing me with different kinds of pressure and friction, learning from my responses what caused the most intense pleasure. And the whole time he murmured the loveliest things, spoiling me with compliments while he spoiled my body, undoing me piece by piece. I writhed against him as he repeatedly drove me toward the edge and eased off just before I got there, doing it again and again until I was mindlessly begging for relief. Only then did he let me have what I needed, his breaths growing ragged as he drove me to that beckoning paradise.

The rush hit me hard, shock waves pulsing through me with a force I'd never felt before, taking me outside my body for a moment. I might actually have died. I definitely saw some kind of light. Possibly a chorus of angels or a set of pearly gates. *Holy shit.*

When I came back down to earth, Bran was cradling me to his chest and nuzzling tiny kisses against my cheek. Everything felt loose, warm, and heavy. I reached up, touched his jaw, and tangled my fingers in his hair as I sought his mouth.

A hum of enjoyment vibrated through him as his tongue slipped through my lips for a languid kiss. I sank into it, falling into him, needing to get closer, greedy for more of him, wanting to hold on and never let go. Knowing exactly how vulnerable that kind of need made me and not giving one damn.

It was unacceptable that he was still fully dressed. How was I supposed to get closer to him with all these clothes between us? I wanted his skin on my skin. Urgency propelled me out of his lap and onto the bed beside him so I could push his jacket off. Our mouths crashed together as I pulled at his tie, loosening it with clumsy fingers. Every stroke of his tongue seared me with a kind of desire I'd never experienced before, something raw and brilliant. If I paused to let myself think about it too much, it'd scare the hell out of me. So I didn't think. I rode the wave and went with it.

Bran's tie pulled loose, and I clawed at his shirt buttons next. This angle wasn't helping me. My fumbling fingers fought with the finicky discs until frustration drove me to climb into his lap, and I straddled his legs, pushing him toward the mattress. He sucked in a sharp breath as he fell back, staring up at me with dazed, lust-dark eyes.

"What sadist invented buttons, anyway?" I muttered as I bared his chest inch by frustrating inch. I'd already unearthed a tantalizing patch of dark hair I couldn't wait to run my fingers through. "Snaps are so much better. One good yank and *bam*, you're in business."

I'd made it halfway down his chest when Bran laid his hands over mine to stop me. "Do you have any condoms?"

My heart screeched to a halt. With a sinking feeling, I mentally reviewed everything I'd packed for the trip. "I don't think so, no."

"Neither do I." Bran groaned like a dying man and laid his forearm over his eyes. "That was what I meant when I said I wasn't expecting this."

CHAPTER TWENTY-THREE

CHLOE

Silly me, I'd assumed Bran's hesitation had something to do with his ex, when he'd simply been focused on the practicalities of prophylaxis. Despite our tragic predicament, I almost laughed.

He dragged his hands through his hair and over his face. "I should have planned ahead, but I didn't think it would happen." A wry, pained laugh tore out of him. "I'm never this lucky."

I leaned down to press my lips against the part of his chest I'd painstakingly exposed. "Me neither."

"I'm so sorry." His fingers stroked the cropped hair at the back of my neck as I laid my cheek against his hairy chest. He let out a despondent sigh. "This sucks."

I rolled off him and crawled across the bed. "Let me check my purse, just in case." Sadly, I'd brought a different one for the weekend trip than the one I usually took on dates, which I knew for a fact had condoms in it. But you never knew…there could be a forgotten one hiding in there. Maybe even one that wasn't expired.

While I dumped the contents of my purse out on the bed, Bran hauled himself upright with a pained grunt. He shifted to the edge of the mattress next to me and double-checked the stuff I'd already picked through while I searched each and every pocket and rummaged through my wallet.

"Nothing," I said, sighing as I shoved everything back into my purse after I'd definitely established it didn't contain a miracle Hail Mary condom.

Nodding in grim acceptance, Bran turned away from the bed and dropped his head into his hands. "Right," he said, blowing out a miserable breath. "Okay, well…"

When he started to rise, I snagged his arm. "Whoa there, buddy. Slow your roll."

He turned to me with an agonized look. "I'm probably going to cry if I can't have you, and I'd rather you didn't see me do it."

I was pretty sure he was kidding. Then again maybe not, since I definitely wanted to cry a bit myself. "You may not be able to have me in one particular way, but that still leaves all kinds of things we can do." I smiled as I trailed my hand down his chest to the bulge straining the front of his pants. "A whole wide world of things, in fact."

"Chloe." He clenched his jaw, covering my hand to still it. "You need to stop unless you want me to come in my pants."

"We can't have that. Obviously those pants need to come off."

"I'm serious," he growled as my fingers explored the outline of what felt like an impressively thick shaft. More data was definitely needed. Immediately.

"Me too," I said in my best no-nonsense tone. Tossing my purse to the floor, I pointed at the dress shoes still on his feet. "Those need to come off. Let's go."

Bran stared at me for a moment before bending over with a wince to pluck at his laces. Once he'd taken his shoes off, I got up and stood in front of him. He allowed me to pull him to his feet and watched me silently as I finished undoing his shirt. Now that I wasn't quite so lust-addled, the buttons weren't nearly as challenging. Go figure. Making quick work of them, I pushed his shirt off his shoulders and paused to admire what I'd uncovered.

"Wooooow," I breathed, awestruck. "Why do you look like this?" I ran my hands through his dark chest hair and over his gloriously firm flesh. "Seriously, how?" Bran's body was unreal for someone who wasn't a professional athlete. This man was out here walking around with an honest-to-God six-pack underneath his starched shirts. *What even?*

"I exercise when I'm stressed," he ground out, his nostrils flaring as my fingers followed the trail of hair leading to his trembling ab muscles. "And I'm stressed a lot."

I could feel the pent-up sexual frustration vibrating through every taut muscle I touched. The poor guy was about to go off like a grenade. I tucked my fingers inside his waistband and tugged him closer. "I happen to know something else that helps with stress."

He shut his eyes, his body shaking as I unbuttoned his pants and carefully slid the zipper down. Set free from its suit-pants prison, his erection was improbably large. How had it even fit inside those tailored pants? He really must have been in agony.

"Chloe," he bit out brokenly when I cupped him through his underwear. He sounded like a dying man.

"Baby," I crooned, tilting my head to kiss his neck as I caressed his swollen cock. "Let me help you with this."

"God, yes." His head bounced with a desperate nod. *"Please."*

"Don't worry," I said as I eased his pants down. "I'm going to take care of you."

Eager impatience drove him to shove his boxer briefs to the floor. He stepped out of his pants and kicked them aside.

Yowza, the man was girthy. My insides clenched, mourning that the lack of a condom prevented me from riding that majestic dick. But I had my work cut out for me right now just getting my mouth around that beast.

I licked my lips as I stared at it, considering my best approach. "Lie down on the bed."

He stretched out on his back in the center of the king-size mattress. As I positioned myself between his thighs, he watched me through pupils blown so wide his eyes looked black. "Just so you know, I'm probably going to go off the second you touch me."

Smiling, I knelt over him and kissed his lips. His arms came around me as he kissed me back hungrily, pulling me against him. His hands stroked my back while I kissed my way down his neck, the stubble already prickly enough to feel like sandpaper against my lips.

He groaned when my breasts dragged across his chest. "You're going to kill me."

I laughed as I moved lower, licking the salty, sweat-dampened skin between his pecs. "No, I'm going to get you off." Veering to one side, I circled his nipple with my tongue before grazing it with my teeth. "When I'm good and ready."

His cock jumped against my belly, and he arched into me, seeking more pressure. "God, Chloe, please. I'm dying."

Taking pity on him, I skimmed my lips over his trembling abs, grasping his hips as I traveled lower. Being eye to eye with his cock didn't make it look any less massive. I wrapped my fingers around it, marveling at the diameter, and my inner walls clenched at the thought of it pushing inside me. Ah well. Hopefully another time. I ran my hand along the hard, silky length, giving it an experimental stroke.

Bran sucked in a breath, clenching fistfuls of the bedspread as he thrust into my hand uncontrollably. "I'm sorry," he rasped. "I know it's— You don't have to—"

He broke off with a strangled sound when I dragged the flat of my tongue along the underside of the shaft. Since I couldn't unhinge my jaw like a snake, there was no taking the whole thing in my mouth, but I'd see what I could do. I licked up and down the shaft a few times, getting it nice and wet, before I fit my lips around the head and sucked while giving him a hard, twisting stroke.

"Oh fuck," Bran gasped, nearly jolting off the bed. "Oh God, that feels so good."

I threw myself into my task with relish, working him with my hand while I swirled my tongue around the tip, teased the sensitive ridge at the base of the head, and sucked down as much of him as I could take until my eyes watered. All the while, Bran moaned a string of desperate-sounding pleas and praise, interspersed with unintelligible, guttural noises as his fingers pushed through my hair, stroking my head to offer comfort and encouragement rather than trying to take control.

Despite his threat to blow at the first touch, he was hanging in there like a trouper. I'd been with enough men and given enough head to feel fairly confident in my skills. It wasn't historically my favorite part of sex, so I'd gotten good enough at it to get the job done quickly. This time, oddly, I didn't feel any urge to get it over with in a hurry.

Doing this with Bran wasn't a chore. For the first time, I understood what other women meant when they said it was a pleasure. The taste of him on my tongue, the feel of him, the satisfied sounds he made—every sensation had me unbelievably turned on. Each rock of his hips beneath me, matching the rhythm of my strokes, sent heat spiraling through my body in a way I wanted more of rather than less.

Happy as I was to keep this up forever, I could sense his growing frustration. It was like he'd been holding everything inside for so long, his body didn't want to let go. I planned to get him there, and I didn't care how long it took. But I could feel my upper arms and neck getting tired from holding myself above him. If I was going to take my time, I needed to get more comfortable. Pausing, I lifted my head, taking a second to enjoy the sight of his strong body trembling with need, the stunning heat and power of him lying there helpless beneath me.

Bran's dark brows drew together as his eyes met mine. "It's okay if you want to stop. You don't have to keep going. I know it's not that pleasant for you since I'm so—"

"Magnificent?" I suggested, smiling. "For the record, I fucking love having you in my mouth, okay? I'm nowhere near done with you. That was just act one. Now close your eyes for me."

He did it without asking questions. What a privilege it was to have him trust me enough to close his eyes and let me do whatever I wanted to him while he lay there naked and vulnerable.

Pushing upright, I climbed over his thigh and turned myself around on the bed so I could lie on my side next to him. My stomach flickered with unease at having my legs up by his head. Even with my knees bent so my lower legs were angled away from him, my scarred shins and ankles felt uncomfortably exposed. That was why I'd asked him to close his eyes. I was used to hiding my legs, not sticking them in front of people's faces. But Bran hadn't acted repelled by them before. If he could trust me, maybe I could try trusting him.

He jolted in surprise when I rested my head on his thigh below his hip, but he kept his eyes closed even as his hands reached out for me. "Chloe, what—"

"Roll toward me onto your side," I said. As he obediently shifted his weight, I tugged the thigh under my head forward to make a comfortable pillow for myself.

"Like this?" he asked, sounding confused.

"Perfect." I wrapped my top arm around his waist and upper thigh to pull his hips toward me as I grasped his twitching cock with my other hand. Oh yeah, this was much more comfortable. All that energy I'd been spending to hold myself up could be put to better use now, allowing me to redouble my efforts. "You can open your eyes if you want," I said and took him into my mouth again.

"Oh God. Chloe." He shuddered against me as my hand squeezed his ass, hauling him closer so I could take even more of him into my mouth. "Holy shit."

"Comfy?" I asked, pulling off to take a breath as I gave him a few slow pumps with my hand.

"It feels…*fuck*." He let out a groan that sounded like I was sucking out his soul when I took him into my mouth again. "How are you so fucking good at this?"

Lots and lots of practice, but I didn't exactly want to tell him that. I wasn't sure how he'd feel about it given his extraordinary record of monogamy. So I only answered with a groan of pleasure as I worked him faster with my tongue and hand. The more I threw myself into it, the more driven I was by primal lust.

I didn't just need to make Bran feel good. I needed to make myself feel good by doing this, having him, tasting him. I wanted all of this. All of him. I pressed my thighs together as need throbbed between them, slicking my skin.

Bran's hands spread over the back of my thighs, and he yanked my legs toward him, spreading them apart as he thrust his head between them. His mouth closed over my pussy, and I moaned around his cock, helplessly rocking my hips against his face. The flat of his tongue dragged over my clit, lashing the aching flesh with rough, frantic strokes that lit up my nervous system like Times Square.

The rhythm of my ministrations faltered as the pressure building inside me abruptly upgraded to orange alert status—escalating unrest with potential for imminent eruption. When Bran stroked two fingers into my pussy, I pulled my head back to cry out his name as the first spasm of my climax hit me. Sucking in a gasping breath, I took him in my mouth again, lavishing him with frenzied attention as waves of pleasure pulsed through me.

"Oh shit, Chloe." His voice shook with an edge of desperation. "I can't— You need to— *Chloe.*"

I sank my nails into his ass cheek, letting him know I wanted him to stay right where he was, then slid a finger along his crack and pressed against the cinched-up entrance. His hips jerked and he came with a shudder, gasping my name against my still-fluttering pussy as he filled my throat. I milked every drop from him, taking everything he had until I felt him go slack.

My head swam as I rolled onto my back, staring at the ceiling in an orgasm-drunk daze. *Wow, oh wow.* That was the best sex I'd ever had. I'd had a lot of sex —more than I liked to admit—and it had never felt anything like that before. *What the hell?*

Bran scooped me up and cradled me against his heaving chest. His fingers skated gently over my face, then tipped it up to bring our lips together. For a man who'd just crossed the finish line, he kissed me with a surprising urgency, cupping his hand around the back of my neck as his mouth claimed me with greedy, possessive, cherishing kisses.

Shouldn't he be lying there inert as he drifted off into a drowsy stupor? Or jumping up to gather his clothes so he could disappear into the shower or out the door? Why was he kissing me like he still needed something from me even after he'd gotten off?

Because he does.

The thought inspired a bright flare of joy in my chest. This was what it was supposed to be like. This was how it felt to be cared for. To be treated like someone who mattered. Someone worth treasuring rather than something to be disposed of at the first opportunity.

"Are you okay?" Bran asked, searching my face as if he could sense my disorientation.

I nodded, smiling at him. "I'm just coming down from the brain sparkles and happy shakes."

"Brain sparkles?" His lips twitched. "Does that mean you enjoyed it?"

Tender instinct drew my fingers up to smooth his hair. "Could you not tell? I thought I was fairly vocal in my approval."

"I just wanted to make sure. If you have any notes—"

"No notes. None at all. It was…" The words *the best sex of my life* threatened to spill out of my mouth, but I swallowed them down. "Perfect."

Bran kissed me with a sweetness that made me squeeze my eyes shut. He was all around me, holding me close, his smell on my skin and his taste on my tongue. I clung to him as a tangle of emotions swarmed around my heart and clogged my throat.

I loved this feeling of being treasured and adored, but I didn't trust it. So we'd had mind-blowingly good sex. That didn't necessarily mean anything. The more I allowed myself to hope for, the more it would hurt not to get it. Bran could still drop me as easily as everyone else did, cast me aside for something more important and leave me reeling. I couldn't afford to expect anything different. I needed to keep my feelings in check.

Assuming it wasn't already too late.

CHAPTER TWENTY-FOUR

BRAN

"Bran."

I jolted awake at the sound of Chloe saying my name. "Whuh? What's wrong?"

As my tired eyes remembered how to focus, her face swam into my field of vision. Her lovely hair all mussed up. Makeup smudged around her gorgeous caramel eyes. Stubble burn reddening her delicate lips. It was the most beautiful sight I'd ever seen.

"Your alarm's going off."

Right. That was the annoying noise I'd only barely registered in the back of my mind. I rolled toward the nightstand and reached out for my phone, which wasn't there.

I was in Chloe's room, not mine. That meant my phone was probably…still in my jacket pocket from last night. And my jacket was…on the floor, lying in a rumpled heap near the foot of the bed. Bending down to snag it, I retrieved my phone and shut off the blaring alarm.

"Thank God," Chloe said. "How can you sleep through that?"

"I have no idea, but I do. Regularly."

Despite the lingering fog of drowsiness, I felt strangely refreshed. Chloe and I had kept each other up late last night, but once we'd fallen asleep I'd slept better than I would have expected.

I'd never had a chance to get used to sharing a bed with another person.

Marisa and I had both lived with our parents during our college summer breaks, which hadn't allowed many opportunities for sleepovers. The few times we'd been able to spend a whole night together, insomnia had kept me awake, and she'd complained about my tossing and turning.

Yet I'd drifted right to sleep with Chloe in my arms and slept soundly until my alarm went off, which almost never happened. *Funny.*

Memories from last night washed back over me. Dancing with Chloe. Kissing her. Watching her come undone as I touched her. How she'd taken me apart in a way I'd never experienced before or even known was possible.

I hadn't appreciated just how different sex could be with a different partner. Nor had I fully understood just how limited my experience had been with Marisa. Our sex life hadn't exactly been a raging inferno. I'd blamed it on the challenges of a long-distance relationship, telling myself things would get better once we were able to be together all the time.

But the truth was, Marisa had never been adventurous or overly enthusiastic in the bedroom. I'd thought she wasn't all that interested in sex, but her infidelity had put the lie to that theory. Apparently, it was just sex with me that hadn't interested her.

Last night with Chloe had been a world-rocking experience. I finally understood just how much I'd been missing out on. It was the difference between a McDonald's Happy Meal and a perfectly cooked filet mignon at a five-star restaurant.

Maybe it wasn't so surprising I'd slept like the dead after that.

According to my phone, we had an hour until my mother's wedding brunch started. I should probably get up and go back to my room to shower and get dressed.

But that meant leaving the beckoning comfort of Chloe's bed. The scent of her on the sheets. The silky softness of her skin. The enticing warmth of her gloriously naked body. How was I supposed to walk away from all that? The urge to hold on to the feeling a little longer was too powerful to resist.

Setting my phone on the nightstand, I flopped back on the bed and rolled toward her. "Hi," I whispered, drinking in the lovely sight of her sleepy morning eyes and kiss-bruised lips.

"Hi," she whispered back quietly.

I reached out to brush a rumpled lock of hair off her cheek, troubled by the uncertainty I saw in her face. She looked like she was waiting for me to let her down. The thought that she expected it pained me almost as much as the possibility that I might.

"I look awful, don't I?" She swiped her fingers under her eyes with a nervous laugh. "I forgot to take off my makeup."

"You look beautiful." I cupped the back of her head to pull her closer and touched a tender kiss to her lips. "You always look beautiful."

The sight of her smile loosened the knots in my chest. "Flatterer."

"You've clearly mistaken me for someone else." I pressed my thumb to the red spot beneath her lower lip. "I'm sorry I gave you stubble burn. I should have been more careful with you."

She laid her palm against my jaw, stroking her fingertips over the prickly skin. "I like it when you're a little rough."

I was already hard, but my cock swelled against my stomach at the flood of memories her words brought rushing back. My voice came out husky. "I noticed that last night."

Chloe's cheeks pinked, but her eyes stayed locked on mine. There was that uncertainty again. That sense of waiting.

I wrapped her up in my arms and rolled onto my back, dragging her on top of me. Her face nestled into the crook of my neck as she wriggled against me, getting comfortable. We both went still when her pussy settled against my erection. Jesus, she was as wet as I was hard. I shuddered as my hips rocked of their own volition, rubbing my shaft against her sex.

It would be so fucking easy to press the tip against her entrance and bury myself inside her.

If we had a condom.

And more time.

"Chloe." I pressed my face into her hair, holding her tight while I fought for self-control. "What we did last night...I wasn't prepared for it to be like that."

I felt her tense, holding her breath. "Like what?"

"Being with you was the best sex I've ever had."

She lifted her head, surprise written on her face—but also pleasure. "We didn't even get to go all the way."

"It still felt better than anything else I've ever done. I didn't even know it could be like that."

It was an embarrassing truth to admit to myself, much less confess to Chloe that I'd nearly committed myself to a lifetime of mediocre sex. It horrified me, frankly, to think I'd been prepared to spend my whole life with a woman who'd never touched me with anywhere near the fervor and enthusiasm Chloe had last night. And yet the admission filled me with an incredible sense of relief, as if the clouds dimming my eyes had cleared, allowing me to finally see the truth of what was—and what could be.

"It's never felt like that for me either." Chloe's eyes shone as she slid her fingers into my hair and pressed her lips to mine.

It was a hell of a rush to know I'd broken the curve despite my lack of experience. I kissed her back with gusto, running my hands over her skin as our tongues slid together. I couldn't believe how natural this felt—kissing her, touching her, having her body wrapped around mine. As if this was where I was supposed to be. Imagine getting to wake up to this every day. What a miracle that would be.

Just not one available to me. I deflated as I remembered I couldn't afford those kinds of indulgences. Not at this point in my life. It would pose too much of a distraction from my goals. I had a hard enough time getting out of bed in the mornings without adding this kind of temptation. The demands of work and school required all of my focus, not to mention most of my days and too many hours of my nights. I'd never be able to give someone like Chloe as much as she deserved. I wouldn't be able to make her happy. And the thought of making her unhappy was unbearable. My fantasies needed to stay fantasies.

My second alarm went off, reminding me where I was *actually* supposed to be. Not here with Chloe. But in my room, getting ready to see my mom and step-father off at a breakfast.

"I need to go," I said with a sigh.

"Okay."

But I didn't go. I kept kissing her as I ran my fingertips over the supple curve of her ass, ignoring the irritating blare of my alarm.

"Should I turn that off?" Chloe asked between kisses.

I groaned. "No, I'm doing it. I really do need to go." I gave her one final kiss and slid out from under her.

She stretched out on her side and propped her head on her hand as she watched me pull my clothes on.

"Enjoying the view?" I asked as I yanked my pants up over my hard-on.

"Very much so."

I thrust my arms into my shirt and let my gaze settle on her as I did up the buttons. The tangled sheet lay loosely draped over her hips, and her bare breasts and one exposed thigh presented a seductive feast for the eyes. "Me too."

"This view, you mean?" She reached one arm behind her head and stretched, arching her back to show off her breasts and graceful figure. "Or maybe you meant this view?" she suggested, twitching the sheet aside to offer a tiny glimpse of the sweet pussy I wanted so badly to sink into.

"Now you're just playing dirty." I winced as I tucked my shirt in around my hard-on. It would have to be a cold shower this morning. A very cold shower.

"I don't know what you're talking about." Another twitch of the sheet, baring even more.

"You're trying to murder me," I growled, snatching the rest of my clothes off the floor. After I'd gathered everything, including my phone and shoes, I paused to give Chloe another thorough look, memorizing the sight of her like this. Thinking about how comfortable and content I'd felt a few minutes ago when I'd still been in her bed almost made me drop everything in my arms and climb right back on top of her.

Perhaps sensing she was in danger of actually keeping me from leaving, she sat up and pulled the sheet over her chest. "I'll see you at breakfast?"

It shouldn't have been a question—we were both invited and we'd both obviously want to see my mom before she and Mike left for their honeymoon—but it sounded an awful lot like one.

Clutching all my stuff to my chest with one arm, I bent and cupped Chloe's face with my free hand. "Of course you will," I promised, giving her a slow, savoring kiss.

Then I forced myself to turn away from her and go. I resisted the urge to look back as I let myself out the door, afraid I'd lose my resolve.

CHAPTER TWENTY-FIVE

CHLOE

The post-wedding brunch was a smaller affair than the rehearsal dinner, since a lot of the guests had left early this morning to catch flights home. I arrived five minutes late after rushing through a shower, twisting my wet hair into a bun, and skipping makeup altogether, but I still managed to get there before Bran.

I chose a seat next to Angie's husband Charles and tried to hide my disappointment a few minutes later when Mike's mother claimed the empty seat on my other side. Not that I minded her company. Mrs. Pilota reminded me a lot of my grandmother. I'd have been glad to be her breakfast companion if I hadn't been hoping for someone else's company instead.

Bran didn't show up for another ten minutes. His eyes briefly met mine as they scanned the room, and his chin lifted in a barely perceptible nod before he went to sit next to Deon.

For the next forty-five minutes I directed a steady stream of cheerful conversation at the taciturn Mrs. Pilota while trying not to look at Bran. Whenever I did let my gaze slide his way, he was always looking at someone else. Never at me. Which didn't help the knot of apprehension sitting like lead in my stomach.

In my room with him this morning, I'd felt happy and hopeful. He'd seemed so comfortable, like he truly wanted to stay there with me. And maybe he had. But as soon as the door had slammed behind him, the afterglow bubble burst and reality came rushing back in.

We hadn't talked about the future or whether we had one. I couldn't shake the feeling that it wasn't likely to involve the two of us being together long-term. Worse, deep down, a part of me thought that might be for the best.

Bran had told me how challenging law school was, how little free time it left him with, and how his first few years as a junior associate would be even more demanding. That didn't sound like someone in the market for commitment. And who could blame him after his last relationship? He deserved to enjoy his freedom, sow some oats, live a little.

Let's be real, I wasn't his next girlfriend. I was his rebound.

Which would be fine if I wasn't falling for him. Stupid feelings. I should have known they'd go haring off and get me into trouble. This was the problem with happiness and hope. It never lasted.

The more I thought about it, the more likely it seemed that Bran had been reluctant to leave this morning because he'd known it would be the end. He was too honest and practical to pretend otherwise. What we'd had this weekend was great, but probably never destined to be more than a vacation fling.

Better to start making my peace with that now, so when he delivered the news I'd be prepared. I'd take it gracefully. I wouldn't let my feelings show and make him feel bad. He didn't deserve that, not after he'd been so lovely and caring. We could stay friends. Or at least remain friendly when we happened to cross paths in the future.

Once the breakfast plates had been cleared, people began trickling out in ones and twos, stopping off to hug Dawn and Mike and say goodbye before they left. A sense of melancholy settled over me as I watched the guests disperse. This was it. The magical wedding weekend was over and we were all heading back to our regular, mundane lives now.

"Did you have a nice time this weekend?" Angie's husband asked me after Mike's mother had left to go finish packing.

"I've had an amazing time," I answered with a wistful sigh. "I wish it didn't have to end."

"I'm with you there," Charles agreed. "I'll be sorry to leave this place. But work beckons bright and early tomorrow. Angie and I are hitting the road just as soon as we get the car packed up after the newlyweds leave for the airport. I can't remember—are you still riding back with us today?"

"I think she might have another ride home," Angie told her husband.

"Uh…I'm not sure, actually." I hadn't thought that far ahead. I supposed I'd assumed I'd ride back with Bran. But if he was looking to treat this as a What

Happens in Michigan Stays in Michigan situation, that could make for an awkward six-hour drive, and it might be best to say our goodbyes here.

Angie gave me a speculative look as she sipped her coffee. "You're not getting home the same way you got here?"

"I need to figure out what the plan is. Can you save my seat until I've had a chance to ask Bran?"

A prickle of awareness climbed up the back of my neck, and I turned to find Bran standing behind me.

"Ask me what?" he said.

Charles smiled up at him fondly. "Ah, Brandon, just the fellow we need. Will you be taking Chloe back to Chicago with you, or is she riding home with us?"

"She's riding with me." Bran's eyebrows snuck together as he looked at me. "Aren't you?"

"We hadn't discussed it, so I wasn't sure."

His frown deepened. "Would you rather ride with Angie and Charles?"

"Sounds like you two have some talking to do." Angie exchanged a meaningful look with Charles and pushed her chair back. "Come on, honey. Let's give them a minute."

"Good idea," Charles said, rising to follow her. He gave me a kind smile. "You just let us know once you've figured it out. We're always glad to have your company."

Angie pointed a finger at me. "Don't forget—I'm calling Roland first thing in the morning, so you need to make up your mind about the exhibition before then."

I nodded distractedly, not wanting to think about that right now.

When they were gone, Bran sank down in Charles's vacated chair. "What does she mean make up your mind? Why wouldn't you do the exhibition?"

"I don't want to talk about that right now."

"Okay." He drew back slightly, looking hurt. "Do you not want to ride home with me?"

I shook my head, swallowing. "I just didn't want to assume or anything."

"You didn't want to assume," he repeated. "You really think, after everything that's happened between us over the last two days, that I would tell you to find your own way home this morning? That's who you think I am?"

"No, that's not— I didn't think that. I just…"

"Couldn't be sure," he finished flatly.

"It's not that." I cast an anxious look around to make sure no one was paying attention to us. "I don't know what you're looking for going forward—if anything. Maybe this was a one-time weekend hookup, in which case it might be better if we part as friends now rather than spend the whole day in a car together right after we've agreed to not see each other anymore."

"I don't want to part now," he said.

"Okay." I blew out a steady breath, tamping down the rush of relief I felt. It was still too soon to be counting any chickens. "Then what do you want? What are we after we get home and our lives go back to normal? Are we dating? Are we sex friends? Is this a casual thing, or are you looking for a commitment?"

His reflexive flinch at the word *commitment* pretty much said everything I needed to know. He tried to hide it, but it blared like a siren.

"So not a commitment, then." My gaze didn't waver and my tone betrayed no disappointment. It was no big deal. This was why I'd prepared myself for this.

Bran opened his mouth, then shut it again as he darted a tense glance around the room. "This isn't a conversation we should be trying to have right now."

"Agreed."

"Can we just—" He wet his lips, searching my face with pained, pleading eyes. "Can we go somewhere and talk about this after we see my mom and Mike off?"

"Of course." I produced a smile, letting him know everything was fine and dandy. Nothing to worry about at all. "Let's do that."

Twenty arduous minutes later, after we'd hugged the newlyweds goodbye and watched them climb into the taxi that would take them to the airport for their honeymoon, Bran followed me back to my room for The Talk.

A leaden silence fell as soon as we were alone together. My gaze hooked on the rumpled bed we'd slept in, then zipped away. I lifted my chin and made myself smile as I turned to face him. "It's okay, you know. This can just be a vacation fling if that's what you want."

Bran's eyes narrowed as they searched mine. "Is that what you want?"

I lifted a shoulder. "It's fine with me if that's all you want."

"Don't," he said, the word sharp enough to make me flinch. "Don't do that thing where you pretend not to care. Jesus, Chloe. I can't take it."

Heat pressed behind my eyes, and I fastened my gaze to the floor. "I'm just trying to make this easier for us. What do you want me to say?"

"I want you to be honest with me. That's all I'm asking."

That was all? Just for me to show him my heart so he could bruise it. A broken laugh tore out of me. "Be fair."

He made a frustrated sound in the back of his throat. "Okay. How about this? What if I go first and tell you what I want? Then you can take your turn."

"Sure." Nodding, I attempted to lift my gaze from the floor but lost courage somewhere around his knees. "Sounds good."

"I want *you*."

The forceful, resolute way he said it yanked my gaze to his face.

"I want you in my life. I want to be your friend, but I also want more than that. I want your kisses and your body as much as I want your company." His chest rose and fell as his eyes closed briefly. "I want to fuck you so bad it's all I can think about. Now that I've had a taste of you, I can't stand the thought of giving you up, so I really hope I don't have to."

"Oh," I whispered. That was all I could manage with everything he'd just declared swirling around in my head. I'd never had anyone say anything like that to me before. Honestly, how was I still standing on these jelly legs and not a puddle on the floor right now?

"But the truth is…" He looked away and drew in a bracing breath. "The truth is, I don't have any idea how to make this work. I don't have free time to spare as it is. I've barely been keeping my head above water with work and school, and I can't afford to lose focus or I'm going to drown."

"I'd be a distraction," I said, understanding.

"The very best kind of distraction, but…yes," he admitted with a wince. "I don't know how much I can offer you. Definitely not as much as I want to—or as much as you deserve. And I don't know what to do about that."

"Right." I breathed in. Then out. Tried to organize my thoughts despite the wild fluttering of my stomach. "Is it my turn now?"

"Yes." Bran watched me warily, braced for bad news. "You tell me what you want."

Instead of speaking, I closed the distance between us. When I fitted myself against him, his arms came up automatically to fold around me. Holding him as tight as I could, I laid my cheek against his chest and closed my eyes.

"Chloe?"

"I want everything you just said." When I felt the relief blow through him, I snuggled even harder.

"But what about—"

"Hold on." I buried my nose in his chest, inhaling deep. "Give me a sec."

"Okay." His hands smoothed down my back while I finished soaking up my fill of Bran-energy.

"I want to be your friend," I said, "but I also want to have sex with you as much as possible. What I don't want is to become a source of stress in your life or a burden. I want you to do all the things you need to do without having to worry about me. So here's what I propose…" I lifted my face to his and smiled at his uncertain, hopeful expression. He'd lowered all his barriers for me, laid himself open when I'd been too afraid to do it, and I planned to reward that trust. He'd taken the leap. Now I was going to be there to catch him. "We play this by ear. No obligations or expectations."

His brow furrowed. "How is that going to work?"

"I don't have any idea. But we'll figure it out together, okay? For now, let's just agree that we want to stay in each other's lives in whatever way we can, however that happens to look for us. I'll take as much of you as you can afford to offer."

"Really?"

I nodded as I smoothed my hands over his chest, then down his stomach. "You have no idea how flexible I can be."

Bran's mouth captured mine in a rough, joyful, devouring kiss, his tongue plunging deep as he jerked my body against his, lighting up every one of my erogenous zones. This man wanted me as much as I wanted him. There was no doubting that. My heart ran wild, set free from its tether as I slid my hand down between us to stroke the growing bulge in the front of his jeans.

"Fuck." He growled against my mouth and thrust his hips against my hand, needy and so damn hot. "I need you."

"Yes," I panted, burying my face in his neck as I wrestled with the button on his jeans. *"Yes."*

"Check my back pocket."

"What?" I muttered, tugging at his zipper.

His hand closed over mine, dragging it off his pants and around to his ass. "There's something for you in my back pocket."

My fingers dipped inside and encountered something crinkly. And flat. And square. I plucked out a condom and stared at it like I'd just unearthed a winning lottery ticket. "How?"

"I drove to the store in town," he said, breaking into a grin. "That's why I was late to breakfast."

I launched myself at him, locking our lips together as my arms wrapped around his neck. He caught me and carried me to the bed, laying me down and covering my body with his.

"Clothes off," I gasped, shoving at his pants. "Naked. Now."

"Good idea." His big hands slid up my body, pushing my shirt over my head, and his mouth latched onto my nipple.

"Bran." Whimpering, I wriggled beneath him, trapped by his weight and loving the hell out of it. My fingernails clawed at his back, tugging his shirt up, trying to pull it over his head. "Please."

He sat up, yanked his shirt off, and shoved his pants and underwear down. "Now you," he said, leaning over me.

"Wait." I grasped his hands when he started to unfasten my pants. "I should do it."

His gaze met mine, softening with understanding. "I'll be careful," he said. "So careful. I promise. Will you let me?"

I nodded and lay back. With steady, gentle hands, he lifted my feet, one at a time, and slipped my shoes off. Then he worked my pants down my thighs, and cautiously eased them off my lower legs, mindful of the sensitive skin. Next he did the same with my underwear, so tender, so protective, so perfect. Tossing them aside, he kissed the inside of my knee.

"You're beautiful," he murmured, dragging his prickly stubble up my inner thigh. "So beautiful." He kissed my hip bone, my stomach, my breastbone, and finally my lips, lowering his weight onto me again, covering my naked body with his. "I'll always be careful with you," he promised between searing kisses. "You know that, right?"

"I know," I panted. My heart felt too big for my chest. It hammered against my ribs, echoing in my ears as I curled my fingers into his hair.

His hips rolled, and we both shuddered as his hard shaft dragged through the slickness between my legs. "You make me so goddamn hard, Chloe. Tell me you want it."

"Yes, please." I rocked against him, restless with lust. "I need it so bad."

He grabbed the condom off the bed and tore it open.

"Hurry, I need you inside me," I pleaded as he rolled it on, and he clenched his jaw so hard a vein throbbed in his temple.

When he had the condom on, he lowered himself over me, settling against my hips. "Are you wet already?"

I arched my back, moaning as he stroked a hand through my wanting flesh.

"Jesus," he hissed. "You're so fucking soaked."

"Give it to me." When I felt his cock notch against my entrance, I squeezed his ass cheeks, and he jerked against me, slipping just a little inside. God, I needed it. I *ached* for him to fill me up, but he wasn't moving. Why wasn't he moving? Instead, he was watching me writhe beneath him, enjoying my frustration. *Freaking tease.* "Bran," I whined. "Please."

He pushed in a little more and stopped. Maddening. "You need it that bad? Tell me, Chloe. Tell me what you want."

I looked into his eyes, which gleamed darkly as they roved over my face. "You want me to tell you to fuck me? Is that what you want? To hear me talk dirty?"

"Yes." He licked his lips and slid a little farther inside with a shudder. "Yes."

The words spilled out of me as the lid came off the well of my inhibitions. "I need your cock in me so bad. Fuck me, Bran. Please, baby. Give it to me rough, okay? Fuck me hard, the way you know I like it."

As if my dirty talk had unleashed something in him, he shoved all the way in with such suddenness and force it drove a cry from my lungs.

"Chloe?" He stilled, his forearms flexing on either side of my head as he gazed into my eyes. Checking in. Being careful, just like he'd promised.

"It's good." I clutched at him, shaking at the overwhelming rush of pleasure, the perfection of it, the startling sense of rightness at the deep, intimate connection. Penetration had never felt anything like this before. It had never been more than a purely physical pleasure. Empty. Sparking no more emotion than a solo session with a silicon stand-in.

This was something altogether different and unexpected. The rich, shimmering warmth spreading through my chest squeezed itself around my heart tight enough to make my eyes water. It was wondrous and terrifying and I never wanted it to stop.

"More," I whimpered, squeezing my inner walls around him, aching to feel him move. "You feel so good. Please, Bran."

"Jesus," he hissed, his body trembling with tension as he held himself above me. "Don't do that. Just be still, okay? I can't—you feel too fucking perfect."

I couldn't be still. Even if I'd wanted to, it wasn't physically possible. Need drove my fingernails into his flexed glutes as my hips lifted to draw him deeper. He made a hoarse sound, pulling back with an undulating roll of his pelvis that pulled a moan from me as he glided against all sorts of incredible places.

With a savage growl, he surged between my legs, driving them apart as he slammed into me, pumping hard and fast. Every fierce, ceaseless drive of his hips rocked the bed, giving me the roughness I loved. He pressed his open mouth against my neck, panting and groaning, his weight bearing down on my body while his frantic thrusts filled all the empty space inside me.

Pressure wound through my core, sparking flares of pleasure that shot up my spine, growing more and more intense until it felt like it was pulling me apart. I wailed his name, and his hand cupped the back of my head as he lifted his head from my neck.

"Open your eyes." His fingers tightened in my hair, pulling hard enough to command my attention. "Look at me."

I couldn't do anything else. He caught me in the intensity of his gaze, and the world narrowed to just the two of us, holding on to each other, locked together as we moved as one.

The pressure cooker inside me burst, swamping me with a wave of bliss that rolled my eyes back in my head, breaking the spell between us. But I could still feel Bran's searing gaze on me, watching intently as I cried out at the pulses of too-intense pleasure.

It went on and on, longer than I thought possible, and it was still rippling through me when Bran's bucking hips stuttered. His hand clenched in my hair as every muscle in his body went taut. Then he broke with a ragged groan and buried his face in my neck, collapsing on top of me.

We clung to each other in a sweaty, boneless tangle, chests heaving as we fought to catch our breaths. Bran shifted, angling my face toward his, and his mouth slanted over mine in a messy, gasping kiss that locked my galloping heart down, cementing his ownership of it and sealing my fate.

I was officially a goner for this man, whether I liked it or not. As of this moment, the matter was out of my hands.

CHAPTER TWENTY-SIX

CHLOE

"Stop that." Bran threw a sidelong look at me, frowning.

"What?" Hard to believe I used to find his frowns intimidating when they were so adorable. The more he frowned, the cuter he was.

"You're staring at me," he said as his eyes watched the road ahead.

I bit down on my lower lip. "What am I supposed to do when you're sitting there looking all hot and sexy? Stare out the window? Boring."

"That's not why you're staring at me. You're trying to tell if I'm getting a migraine."

"Excuse you. Your hotness is at least fifty percent of why I'm staring at you."

"I told you I'm fine."

There were scattered thunderstorms in the forecast across most of Michigan today, and Bran had insisted on driving despite my concerns about it giving him another migraine. So yes, maybe I was watching him like a hawk for early signs of a migraine. Guilty as charged.

"Are you though?" I asked, narrowing my eyes. "Would you even tell me?"

He reached across the console for my hand. "I promised I would, and I meant it."

"Fine." I sighed, tangling our fingers together in my lap. I loved holding his hand. And I loved that he seemed to like holding mine almost as much, not out of obligation or as a performative gesture, but simply for the sake of touching me. "I guess I believe you."

"It's not sunny enough for glare to be a problem, and thanks to you there's not an atom of tension left in my body." He darted a smile at me as his thumb stroked the back of my hand. "The chances of me getting a migraine right now are infinitesimal."

"I'm glad to hear it."

"Where do you think we should stop for lunch?"

"What does the spreadsheet say?"

"I didn't make a spreadsheet."

My jaw dropped in only partially feigned shock. "No spreadsheet? What about the schedule? The detailed travel plan? Where did you organize your return trip research if not in a spreadsheet?"

He smiled. "There's no plan or schedule today. We're winging it."

"Winging it? What? That's crazy talk."

His smile twitched wider. "We're improvising. Flying without a net. Playing it by ear. Taking it as it comes."

"I don't know what to say. I didn't even realize those phrases existed in your vocabulary, and here you are saying them with a smile on your face. It's like you're a completely different person."

"You make me feel like one."

"Is that a good thing? Because now I'm worried I'm a bad influence on you."

His hand squeezed mine. "It's a very good thing. I haven't felt this happy and carefree in…I can't even remember. God, how sad is that?"

"Here's a thought—maybe you should take vacations more often."

"Maybe," he agreed. "Or maybe I just need to spend as much time as possible with you."

"Sounds good to me."

"Let me know if you get hungry or see somewhere you want to stop."

"Look at you, embracing spontaneity." I reached over and pushed the collar of his shirt open as I leaned forward, squinting at his exposed chest.

"What are you doing?" he asked, swatting my hand away.

"Checking you for stress hives."

"Very funny," he said with a grunt as he fought to suppress a smile.

"I agree. It was pretty funny."

He captured my hand again and dragged it into his lap. "Hey, listen, speaking of stress hives…"

"Uh oh. That's not a fun-sounding segue."

"I want to talk about that art exhibition." I stiffened reflexively and tried to pull my hand away, but Bran held tight, refusing to let me go. "Tell me why it makes you so tense? I thought you'd be excited about an opportunity like that. Isn't this what you want?"

I stared out the windshield as my jaw clenched. "Eventually."

"But not now?"

"I'm not ready."

"I get that it's short notice," he said gently, "but Angie seems to think a month is enough time for you to get ready. Or do you mean you're not ready to show your work to this Roland guy who owns the gallery?"

"I don't feel ready for any of it," I admitted. "I'm supposed to get my MFA before I start showing my art in public."

"Why?"

"So I can improve myself and produce better work. So people will take me seriously."

He was quiet for a moment, his brow furrowing as he took that in. "You don't think you're good enough now?"

"No." I wasn't sure I'd ever be good enough, but I definitely wasn't yet.

"Angie thinks you are. If this guy who's putting on the exhibition says you are, maybe that means you are. Don't you think they know what they're talking about?" Bran's fingers tightened around mine. "It's possible yours might not be the most objective opinion here."

I kept my mouth shut. While some part of me saw the sense in what he was saying, the rest of me was in no way ready to admit that. Because if I did—then what? I'd have to *do* something about it. It was much easier to keep telling myself I wasn't good enough and using that as an excuse to take myself out of the game before I had a chance to lose.

Bran let the silence linger awhile before he tried again. "Is it possible you're scared?"

I snorted. "I'm definitely scared."

"Because it means people will be judging and critiquing your work, and that's something that's especially hard for you to deal with." It wasn't a question. He was telling me he understood exactly what had me paralyzed, even though I'd never come right out and said it out loud.

"Yes." I hated that he knew me so well. Most of the time I loved it, but right now I hated it.

"Criticism is something you'll have to get used to enduring if you're serious about being an artist, isn't it?"

I said nothing. He'd just landed on the big, scary thing that kept me up at night. What if I couldn't endure it? What if I wasn't strong enough? Maybe I wasn't cut out to be an artist, and I'd been fooling myself all this time.

Bran squeezed my hand again. "I think you're a lot tougher and a lot more accomplished than you give yourself credit for." His tone was gentle, but there was force behind the words, letting me know how much he meant them. "The fact that you feel things so deeply makes all of this more difficult for you, but it's also what makes you such an incredible artist, Chloe. It would be a shame if the world never got to see how much you have to offer."

God, he was convincing. That quiet passion in his voice almost had me swayed. I could totally picture Bran in court one day making rousing arguments in that same voice and winning over everyone with the strength of his convictions.

Imagine thinking I was a worthy use of that passion inside him. But he did. He'd told me with his words and shown me with his actions, over and over again, how much faith he had in me. He'd opened himself up, put himself in my hands, and tried new things that scared him simply because I'd asked him to.

Now it was my turn to step up. All I had to do was put my faith in him, which wasn't actually such a hard thing to do. If someone as smart and genuine as Bran believed in me this much, that had to mean I was worth believing in.

"Fine," I said, reaching into my purse for my phone. "You win."

"What do I win?" he asked, releasing my hand reluctantly when I tugged it out of his grasp.

"I'm texting Angie to tell her I'll do it," I said as I typed the message. "I'll meet with her friend Roland and see if he thinks I'm good enough for his exhibition."

"You *are* good enough," Bran said, sneaking a proud look at me.

At that moment, fueled by the warmth of his unwavering support, I felt invincible. Like I could take on the whole world without even breaking a sweat.

The drive went way too quickly. Of course today, when I wanted to have as much time with Bran as possible, we hadn't run into a single traffic jam or thunderstorm. It'd been smooth sailing all the way home.

I wasn't ready for it to be over. But here we were, parked in front of my grandmother's house. As I stepped out of the car, I had that same jarring feeling you got when you first walked out of a movie theater and realized you were in the real world again instead of the fantasy world you'd been immersed in for the last three hours. The credits had rolled on our weekend getaway, and we'd been dumped back into our old lives and routines.

Bran retrieved my bag from the trunk and carried it up the stoop. When I let myself into the house, my grandmother was in her usual spot, kicked back in her recliner in front of the television. She looked up from *America's Funniest Home Videos* long enough to give me an understated greeting and Bran a disinterested once-over before returning her attention to the TV screen.

I tugged Bran into my room and shut the door behind us. He looked as out of place in my messy bedroom as he had two days ago when he'd come to pick me up. Everything had changed since then, but right at that moment it felt like nothing had. Bran didn't fit in my world any better now than he had before.

Until he pulled me against him. As soon as his arms came around me and I sank into the firm warmth of his body, everything felt right again. *This* was where we fit. In a little private world of our own making.

"I've been wanting to kiss you for the last two hours." His lips slanted over mine, his mouth already opening as if he'd been starving to death for the taste of me.

My knees turned to rubber as his tongue delved deep, and I slid my hands over his chest, up his neck, and into his hair, pulling his head down and holding on for dear life.

"I should go," he said on a shaky exhale.

"My grandmother's hearing isn't that great. Just putting that out there in case it changes anything."

He looked torn, and for a second I thought I'd hooked him. Just when I was about to reel him in, he shook his head. "I have work in the morning and about a million things I need to catch up on tonight."

I nodded in understanding, doing my best to hide my disappointment. This was the arrangement we'd agreed to. All I got to have of him was what he could afford to offer me.

That was enough. I could be just as strong as he was. I would be. We were going to make this work.

"I'll walk you out." Threading our fingers together, I led him out of my room and past my grandmother, who barely acknowledged Bran's polite goodbye.

Out on the front stoop, I pulled the door closed and tugged him off to one side, away from the window in the door. A lump rose in my throat as I gazed up

SUSANNAH NIX

into his green-gold eyes, but I smiled around it, trying not to act as clingy as I felt.

He gathered me into a tight hug, and I clutched at him as I pressed my face into his neck, soaking up as much of the feeling as I could to tide me over. Loosening his hold, he lifted a hand to cradle my jaw and kissed me softly, his lips moving over mine with such tenderness my heart slammed up against the inside of my chest.

"I'm going to miss doing that tomorrow," he whispered, pressing our foreheads together.

"There will be more waiting for you whenever you're in need of a top-up."

He kissed my temple and let me go. "I'll text you, okay?"

I nodded, managing to keep a smile on my face until he turned to walk away.

When I let myself back into the house, my grandmother peeled her attention away from the TV to squint at me. "You like this one, don't you?"

"Yeah, I do," I admitted, sinking onto the couch with a sigh.

"Take care with that heart of yours," she said. "Make sure you don't give him more than he's willing to give you back."

"I know," I said. It wasn't the first time she'd given me similar advice. "I'll be careful."

She nodded and turned back to the TV.

For my grandmother, that constituted a voluminous heart-to-heart talk. She wasn't an effusive person, but that didn't mean she didn't care. She just didn't express it much.

I sat with her for a while and told her about my weekend during the commercial breaks. As per usual, she didn't comment much about any of it, except to say "good for you" when I told her how I'd done part of the driving on the way there.

When *Supermarket Sweep* started, I left her to it and went into my bedroom. I needed to review my existing portfolio and decide what pieces to show this Roland person. I forced myself to get started, even though I wasn't feeling it.

Saying goodbye to Bran had left me low-key depressed. The balloon of happiness that had fueled my confidence earlier had deflated now that he was gone. I couldn't even look forward to seeing him again because he hadn't given me any indication when that might happen.

When he said he wouldn't have much free time, what did that actually mean, practically speaking? Once a week? Once a month? Even less than that? I'd

206

vowed not to put any pressure on him, but it sure would be nice to have some idea how long I'd have to wait.

As I moved around my room, it started to feel like Bran had never been there. Like I'd dreamed him up and he'd been a figment of my imagination the whole time.

Thirty minutes later, I got a text from him.

One of the partners is hosting a cocktail party for the summer associates Saturday night. I can guarantee you'll have a miserable time, but I don't suppose you'd want to come as my date anyway?

A giddy smile spread across my face as I typed my reply.

After that sales pitch? How could I possibly say no?

CHAPTER TWENTY-SEVEN

BRAN

"It's you again," Chloe's grandmother said, standing in the doorway with one hand resting on her hip.

"Yes, ma'am. I'm here to pick Chloe up for a date."

Mrs. Carpenter turned and headed for her recliner, leaving the front door open by way of an invitation to come inside.

"I'm almost ready!" Chloe shouted from the back of the house.

I followed the sound of her voice to the bathroom and found her leaning over the sink putting on makeup. The relief of seeing her again practically bowled me over, and my thoughts fuzzed into an incoherent electric hum as I paused in the doorway to take in the sight.

We'd texted every day, spoken on the phone a few times, and she'd even sent a couple of photos that I'd spent more time staring at than I wanted to admit. But it wasn't the same as seeing Chloe in person. It wasn't the same as breathing in the scent of her shampoo. It wasn't the same as knowing I could reach out and touch her.

Her face lit up as she turned toward me. God, that smile. It was better than oxygen. I'd never get tired of breathing it in.

"You're a sight for sore eyes," she said as I moved into the bathroom.

"That's supposed to be my line." My hands slid around her hips, and she angled her face up to me as I bent my head to give her the kiss I'd been holding in for the last six days.

I'd never in my life experienced this kind of yearning for anyone before. Six days wasn't even a long separation. Didn't most newly dating couples go that long between dates as a matter of routine? Marisa and I had gone far longer than that regularly, and while I'd eagerly anticipated seeing her again, it had never been with this sort of all-consuming urgency.

Chloe had awakened something in me, and it scared me almost as much as it thrilled me. Every night this week, it had taken all my willpower not to invite her over. The mental tug-of-war had played hell with my focus. I'd gotten less work done, made more mistakes, and wasted way too much time daydreaming. The long hours spent in the company of my fellow summer associates felt even more dismal and unpleasant in comparison with the time I'd spent with Chloe last weekend.

Just as I'd feared, she was a distraction. But since I wasn't willing to give her up, I'd just have to adapt. It couldn't be like this forever, right? Eventually the first unruly rush of attraction would fade into something more manageable, and going about my usual routine without her wouldn't feel so much like torture.

I broke off the kiss before it got too heated, remembering her grandmother was just a few steps away. Although I wasn't entirely convinced Mrs. Carpenter would notice if a meteor struck the house. It hurt my heart to think of bright, bubbly, sensitive Chloe growing up with someone like her as the closest thing to a nurturing caregiver in her life.

"Good thing I hadn't put my lipstick on yet," Chloe said, rolling her lips together. "You get enough kissing in for now? Because once I do these lips, they're off-limits until after the cocktail party."

"Shit," I muttered, kissing her again. And again. And one last time for good measure. "Okay," I said, backing off finally. "I think I'm good to go for a while."

I planned to take Chloe back to my apartment after the party, and I hoped she'd be willing to spend the night. I'd have hours and hours to kiss her to my heart's content—not to mention all manner of other things—later. If we were lucky, my roommate would be out so we wouldn't even have to be quiet.

I waited while Chloe applied her lipstick, then followed her into her bedroom while she searched through the chaos for a pair of shoes. Good to see her room was just as messy and utterly Chloe as before. In fact, it was even more cluttered, with a few new boxes of old art projects added to the chaos, as well as a brand-new work in progress spread out over the craft table.

Angie had taken Chloe and some of her portfolio over to her friend's art gallery on Monday, and he'd offered Chloe a space in his exhibition on the spot.

Now she had less than four weeks to prepare for the show and was scrambling to get some new pieces completed by then.

"Is this for the exhibition?" I asked, crossing to the table for a closer look.

"Yes," she said as she peered under the bed, still searching for her shoes.

It was similar to the wedding present she'd made for my mother. Though it wasn't very far along yet, I could make out an eye and part of a face coming into shape already. A sketchbook lay beside it, open to a drawing of a young girl that seemed to be a reference sketch for the crochet piece.

"Who's the girl?" I asked. "Is that you?"

"Mmhmm," Chloe said, coming to stand beside me. She shifted the sketchbook aside to reveal a photo underneath.

It was a school picture of her. She looked to be roughly ten years old, grinning at the camera against a plain gray backdrop. The Chloe in the photo looked like a happy, ordinary kid. The girl in the sketch was nearly identical—same pose, same smile, same everything—but she somehow looked much sadder. The drawing had a feeling of melancholy that wasn't in the photo. The same sadness was present in the crochet portrait as well. I could already see it in just that one little portion of the face.

"That was the year my mom left," Chloe said. "She moved out the weekend before picture day."

"You drew yourself the way you felt on the inside that day," I said, blown away by the skill that allowed her to capture so much emotion with such subtlety.

"I'm doing a series like that." She flipped to the next page in the sketchbook and plucked another photo out of the clutter. "This is my grandmother holding me for the first time."

In the photo, a younger version of the steely-eyed woman in the living room glared at the camera while holding newborn baby Chloe in her lap. Yet in the sketch, although she wasn't smiling, Chloe had somehow made her look joyful, proud, and even warm. She'd drawn her as the loving grandmother Chloe saw when she looked at her, the woman who'd always been there to care for her grandchildren when their parents hadn't.

"That's incredible," I said. "How do you do that?"

Chloe shrugged and flipped the page again as she reached for another photograph. "This one is my parents on their wedding day."

It was a typical wedding portrait of a young bride and groom smiling attractively at the camera. But in the sketch, despite the smiles they wore, Chloe's parents both looked utterly miserable, her mother's expression regretful and despondent while her father had a cold, uncaring look to him.

"Jesus," I breathed. This was how Chloe saw her parents. Looking at the drawing, I could feel the unhappiness of her childhood so palpably that an iron band clamped around my chest.

"Yeah, if they actually come to my show, they're probably not going to be too pleased about that one." Her voice sounded light, but there was brittleness beneath it. "Assuming I have time to finish it. We'll see."

I looked at her in surprise. "You're inviting your parents to the exhibition?"

She flipped the sketchbook closed and moved it back on top of the photos, covering them up. "They probably won't come."

Not knowing what to say, I folded her into a hug and pressed a kiss to her temple. "I'm sorry your parents are like that."

Her fingers curled in the back of my shirt as she exhaled a breath. "They've been this way my whole life, so I got used to it a long time ago."

She'd said the same thing about her skin condition, but in this case I didn't buy it. Not for a second did I believe Chloe was as used to her parents' indifference as she pretended. She wouldn't be inviting them to her art show if some part of her didn't still hold out hope that one day they'd act like the parents she wanted them to be, the parents the little girl in that sketch should have had. As long as they kept disappointing her, Chloe would keep on being hurt by it.

I leaned back to catch her eye. "You are an amazing artist, you know that? I've never known anyone as talented as you."

"That's very sweet of you to say, but is it possible you're not the most objective authority?" Her eyes shone playfully as she threw my words from last weekend back at me.

"Maybe," I agreed, brushing a trail of kisses along her jaw. "But I still stand by my statement."

"I need to find my shoes," she said, shivering as she pushed out of my arms. "We're going to be late."

I caught her hand before she could drift away, twining our fingers together. "I don't want to go."

The abject truth of the words hit me even more sharply as I said them out loud. I hated these sort of work social events where everyone was trying to outdo and impress everyone else in order to get ahead. This wasn't how I wanted to spend my time. I loved the law, but not all this other bullshit. Why couldn't I just do my work and be judged by that? The thought of all the events like this that lay in my future depressed the hell out of me.

"I know." Chloe rose up on her toes to kiss my cheek as her fingers stroked the back of my neck. "But you'll have me right beside you acting as your buffer. I'll keep the conversation going to make it easier for you."

"I hate that you have to do that."

"I don't mind." She wiped away the lipstick she'd left on my cheek and slipped out of my grasp to renew her search for her shoes.

"Which shoes are you looking for?" I asked, casting my gaze around the room.

"Black ankle boots," she said with a sigh.

I pointed to a pair of black shoes peeking out from underneath the open top of her still-not-unpacked suitcase from last weekend. "You mean those there?"

"Ha! I knew they were here somewhere."

As she bent over to retrieve them, I drank in the view of her luscious back-side with an ache of longing. My hands twitched to take hold of those gorgeous curves, but if I let myself do that we might never leave. Also, as the sound of the television reminded me, Chloe's bedroom door stood wide-open and her grand-mother was just in the living room. My explorations of Chloe's curves would have to wait until after the party.

She straightened after she'd slipped her boots on and turned to face me. "How do I look?"

I swallowed as my gaze skimmed down her body. She wore the same bright purple jumpsuit she'd worn to my mom's shower, the one that had consumed much of my attention that night. "So sexy I don't know how I'm supposed to keep my hands off you tonight."

Her cheeks flushed at the praise, but her smile remained uncertain. "But is this outfit okay? Do you think I'll fit in with everyone else there? Should I cover up my tattoos?"

In no way whatsoever would she fit in, tattoos or no. The law profession was historically one of the most conservative, right up there with banking on the stodginess scale. It wasn't that long ago that female lawyers were still required to wear skirts, heels, and pantyhose to work. Some of the older partners still looked down on women for wearing pants. They just weren't allowed to say so outright anymore.

Chloe was going to stick out tonight like a wild tropical bird in a flock of domesticated gray pigeons. Even aside from her nonconformist haircut, extra ear piercings, and tattoos, she was too bright, too beautiful, too sweet, too uniquely herself to fit in with the crowd we'd be socializing with tonight. I could tell she'd already tried to tone herself down with subtler makeup, and I absolutely fucking hated that she'd felt the need to do that. I didn't want her to change herself to fit in with my professional colleagues. I wanted more of Chloe's sparkle in my life, not less.

But she was nervous and fitting in seemed to matter to her, so I tried to put her at ease. "You're perfect exactly as you are. Everyone's going to love you tonight."

As predicted, my arrival at the party with Chloe on my arm made quite a splash. The house was exactly what you'd expect—pretentious, overly grand, and lacking real character. Just like most of the people rubbing elbows in the luxuriously furnished living room. You could smell the ambition hanging over the room like a cloud of cigarette smoke.

I'd never brought a date to one of the program's social functions before, and that fact alone attracted the curiosity of my colleagues. That I'd brought someone who didn't fit the mold of a future lawyer's wife only added to the novelty. I often found myself ignored at events like this, but tonight they swarmed like sharks as soon as they saw Chloe, plying her with phony friendliness and pointed questions. It put my hackles up and made me want to sweep her into my arms Batman-style, fire a grappling hook gun at the ceiling, and fly us both out of there to safety.

It quickly became apparent Chloe required no such saving. I should have known. She was a natural people pleaser. In no time at all, she had everyone eating out of the palm of her hand with her relentless cheerfulness and uncanny ability to turn the conversation back around on them. The truth was, she fit in a lot better than I did because she seemed to understand instinctively how to give people what they wanted.

I watched in awe as she wove her magic, charming everyone she talked to, from summer associates up to senior partners and their spouses, drawing them out with earnest questions skillfully aimed to appeal to their egos. She made it look so effortless, the way she deflected supercilious attitudes with sincere-sounding flattery, and melted cold demeanors by encouraging people to talk about themselves. She even drew me into the conversations by lobbing equally adept questions and compliments in my direction to make me look good.

It was both impressive and an incredibly supportive thing to do. And I fucking hated watching it. A vein throbbed in my neck every time Chloe laughed along with someone's condescending comment or thinly veiled derision as if she wasn't aware of their meaning. I couldn't stand to see her catering to their snobbishness by pretending to be the clueless flake they assumed her to be, making herself smaller and dimming her brilliance to fit into the box of their expectations.

Every time I raised the subject of her artistic talent, she laughed that off as well, dismissing my compliments as if her art was nothing more than a silly hobby and quickly turning the subject to someone else's accomplishments. God, it made me want to scream—at her to stop diminishing herself, at everyone else for underestimating her, and at myself for letting her do all of this to help me. I had to bite the inside of my cheek to control the impulse, knowing how unhappy it would make her if I caused a scene.

"Is everything okay?" she asked me quietly during one of the rare moments the two of us were left to ourselves.

"Everything's fine," I said, trying to muster a smile I didn't feel.

She frowned, seeing right through me. "Bran—"

Before she could finish the sentence, we were interrupted by the managing partner herself, saving me from a conversation I wasn't prepared to have right now.

I knew one thing for sure. I wasn't ever bringing Chloe to another one of these events again.

"You didn't enjoy yourself," Chloe said as we walked toward my car. She sounded disappointed, and it hurt to think she actually believed I could have enjoyed watching her do that.

I stopped on the sidewalk and pulled her into a hug. "Thank you for coming with me tonight. I appreciate how supportive you tried to be."

"But it didn't work," she said, leaning back to search my face. "I didn't help."

"You did help." I grasped her hand and towed her toward my car. "Everyone loved you, just like I knew they would."

"But you still didn't have a good time."

I didn't say anything, afraid if I tried to explain I'd say the wrong thing and hurt her feelings. This wasn't a good place to talk about it anyway, out on the street where other people from the party might overhear. Besides, I was still too upset. The experience had actually left me feeling physically ill. I needed to calm down and get my head together before I tried to talk to Chloe, or I'd screw it all up and say something I didn't mean.

We got to my car, and I held the passenger door open for her before I walked around to get behind the wheel. "I was hoping to take you back to my place," I said as I fastened my seat belt. "Are you okay with that?"

"Yes, of course. I'd love that." In contrast with her words, her voice sounded tentative in the quiet inside the car.

"Okay, good," I said, my stomach churning as I started the engine.

"Bran, please tell me what's wrong."

"Can we talk about it later?" I asked, pausing with my hand on the gearshift. "I don't want to do it in the car."

"Are you mad at me?"

I reached for her hand and brought it to my lips. "No. I'm not mad at you. Not even a little bit."

"Promise?"

I leaned across the console and stroked her cheek as I pressed a soft kiss to her lips, trying to make her believe me. "I promise."

"Okay," she said, letting out a breath. "We can talk when we get to your apartment."

We passed the drive to Hyde Park in silence. The atmosphere in the car wasn't exactly tense, but it wasn't peaceful either. I could sense Chloe's restlessness. My foul mood had made her anxious. But I appreciated that she didn't try to press me to talk in the car.

I lived in one of the big high-rise buildings near the UChicago campus. As I turned into the entrance to the parking garage, I saw her peer up at the building curiously. I reached for her hand as we walked through the garage and kept hold of it on the ride up in the elevator.

The apartment was dark and quiet when I unlocked the door. Thank God for small favors.

"Is your roommate here?" Chloe asked in a hushed voice as I flipped on the kitchen light.

"Doesn't look like it." Tori was a third-year chemistry PhD student who spent most of her time in the lab or out with her friends. We rarely crossed paths, which made her an ideal living companion.

"This is your apartment, huh?" Chloe's gaze wandered over the sparse living room, which contained only a secondhand sofa and a beat-up dining table with four mismatched chairs. "It's not what I expected."

"How so?"

"It looks like a student's apartment."

"That's because I am a student. Just because I have to wear suits to my summer job doesn't mean I can afford nice furniture."

"You're shattering my illusions," she said, shooting me a teasing smile. "I thought you were this super-accomplished grown-up with all your shit together."

I snorted at how far from the truth that was. "Hardly. You want anything to eat or drink?"

"No. I want to see your room."

"All right." I led her down the hall, past my roommate's bedroom to mine, and switched on the lamp next to my bed.

"Okay, this is much more like it," Chloe said as she spun around to take in the cramped but tidy space. "Look how neat everything is! Of course you actually make your bed. And my God, this whiteboard calendar with all the Post-it notes. It's all so you."

"Glad I can fulfill your expectations."

She swiveled to face me, her smile fading as she studied my face. "Are you ready to tell me why you didn't have a good time tonight?"

I'd been waiting all week to get Chloe alone. Now that I finally had her to myself, the last thing I wanted to do was talk about that fucking cocktail party. But I knew we had to.

"Did *you* have a good time?" I asked her after I'd shut the bedroom door.

"Yes."

"I hope to God that's not true," I bit out.

She drew back in bewilderment. "I don't understand. I thought tonight went great."

"Oh, it did," I agreed. "It couldn't possibly have gone more smoothly. You had everyone charmed."

"So then what's wrong?"

"You can't expect me to believe you actually *liked* talking to all those condescending assholes."

"They weren't that bad. Most of them were perfectly nice."

"They weren't nice, Chloe." My voice shook as I tried not to shout my frustration at her. "They were looking down their noses at you. Don't pretend you didn't notice. I sure as fuck did."

"Fine. Some of them were awful, okay? Is that what you want me to say? Of course I noticed. I'm not stupid."

"Then why were you acting clueless and letting them think you were?"

"To get along! Because when people pull that shit, they're trying to provoke a reaction to make themselves feel even more superior. I'd rather pretend not to notice than give them the satisfaction of knowing it bothers me."

"That's just letting them get away with treating you like shit."

She threw her hands in the air. "They're your professional colleagues, Bran. What did you want me to do? Make a scene? Of course I wasn't going to do that. I didn't notice you calling them out either, no matter how upset you might have been."

My back teeth snapped together with a click. She was right, I hadn't stood up for her. Getting into an argument at a social event in a senior partner's home would have put a swift end to my future at McCurdy Becker. The most I'd felt able to offer in Chloe's defense were a few surly glares and cold silences. That was the real reason I was so angry. Because I'd felt helpless to protect her. I'd just stood there like a useless lump and watched it happen. "I'm sorry I didn't defend you. I should have."

"No you shouldn't have, and I'm glad you didn't. You know how I feel about conflict. No one did anything tonight that was worth jeopardizing your career over. It was just petty, passive-aggressive power games. The private schools I went to were full of that shit. I figured out a long time ago that if I'm aggressively nice enough to someone who's not being nice to me, nine times out of ten they'll start to feel bad about acting like a dick and stop doing it."

"You've weaponized niceness," I said, grudgingly impressed.

She ducked her head. "I just wanted to make them like me, so they'd like you. Because it's important for your career. I was trying to help you."

Something pulled tight around my heart. I stepped closer, taking hold of her shoulders as I kissed her forehead. "I don't ever want you to help me by pretending to be anything less than you are. I don't want you to feel you have to kiss anyone's ass for my sake or go places where you're miserable just to be with me."

"But I wanted to be there for you. I just wanted to prove I can fit into your life."

"You already do." I tipped her chin up so she'd give me her eyes. "You don't have to change yourself or pretend to be something you're not to fit into my life. I like you—the real you—exactly the way you are. I can't fucking stand most of those people. Why would I want you to fit in with them?"

"*You* have to."

"That's my problem. I don't want that for you."

She opened her mouth, then hesitated, her teeth worrying at her lower lip. "Are you sure this is really what you want for *you*?" she asked finally.

I reared back. "Of course I am."

"If it makes you this miserable, why would you want to spend the rest of your life doing it? Is it really worth it?"

I scrubbed my hands over my face, hating this conversation and everything that had precipitated it. She was asking me to justify all the life choices that had led me here. This wasn't how I wanted to spend the precious time we had together tonight.

"I'm sorry." Chloe's arms slipped around my neck. She tucked her head under my chin, her breasts pressing against my chest as she sighed. "I shouldn't have said that. I didn't mean to upset you."

"You didn't." I held her so tight my arms trembled. "Everything else upsets me. You make it bearable."

Her lips caressed my neck, and she angled her face up, seeking my mouth. I nuzzled her lips before slipping my tongue between them to taste her sweetness. When the kiss ended, we stayed clasped together, our lips still touching as we breathed the same air.

"I need you," I whispered as my hands roamed over her body, petting and stroking her, feeling my tension melt away as she did the same to me. "All I've wanted to do all week is hold you."

Before Chloe came along, I never realized how much I needed to be touched. I hadn't had any idea my life had been lacking something so essential all this time. Her touch eased something deep inside me. Now that I'd experienced it, I craved that physical connection all the time. It was a constant ache that plagued me every minute we weren't together.

She pressed a heartbreakingly tender kiss to my cheek. "You can have as much of me as you want."

"I want all of you." I took a breath. "It hurts how much I want you."

"I'm all yours."

My hands squeezed the luscious curves of her ass, jerking her against me as our mouths crashed together. She tugged my shirt out of my waistband, hitching it up to smooth her hands up over my stomach. Seized by new urgency, I let go of her to yank at my tie. While I unbuttoned my shirt, she went to work on my belt. When we'd finished getting rid of my clothes, she helped me peel her jumpsuit off.

We fell onto the bed, my fingers stroking her silky skin while I feasted on her mouth. As soon as I had the condom on, she drew me into the cradle of her thighs. Shivering heat licked down my spine as my cock slid through the evidence of her slick desire.

She was so soft and warm and giving. I loved the way she reacted when I touched her, the way she touched me back, the little sounds she made. I wanted to devour every one of her lovely little whimpers.

"Mine," I growled as I sank into her. So hot, so slick. Squeezing me so fucking hard.

"Yes," she breathed, lifting her lips to take me deeper. "And you're mine."

I rocked against her, sliding in and out of her welcoming body. Making love to her was like coming home. It healed me. Made me whole again.

Her breath hitched when I hit a certain spot inside her, so I did it again, watching her face go slack with pleasure. Over and over, I thrust into her, giving her more until she was straining against me and pleading. My mouth clamped over the stiff peak of her nipple and I sucked it between my teeth.

Chloe cried out, her fingernails digging into my shoulders, and I fell with her, dropping my head between her breasts as I came so hard the only thought I could hold on to was her name.

———————

I woke sometime in the middle of the night, jerking out of the throes of a stress dream. As consciousness flooded in, the details of the dream disappeared like wisps of smoke, leaving behind only a black, oily residue of fear, a racing heart, and a sheen of sweat on my clammy skin.

In the semidarkness I could just make out Chloe beside me, her arms and legs flung wide, her golden hair spread out around her head. I reached out, needing to make sure she was real, that this wasn't still part of a dream.

My fingers brushed against her warm skin, and the tightness in my chest loosened, allowing me to draw a deep breath. Emotion clogged my throat, an overwhelming sense of gratitude to have her here.

She let out a soft snore and turned toward me, as if seeking me out in her sleep. Rolling onto my side, I banded my arm around her waist and pulled her up against me, nestling her back against my front. She relaxed, going slack again with a contented sigh.

I held her close, breathing in the comforting scent of her, letting the warmth of her skin seep into mine. It felt so good to hold her in my arms. I liked having her here in my apartment, in my bed, in my space. The two of us together just worked. It was the one thing in my life that felt right. A sense of peace washed over me, and I fell back asleep before I knew it.

CHAPTER TWENTY-EIGHT

BRAN

"Move it, buddy, or get out of the way."

Snapping out of my daze, I sprang forward to join the herd of pedestrians that had surged past me into the crosswalk. I had a lot on my mind today, but the downtown streets were no place for absentmindedness unless I cared to get mowed down by a bike messenger or delivery van. I pulled my head out of my ass and paid better attention to my surroundings as I walked the last two blocks to my dad's favorite restaurant near the hospital where he used to work.

"Reservation for Botstein," I told the maître d' as I smoothed my windblown tie and hair back into place. "Table for two."

"Yes, sir. Dr. Botstein has already arrived. This way, please."

Although I was five minutes late, I hadn't expected my dad to be here yet. Like me, he almost always ran late. Not because of ADHD, but because he was a busy renowned physician and researcher whose time was in high demand. Even after retiring from his full-time position at Chicago General Hospital, between serving on the boards of several nonprofits, all the volunteer work he did, and the active social life he'd embraced since the divorce, he was as occupied as ever.

My dad stood and greeted me with a brisk hug. Because of our crowded schedules, we only spoke on the phone every few weeks and saw each other in person even less than that. Truthfully, I didn't make as much of an effort with him as I did with Mom. The long, irregular hours his profession had demanded made him an inconstant presence in my life when I was growing up. I had the sense he didn't miss seeing me as much as Mom did.

I was the one who'd suggested we meet for lunch today because I needed his advice about something I'd been wrestling with. The question Chloe had posed after the cocktail party two weeks ago had stuck with me like a splinter, worming its way deeper into my head.

Was my current career path the right one for me? Did I really want to spend the rest of my life working at a firm like McCurdy Becker?

I used to think so. I'd put a lot of forethought into the choices I'd made, but now that I'd had a taste of the Big Law life, I wasn't so certain anymore.

There were other ways to put a law degree to use than going to work for a large firm. There were other types of private practice settings with vastly different cultures depending on their size and specialty. Or I could go to work for the government, join an in-house corporate legal department, or try to find employment at a nonprofit organization. Thinking back on my law school experiences, the ones I'd found most rewarding had all involved public interest work of some type. Maybe that was a sign I needed to reevaluate my goals.

But I wasn't sure I could trust my gut. Was I looking for an easy way out rather than rising to meet a challenge? Were my feelings for Chloe clouding my judgment and causing me to doubt myself? I already knew what my mom would say—that I should give myself a break and do whatever made me happiest. What I needed was a gut check from my dad, who could be relied upon to give me his candid opinion without trying to coddle me.

While I deliberated over the menu, Dad told me all about the latest volunteer endeavors that had been keeping him busy. I listened with only half an ear, waiting for an opportune moment to raise the subject on my mind.

"How was the wedding?" he asked after the server had departed with our lunch orders.

"It was nice," I said cautiously, unsure how much I should say. The subject of my mom and her post-divorce life was an awkward one to navigate with Dad.

Growing up, I'd never spent that much one-on-one time with him. It was only after my parents' divorce that I appreciated how much heavy lifting Mom had done to facilitate my relationship with Dad. Without her around as a buffer, I found interactions with him more awkward. He didn't always seem to know how to relate to me. Sometimes he'd lecture me like I was still a teenager, and at other times he'd overshare details of his personal life I'd prefer not to know.

The worst was when he tried to talk to me about Mom or his feelings about her. He seemed to want me to take his side, which left me caught between my loyalties to both of them. I preferred not to discuss Mom with him if I could avoid it.

"So she really went through with it." Dad shook his head as if he found it hard to believe.

"Did you think she wouldn't?" I asked, surprised by his surprise. Mom was one of the most reliable people I knew, hardly a runaway bride candidate.

"I honestly don't have any idea what's going through your mother's head these days. It's hard to understand what she sees in this guy she's with now. He didn't even finish college. Did you know that?"

I fiddled with my silverware, lining the fork up with my knife so they were parallel. "He's been taking classes to finish his degree. I think he's almost done."

"It's all so out of character," Dad went on as if I hadn't spoken. "Your mother never used to be the type to choose brawn over brains. To tell you the truth, I feel a little guilty. I can't help thinking this whole thing is a reaction against me. It's like she's trying to get back at me or show me up. I don't know." He gave a troubled shake of his head, appearing mystified. "Maybe she's going through some sort of female midlife crisis. Some women experience personality changes with menopause, and she took up with this new boyfriend right after her hysterectomy last year. I'd hate to think he's been taking advantage of her vulnerability and low self-esteem."

"Mike's a decent guy," I said stiffly. "He treats Mom well." Listening to my father talk about Mike made me uncomfortably aware of the similar sentiments I'd held until recently. It was possible I'd let my father's sour grapes influence my opinion of Mike more than I'd realized.

"Well I hope to hell he does," Dad grumbled. "Did you know this is his third marriage? He's already been divorced twice. Absolutely boggling, but I suppose your mother's allowed to make her own choices." It sounded like he didn't really think she should be, which was a bit rich considering Dad had been the one to initiate the divorce and had done his fair share of dating since. He seemed to forget that sometimes in his brooding over the fact that Mom had moved on, as if he'd expected her to sit around pining for him.

"Are you still seeing Jennifer?" I asked, bringing up his latest girlfriend in the hopes he'd take the hint.

"That's been over for a while now," Dad said, shaking his head sadly.

"I'm sorry to hear that." I'd noticed he seemed happier when he had a girlfriend, but he'd never stuck it out with any of them for more than a few months.

"What about you?" he asked, eyeing me over his water glass. "Have you managed to do any dating yet?"

Since my breakup with Marisa, Dad had been pushing me to put myself back out there. He was the one who'd suggested I make an effort to go on some low-risk trial dates now, so my dating skills wouldn't be so rusty later when I needed them. It had seemed like sound advice coming from someone who'd recently had to reenter the dating market after twenty-five years of marriage.

"Actually, yes. I've been seeing someone for a few weeks." I hesitated. "Since the wedding, in fact."

"Really?" Dad's carefully blank expression gave away nothing.

"Her name's Chloe." I hesitated again. "She works in Mom's store."

I'd expected some kind of reaction to that information, but he betrayed none. "How old is she?"

"The same age as me."

"Where did she go to college?" he asked, reaching for his water glass.

"University of Michigan. She studied art."

Dad set his water down and turned it in the ring of condensation on the table-cloth. "I see."

"She's a textile artist," I said. "A brilliant one."

"And she works in your mom's store." His tone remained neutral, but the judgment still came through loud and clear.

"She's about to have her first art show at a gallery here. It's a huge opportunity for her."

"Well." Dad sat back in his chair and smiled. "She certainly sounds like an interesting young woman. I'm glad to see you finally getting back on the horse again. Now's the time in your life when you should be casting a wide net and trying out different kinds of fish to see what's out there. Dating around will help you figure out what you want before you're ready to settle down with a serious partner."

"She's not a fish," I said, my voice tight.

"No, of course not." He offered me a conciliatory smile. "It's only a metaphor, obviously."

"The thing is, I think I might be serious about her." I wasn't yet ready to call what I felt for Chloe *love*, but it certainly felt like things were headed that way.

"Is that right?" Dad regarded me for a moment. "That seems a little fast, don't you think?"

I responded with an uneasy shrug, unwilling to admit I'd had the same thought myself.

"You've known this girl for what? Three weeks? How much time have you actually been able to spend together? It can't be all that much with the hours you've been putting in at your summer internship."

"We've been doing a lot of texting and talking on the phone." It didn't make for a very compelling argument when I said it out loud. But it didn't matter what my dad thought. I knew how I felt about Chloe. The connection between us was real, even if we hadn't been able to see much of each other. She'd been just as busy as me the last two weeks, prepping for her show. What we had was working. Mostly.

Dad remained silent as the server appeared to set our food in front of us. Grilled tuna salad for me and clam chowder with half a club sandwich for my dad.

After the server departed, my dad picked up his spoon and slowly stirred his soup. "You know, Brandon, you don't have to throw yourself into a serious, years-long commitment with every girl you happen to like. It's okay to keep things casual and just have a good time together. Not every relationship is meant to last."

My knife clattered loudly against my plate as I cut up the lettuce in my salad. "I'm aware of that."

He glanced up at me. "Didn't you say you couldn't afford the distraction of a serious girlfriend while you were still in law school?"

"Yes." I stabbed a piece of tuna with my fork. "I didn't plan on meeting Chloe or feeling this way about her. Sometimes things happen when we're not looking for them."

"They certainly do," my dad agreed with a rueful grimace. "I'm just concerned you're taking on more than you can handle. It's easy to get swept up in the excitement of a new infatuation and lose sight of what's really important."

I cleared my throat as his warning resonated a little too much for comfort. "There's actually something else I wanted to talk to you about today."

"What's that?" he asked, blowing on a spoonful of chowder.

"Recently I've been having second thoughts about going to work for a large law firm after graduation."

Once again, my dad betrayed no visible reaction. "Why's that?"

"The internship with McCurdy Becker isn't going how I thought it would."

He gave the faintest of nods. "Are you struggling to keep up?"

"No more than usual." Ironically, I'd become more adept at navigating the social aspects over the last few weeks, thanks in no small part to Chloe's influence. Her performance at the cocktail party had opened the door for improved relationships with my peers and some of the higher-ups at the firm. I'd endeavored to suppress my lingering ill feelings and adjusted my approach to social interactions based on her advice and example. But the better I got at pretending to enjoy socializing with my summer associate peers, the more I disliked doing it and the more I loathed the idea of having them as my permanent coworkers.

"Is it the work they've got you doing that you're not enjoying?" Dad asked, dabbing at his mouth with his napkin.

"Partially. The actual legal work is boring but fine. It's more the culture I'm starting to think isn't a good fit. The competitiveness, but also how performative it is. There's more focus on billable hours and stroking egos than the quality of work you're producing."

"Isn't that the reality of practicing law? It's what you signed up for."

The note of disapproval I detected in his voice struck a familiar chord. It was the same disapproval I'd felt when I told him I wanted to be a lawyer rather than a doctor. He'd not-so-secretly wanted me to follow in his footsteps and had never quite gotten over the disappointment.

Nevertheless, Dad had accepted and supported my choice. He'd always pushed me to strive for more, to go the extra mile, to never let up or settle for the path of least resistance. I was as grateful for the pressure he put on me as I was for my mom's encouragement and support. I never would have realized so much of my potential without my dad's high expectations driving me to work harder.

"In a large firm, yes," I said. "They all tend to be like that to some extent. That's why I'm questioning if it's right for me. I've been thinking I might like to go into public interest law instead of private practice. Maybe work for a nonprofit advocacy organization that's doing real good in the world."

"That's a big one-eighty," Dad said with a look of surprise. "Especially this late in the game."

"It's not completely out of left field. I volunteered for the ACLU for years before I got too busy, and I did a civil advocacy clinic my first year that I loved. Plus my internship last summer with the city family services department. That's all relevant experience. The little bit of pro bono work they've let me do at the firm this summer has been the best part of the whole program, and it's got me thinking maybe that's what I was meant to be doing."

Dad's eyes narrowed as he considered me for a long moment. "I don't suppose this artist you're dating has anything to do with your sudden career change of heart?"

"No." It wasn't exactly a lie. She might have planted the initial seed, but that was all. It wasn't what Dad was obviously thinking—that I'd taken up with a free-spirited do-gooder who'd pressured me into eschewing the evil corporate money machine to make the world a better place. "I haven't talked to her about any of this. She's been too busy getting ready for her show the past few weeks."

He nodded, seeming mollified. "Isn't it a little late in your law school career for this kind of swerve? Everything you've done up to now has been about getting *this* internship so you'll have the security of walking into a job after graduation. Are you afraid they won't make you an offer in September? Is that what this is about?"

"I don't know if they will or not," I admitted, although it wasn't about that. "But if they do, I don't know if I want it."

"You'd actually turn down a guaranteed job you've had your sights set on for two years so instead you can...do what? Start over from scratch at the last minute? You'd rather scramble to find a job at some underfunded organization that can't even afford office supplies than capitalize on the opportunity you've already got in front of you?"

Was that it? Would I really turn down a guaranteed job if McCurdy Becker offered me one? Some of my law school cohort would be starting their third year with a postgraduation job offer in hand, and I'd always planned to be one of them. Did I seriously want to trade that security for the uncertainty of a months-long job search in a field of law I didn't have as much relevant experience in?

I sighed and rubbed my forehead. "I don't know what to do, Dad. All I know is McCurdy Becker doesn't feel like the right place for me."

"Are you sure this isn't simply a case of cold feet? Now that you're close to achieving your goal, it's common to experience second thoughts. I know this internship has been challenging, but it's good to do things that take you out of your comfort zone. That doesn't mean you can't handle it, even if it takes some adjustment. Don't quit the marathon ten paces from the finish line, son."

"It's not about this marathon so much as the one I'd be automatically signing up for after it," I said. "I'm not sure I want to stay in this kind of race forever." I'd been driving myself so hard for so long, I couldn't even remember what it felt like to stop and rest. Those three days at Mom's wedding and the few stolen moments I'd had with Chloe since were the only times I hadn't felt like I was being slowly crushed to death.

My father's disappointment etched the lines on his face deeper. "You've got great things in you, Brandon. I'd hate to see you settle for less than you deserve because you don't believe in yourself."

"So you think I should stick with it?" I already knew he did. Hadn't I known all along what he was going to tell me? I'd just needed to hear him say it. That was really why I'd come to Dad, wasn't it? Because I wanted him to keep me on track like he always did.

"I think you knew what you were doing when you chose this path, and you should see it through."

I nodded grimly as I internalized his answer, making my peace with it. "Okay."

"If it's really not for you, no one says you have to stay there forever. You'll have the whole rest of your career to change jobs. At least give this one a chance before you give up on it. Maybe just try it for a year, pay down your loans some, and if you still feel the same, then you can start looking for something else. Won't it be easier to find a job with a year of experience on your résumé?"

What he was saying made good, solid sense. I didn't have to change course right this minute. That was fear and weakness trying to turn me into a quitter, making me want to give up when things got hard. That wasn't me. I was stronger than that. Sticking it out was the smart move. Then I could take my time finding something else with the security of a paycheck and a good job to help smooth my way.

"Look, you're stressed," Dad said more gently. "I can see that. You know how you get when you're overwhelmed. You've had a lot going on with this internship, not to mention the emotional upheaval of your mother's wedding, and now this new girlfriend. You're clearly stretched too thin right now. You're probably right that something's got to give." His gaze held me fast. "I think deep down you know what that something has to be, even if you don't want to admit it."

Unfortunately, I did. Dad was right, as usual.

CHAPTER TWENTY-NINE

CHLOE

Three days. That was how long I had left to finish my last two projects for the exhibition. Seventy-two hours. Less than that really, since they'd need to be mounted before the opening night party, and I should probably leave myself some time to, you know, actually shower and wash my hair.

Speaking of which—*eesh*—when was the last time I'd done that anyway? I was getting a bit whiffy.

I'd been working nonstop to finish the three new projects I'd started. My wrists ached, my fingers were cramping, and my eyes were tired. I'd been living on Advil, nut-free granola bars, and too little sleep for the last two weeks. The childhood self-portrait was all done, and the portrait of my grandmother was nearly there. The one of my parents had a ways to go, however. Two faces meant twice as much work, plus there was all the detail required for my mother's wedding dress. It was possible I'd been a tad overambitious, but at this point the programs were printed and space in the gallery set aside for all three pieces. I had to finish.

When my phone buzzed, I scrambled for it, glad for any excuse to take a break but also really hoping it was Bran. He'd been at a retreat all weekend, so I hadn't been able to see him or even talk to him. He'd barely even texted, which probably meant they'd kept him busy with a full schedule of outdoorsy bonding activities.

We hadn't seen each other in almost two weeks. He'd been working extra-long hours to finish a special project for one of the partners before the retreat this weekend. But it was fine. I'd been equally busy getting ready for my show, so it wasn't like I'd had free time to spend with him either.

I missed him though. So much it made my chest feel hollow, like some of my insides were missing. How could he already feel like such an essential part of me? I prided myself on my self-reliance and not being clingy. But God, how I wanted to cling to Bran and never let him go.

To my immense disappointment, it wasn't Bran calling. It was my father.

I'd emailed both my parents an invitation to the opening night party. Mom had replied back promptly with the usual excuses and apologies, just as I'd expected she would. Dad hadn't responded, which was also typical. I'd given him a week, then texted on Friday to ask if he'd seen my email. He was finally getting back to me on Sunday night, no doubt to tell me he couldn't make it.

Bracing myself, I accepted the call and held the phone to my ear. "Hi, Dad."

"Hi, sweetheart, how are you?" The sound of his brisk, deep voice never failed to make me feel small and brittle. He always sounded impatient, rushed, preoccupied. It seemed like he only ever called when he was about to do something else—walk into a meeting, get on a plane, sit down to dinner—that always cut the conversation short. Forever reminding me I was something to be squeezed in between other things that were more important to him.

"I'm good," I said, rolling the stiffness out of my shoulders. "Great, actually. Busy getting ready for my art show."

"That's what I'm calling about. I saw your email. Sounds like you found someplace to sell your little art projects, is that it?"

My back teeth ground together as I breathed in through my nose. "I'm one of the featured artists in a brand-new exhibition at an established gallery in the River North art district."

"Really? Well, congratulations. At least you're doing something with your college degree finally."

He was trying to be encouraging, I told myself. Although he'd never come right out and said it, it had always been obvious he didn't take my artistic pursuits seriously. I couldn't even blame him since I hadn't exactly been pursuing them seriously up to now.

"Like it said in the invite, there's an opening night party this Wednesday, if you'd like to come and see for yourself." I tried not to sound too hopeful. Experience had taught me to expect disappointment when it came to my dad.

"I've got a lot going on this week, Chloe. I'm in the middle of a trial right now."

"Oh well," I said. "Okay."

"You said it was Wednesday? I could probably swing by for a little while. I wouldn't mind seeing this gallery for myself. I'm sure whatever exhibition you've gotten into will be interesting."

Slightly insulting, but still better than I'd expected. He hadn't flat out said no.

"It's on my calendar. I'll try to make it," he said.

"That'd be great, if you could."

"It's a big night for you. I'll do my best."

"Thanks, Dad."

"I have to get back to trial prep now. Good talking to you."

"Yeah."

"Bye, sweetheart. See you Wednesday."

"Bye." I set the phone down and rubbed my breastbone. That had been unexpected. I didn't usually make it as far as Dad's calendar. He might actually come. Although I knew better than to let myself feel too optimistic. Still, even a chance was better than nothing.

I picked up my phone again and checked my text chain with Bran. As if a new message could have come in without my seeing it somehow. I thumbed through our most recent texts, smiling at all his regular check-ins reminding me he was thinking of me and missing me like I missed him.

But did he miss me *as much* as I missed him? That I couldn't say. I should probably hope not, for his sake, knowing how hard he already found it to focus on work.

Speaking of which, I needed to get back to mine. I couldn't afford to sit here all night pining over him. Swallowing the longing in my chest, I set my phone down and picked up my crochet needle.

An hour later my phone buzzed again. This time it actually was Bran.

My heart tripped against my ribs as I answered it. "Hey, handsome. Are you back?"

"I just got home a minute ago."

It felt good to know he'd called almost as soon as he'd walked in the door. That had to be a good sign, right? "How was Lake Geneva?"

From the sound of his sigh, I could picture the beleaguered scowl on his face.

"The cabin smelled like mildew, my cabinmate snored, and I've got a rash on my arm that I'm hoping is stress hives and not poison ivy."

"That fun, huh?"

"I missed you like crazy. How was your weekend?"

"Fine except for the part where I missed you like crazy too."

"How are the new pieces coming along?"

"Okay," I said. "I'm only panicking a little."

"You'll get it done." He sounded so confident. At least one of us was.

"Oh hey, guess what? My dad called and says he might actually come to the show."

"Really?" Bran said. "Wow."

"Wow is right. I mean, I'm still not holding my breath or anything." I'd learned my lesson about that a long time ago.

"But you'd like to have him there, wouldn't you?"

"I guess I would." I gave a little sigh. "It'd be nice if he showed up for me for once."

"Chloe…" Bran's voice sounded pained. Ominously so. "I have to tell you something."

A weight dropped through my stomach. I could already sense where this was going. "Okay."

"The managing partner is taking all the summer associates out to dinner." He paused. "On Wednesday."

Shit, shit, shit.

Of course. The night of my show. It was too much to hope that Bran would be free when I wanted him to be. I should have seen this coming. Why hadn't I?

I squeezed my eyes shut. "The managing partner, she's the big cheese, right? You can't miss that."

"I'm so sorry."

Fuck, my throat hurt. I wanted to cry, but I wasn't going to. *Hell no.* I was keeping my shit together. The last thing I wanted to do was make Bran feel bad for something he couldn't help. I'd always known what the score was.

"You don't need to be sorry," I said. "I understand. You have to go."

"I feel terrible. I'm letting you down."

I almost lost it at the sorrow in his voice. I couldn't stand to have him feeling sorry for me. What good would that do? Making him feel guilty would only push him farther away.

Never mind that I was scared out of my mind about this exhibition. Or that

I'd only said yes to the whole thing because Bran had pressured me to do it. Knowing he'd be there with me had been the only thing keeping my panic levels manageable.

Too bad.

I was on my own. Like always. I should have known better than to think otherwise. He'd told me up front he couldn't commit. I didn't have any right to expect him to make me a priority now.

"No, you're not letting me down," I said, forcing lightness into my voice to hide how much I hurt. For the first time, I was grateful he was on the other side of the city so he couldn't see my face. "It's fine. Really. It's not like you're required to come to my opening."

"I wanted to be there. You have no idea how much. It kills me to miss it."

"Sure, I know. But you've got other things you need to do. You don't have to feel bad about it. That's what we agreed—no obligations or expectations, remember? We're just hanging out. Keeping things casual with no pressure. So don't worry about me. I'll be fine."

The long silence on his end of the line scraped over my skin. "Are you really okay?" he asked. "Tell me the truth."

My heart pounded as I gripped the phone, squeezing hard enough to make my fingers hurt. "Of course I am. I'll have other people there on Wednesday if I need anything. But honestly, I'll probably be so busy I wouldn't be able to talk to you much anyway. So go to your dinner and impress the hell out of that managing partner for me, okay?"

"Okay." He didn't sound like he was buying it. In the silence, I heard him take a breath.

"I should probably get back to work," I rushed on before he could say whatever he'd been about to say. "I can't afford to take a long break, and you should get some sleep."

"Chloe," he said, so softly my heart nearly broke open.

"It was nice to hear your voice." I hugged myself around my middle. "I'll text you tomorrow, all right?"

"Yeah."

"Good night." I disconnected before he could hear me sob.

CHAPTER THIRTY

BRAN

"Hey!" I heard Donal call out as I passed by the open door of his glass-walled office. "Bran!"

Halting my journey back to my cubicle, I did an about-face to see what he wanted. He waved at me through the glass, beckoning me inside.

As I passed by her desk, I smiled at his legal secretary, who rolled her eyes and shouted, "You're going to be late!"

"I know," Donal shouted back as I came to a stop in his doorway. "What are you still doing here?" he asked me as he stuffed things into his briefcase. "I thought you'd be at the gallery by now. Didn't Chloe's opening start at six?"

I shoved my hands deep in my pockets, swallowing around the knot of guilt that had been lodged in my throat for the last three days. Ever since I'd told Chloe I couldn't make it tonight.

We hadn't talked since. She'd been texting me as usual, pretending everything was fine, but whenever I tried to call I got her voicemail. She always texted me back with a perfectly reasonable excuse. One time she was sleeping. Another she hadn't noticed her phone's battery had died. Last night she'd said she didn't have time to stop working long enough to talk. But I was pretty sure she'd been avoiding my calls on purpose. If she answered the phone and talked to me, I'd be able to hear how upset she was. She wouldn't be able to hide it like she could over text.

I'd heard it the last time we talked, the quaver of hurt in her voice. I'd done that. To her. To bright, bubbly, sensitive Chloe. I'd crushed her, and she didn't want me to know because she was still trying to take care of me even though I'd disappointed her like every other unmitigated asshole in her life.

"I'm not going," I said. "Angela Navarro is taking all the summer associates to Maple & Ash tonight."

Donal stopped his harried shuffle through a stack of files and looked up at me. "You're skipping the opening of Chloe's art show?"

"I don't have a choice. It's not like I can skip dinner with the managing partner."

"You always have a choice," he said.

"Oh yeah? You wanna explain that to Angela Navarro for me?" I shot back more sharply than I should have. Donal might be a friend of my mom's, but he was also a senior partner here who'd gone out of his way to help me more than once. "Sorry," I muttered, wincing. "I'm just…" *Defensive, bitter, and feeling like a piece of shit for disappointing my girlfriend.*

"Debra!" Donal shouted, looking past me.

"Yes?" His secretary materialized at my elbow like a ninja, startling the hell out of me.

"Can you please text Tess for me and let her know I'm running late?" Donal asked.

"I already did," she told him.

"Thank you." He pressed his palms together in front of his chest. "You can go home now. Have a good night."

Debra aimed a warning look at me as she turned to go. "Don't let him stay more than five minutes."

"Close the door and sit," Donal told me, inclining his head at the chair across from his desk.

I did as ordered, feeling as if I'd just been called to the principal's office.

Donal sank into his desk chair and gave me a long look. "I was under the impression tonight was a big deal for Chloe. Like a once-in-a-lifetime kind of big deal."

"It is," I muttered at the floor, feeling shittier by the second.

"But you're missing it." The censure in his tone didn't pull any punches. It went straight for my jugular, which was pretty unfucking fair, coming from him.

"You're the one who told me how important the social aspects of the program are if I want to get an offer at the end of the summer. What am I supposed to do? Blow off dinner with Navarro? You really think she'll understand if I tell her I have to go to a thing for my girlfriend instead?"

Donal cocked his head to the side. "Maybe."

"Really?"

"Hell, I don't know." He let out a tired sigh and rubbed his hands over his face. "Maybe not."

"I can't afford to take that risk if I want to work here."

He leaned back in his chair, studying me as he chewed on the inside of his cheek. "How serious are your feelings for Chloe?" When I hesitated, he held up his hands. "It's not any of my business, I know. Humor me anyway."

I hedged. "It's kind of hard to have a serious relationship in law school."

His mouth twisted wryly. "Oh believe me, I know. But that's not an answer to my question. Is Chloe someone you think you might want in your life long-term?"

"I'm not sure yet." It was both the truth and a bald-faced lie. I absolutely wanted Chloe in my life forever. I just wasn't convinced it was a good idea—or a realistic one.

I'd almost deluded myself into thinking I could make it work, but talking to my dad had knocked some sense back into me. I couldn't throw away everything I'd worked for just so I could spend more time with my girlfriend.

But this no-obligations arrangement I had with Chloe wasn't fair to her. What kind of relationship was that? Where she wasn't allowed to expect anything from me and couldn't ever count on me to come through for her? She deserved a hell of a lot better, but I couldn't give it to her. The knowledge had become a weight on my chest, and I didn't know what to do about it. I was too selfish to let her go, but I cared about her too much to keep hurting her like I had tonight. I was at an impasse.

The sympathetic look Donal gave me only made the anvil on my chest feel heavier. "I recommended you for this internship as a favor to your mom. But I offered to mentor you because I like you, Bran. The better I've gotten to know you, the more I see myself in you."

"Really?" I'd always thought of Donal as an older, wiser, less insufferable version of my brother Zach. They had similarly easygoing personalities and charm to spare. Nothing at all like me, in other words.

"Yeah," Donal said, flashing exactly the kind of grin that made me think of Zach. "Maybe not so much on the surface. I'm talking about what's underneath —the parts of myself I don't usually let people see."

I looked at him more closely, trying to suss out what he meant by that.

He cleared his throat as his smile faded. "That's why it's hard for me to see you making the same mistakes I did."

"What do you mean? What mistakes?" As far as I could tell, Donal had it all. The perfect career. The perfect relationship. The perfect life. Not to mention he was one of a handful of people here I genuinely liked. He was everything I aspired to be one day, and he gave me hope I could make as good a life for myself at McCurdy Becker as he had.

His gaze skated away from me, drifting to a picture frame on his desk. "You know I'm divorced, right?"

I nodded. My mom had been friends with Donal since they were kids, so I knew a lot about his personal life through her, probably more than most of his colleagues knew. I knew he and his current girlfriend Tess had briefly been a couple back in high school. And I knew the two of them had gone their separate ways after Tess had gotten pregnant and given the baby up for adoption. Donal had married someone else, had a couple of kids, and gotten divorced around the same time my parents had. Then last year, the daughter Tess and Donal had given up for adoption tracked them down. Getting to know her had brought the two of them back together, and they'd started dating again.

But I wasn't sure what his divorce had to do with anything. Mom hadn't told me much about that particular chapter of Donal's life.

"I was in my third year of law school when I met Wendy," he said, leaning back in his chair. "About the same age as you and Chloe, as a matter of fact. We got married when I was a newly minted first-year associate fresh off the assembly line. You think law school's hard? Wait'll you're working full-time while studying for the bar. Or working sixty-hour weeks to meet your billable hours requirement and juggling projects for three different partners with the same deadline. The challenges of managing difficult clients and appeasing supervising associates out to make you miserable, not to mention keeping on top of changing case law and statutes, will eat up your whole life. And just staying on top of everything isn't enough. You have to look like a superstar if you want to stay ahead of everyone else you'll be competing with on the partner track."

None of this came as a shock to me. I'd heard it all before. It was the future I'd knowingly chosen for myself. But listening to Donal describe it now made my throat feel like it was full of sand.

"I thought it'd get easier after the first few years, once I'd proved myself." He leveled me with a look. "But the reality is it doesn't ever let up. The farther ahead you get, the higher the expectations are, and the bigger the price of failure becomes."

"Why are you telling me this?" I asked, trying to swallow around a choking sensation. "Because you don't think I can handle it?"

"No, not at all. I know you can handle it. You've already proven that as far as I'm concerned." He paused. "But I get the feeling you're not happy here. Am I wrong?"

I pressed my lips together and stared down at the floor, not wanting to lie to him but unwilling to admit the truth.

"That's not a criticism," Donal said. "This isn't about what you can or can't do. It's about what you *should* do. What kind of life you want to have. I'm talking to you as a friend right now and not a partner at this firm, okay?"

"Okay," I said, looking up at him again.

Donal had one of those faces that always seemed to be either smiling or on the verge of smiling, but an uncharacteristic grimness shadowed the lines carved around his eyes. "When I was your age, I made the same choices you're making right now. I didn't just live for work, I ate, slept, and breathed it because it was what my dad had done, so I thought it was what I was supposed to do. I put so much of myself into this job there was nothing left over for my wife and kids. I was so focused on getting ahead and being the best that I failed the people I loved the most in this world." Regret twisted his expression as his gaze went to the picture on his desk again. "I didn't even realize how much I was hurting them until it was too late. I let them down over and over again by choosing my job over being there for them because it was what I had to do to get here"—he cast a contemptuous glance around his spacious executive office—"and it got me everything I wanted except the things that mattered most."

My nails bit into my palm as his words sank into the pit of my stomach. "You're saying it's not worth it? Working here?"

Donal's gaze wandered to the glass wall of his office. "I can't tell you that. You have to figure out for yourself what your priorities are. For some people, maybe professional success is what feeds their soul." His eyes pinned me in place. "I get the sense from your mom that your dad's one of those people."

I dropped my gaze to my lap as I rubbed my thumb across my palm. I'd never questioned my dad's devotion to his work or how much he'd let it take him away from us. His absences had simply been a fact of life, an immutable reality of who he was and how our family worked. It never occurred to me it was a choice he'd made, or that he could have made a different one.

Truthfully, I hadn't missed having Dad around that much. We'd had Mom for anything we needed, and between his exacting nature and rigorous expectations, things were often easier and more fun around the house without him. Which was pretty fucking sad when I thought about it. How would it feel to know your family was happier when you weren't around?

I doubted Dad even had a clue. Hearing him talk so obliviously about Mom had underscored how one-sided their marriage had been. She'd sacrificed her own needs and ambitions so he could throw himself into his career. But he'd never given up anything for her in return. He'd taken her support for granted, growing so self-absorbed that even now, after the divorce, he couldn't see the double standard.

The possibility that I might do the same thing to Chloe had haunted me since that lunch with my dad. I didn't want to be that kind of man. But the only way I knew how to avoid it was to give her up before I hurt her even more, which made me feel sick to my stomach.

"Maybe that's you too," Donal said. "You're clearly very driven, and you've worked your ass off to get here. Just make sure you're doing it for the right reasons. If you're having doubts, maybe it's time to reevaluate your goals."

"It feels a little late for that," I said. "Unless you think they're not going to make me an offer?" Honestly, I sort of hoped they didn't. Then the decision would be out of my hands. It was possible that was why Donal was telling me all this, to prepare me for it and soften the blow.

His expression gave nothing away. If he knew something about my future prospects here, I couldn't tell. "You don't have to take it if they do."

"It feels like I do." I couldn't imagine turning down that kind of money with all the law school debt I was carrying. Not to mention what a relief it would be to know I had a job waiting for me after graduation. I could enjoy my final year of law school without the added stress of finding a job.

"Is it because you think you've invested too much to change your mind now?" he guessed.

"Something like that," I mumbled.

Donal nodded in understanding. "You know what that is, don't you? That's the sunk cost fallacy. It's an emotional reaction, not a rational one. Doubling down on a small misstep is a surefire way to turn it into a big one."

Fucking hell. He was right. I hadn't even realized that was what I'd been doing. I'd had a whole freshman seminar on cognitive biases at Princeton, but I'd let myself get lured into fallacious reasoning anyway.

"Your choices aren't lifelong contracts," Donal said. "It's okay to reconsider, regroup, and make a different decision when there's new information to support it. The whole point of the summer associate program is to give you a chance to try this place on for size and see if it's a good fit for you. Now is exactly the time to change your mind if that's what you want to do."

I was starting to think I'd made a mistake putting so much stock in my dad's advice. I knew he meant well and wanted the best for me, but when it came down to it, he didn't really understand me. Hell, he didn't even understand himself all that well. It wasn't as if he seemed all that happy with the choices he'd made. So why was I letting him tell me what my priorities should be? After spending my whole life wishing I could be more like my accomplished, successful father, it was a cold-water shock to my system to suddenly realize I didn't actually want to be like him after all.

"I just want you to be sure you're making the right choice for you," Donal said gently. "Because let me tell you, no matter how much you give it, this job isn't ever going to love you back or be there to take care of you when you're down. It's cold fucking comfort when you're here by yourself every night with no one waiting for you at home. I'd hate for you to wake up one day and realize that in your race to get ahead you've lost everything in your life that makes it worth living."

Hadn't my mom tried to give me the same advice? And I'd disregarded her wisdom in favor of my father's. But of the two of them, she was the one who seemed genuinely happy these days. Maybe I should have listened to her more instead of trying so hard to please my father. Jesus, he'd almost had me convinced I should give up the best thing that ever happened to me in favor of a job that made me miserable.

My heart beat in my throat as my head filled with images of Chloe. Beautiful, smiling Chloe holding my hand. Cuddly, sex-mussed Chloe in my bed. Courageous Chloe gripping a steering wheel in the rain. Vulnerable Chloe with her legs dangling off a massage table. Angry Chloe storming out on our first date. Every moment I'd spent with her, even the painful ones, had been infinitely better than any I'd spent working in this building.

When I tried to imagine my life without Chloe in it, I wanted to curl up and die. But when I imagined not getting an offer from the firm at the end of the summer and having to find another job, I felt only mild trepidation.

Having Chloe in my life made me happy. It was the only thing that had in a very long time. My life before her seemed like a gray fog of joyless exertion.

She'd brought more light and color into my world than I'd even known existed before I met her. The thought of losing that feeling—of losing *her*—made my lungs burn with panic.

I swallowed glass as I stared at Donal. "I think I might have really fucked up."

CHAPTER THIRTY-ONE

CHLOE

I'd been working so hard to finish the new pieces for the show that I hadn't had time to get scared in advance. Only now that all the pieces were done, the opening was actually here and I was so nervous I wanted to throw up.

Do not vomit. It'll ruin your makeup.

This show was everything I'd wanted. Visibility. Legitimacy. Publicity. It was a dream come true to be at the opening night party of an exhibition featuring my art.

While I reminded myself of all that, I tried to breathe in inner stillness and breathe out my irrational fears. But I only succeeded in making myself hyper-ventilate.

"Everything looks fantastic," Angie said, squeezing my arm. "Try to relax and enjoy yourself tonight."

"Oh sure," I said, fanning my armpits as I watched people stream through the recently opened doors of the gallery. "No problem. Very doable."

There were *a lot* of people here. I'd been afraid no one would turn up and I'd be standing around in an empty gallery all night like a chump. No need to worry about that. Nope, this place was hopping and it'd barely even started.

My installations were in the far back corner, so not many people had mean-dered their way over here yet, but it was just a matter of time. Any minute now they'd stroll by and their withering gazes would light upon my work, the creations I'd poured so much of myself into, digging a needle into my deepest hurts and letting them bleed out onto the fibers I'd woven together. All these strangers crowding into the gallery would stand around calmly sipping their wine as they scrutinized and discussed my art, comparing it to the other works on display tonight and assessing its value. Assessing *my* value, because it might as well be me hanging on these white walls in the unsparing beams of LED gallery lights. It made me feel stark naked. Worse than naked. Naked and strapped to an operating table with a crowd of people standing over me holding scalpels, eager to cut me open and dissect my insides for sport.

Don't vomit, don't vomit, don't vomit.

"Here, I got you some wine." Dawn appeared in front of me and put a wineglass in my hand. "Why do you look so green?" She looked at Angie as she handed another glass to her. "What happened? What's wrong?"

"Nothing's wrong," Angie said. "Everything's perfect."

"Ah." Dawn nodded sagely and gave me a sympathetic look. "Opening night jitters. You'll be fine."

"I might throw up," I said, staring around the gallery at the works of the other artists in the exhibition. They were all so much better than mine. More professional. More mature. More complex. My little corner of the room looked like an elementary school art show by comparison. Crude. Amateurish. Naive.

Dawn took the glass away from me. "Maybe no wine, then."

What was I doing here? It was so obvious I was out of my league. I wasn't good enough to be standing alongside these other artists. Pretty soon everyone here was going to realize that. They'd take one look at my work and see it didn't measure up. I'd never felt more like an imposter in my whole life.

"No, she needs it." Angie took the glass back from Dawn and put it in my hand. "Take a drink. It'll numb the nerves a little."

I did as she said. It made my stomach burn but also made it feel less queasy. On balance, I considered that an improvement.

Oh God, people were coming this way and starting to look at my installations. I downed another gulp of wine.

"Okay, that's enough for now." Angie took the glass away again. "Don't want to get too numb. We need you coherent."

"Tonight's going to be wonderful," Dawn said, pulling me into a hug. "Your work is amazing, and everyone's going to fall in love with it. I'm so proud of you."

I clung to her, trying to absorb some of the confidence she had in me through osmosis. But then my phone vibrated in my pocket, and I had to pull out of her arms to check the screen.

I'd really hoped it might be Bran calling to wish me luck, but instead it was my father. I tried not to be too disappointed. Bran was busy impressing the managing partner tonight. He probably wouldn't be able to call.

Thinking about him made my heart hurt. It sucked that he wasn't going to be here tonight. It sucked a lot. I could seriously use his solid, reassuring energy right about now. But it was what it was. Things came up. People weren't always there for you. That was life. I knew that well enough by now. My heart would have to get over it.

"It's my dad," I told Dawn and Angie. "I'll be right back." I wandered in the direction of the bathrooms where it was a little quieter, ducking behind a pillar as I answered the call. "Hi, Dad."

"Hi, sweetheart." He sounded harassed, and my stomach sank as I guessed why he was calling. "Listen, I know I said I'd try to come to your thing tonight, but it turns out I can't make it."

"I get it," I said, chewing on my fingernail. "It's fine."

He kept talking, explaining whatever work emergency had come up that was more important than my art debut, but I didn't pay attention because it didn't matter. I'd known it would shake out like this, even if I'd hoped otherwise. There was always something more important than me. One day I'd figure out how to stop letting that hurt me.

On the bright side, I didn't have to worry about his reaction to seeing my take on his wedding picture. Neither he nor my mom would ever see it. It was probably just as well.

At least I had Angie and Dawn here. And my grandmother would show up eventually. She could always be counted on to come through. I hadn't bothered inviting anyone else. My brother obviously couldn't make it home from Bloomington in the middle of the week, although he'd texted earlier to wish me luck. That was nice. I might not have a big group of friends and family here to support me, but I wasn't alone. That was something to be grateful for.

Taking a deep breath, I straightened my spine and peered around the pillar. The crowd had spilled all the way to the back of the gallery by now. People were walking past my installations at this very moment. Some hardly slowed down at all, giving my work only a cursory glance as they cruised past on the way to something more interesting. But other people had come to a full stop in order to study them more closely, forming small clumps directly in front of several of the installations.

My stomach started to churn as I stood there watching people size up my work. I tried to guess what they were thinking, but it was hard to read their expressions from way over here. Angie was talking to a few of them, gesticulating at my picture day self-portrait. I should join her. Put on a smile and go introduce myself. Talk up my work, explain my process, try to sell something.

But I couldn't seem to make myself do it. I stayed where I was, watching from a distance, caught between fascination and abject terror. No one paid me any attention as they wandered past me. For the moment, my anonymity offered me protection. If I went over there and outed myself as the artist, I'd have to act like I thought I belonged here. I'd have to pretend to believe I was good enough.

You can do this. You're good at faking things. Just do that.

"Some of it's intriguing, but so much of it stinks of vapidity," I overheard a male voice say behind me. "Like those yarn portraits. Good God. What was Roland thinking?"

The random snippet of conversation froze me in place.

"Embarrassingly pedestrian," agreed another voice, this one female. "They look like those craft kits they sell at Hobby Lobby."

"Unsophisticated fluff," proclaimed the male voice. "Kid stuff with nothing to say."

The voices drifted away, along with everything else around me as an icy numbness swarmed my stomach. It spread through me like a living thing, crawling up my esophagus and filling my ears with a fuzzy roar. I stood on shaky legs, wishing it would swallow me whole so I could disappear from the face of the earth.

Unsophisticated.

The word reverberated through me like a bass drum as an image of it spelled out in a black sans serif font against the white background of Bran's phone screen filled my mind's eye. Other words joined it, crowding each other out. *Fluff. Pedestrian. Vapid. Embarrassing.* The ceaseless cascade of sharp black letters piled up in my head and filled the back of my throat with nails.

I couldn't breathe.

I needed to get out of here, away from all these people.

A hiccuping sob tore its way out of me as I turned and ran.

CHAPTER THIRTY-TWO

BRAN

The art gallery was packed when I pushed through the doors. *Jesus, what a scene.* I hadn't realized it would draw this much of a crowd. Ambient dub techno pulsed beneath the noisy buzz of conversation as I dodged through the mass of wine-sipping art enthusiasts.

I had to find Chloe. Knowing how terrified she'd been to do this show, I could only imagine how she must be feeling right now surrounded by all these people. I couldn't believe I'd left her to fend for herself tonight. I was supposed to be here to support her. That should have been my job, and I'd utterly fucking failed her.

This was one of the biggest nights of her life—her professional art debut—and I'd blown her off to go to a fucking dinner. The worst part was I'd done it even though I knew what Chloe's childhood had been like, how her parents had never made her a priority, never been there for her, how they'd neglected her emotional needs, making her feel deserted and unimportant. And then I'd turned around and done the exact same thing. It made me feel sick with shame.

Fuck, where was she? I needed to make it right. I had to show her how important she was. She was my brilliant, gifted, one-of-a-kind girl. Her creativity and her generous, loving nature shined on everything and everyone around her. She made everyone's life richer, but especially mine.

I loved her.

Fiercely. Indelibly. Uncontrollably.

I had to tell her that. She needed to know I'd chosen her tonight, and I was going to keep choosing her. I'd make sure she never had a reason to doubt how much she mattered ever again. I'd devote the rest of my life to it if she let me.

I'm here, Chloe. I fucked up, but I'm here now. Where the hell are you?

Relief blew through me when I recognized one of her pieces hanging on the wall. I didn't see her anywhere, but I spotted my mom standing near it and made a beeline for her. "Mom!"

She spun around and broke into a smile when she saw me coming toward her. "Brandon, there you are! Where's Chloe?"

"I just got here," I said. "What do you mean where's Chloe?"

Her smile disappeared. "You just got here? Where've you been? The opening started an hour ago."

"I was at work."

"Of course you were." Her tone brought to mind every time Dad had been paged to the hospital at an inconvenient moment or called to say he couldn't make it somewhere Mom was counting on him to be. She was looking at me the same way she used to look at him, and it fucking gutted me where I stood.

"What happened to Chloe?" I asked, swallowing down the bitter pill. "Isn't she here?"

"She was. I'm sure she's around here somewhere. She got a call from her father a little while ago and wandered off to take it. I haven't seen her since."

"Her father called? So he's not here yet?"

"Not that I've seen. Maybe he's with Chloe."

I doubted that somehow. My guess was he'd called to cancel. After the opening had already started, no less. *Dammit.* Chloe had said she wasn't holding her breath, but she'd wanted him here. She'd let herself hope he'd come through for her this time. It would have hurt her when he didn't.

First I'd let her down, then her father had turned around and done the exact same thing. The ugly realization that I was no better than him sliced through my gut like a hot knife.

"How long ago was that?" I asked my mom.

"A half hour, maybe?" She looked around. "It's hard to find anyone in this crowd. I didn't realize there'd be so many people here."

"Neither did I." When I'd imagined it, I'd pictured it as a more sedate event in a much smaller space, not this packed house in what appeared to be one of the more prestigious art galleries in Chicago. I'd underestimated how impressive an achievement this was for Chloe. No wonder she'd been so nervous.

"Roland's openings always bring in a big crowd," Angie said, appearing beside us. "Not to mention lots of press." She directed a sour look at me. "I see you decided to show up after all. You get some points for that, I suppose."

I winced at the justified reproof, then winced again as my mom turned a shocked look on me.

"What does that mean? Were you not planning to come tonight?"

"He told her he had a work thing." Angie's lips pursed as she folded her arms. "Like father, like son, I suppose."

Brutal, but no less than I deserved.

"Why didn't I know that?" my mom asked, frowning at me. "Chloe never said you weren't planning to come."

"She asked me not to tell you," Angie said. "She didn't want you to try and talk some sense into him."

My mother gave me her most disappointed look, the one that always made me want to sink through the floor. But she was too late. It wasn't possible to feel worse than I already did. "I can't believe you, Brandon. Do you have any idea how much Chloe could have used your support tonight? What was so much more important that you'd pick it over being here for her?"

Shame coiled through my insides as I rubbed the back of my neck. "It was a dinner with the firm's managing partner. I was afraid missing it would hurt my chances of getting a postgraduation offer, but I had a talk with Donal tonight and realized Chloe means more to me than getting that job does."

"Well thank God for Donal." Mom shook her head as she twisted her hands. "No wonder Chloe was so upset earlier."

"She was upset?" I asked, my stomach plummeting.

"Opening night jitters," Angie said. "Poor kid was a bundle of nerves, as you must have known she would be when you decided you didn't need to show up for her. That was a real kick in the teeth to someone who was already feeling shaky."

"I know," I said miserably. "I screwed up and I regret it. But I'm here now, and I've got my priorities straight. I'm going to make it up to her."

"Where's my granddaughter?"

I spun around to find myself face-to-face with Chloe's grandmother, flanked by three other women close to her age.

"You're Chloe's grandmother?" my mom said, eagerly inserting herself in front of me. "It's so lovely to meet you."

I cleared my throat to make the introduction. "Mrs. Carpenter, this is my mother—"

"Dawn Botstein," Mom said, pressing Mrs. Carpenter's hand warmly. "You have such a wonderful granddaughter. I absolutely think the world of Chloe."

"So do I," Angie piped up. "I'm Angie. I work with Chloe at the store. That girl's one of the most gifted artists I know."

"You must be so proud of Chloe," my mom said.

"Damn right I am," Mrs. Carpenter replied gruffly. "I meant to get here sooner, but I had to pick up my friends so they could see for themselves what a star my granddaughter is."

While Mrs. Carpenter introduced the women with her to Mom and Angie, I craned my neck to peer around the gallery, hoping to spot Chloe. I didn't see her anywhere, and I was getting seriously worried.

Just how upset had Chloe been earlier? Upset enough to leave her opening without telling anyone? I'd never forgive myself if tonight was ruined for her because of my stupidity.

"Hey." Mike's hand landed on my shoulder, drawing my attention. "What's wrong?"

"I fucked up," I blurted before I noticed his mother and sister standing just behind him.

"Come on, Kelly," Mrs. Pilota said, cocking her head. "Let's go say hi to Dawn."

"What happened?" Mike asked me when they were out of earshot. "Tell me."

The words poured out of me in a rush, how and why I'd let Chloe down, how she'd been nervous and upset earlier, and how no one had seen her since she'd gotten a call from her dad. Telling the whole story again drove home the immensity of how badly I'd failed her.

"I should have been here," I said, as much to myself as to Mike, who'd been listening to the sorry saga with a grim look on his face. "She's the best thing that ever happened to me, and I wasn't here when she needed me. What if she's off somewhere alone crying because she thinks I don't care?"

Mike's massive arms folded around me, and my throat tightened as he clenched me in a firm hug. "We'll find her," he said gruffly, giving me a few hearty thumps on the back before letting go. "It's gonna be all right."

I nodded, as surprised by his reaction as I was grateful for it. Instead of blaming me or giving me a lecture or going over everything I'd done wrong, he'd simply tried to make me feel better and offered to help.

"What's going on?" Donal materialized out of the crowd with Tess in tow and gave me a questioning look. "Where's Chloe?"

"She's gone AWOL," Mike explained. "Dawn says she wandered off to take a call from her dad thirty minutes ago and hasn't come back."

"Maybe she's just in the crowd somewhere," Tess suggested hopefully. "With all the people here it'd be easy to lose track of her."

"She was having pretty bad opening night jitters," I said, wishing I could believe Tess was right. "Mom said she seemed upset—probably because of me," I added, darting a guilty look at Donal. "And I'm pretty sure the reason Chloe's dad called was to tell her he wasn't coming tonight either."

"Which would have made her even more upset," Tess said, biting her lip.

"We need to split up and see if we can find her," Mike said.

"I'll check the women's restroom. That's where I'd go." Tess gave my arm a sympathetic squeeze before she set off into the crowd.

"We should get the others to help too," Donal suggested. "We'll cover more ground if we all spread out."

"Good idea. And let's make sure she hasn't texted anyone before we send out the search party." Mike clamped his hand on my shoulder and steered me toward my mom as Donal fell into step on my other side.

The group of people with Mom had swelled in the last few minutes. I recognized a lot of faces from the wedding, both friends of my mom's and friends of Mike's. They'd all come out to support Chloe tonight. Because she meant something to them. She'd worked her way into their hearts. Because that was what she did. She shined her light on people everywhere she went. I doubted she had any idea how much affection and loyalty she inspired.

Flanked by Mike and Donal as they asked the group if anyone had seen or heard from Chloe, I felt a little steadier. With so many people who cared about her looking, someone would surely find her. Then she'd know how loved she was. How special. And I'd throw myself at her feet and beg for her forgiveness. If I was really lucky, maybe she'd even offer it to me.

As long as she was okay.

She had to be okay.

CHAPTER THIRTY-THREE

CHLOE

The only thing grosser than throwing up was throwing up in a public restroom. *Ugh.* Talk about unsanitary. I hated having my face so close to something strangers had put their naked butts on. Vomiting was bad enough without the added challenge of trying not to touch anything around you while you were doing it.

After I'd finished heaving up everything in my stomach, I flushed the toilet and pulled myself to my feet to wash my hands. Thank God for single-person unisex bathrooms. At least I didn't have to worry about anyone coming in or overhearing me from the next stall. There were two other bathrooms just like this one for everyone else to use. I could stay in here undisturbed as long as I wanted. All night even.

Maybe I would. The last thing I wanted to do was go back out there. Just the thought of it made my gorge start to rise again.

Besides, I officially looked like warmed-over hell. Crying and throwing up at the same time was murder on even waterproof makeup. No way was I going back out there looking like this. Everyone would know I'd been crying. They'd all see how weak I was. Not only was I a vapid, unsophisticated maker of pedestrian fluff, but I was a gutless, overwrought nervous wreck who fell completely to pieces at the drop of a hat.

I didn't belong here. I'd never been cut out for this life. I should have trusted my instincts. I didn't have what it took to be an artist. If I didn't know it before, I sure as hell did now.

Best to call it a night and go home. I took my shot and failed. *Oh well. Lesson learned.* No reason to stick around for the rest of the night and subject myself to more torture.

Unfortunately, about a million people stood between me and the door. But also, as much as I ached to crawl into my bed and hide under the covers, it didn't feel right. Dawn and Angie were out there doing everything they could to support me. And my grandmother was probably on her way too. I couldn't just leave, no matter how much I wanted to.

I'd have to go out there again, at least for a while. Long enough to face Dawn and Angie and thank them for believing in me. Even if their faith in me had been misplaced, it meant a lot to know I'd had it.

I rinsed my mouth out and dabbed a paper towel around my eyes, cleaning up my smeared eye makeup as best I could. It wasn't great, but it would have to do. After popping one of the minty breath strips I'd thankfully had the foresight to stash in my pocket, I stared at myself in the mirror.

I could do this. I could pretend to be strong. So what if everyone out there thought I was a fraud? At least I tried, right? I'd put myself out there in spite of my crippling fear. Shit, that was something to be proud of rather than embarrassed about.

And you know what? Roland might only have given me a spot in the show out of last-minute desperation, but he'd still deemed me good enough to be a last-minute desperation choice. Considering what a big deal he was, that wasn't too shabby. It was more than a lot of people could say. I was doing pretty good.

Why did it matter what those people I'd overheard thought of me anyway? I didn't even know who the hell they were. Who died and made them the unimpeachable arbiters of artistic merit? They were just two random strangers. Who was to say they even knew what they were talking about? Their opinions didn't have to mean anything to me. They didn't have the power to hurt me unless I let them.

They weren't the only opinions that mattered. My grandmother's opinion meant a lot more. So did Dawn's. And Angie's. And Bran's. Even if he wasn't here, I knew he still believed in me. So what if my parents didn't? Their good opinions weren't worth having.

I was going back out there, and I was going to hold my head up high. I owed it to the three people who'd showed up for me. But even more than that, I owed it to myself.

So there.

After one last check in the mirror, I unlocked the bathroom door and ventured back into the gallery. Back straight, boobs out. I had this under control.

Holy hell. It'd gotten even more crowded while I was in the bathroom. Like, crazy crowded. An anxious flutter stirred in my stomach at the sight of so many more people, but I gritted my teeth and stubbornly ignored it.

"Chloe, thank God." Tess stepped in front of me, her expression anxious as she grasped my hands. "Are you okay?"

"I'm fine," I said, surprised to realize how true it was. I *was* okay. I'd pulled myself out of my tailspin.

"That's a relief," she said. "Everyone's looking for you. You had us all worried."

"Who's everyone? You mean Dawn and Angie? Is my grandmother here already?" I hadn't even realized Tess was coming tonight. Dawn must have told her about it. Who else had she told? Were other people here too?

"I mean *everyone.* Come see." Tess took my hand and led me back toward my corner of the exhibition, bobbing and weaving through the crowd. Then she stopped and pointed. "Look."

My mouth fell open when I saw all the familiar faces standing in a big group with Dawn and Angie. So many more people than I'd ever expected. People I'd never thought to invite, assuming they wouldn't want to come. Mike was here, which wasn't such a surprise, but his mother was here too and so was his sister. My grandmother had brought three of her friends from the neighborhood. Tess had brought Donal. And there was their daughter Erin with her husband who was wearing their baby in a carrier on his chest. There were so many others. The longer I looked, the more people I spotted. Charles. Linda. Deon and Andrew. Stan. Sandra and Alex. Marie and Matt. Fiona and Greg. Janie and Mr. Sullivan. Elizabeth and—

Oh my God, Nico Moretti came to my art show! What the heck?

And there were others too, standing at the back or behind other people, who I couldn't see well enough to identify. So many people. I couldn't believe it.

"What are they all doing here?" I asked, absolutely gobsmacked.

"They're here for you," Tess said. "Dawn emailed the invite out, and we all wanted to be here to celebrate your big night."

"I can't believe it." Tears stung my eyes, but this time they were happy tears instead of sad. Never in my life had so many people turned up anywhere for me. Not ever.

"Hey, guess what?" Tess slung an arm around my shoulders and gave me a shake. "You have a lot of friends who like you an awful lot."

It almost made up for Bran not being here. *Almost.* Nothing could truly make up for that. He was the person I wanted to have with me most of all. I would have traded everyone here in a heartbeat to have Bran instead. But still. This was a pretty awesome consolation prize.

Tess lifted her other arm and waved to get everyone's attention. Angie was the first to notice. She nudged Dawn, who nudged Donal, who nudged Mike, and then everyone was turning to look and waving back at us. At *me.* They started cheering and whistling and shouting my name, and I buried my face in my hands because now everyone else in the gallery was looking to see what the ruckus was about, and I was a little embarrassed but also really happy and kind of crying, and I didn't want everyone to see my nose drip.

Tess's arm dropped away while I tried to pull myself together. When I felt her leave my side, I lifted my head and that was when I saw Bran walking toward me.

Oh my God. Oh my God.

It was really him, looking relieved but also distressed and so handsome it stole my breath away. His eyes were unbearably sad for some reason, especially when he said my name. His voice was swallowed up by the noise of the party, but I didn't need to hear it to recognize the sight of my name on his lips.

A big fat tear rolled down my cheek, and he started moving faster, almost running, so by the time I'd taken a step toward him he was right in front of me, reaching out for me as I reached for him.

"You're here," I whispered against his neck as he locked his arms around me.

"I'm sorry." He held me tight as he kissed my hair, my temple, my forehead. "I'm so sorry, Chloe."

I didn't know what he was sorry for or why he looked so sad when he was *here.* He'd made it after all, and now that I was in his arms everything felt right in the world again. A wet laugh bubbled out of my chest as it overflowed with happiness, and I tipped my head back to kiss him.

Before I could, people closed in around us, and Bran's arms slipped away, replaced by others. Dawn pulled me in for a hug, followed by Angie. My grandmother gave me one of her rare brisk hugs, mumbling that she was proud of me as her friends crowded around to coo over me. Others followed suit, a succession of blurry faces appearing in front of my tear-streaked eyes as everyone gathered around, eager for their turn to give me a hug, a cheek kiss, a pat on the back, or some combination of all three as they offered their congratulations. I'd never had so many hugs in my whole life. It was astonishing, wonderful, and over-whelming.

All these people had come here just for me. I didn't know what to do with this much attention. It made my head spin. As much as it was a lifelong dream come true, all I wanted was to bury myself in Bran's arms again. His was the attention I wanted most, but I'd lost sight of him completely.

Oh Lord, Nico Moretti was hugging me now, and I couldn't even properly appreciate it. He handed me off to his wife, and when she let go Angie was back again with Roland, who told me he'd already sold almost all my pieces and had multiple offers for the portrait of Dawn and Mike if I wanted to change my mind about selling it.

"Absolutely not," Mike cut in, grinning as he draped an enormous, muscular arm around me. "That's my favorite wedding present, and I'm not giving it up for anything."

"However, I suspect the artist might consider taking on commissions," Angie added, jabbing me with her elbow. "Isn't that right?"

"Yes?" I said, unable to believe it. People were actually buying my art? It had shocked the hell out of me when Roland told me what he'd be asking for them. I never imagined a single one would sell at those prices.

"Excellent," he said. "I'll let them know and collect their info for you. Oh, and the critic from the *Chicago Reader* wanted to talk to you later, so be ready for that."

"Wants to talk to me?" I asked in disbelief.

Roland laughed. "Of course she does, honey. You're the star of the night. I owe Angie a steak dinner for throwing you into my path."

"Damn right you do," Angie called after him as he disappeared back into the crowd with a wave. She turned to give me an appraising look. "How do you feel?"

"Utterly shocked." My legs were so shaky, if it wasn't for Mike's arm holding me up I almost definitely would have slid to the floor already. "It's not really true what he said about me being the star of the night, is it?"

"It fucking well is," Angie said. "Better get used to all this attention because your art debut's a smash hit."

"You look like you could use a minute to regroup," Mike said as he guided me away from the crush of enthusiastic supporters. "Oh hey, here's someone I bet would be happy to take you outside for some fresh air."

Suddenly Bran was there, and I was in his arms again, sighing against his chest and exactly where I wanted to be. And then he was hustling me through the gallery, out the front door, down the sidewalk, and around the side of the building to a quiet alley. Once we were alone, he stopped and gathered me to his chest, banding both his arms around me.

"I'm sorry I wasn't here sooner," he rasped against my hair.

"You're here now," I said, holding him as tight as I could so no one would be able to take him away from me again. "All I wanted tonight was you."

"You've got me, and I swear I won't let you down like that again. I fucked up, Chloe. Can you forgive me?"

"Of course I forgive you." There was nothing to forgive as far as I was concerned. "It's okay."

"No, it's not okay." He sounded angry, but his hands were gentle as they cradled my face. "You should be able to expect more than that from me."

I touched his cheek, wanting to soothe away his fears. "Bran, you had a work thing. That's more important. I understand."

"I don't want you to have to understand that. My job isn't more important than you. *Nothing* is. You're the best thing in my life, dammit. I love you, Chloe."

Emotion clogged my throat and flooded my eyes with tears. "No one's ever said that to me before," I choked out.

His deep green eyes held mine as he thumbed away my tears. "Which part?"

"All of it. Any of it." My whole life, no one had ever said "I love you." Not my parents or my grandmother. Even if they felt it, it wasn't in their nature to say it out loud. I'd never been the most important thing in anyone's life before.

Bran leaned in to rub his nose against mine. "I love you. If you let me, I'll tell you every day, over and over again, until you get tired of hearing it."

Never, I thought, squeezing my eyes closed. *I'll never, ever get tired of it.*

"I don't just want you in my life when it's convenient." His deep, husky voice hummed over my skin as he kissed the tears from my cheeks. "From now on you're my number one priority, okay? I'm going to show you how important you are."

A tremor ran through me, and I clutched at his neck as my lips sought his. His mouth opened to meet mine and we traded breath, sinking into each other.

"I love you," I whispered as my lips trembled against his, getting used to saying the words I'd never spoken before. "I love you, Bran."

"Thank God." His whole body sagged with relief as he kissed me, hard and a little frantic. "Thank God. I don't know what I'd do without you. It scared the shit out of me when I thought you'd left the opening."

"I almost did," I admitted, ducking my head. "I wanted to, but I talked myself into staying." I took an unsteady breath. "My dad called to cancel."

"I thought he might have." Bran kissed my forehead. "I'm so sorry."

I shrugged, not wanting to meet his eyes. "I knew he would."

"But it still hurt." At my jerky nod, he gathered me to his chest. "Baby," he murmured, stroking my hair. "Baby, I'm sorry."

"After I got off the phone with my dad, there were these people behind me…" I didn't want to say it, but I knew I could tell him. Bran was my safe space. My strength. "I overheard them talking about me and I might have spiraled a little. That's why I was hiding in the bathroom."

He drew back, his expression fierce and protective. "What people? What did they say?"

"I don't know who they were. Just two random strangers who happened to be standing behind me." I sucked in a breath. "They were saying all these awful things about my work."

An anguished, furious sound tore out of him, but I shook my head, pressing my thumb against his lips to silence him.

"I'm okay. I mean, yes, I may have freaked out and cried in the bathroom a little. But you know what? After that I pulled myself together and went back out there all on my own. I did that." I smiled up at him through tear-spangled eyes. "I guess I am pretty strong after all. I think I needed to prove that to myself."

He nodded and hugged me, pressing a kiss to my temple. "I still hate that you were crying and I wasn't here to hold you."

"I didn't love that part so much either. But I love you, and I love that you're here now." A joyous smile broke over my face as it hit me anew. "You showed up for me."

"I'll always show up for you when you need me. You can count on that."

"We'll count on each other." I reached up to touch the frown lines on his face, dragging my finger down the two little creases between his brows before tracing the beautiful curve of his lips. "I don't suppose we can stay out here all night, can we?"

Bran shook his head. "We probably shouldn't. It wouldn't be fair to all your new fans who are inside waiting to talk to the star of the night."

My stomach dropped at the reminder, but not with fear or anxiety this time. With excitement.

"Are you ready to go back in and face your adoring public?" he asked. "Or do you need a few more minutes?"

"I'm good," I said, realizing it was true. "I can handle this."

"I never doubted it for a second." He pressed a kiss to my cheek. "Lead the way. I'll be right behind you."

We walked back into the gallery hand in hand. Bran's fingers felt so good against my skin it was impossible to feel anything but utterly, incandescently happy.

I had it all. Everything I'd ever wanted. What was there to be nervous about?

EPILOGUE
CHLOE

I stood in front of the oven, peering through the dark, double-paned glass. Radiant heat warmed my face as I inhaled the herb-rich scent of roasting turkey. The sound of a football game drifted beneath the steady babble of conversation that filled the kitchen, wrapping itself around me like a cozy blanket.

"How's it looking?" Dawn asked me as she stood at the island forming dough into balls for homemade dinner rolls. On the counter beside her, the pies we'd baked earlier this morning sat cooling under tea towels.

"One hundred twenty-five degrees," I read off the thermometer sticking out of the giant bird. "Is that good?"

"It's excellent." Dawn reached up to brush a tendril of hair off her face and left a streak of flour across her cheek. "We're right on track."

She'd showed me how to dress the turkey before it went into the oven, and I'd been watching its progress for the last three hours like a proud parent. I'd never had a home-cooked Thanksgiving turkey before, much less helped to make one. Grammy wasn't big into cooking, so we'd never done much for holiday meals in my family. If we were lucky and Dad didn't happen to be working, he might take us out to a restaurant. More often, my brother and I had spent Thanksgivings eating Boston Market frozen turkey dinners in front of the TV at Grammy's house.

This year was different because Dawn had invited me to spend Thanksgiving at her house. Not just me, but Grammy and my brother Noah, who'd come home for Thanksgiving break. Dad was working, of course, but for once I honestly didn't care.

I'd spent last night at Bran's apartment, and we'd come over early today to help his mom and Mike with the cooking. Bran had chopped vegetables and peeled potatoes while Dawn and I baked pies and Mike made the stuffing. Just the time the four of us had spent working in the kitchen together had already made it the best Thanksgiving ever. And it had only gotten better when the rest of the guests showed up and filled Dawn's house with noise and laughter.

A chorus of cheers and exuberant shouts erupted from the den where people were watching football. Dawn cast a fond smile over her shoulder at her husband's boisterous celebration of whatever had just happened in the game. Noah and Grammy were in there crammed onto the couch in front of the TV with Mike's mom, sister, and brother-in-law, while Mike, Donal, and Angie's husband Charles hovered behind the couch sipping beers.

"You've got something on your face," Tess said to Dawn as she helped her shape the dough for the rolls. "Here, I'll get it for you." She reached up and smeared a flour-coated finger across Dawn's other cheekbone to give her a matching smudge. "Much better."

"Thanks very much," Dawn said, laughing as she wiped her cheeks with the back of her hand.

On my way to the sink, I stole a handful of mini marshmallows from Angie, who was assembling a sweet potato casserole next to the stove.

"Quit that," she said, bumping my hip with hers. "There won't be any left for the topping."

Grinning, I shoved the mini marshmallows into my mouth and looked out the window over the sink. Bran and Zach had taken Mike's two nephews into the backyard to play football in an attempt to burn off some of their boundless little kid energy. The four of them seemed to be enjoying themselves out there despite the cold. We hadn't had our first snow of the season yet, but there was a chance we might get a light dusting today. The overcast skies sure looked ripe for it.

As I stood at the sink watching them, Bran glanced up and saw me. The slow, broad smile he broke into was a thing of beauty. He'd been smiling more the last few months and I loved to see it. He seemed a lot happier since his internship had ended. He'd turned down the postgraduation job the firm had offered him and decided to pursue public interest work instead. On top of his classes this semester, he'd signed up for economic justice clinical work representing clients in workers' rights cases, and also started volunteering for the ACLU again.

It all kept him pretty busy, but these days I was just as busy as he was. The exhibition at Roland's gallery had gotten a big write-up in the *Chicago Reader* that had been particularly kind to me, highlighting my work with a glowing review and calling me a rising star to watch. Since then, I'd been overwhelmed with commission requests, which meant I didn't have to pick up waitressing shifts anymore, but also meant I'd had to cut back on my hours at Dawn's store.

Bran and I still didn't get to spend as much time together as we would have liked, but we'd been making an effort to carve out regular couple time. It wasn't always easy. There were still plenty of nights I went to sleep in an empty bed, missing him, and days I didn't get to see him at all. But it was worth it because we were both doing what we loved, and because, no matter how busy we got, we belonged to each other. Wholeheartedly and above all else.

As I lifted my hand to wave at Bran through the window, Zach nailed him right in the stomach with the football. Good thing he hadn't aimed a few inches lower because I'd hate to have to murder Zach for damaging my boyfriend's precious goods. Poor Bran clutched the football as he doubled over, and Mike's nephews barreled into him, tackling him to the ground and piling on like a pair of hyperactive monkeys.

I let out a relieved breath when I saw Bran rear up again, laughing as he play-wrestled them for possession of the football. Eventually Zach waded into the fray, pulled the boys off his older brother, and gave him a hand up off the ground. After Bran stood and dusted himself off, they herded the kids into the house.

The back door flew open and the boys charged inside, but Zach snagged them before they could run off and made them remove their shoes and hang up their jackets. As Bran edged inside around them, I went to meet him.

"You good?" I asked, curling my hands into the front of his fleece jacket to pull him against me.

"Nothing wounded but my dignity," he murmured, leaning in to fit his mouth against mine. He tasted salty and warm, but his lips were cold, and I slipped my hands around his neck and pulled him closer to warm him up.

Letting myself love Bran with everything I had, and knowing I was just as loved in return, was a comfort I'd never had the luxury of before. It gave me a sense of security I'd been missing my whole life.

It was funny, because I used to think finding my soul mate would make me whole. But I realized now that wasn't how it worked. I didn't need a man to fill the holes in my life or fix the broken parts of me. It was on me to figure out my own crap and make my life what I wanted it to be.

But having Bran in my corner made the hard work easier. He lent me some of his strength when I needed a boost and some of his confidence whenever I started to doubt. He inspired me to fight for myself, and he gave me the courage to keep at it because I knew he'd be there cheering me on, believing in me, and loving me even when I failed. Just like I was there for him. What a privilege.

"Break it up," Zach groaned at us as the boys stampeded into the den. "Our mother is standing right there, for the love of everything holy."

"Go away," Bran replied, rubbing his freezing cold nose against my warm one. "I'm saying hi to my girlfriend."

Dawn laughed. "Zach, honey, I'm afraid it'll take a lot more than kissing to scandalize me."

"Please, can we not find out how much more?" Zach hung his jacket up and shuddered dramatically as he dodged around us. "Won't anyone think of my trauma?"

"You smell like snow," I told Bran, ignoring Zach.

"I think we might get a white Thanksgiving after all." He kissed me again, his lips curving against mine. "You doing okay? Having a good Thanksgiving?"

A blissful smile bloomed across my face. "Only the best Thanksgiving ever."

"I'm glad." He bent his head to nuzzle my cheek.

"Do you think your mom will let me come over for Christmas too?"

"Of course she will." He pulled back, his gorgeous green eyes narrowing with faux suspicion. "Wait a second. You're not dating me just to get closer to my mom, are you?"

I gasped. "No, but that would have been a great idea. I wish I'd thought of that."

He shook his head, failing to hide the smile sprouting at the corners of his mouth. "Unbelievable."

"Don't worry," I said, threading my fingers through his hair as I pressed a trail of kisses along his prickly jaw, "your mom's only the second-best thing about being your girlfriend."

"What's the first?" he asked, ducking his head to arch a heavy eyebrow at me.

"You are," I said. "Duh."

A laugh rumbled out of him as he tightened his arms around me, lifting me off the floor. "Good to know."

"Every day with you is the best day ever," I whispered into his ear, feeling so safe and loved and happy I could barely stand it.

Bran made a sound in the back of his throat and reached up to cradle my jaw, devotion shining in his eyes so brightly it blurred my vision with tears. "Then I hope you don't mind that I plan on keeping you forever."

ABOUT THE AUTHOR

SUSANNAH NIX is a RITA® Award-winning and *USA Today* bestselling author who lives in Texas with her husband, two ornery cats, and a flatulent pit bull. When she's not writing romances, she enjoys reading, cooking, knitting, and watching lots of sad British mysteries on TV.

Sign up for Susannah's newsletter: https://www.susannahnix.com/newsletter

---

www.susannahnix.com

Facebook: https://www.facebook.com/susannahnix/
Goodreads: https://www.goodreads.com/susannah_nix
Twitter: https://twitter.com/Susannah_Nix
Instagram: https://www.instagram.com/susannahnixauthor/

Find Smartypants Romance online:
Website: www.smartypantsromance.com
Facebook: www.facebook.com/smartypantsromance/
Goodreads: www.goodreads.com/smartypantsromance
Twitter: @smartypantsrom
Instagram: @smartypantsromance
Newsletter: https://smartypantsromance.com/newsletter/

ALSO BY SUSANNAH NIX

Chemistry Lessons Series

Remedial Rocket Science

Intermediate Thermodynamics

Advanced Physical Chemistry

Applied Electromagnetism

Experimental Marine Biology

Elementary Romantic Calculus

King Family Series

My Cone and Only

Cream and Punishment

Pint of Contention

Mint to Be

Kilt Trip Series

Kilt to Order

Starstruck Series

Star Bright

Fallen Star

Rising Star

Lucky Star

Smartypants Romance

Mad About Ewe

Not Since Ewe

Ewe Complete Me

For the most up-to-date book list, CLICK HERE.

ALSO BY SMARTYPANTS ROMANCE

Green Valley Chronicles

The Love at First Sight Series

Baking Me Crazy by Karla Sorensen (#1)

Batter of Wits by Karla Sorensen (#2)

Steal My Magnolia by Karla Sorensen (#3)

Worth the Wait by Karla Sorensen (#4)

Fighting For Love Series

Stud Muffin by Jiffy Kate (#1)

Beef Cake by Jiffy Kate (#2)

Eye Candy by Jiffy Kate (#3)

Knock Out by Jiffy Kate (#4)

The Donner Bakery Series

No Whisk, No Reward by Ellie Kay (#1)

Dough You Love Me? By Stacy Travis (#2)

Tough Cookie by Talia Hunter (#3)

The Green Valley Library Series

Love in Due Time by L.B. Dunbar (#1)

Crime and Periodicals by Nora Everly (#2)

Prose Before Bros by Cathy Yardley (#3)

Shelf Awareness by Katie Ashley (#4)

Carpentry and Cocktails by Nora Everly (#5)

Love in Deed by L.B. Dunbar (#6)

Dewey Belong Together by Ann Whynot (#7)

Hotshot and Hospitality by Nora Everly (#8)

Love in a Pickle by L.B. Dunbar (#9)

Checking You Out by Ann Whynot (#10)

Architecture and Artistry by Nora Everly (#11)

Scorned Women's Society Series

My Bare Lady by Piper Sheldon (#1)

The Treble with Men by Piper Sheldon (#2)

The One That I Want by Piper Sheldon (#3)

Hopelessly Devoted by Piper Sheldon (#3.5)

It Takes a Woman by Piper Sheldon (#4)

Park Ranger Series

Happy Trail by Daisy Prescott (#1)

Stranger Ranger by Daisy Prescott (#2)

The Leffersbee Series

Been There Done That by Hope Ellis (#1)

Before and After You by Hope Ellis (#2)

The Higher Learning Series

Upsy Daisy by Chelsie Edwards (#1)

Green Valley Heroes Series

Forrest for the Trees by Kilby Blades (#1)

Parks and Provocation by Juliette Cross (#2)

Letter Late Than Never by Lauren Connolly (#3)

Peaches and Dreams by Juliette Cross (#4)

Story of Us Collection

My Story of Us: Zach by Chris Brinkley (#1)

My Story of Us: Thomas by Chris Brinkley (#2)

Seduction in the City

Cipher Security Series

Code of Conduct by April White (#1)

Code of Honor by April White (#2)

Code of Matrimony by April White (#2.5)

Code of Ethics by April White (#3)

Cipher Office Series

Weight Expectations by M.E. Carter (#1)

Sticking to the Script by Stella Weaver (#2)

Cutie and the Beast by M.E. Carter (#3)

Weights of Wrath by M.E. Carter (#4)

Common Threads Series

Mad About Ewe by Susannah Nix (#1)

Give Love a Chai by Nanxi Wen (#2)

Key Change by Heidi Hutchinson (#3)

Not Since Ewe by Susannah Nix (#4)

Lost Track by Heidi Hutchinson (#5)

Ewe Complete Me by Susannah Nix (#6)

Meet Your Matcha by Nanxi Wen (#7)

All Mixed Up by Heidi Hutchinson (#8)

Educated Romance
Work For It Series

Street Smart by Aly Stiles (#1)

Heart Smart by Emma Lee Jayne (#2)

Book Smart by Amanda Pennington (#3)

Smart Mouth by Emma Lee Jayne (#4)

Play Smart by Aly Stiles (#5)

Look Smart by Aly Stiles (#6)

Smart Move by Amanda Pennington (#7)

Lessons Learned Series

Under Pressure by Allie Winters (#1)

Not Fooling Anyone by Allie Winters (#2)

Can't Fight It by Allie Winters (#3)

The Vinyl Frontier by Lola West (#4)

Out of this World

London Ladies Embroidery Series

Neanderthal Seeks Duchess by Laney Hatcher (#1)

Well Acquainted by Laney Hatcher (#2)

Love Matched by Laney Hatcher (#3)

Made in the USA
Thornton, CO
07/23/24 07:53:54

4ae3cf7e-b058-4bec-9277-123e17c89880R01